IN THE
*Presence* OF MY
ENEMIES

A NOVEL

Renée Allen McCoy

# ACKNOWLEDGMENTS

*"Let the redeemed of the LORD say so, whom He has redeemed from the hand of the enemy,"* Psalm 107:2.

I graciously thank my God, the God of Abraham, Isaac, and Jacob; the God who has saved my soul through His Son, Jesus Christ, and comforts me by His Holy Spirit. Words cannot possibly fully express my gratitude and love for You. In the midst of all the turmoil in this world, I know that You are still on the throne, interceding on my behalf. For that and so much more, I owe You my life.

I also thank my family members and friends. Without positive people in life, for me, this world would be practically unbearable to live in. I thank the Lord that He has blessed me to be born into the Moultrie & Allen families and to marry into the McCoy's. Additionally, God has blessed me with wonderful friends who are as close to me as blood relatives. Thank you for a lifetime of love.

As I wrote *In the Presence of My Enemies*, I was constantly reminded that no matter what we go through, as long as we have Christ, we'll get through it. To all who have been unjustly hurt, heartlessly discarded, and ridiculed for your faith in Jesus, keep pressing forward. When it is all said and done, God has the final say.

It is a pleasure to write for the glory of God and I thank every person who has picked up this novel to read. May we all remember that no matter how many bestselling books are out there, the Bible is still the greatest story ever told.

In His Name,

*Renée Allen McCoy*

*You prepare a table before me*
*in the presence of my enemies...*

Psalm 23:5

# PROLOGUE

STIRRING FROM HER sleep, Gwendolyn dragged the back of her hand across her dampened forehead. It had been a sultry summer's day in northern Mississippi that mercilessly poured into the evening. Regardless of the elegant new negligée she wore crafted with sheer material, Gwendolyn fought off the notion that she may be having premature hot flashes. At the age of forty-four, she didn't expect her body to go through such a change for at least another five years or so.

"Did you turn the air off?" Gwendolyn groggily questioned her comatose husband. "Ken, did you hear me?" She lightly nudged him in the side as her eyelids briefly fluttered, barely allowing enough time for the light from the dimmed corner lamp to penetrate her pupils. "It's hot in here. Make sure the air didn't go out."

Kenneth groaned as he rolled over onto his side.

Spent from the day's event of entertaining family and friends at their housewarming, Gwendolyn and Kenneth Bentley both drifted back off to sleep.

Abruptly, the quietness of the night was disturbed by a growing noise in the hallway.

Gwendolyn's eyes shot open as she coughed uncontrollably.

"*Oh no!*" Kenneth's sleep haze cleared as he jumped up from the bed and ran to the door.

With a deafening scream, Kenneth snatched his hand from the scorching doorknob that instantly formed blisters on the tips of his fingers. The searing blood coursed through his veins as he hollered in pain. With sweat trickling down his flushed skin, Kenneth's dread-filled eyes quickly surveyed the room. He searched for a towel, a jacket, a sock, anything that would protect his hands so they could escape the dark, smoky deathtrap. Having spotted a glimmer of hope a few steps away, his pasty bare feet clamored across the hardwood floor. He hurriedly grabbed the decorative cloth runner from the dresser-top to pad his hand from the fiery handle. Just as he got within inches of the exit again, Kenneth watched in horror as an orange glow blazed underneath the door. With defeat in his eyes, he glanced back at his wife who had fear in hers.

"We have to get out of here!" Gwendolyn shrieked as her eyes searched for refuge. "The bathroom!" The illuminated plug-in from the bathroom shed an additional sliver of light that allowed them to maneuver through the haze in the room.

Just as Gwendolyn rounded the foot of their bed, a part of the ceiling collapsed in front of her and blocked the bathroom door. She screamed hysterically. Kenneth shouted for her to wrap herself in the housecoat he had just yanked from the rocking chair in the corner. The fire was spreading quickly as the air steadily grew thin.

"What are we going to do?" Gwendolyn cried. "I thought you said this would never happen!"

Kenneth tried to calm his wife down as he took another try at breaking the jammed window. "Somebody blocked it from the outside!" He fiercely jabbed a curtain rod that had been torn from the wall against the tempered glass. "*Oh my God, oh my God, I never thought he would go this far.*" The rod folded in his hands as his mind incessantly repeated his wife's brother-in-law's dismissive comment from a casual conversation earlier in the day: *What the mayor wants he usually gets ... he never lets go without a fight.*

Gwendolyn shook uncontrollably as her entire body erupted with beads of sweat from the sweltering heat. The blankets they tossed on the growing fire only seemed to boost the flames. "This isn't working!" Gwendolyn shouted as she tripped, accidentally ripping the hem of her nightgown in the process.

Kenneth soon realized that the bedding he threw on the fire was laced with some sort of combustible fluid. In suspicion, his mind immediately flipped back to the woman who had laundered two of his wife's hand sewn blankets. The bedspreads fashioned with average material, but lots of love, were a housewarming gift to themselves. Gwendolyn had spent a year and a half stitching in between her day job at the bank and caring for her family at night to assemble those covers. Kenneth didn't want Gwendolyn to know they had been ruined a few days prior when their daughter, twelve-year-old Kara, accidentally spilled grape juice on them. So, he took them to be cleaned before she returned home that day from an appointment at the out-of-town law office they had previously visited.

After legally finalizing ownership of a sizeable acreage of land where it was rumored that items dating back to slavery may have been located, those suspicions proved to be true. Professional artifact recovery diggers who paid the Bentleys to rent use of their land just weeks before their home was to be built found numerous relics buried beneath the ground. The percentage profited from the found items surprised both Gwendolyn and Kenneth.

During a subsequent visit to the law office while their house was being built, the Bentleys signed off on paperwork that protected their children if anything should happen to them. It was a precautionary measure they hoped would never have to be used. With money in the bank from ownership of that property, they had secured their family's financial future.

"Oh honey, I'm sorry." Kenneth clutched his wife in his arms as they cowered in a clearing of the bedroom's walk-in closet still partially occupied by stacks of unopened cardboard boxes. "I never thought it would come to this." The sorrow in his eyes barely began to describe the grief in his heart as he wept, "Let's just pray that the girls got out all right."

Kenneth regretted the day that he convinced his wife to move back into the small town of Dadenville. His wife was right about the racism, despite their prerogative to buy land available to the public; in that town many unjust benefits came with generations of political clout. Kenneth never thought that securing a successful land bid over Mayor Jenson would cost them their lives.

Gwendolyn sobbed with heavy pants, "*Lord, p-p-please watch over my girls.*" Her eyes focused on the wooden framed picture of her daughters, Kara and Miriam, which inadvertently tumbled to the floor. Gwendolyn's fingers trembled as she ran them across the cracked glass overlaying the image of her children's faces. The reflection of the flickering flame bouncing off the glass caused her to look away. Crushed, she buried her face in Kenneth's chest.

"God will make sure that they have each other," Kenneth said, yanking the closet door closed. He then tightened the grip on his wife as the sound of crackling wood pierced their ears and choking smoke ballooned in their lungs. "Don't worry," he fought to say in between violent coughs, "Miriam will be there for Kara."

# CHAPTER 1

*New York City, five years later ...*

THE KEYSTROKES BLENDED beautifully into an edifying combination that would have delighted the most famed composers. Kara Bentley sat at a Louis XV Grand piano with a slightly arched back confidently stroking a masterpiece. Her uniquely draped evening gown cascaded just inches above the mystic black, marble stone flooring. She mesmerized the audience with her awe inspiring, medley rendition of classical music. As Kara's captivating performance concluded, the crowd erupted into a standing ovation. Wendell McGuire was among those who had catapulted to their feet, briskly clapping his hands together.

Kara modestly stood with one hand lightly atop the ivories and took a bow. She raised her head in relief that she had once again defeated the odds. Only one person believed in her enough to daringly submit the videoed raw version of her selections for a previous audition—Wendell. That submission to the theater's owner only guaranteed a possible chance to be a part of tonight's performance. That possibility became a reality.

In the heat of excitement Wendell met her backstage.

"My goodness, you were great out there!" he exclaimed, extending his arms towards her. "If I didn't know any better, I'd say you were holding out on me, girl."

Kara unassumingly blushed, falling into his waiting arms. "Thank you ... thank you for everything." She peered up at him, and then graciously admitted, "I couldn't have done this without you, Wendell."

For a moment, Kara had forgotten all of her troubles. She allowed herself to be swept into a celebratory night. It was what she had worked so hard for and now she could assertively declare that she had performed before one of Juilliard's most notable faculty members.

"So, did you see her? Did she say anything about my performance? It was so nice of you to do this for me." She briefly glanced away before meeting eyes with him again. "I know it wasn't easy to convince your aunt to allow me this opportunity, especially on opening night of her theater."

Wendell methodically stroked his chin, pleased at how impressively humble Kara was. "You've thanked me enough by that performance out there. My aunt trusts my recommendations and don't forget that you did a dynamite job with that showcase last week." He winked at her. "But I think tonight's performance may have been enough to get her friend at the college to notice your skills. That was gutsy to switch things up and toss in a Brahms waltz instead of a Mozart or Hayden sonata."

Kara stood back, surprised that he knew anything detailed about classical music. "You know composers? After all this time, I had no idea."

"Hey, you couldn't grow up in the McGuire household and not know your composers," he jested. "We had very limited choices for summer hobbies, but truth be told after all was said and done, I just couldn't let go of learning about film production."

Kara gave him a wary eye. "Film production as a hobby?"

"Yeah," Wendell said with a convincing nod. "But I had to learn about the other arts before my parents even allowed me to make a decision.

I guess they wanted to ensure that I learned as much as I could before leaving home. My parents always reminded us that just because they're rich don't mean that we, me and my sister, are." Wendell chuckled. "They drilled into our heads that we better make a way for ourselves because all they were responsible for doing was giving us a head start."

"*Man*, I thought I had it rough," Kara joked.

Wendell grinned. "Hey, it made me a well-rounded person. At least I know that sonata wasn't just my swim instructor's name."

They both erupted into laughter. Kara shook her head at Wendell who playfully shrugged.

"Oh before I forget," he casually began.

"What is it?"

"I have a little something for you." With a growing smile, he reached inside of his tailored fit sport coat and pulled out a playbill.

"I'm in there?" Kara's eyes widened as she bubbled over with joy, bouncing up and down like an elementary school-aged girl while quietly clapping her hands together. "But I thought your aunt said I was only the prelude to the show." She peered at the inside cover and excitedly gasped, "*Wow!*"

"Well, when you get to know my aunt you'll find that she doesn't do anything small nor conventional. If she believes in you, the world will know." Wendell flashed his gorgeous smile. "Besides, the way you played tonight sounded like a seasoned professional."

"I don't know what to say." With her lips slightly parted, Kara gazed into his mesmerizing brown eyes.

"You don't have to say anything," he replied, slowly wetting his bottom lip as he confidently folded his arms across his chest, "just let me take you to dinner."

Kara's radiant olive skin became flushed. Wendell took notice, but didn't speak on it.

"I think my aunt and her friend will be having an interesting conversation about you later tonight. Don't be surprised if you get a call first thing in the morning."

Kara instinctively pecked Wendell on the cheek, recoiling as quickly as she had reached out. "Oh, I'm sorry." She nervously swayed her limp wrists back and forth. "I shouldn't have done that."

Wendell grinned at her glowing innocence. "You don't hear me complaining."

Kara shyly smiled as he escorted her to his vehicle.

Moments later the two entered a quaint restaurant facing the Hudson River in Manhattan's West Village. On a date with an attractive, older guy, Kara was now the complete opposite of the confident young woman who had just brilliantly mastered Frederic Chopin's Etude in C# minor Op.10 No.4 after an excerpt arrangement featuring the famed 1812 Overture from the repertoire of Tchaikovsky. With a deflating poise, Kara timidly tapped her fingertips on the tabletop.

Wendell's eyes rotated upward from Kara's slender fingers to her strikingly beautiful face. She wore her youth well. His romantic advances towards her remained hidden as he carefully planned out the right moment to share his affection towards her.

"Are you practicing?" Wendell prompted his eyes towards her pattering fingers.

Kara easily smiled, quickly withdrawing her hands from view. "Oh, I'm sorry. It's just that I've worked very hard on that piece and now I can't seem to get it out of my head."

Wendell irresistibly looked on as she pushed a pin back into place of her attractively arranged hair. He then reached across the table with open palms and Kara hesitantly allowed hers to rest on top of his. "Stop saying that you're sorry. You have nothing to be sorry about. You did a wonderful job, and you know I don't give out compliments unless I mean it." He winked.

Wendell drew a smile from Kara, overshadowing the serious expression she wore.

"Now, that's what I like to see, your beautiful smile."

Kara could do nothing to keep from blushing as a lock of her wavy hair rested gently beside her distinguishing cheekbone. He knew all of the right words to say and when to say them. Kara had never had a serious boyfriend, but at the age of seventeen she hadn't expected to. In between classes at school and long hours of practicing the piano there was barely enough time to do much else.

"So, do you honestly think I have a chance? I mean, there are so many talented hopefuls—"

"And you're one of them." Wendell's deep voice held confidence.

Kara contained her excitement of how highly he thought of her.

"Don't sell yourself short. I mean it," Wendell urged. "Your hard work is really paying off. Mark my words, you're getting into Juilliard," he persuasively said, pointing a finger at her while still holding her hands.

Kara's hazel eyes beamed at the thought of being a Juilliard graduate. She had proficiently performed many recitals as a child and the buzz around her distant and rural hometown in northern Mississippi deemed her a child prodigy. Not to mention being a finalist of a major international piano competition just before her parents' untimely demise.

"I sure hope so. I've worked and prayed really hard for this. It hasn't been easy over the past couple of years, but I've never lost the passion for music ..." She began to choke on her words, but quickly composed herself. "My parents sacrificed so much for me to succeed."

Wendell nodded knowingly. He gently released the grip on her hands as the waiter placed their dinner selections before them.

"Kara, will you do the honor?" Wendell asked her.

Kara respectfully nodded and prayed over the food.

The two sat for nearly an hour talking about the performance and how well received Kara was by the audience. They chuckled at the fact that they had skipped out on the remaining program, simply excited about celebrating her performance and privately being in the company of one another.

"I guess that Miriam didn't make it. Why wasn't she there?" Wendell asked about Kara's older sister.

"Well, she's just not the biggest fan of classical music," Kara reasoned.

"I guess it's not for everybody." Wendell complacently shrugged his broad shoulders as he cut into his porterhouse steak. "But I would think that since her younger sister was so good at it, she'd at least show a little support."

Kara warmed even more from the attention he was showering upon her. It hadn't been since she was twelve years old that she'd received such acceptance. Kara remembered her parents as the most loving couple anyone would ever want to meet. After all, they had groomed their biracial daughter to dream big and never settle for less. Kara took every positive word they had instilled in her to heart. Lately, it just always seemed to tarnish in the presence of her older sister.

Miriam, ten years Kara's senior, took custody of her younger sister just after finishing college. She had been home that summer after graduation, searching for full-time employment. Just moments after their new family home caught fire from what the fire department reported as a faulty wire in the hallway bathroom, Miriam promised to be there for Kara. When she was awoken by the frantic screams of their mother, Miriam snatched Kara from her room and helped her through a window to safety as black smoke rose all around them. Miriam wanted to go to her parents' bedroom, but she had only moments to save herself from the licking flames.

"How's your food?" Wendell asked.

Kara nodded with a smile. "It's very good. How was the steak?" She pointed at his plate with her fork.

Wendell gestured at the scraps of vegetables left behind on his otherwise empty plate. "You tell me."

They joined in laughter.

Wendell's hearty appetite got the best of him tonight as opposed to Kara's. She instead asked for a take-out box, having barely touched her roasted garlic chicken, seasoned red potatoes, and lightly buttered asparagus. After refusing dessert and paying the bill, Wendell followed Kara out into the night. They received pleasant stares along the way due to their formal attire.

"Oh, I'll be sure to return the dress after I have it cleaned," Kara offered.

"Nah, don't worry about it. My sister won't be attending any more cotillions. *Not at her age.*" Wendell chuckled, gently touching his neatly trimmed goatee that extended from his thin mustache. "Besides, she's no longer a size six," he added with a smirk. "You can have it, the shoes too. She said so."

Kara graciously accepted the gift. "Tell her I said thank you. I'll be sure to save it for another event." She glanced down at the flowing, amaretto gown with the incredibly warm inner lining. The satin straps graced her shoulders perfectly. Wendell quickly draped the matching shawl wrap across her partially exposed back to shield her from the nippy November air.

After he snapped from his hypnotic gaze on Kara, Wendell opened his car door for her. Once she was safely inside, he dashed around the graduation gift from his generous parents—a liquid platinum G37 Infiniti Convertible—and slid behind the steering wheel.

Wendell McGuire, the twenty-two-year-old who had successfully completed a directing apprenticeship after his undergraduate years at one of New York's most prestigious film academies, was absolutely smitten with the striking, but young Kara Bentley. He had noticed her while she waited for her best friend at a casting call for a short film he was working on during the summer. His approach was an unorthodox one that not only caught Kara off guard, but him as well. After shamelessly interrupting a conversation Kara was having with her friend, Wendell was disappointed to find that she was only seventeen. Although drawn by her outward beauty, Wendell was absolutely captured with her inner charisma.

Initially he had assumed she was there for the leading role, but soon found that Kara's abilities rested within the art of producing beautiful music.

"So, what's the address again?"

Kara repeated the street address of her destination and Wendell relayed it into his GPS. Moments later, they arrived in front of an elegantly renovated historic mansion. Kara stepped out as Wendell held her hand for support.

"This is a beautiful home, Kara." Wendell's gaze drifted from the exquisite front door design to the aesthetically landscaped entrance. "Now, I kind of feel foolish for offering you my sister's old dress."

"Oh no, you shouldn't. And it's not old ... really, I appreciate it."

Wendell nodded as he glanced down. "So, why haven't you invited me over sooner?" He then curiously looked at her for an answer.

Kara timidly skirted her eyes away to the cars passing on the street.

"We've known each other for over three months, and I haven't even met your sister yet." Wendell gently touched her on the arm, drawing her attention back to him. "I know we're just friends, but I would still like to get to know you better."

Kara slowly exhaled and gently bit the corner of her bottom lip. "Wendell, I just don't think it's a good idea for you to come inside," she cautiously answered. "Besides, you don't know my sister. If you met her, she'd automatically assume that we're dating and that you're too old for me."

"But you're an honors senior who'll be eighteen in a few months," Wendell interjected.

"You remembered?" Kara easily blushed. "I must've told you that ... I think just after we met."

"Yeah, it was on my birthday that you told me. I wrote the date down. February twenty-fifth." Wendell's shoulders then shrunk in embarrassment. "Uh, I don't believe I just said that ... *wow* ... I'm sounding like a girl with a diary." He ashamedly lowered his head as he slid one side of his sport jacket behind a hand parked at his waist.

"I know right, not just any diary, one with dancing dandelions on the cover." Kara giggled at his obvious shame. "Don't worry, I won't tell anybody." She playfully tapped him on the forearm.

Wendell looked up with the slight raise of a brow. "*Gee thanks.*" He awkwardly chuckled. "I don't think this would go over too well with the fellas. Especially my boy Tim."

"That's right, you told me how hard your friend, Tim, *the detective*, is on all of you guys. He would never let you live it down." Kara giggled again before peering back at the house. "Look, thanks for seeing me here." She then tightened the shawl around her body. "I guess we'll talk on tomorrow."

He pressed her to let him walk her to the door, but she adamantly refused. Wendell caved in to her request and waited on the sidewalk near his vehicle until she was safely inside.

There was something mysteriously peculiar about the beautiful Kara Bentley, a young woman who was intellectually mature beyond her years. She was attractively innocent like a delicate, untouched flower in bloom. He desired more from her and to know more about her, but tonight Wendell reluctantly dismissed the oddities and drove home.

# CHAPTER 2

"HONESTLY MELISSA, THIS is not a shelter. I wish you would stop bringing home strays." The mother of Kara's best friend spoke coldly as she stood at the bottom of the majestic staircase. "Now, I'm leaving for my weekly game of tennis. The girls are coming back for brunch, and I don't want them to see her here." She casually cleared strands of hair from her long eyelashes. "*Do you understand me?*" Talia's snobbish tone reeked of arrogance. She spun around in her perfect length, white pleated skirt with matching tights underneath and form fitted zipper front sweater.

Melissa stood shaking her head as her mother exited the front door with a small purse casually hanging from the bend in her elbow. Franklin, Melissa's father, came alongside his daughter carrying a thermos filled with chai tea in one hand. She rested her head on his chest and miserably muttered, "Daddy, why is she like that?"

"Don't take it personal, sweetie." He kissed her on the forehead. "Your mother just wants to make sure that you have the best."

Melissa raised her head, making direct eye contact with her father who shared the same deep toffee colored skin she had and said, "But Daddy, I do. I couldn't have found a better friend than Kara. How am I going to tell her that she can't come over anymore?"

"Oh honey," Franklin sighed and squeezed his daughter's shoulder, burying her further into his chest. "Now don't you worry about that. You know how your mother is always in and out of town on sporadic shopping trips. She sure loves those Paris fashions," he mentioned as a faraway gaze momentarily washed over his face, "and my pocket pays for it." He let out a soft chuckle and then quietly cleared his throat, focusing back on his daughter. "So, when her schedule puts her out of town, how about you and Kara make a weekend of it?"

Melissa's eyes beamed. "Every time, Daddy?"

"Every time, sweetheart," he assured her. "Now, will you have some free time to spend with me this afternoon?"

Melissa slowly shrugged. "I guess so since Kara has to leave."

"Douglas will get her home safely. Now go on up and tell her to get ready."

Franklin Peterson was a gentleman to the core who had accumulated his wealth from good, old-fashioned hard work. He carefully planned on many occasions to instill in his daughter the mechanics of his successful investment firm and today was no different. It saddened him that he never had a son to pass the company on to, but after suffering with his wife through three miscarriages since the birth of Melissa, he had long since given up on that dream. Franklin simply threw himself into his work to get his mind off of their losses.

Franklin and Talia Peterson, married for nineteen years, now enjoy the wealth from his boutique investment firm that catered to the city's elite. They are strong financial supporters in their local church where Talia actively participated by teaching the church etiquette portion of new member classes—a position she accepted just eight months ago.

When the two initially got married, it was like a honeymoon for the first year. During their humble beginnings, Franklin and Talia had some of their best times. They used to spend hours laughing while at the local laundry mat. As their clothes washed, they would often devour pizza slices and chicken wings from the neighborhood eatery. Then things changed after Melissa came along, but for the better. Franklin became more driven to provide for his growing family. A few smart investments just after their daughter was born helped build the business and his bank accounts to what they are today.

Just before the September 11th attacks, Franklin had removed most of his holdings from the stock market and reinvested primarily in short and long-term certificates. It didn't strike him how blessed he was until he saw the devastation of the economy in the subsequent months and years. Franklin soon realized that God had blessed him to be a blessing, so for years now he has given back generously through foreign missions and local charities.

"Well, I'll be glad when Mom takes her next trip." Melissa released her father's embrace. "Thanks again, Dad."

Franklin softly smiled as he replied, "You're welcome." Pondering his own issues with Talia, he turned and walked away.

Melissa took large strides up the staircase to her room, excited that she didn't have to banish her dear friend from their home all together. She couldn't understand how her mother, an active member at Faithful Christian, could treat Kara in such a way.

The entire Peterson household has attended the Faithful Christian Center for well over ten years now. Melissa has starred in several of the church plays while her father offered his skills as a member of the trustee ministry. Although Franklin enjoyed traveling on certain foreign mission trips whenever his schedule allowed, he felt more at home in the financial office.

Melissa slipped inside of her spacious bedroom adorned in fun pastel trimmings. Her eyes moved from one corner where two zebra-print bean bags rested around to the cushiony soft Melrose pillows thrown in front of her pink laptop computer.

"Kara?" Melissa called out as she glided across the plush carpeting to the partially open French doors leading to one of the three private gardens located on the property. Although it was nippy outside, she had momentarily left Kara sitting in the garden before she had skipped downstairs to tell Douglas, the long-time family attendant, that she was going to have breakfast upstairs with her best friend. As Melissa stared at the empty chairs on the terrace she wondered where Kara had disappeared.

"Yeah?" Kara emerged from behind the bathroom door with a vibrantly decorated monogrammed towel tucked securely around her body.

Melissa walked back inside of her room. "There you are."

"I was just about to get in the shower," Kara replied. "What'd you need?"

Melissa closed the terrace door as she smiled at her best friend of two years. "Douglas will be up in about fifteen minutes. We're having fattening buttermilk pancakes and cholesterol clogging eggs." She released a sinister giggle as she playfully tapped her fingertips together.

Kara chuckled. "Your mother will have a fit if she saw you eating that."

"Well, she'll be gone for at least two or three hours. She'll never know." Melissa reached out and gave her friend a pinky shake. "It'll be our little secret."

"Why don't you tell her that you don't want to model?"

Melissa steadied her eyes onto her oblivious friend. "The same reason I can't get my father to understand that I'm not going to be a business major. I mean *hello*, I have an acting coach and audition for parts every chance that I get."

The two close friends laughed in unison.

Melissa then added, "Not to mention that I'm in a specialized high school for music and performing arts."

"Girl, I'm so glad that we're in the same high school or we probably would've never met," Kara admitted.

"Let me tell you, it was no small feat getting my parents to allow it," Melissa confessed. "I've been in private schools all my life, *all girls* private school might I add," she stressed. "I just felt that it was time for something different. Mom and Dad finally agreed that since this public school has stringent admission criteria, and better ratings than some of the private schools," she intermittently laughed, "they'd let me give it a try."

"Well, thank the Lord for that," Kara praised.

Melissa returned an endearing smile. "Not to mention that it's near *Juilliard*," she hummed. "Living here with my parents in this beautiful house is nice, but I can't wait to get out of here and be on my own. At least being at our school helps to be around other people like me. You know what I mean, I get to *really* immerse myself into acting without having to wonder if my mother is going to pull me aside to talk about modeling or if my father is going to do the same thing to talk me into the family business."

"I hear ya, Mel, acting is your thing. I could only dream of being that confident on my feet." Kara pulled her soft hair up into a turquoise scrunchy.

"Girl, please don't start. You got me beat hands down with your musical skills. How do you learn how to play such difficult pieces so quickly?"

"I guess it's just natural, my dear," Kara teased in a British accent.

"Oh, you got jokes." Melissa tossed a squishy stress ball in Kara's direction that tapped her on the arm. "I don't know what I was thinking playing that British role. I did well at the auditions, but I got a bad case of the giggles when shooting actually began. I couldn't even keep a straight face."

"I know and the director kept yelling '*cut, cut*'!" Kara kidded.

Melissa collapsed onto her king-sized bed, laughing to no end.

"But I'm glad you had me along. Wendell has been a dream come true! Can you say F-I-N-E?" Kara dramatically rested her hands across her chest as she dropped against the door frame.

"Girl, I know," Melissa agreed. "That brother has got it going on."

"Don't you know that I accidentally kissed him last night?"

"*What*?" Melissa sat up with wide, piercing eyes. "You kissed him?"

Kara giggled before rushing to her friend's side, quickly spilling the details of what had happened the night before.

Melissa leaned in and listened attentively as each word poured from her friend's lips. "Well, you better not let Miriam find out."

"I know." Kara's excitement fizzled at the thought of her overbearing sibling. "She's always up in my business as if I'm still twelve years old. I'm almost eighteen. And she always has a way of reminding me about why she's in that wheelchair. But as soon as I graduate I am out of there."

Melissa sat speechless in her form fitted lime green and black warm-ups. She had missed Kara's performance last night because she herself was busy at a meeting for the spring drama festival at school. When she got in, Kara was already fast asleep.

Melissa pitied Kara and all she had gone through with losing her parents at the age of twelve. After becoming such close buddies at school, Melissa aimed to share whatever she had with Kara just as she had been taught at church.

There was a light tap at the door before a properly spoken voice said, "Melissa, breakfast will be served in five minutes."

"Thank you, Douglas," Melissa answered.

The two listened as his footsteps tapered away.

"Well, I better get to my shower. I'll tell you more about Wendell later." Kara tapped her friend on the hand before standing up.

"Okay girl, but I want more details." Melissa pointed at her, adding, "And not that rushy-rush stuff either."

Kara smiled as she grabbed her toothpaste and toothbrush from her bag. She then quietly sighed as she zipped her bag closed. With slightly downcast eyes, Kara timidly began, "Uh Mel, do you think I could—"

Melissa held up a hand. "I got you. Don't worry, I'll take care of it."

Kara exhaled in thanksgiving. "You'll never know how much I appreciate this."

"You're my girl. If it were me, you'd do the same thing."

Kara gently nodded before disappearing to the bathroom.

Melissa looked toward her closet overflowing with designer clothes, handbags, and shoes. After a heavy sigh, she quickly grabbed her friend's duffle bag from the floor and rushed it down to the laundry room. With a compassionate heart, Melissa felt that washing a load of Kara's clothes was the least she could do for her friend.

Perched on the edge of the garden-style jet-stream tub, Kara ran her fingers across the polished granite tiles. She giggled as she wiggled her toes through the fibers of the posh bath rug. Her shoulders relaxed as she tilted her head backwards. This was a life she could get used to.

"*Ugh!*"

Startled by the noise outside, Kara peeked out of the bathroom window and saw Melissa's mother standing behind the trunk of her convertible Mercedes while her tennis racquet lay on the cement sidewalk. Talia shook her head as she pulled her cell phone from her ear.

Kara thought Talia was a beautiful lady with a lot of class. She often thought of what it would be like if she and Melissa were sisters. But when Talia stared up to the bathroom window and didn't return her pleasant gesture of hello, Kara's admirable thoughts of her soon passed away.

# CHAPTER 3

*LORD JESUS, GIVE me the strength*, Talia's thoughts continuously pulsed through her mind.

It was uncustomary for the fashionable, fair-skinned wife of a successful businessman and mother of a studious teenager to entertain anything that may shatter her seemingly perfect life. But as Talia sat at an attractively adorned round table, that's exactly what she was doing.

"Have you given any more thought to my proposal?" Donovan Carson reached across the table with slightly callus ridden hands and tenderly grasped Talia's soft, manicured fingertips. "You know no one will ever find out." His eyebrows danced in a mischievous way.

"Stop it, Donovan," Talia brashly whispered, yanking her hands away from his. It had taken her years to get this man out of her system, but there was something unseen drawing her to him. "I can't do this." She adamantly shook her head. "No, things are different now ... things are good between me and Franklin," she tried to convince him.

Donovan arrogantly scoffed. "Just like last time?" he bitterly questioned.

Those words drove nails into Talia's heart. She lowered her head with regret. Talia had since asked God's forgiveness for her past indiscretions and believed that He had done just that. But now as she sat in front of the man who had convinced her to break her marital vows years ago she wondered if she could truly remain loyal to Franklin. It was a challenge to think with a pure heart as Donovan's muscular physique reminded her of how weak her flesh really was around him.

"Look, I'm sorry. I shouldn't have said that," his smooth voice serenaded her ears. "I know that he's your husband, but you can be honest with me. I know you, Talia ... we have history." Then in a patronizing way he added, "We've been together on *many* occasions."

Talia folded in a portion of her bottom lip as her eyes drifted away from his. Their connection, as she would call it because she'd never admit that it was a relationship, was bittersweet. During the most challenging moments in her marriage, Donovan was there. She found solace in his arms. Talia felt that Donovan understood as he similarly experienced the same dissatisfaction at home with his wife.

"We're good together," Donovan continued. "We understand one another like no one else. You have your own life and so do I, but when we come together, *it's just right*," he quietly moaned.

Talia fidgeted uncomfortably as his words attempted to embed her heart. She didn't want to go back from where God had delivered her. It was a long road to recovery and on her seventeenth wedding anniversary to Franklin—roughly two years ago—she'd say that they had salvaged what was once lost. After five long years of privately working through their marital problems things were finally back on track. Franklin had begun paying more attention to her than his demanding workload, and she had promised to never again violate the trust her husband had regained in her. In hopes that their marital vows would be restored that pledge was made seven years ago.

Donovan scooted his chair closer to the table and whispered, "I know what a woman like you needs." He wetted his lips and in an obnoxious tone added, "And let's be honest, he simply can't give it to you."

Talia tightened her lips before she rebutted, "That's not true." She abruptly hit the bottom of her fist on the tabletop. She glanced around the solarium at several patrons who momentarily shifted their attention to her. As they gradually looked away, Talia then whispered to Donovan, "Things are better between us."

"Then why did you answer my text the other day?" He mocked her with a raised eyebrow.

Talia sighed as she did not have a response for him. It was true that Donovan knew what she desired in certain areas of her life, but Franklin was the man to provide it. He was the one whom she promised to be with until death separated them. And as much as Donovan taunted and teased her, Talia was determined to stand firm on doing right by her husband.

"Why did you come here? I thought you didn't do work in this area anymore." She glanced at her watch, wanting to finish their conversation before her friends showed up for their weekly tennis match. "You really shouldn't have come here, especially to this club where my husband also has a membership."

"No worries," Donovan said, holding his hands up in defense before lowering them again with a smirk, "I'm not going to cause any trouble. I'm just relaxing and soaking up the atmosphere. The food here is great and the big screen television beats the one in my hotel room. What better way to pass the time while on a work assignment?" He slyly grinned. "Besides, I'm only on a temporary pass until my contracts are completed. But I am glad that you had mentioned it before or I would've never known that this place even existed." His eyes roamed from the intricately designed full-service interior to the manicured lawn leading out to the golf course. "Too bad the weather isn't conducive for my golf game." He chuckled. "But I bet you're enjoying the indoor tennis courts. You always liked to play tennis." Donovan grinned, shamelessly peering down at her crossed legs. "I can see how it's been keeping you in good shape."

Talia leaned closer to him as she questioned, "How did you know that I'd be at here?" Her eyes narrowed. "Were you following me?"

Donovan smugly shifted his eyes away again before burying them back onto Talia. "I don't have to follow you, Tee, you read like an open book. You always come to the club on Saturday mornings. I remember many things about you. Like I said, it just happened that I've secured a few construction contracts since that terrible storm and now have a temp pass," he said, casually tossing his hands in the air as he sat back in his chair. "That's all."

"Oh, *that's all* huh?" Talia shot a suspicious stare. "Well tell me, Donovan, what would your wife say?"

"Why bring her into this? You never cared about her before." Donovan sat up as he grunted. "Besides, we're not together anymore." As he twiddled his thumbs, Talia glanced at the fourth finger of his left hand. It was indeed absent of a ring. "We've been divorced for six months. The truth is that I figured you'd be divorced by now too. Let's be honest, physical intimacy is a big factor in any marriage."

Talia shook her head, having made up her mind that this was the last meeting she would have with this man. She couldn't believe that Donovan had the audacity to challenge her by alluding to Franklin's prior bout of impotence. Talia regretted ever revealing such a private matter to him. That's how the affair started between them. When she should've confided in her husband about how the lack of intimacy affected her, she turned to another man for comfort. This served as a reminder that being with Donovan was the biggest mistake of her life. Talia hated that she had cheated on Franklin during the months when he needed her support the most. It was an embarrassing issue to even discuss, but not talking about his erectile dysfunction sadly led to her drifting heart.

"Talia, I just want to show you how a *real* man would treat a woman like yourself." His eyes roamed from her thinly arched eyebrows down to her plunging neckline. "I see that you still have the necklace." Donovan quickly regained eye contact with her. "Did you ever work up the nerve to tell him the real meaning behind it?"

Talia closed her eyes as she clutched the heart pendant and pulled in a deep breath.

"Look, just tell me to leave and I won't bother you again. I only stopped by because I was in town." He then crassly mentioned, "I have money now, so you don't need him anymore. Those other contracts I used to talk about have all been secured. They've paid off in a *big* way. The dream home you always said that you wanted right off the water, I've built." He proudly patted his chest.

"*Do you think that's why I'm with my husband?*" Talia grimaced. "How dare you?"

"Let's face it, you're a woman with fine taste," he complimented her with a wink, "and there's nothing wrong with that, but you and I both know that his money was why you stayed with him."

"Donovan, I can't have this conversation with you here." She stood and grabbed her designer bag from a nearby stool.

"Tell me where and I'll meet you." He stood, towering above her.

Talia nervously looked out of the wood framed glass wall behind Donovan where she saw two of her friends walking towards the entrance. "Just leave or something, I can't be seen with you." She tried to push him in the opposite direction.

Donovan gently stroked her arm with his forefinger as he caved in to her request. Talia waved him off as she smiled in the direction of her friends. She distanced herself from Donovan and greeted the women near the health food bar.

"I hope we haven't had you waiting long," Helen said as she hugged her dear friend. "I had to see Vincent off this morning."

Talia shook her head, relieved that they hadn't seen her talking to Donovan.

"And I was just waiting for my neighbor to tell her husband goodbye for the *third* time before she finally let him go." Marissa smiled as she took her turn at hugging Talia. "You know how Helen is when he has to leave town."

The three women chuckled.

"So, did either of you talk to Rhea?" Talia asked as she glanced at her watch. "I spoke to her just before leaving home, but our call dropped. I hope the directions I gave her were clear enough for her to follow."

"Why doesn't she just use her GPS?" Helen asked.

"You know her, she complains about that thing getting her lost more times than she'd care to admit," Talia replied.

"Oh, well I can understand that. But no, I didn't talk to her, but then again, my phone was turned off. I didn't turn it on until Vincent left," Helen said with a smile. "Besides, you know how she hates leaving messages."

Talia then looked to Marissa who shrugged, and then replied, "She didn't call me either."

"Well, we may as well have a seat at the bar. Ever since we met her, she's always been fashionably late anyway," Talia joked. "I'll be glad when she gets the hang of living here."

The women chuckled again as they sat at the counter to the full-service health food bar. The club's posh amenities drew an elite crowd ranging from those who were wealthy business owners to savvy investors. The atmosphere was a comfortable one Talia had grown accustomed to. She reveled in the fact that she could afford this hobby as part of her lavish lifestyle.

"So Helen, how long is Vincent going to be gone this time?" Talia asked as an attendant slid her usual Saturday morning beverage to her. "I know how you are when he's out of town." She grinned as she sipped on her lime-infused water.

"Just a few days and then we're off for our annual vacation to Australia." Helen drew her head back and smiled endlessly. "I can't wait to relax and unwind with Vincent. We're going to have a *wonderful* time." She then raised her head and winked at her friends. "I'm going to personally see to it."

Marissa chuckled but couldn't relate as she was a single mother of a teenaged boy and girl. "Talia, do you hear her? She swoons over her husband like they just met."

"I hear her," Talia responded, somewhat disconnected from the conversation, trying to ignore the fact that Donovan was still lurking somewhere in the building. "But it's nice to see a couple still in love after twenty years of marriage."

"What about you?" Marissa reminded Talia. "You and Franklin have been solid for almost as long. I'm the one who should be taking notes. You both have married *very* well." She tapped her fingernails on the counter, admiring her friends' long-lasting relationships.

Talia took her words to heart, but instead of commenting she hesitantly nodded.

"Your prince charming will come along soon enough," Helen assured as she gently tapped Marissa on the forearm.

Marissa quietly sighed. "I'm sure that he will. Ever since I gave up on dating *projects*," she giggled intermittently, "just to clean them up for another woman to reap the benefits, I've decided to only go out with men who know *exactly* what they want. I want a man who doesn't mind opening doors and buying flowers instead of just flaunting his money around like my ex-husband did. I mean, is that too much to ask?"

Helen shook her head. "Girl, don't settle for less than what you want. He's out there and he'll love you *and your children* just the same. Trust me. Vincent embraced my Emily as if she were his very own. And she was only two when we met."

"I hear you," Marissa modestly agreed.

Just then Talia's phone began to ring. She looked up at her two friends and said, "It's her calling." She then answered the call in a singing voice, "*Hello, Rhea.*"

As Talia took Rhea's call, Donovan sauntered in the women's direction. His crisp polo shirt was slightly fitted, accentuating his bulging biceps. Marissa was immediately infatuated with him. She discreetly nudged Helen on the arm as he stopped near where they were seated and retrieved a complimentary bottle of water from the attendant.

"*Wow ...*" Marissa practically drooled at the sight of him. She watched as he gulped the water, polishing it off in a matter of seconds. "*Hmm*, he must have been rather thirsty." Marissa gently rubbed the collar of her V-neck shirt.

Helen glanced between Marissa and Donovan as Talia, who had ventured away from them and had her back turned, rattled off directions to Rhea who had taken a wrong turn on her way to the club.

"Why don't you say hi?" Helen urged her friend.

Marissa defensively drew back. "*What?* And sound like a desperate woman?" She shook her head while simultaneously waving a single finger. "No, not me. I am not the one."

"You're not desperate nor will you sound that way." Helen stared in Donovan's direction. He looked up after tossing the empty water bottle in a nearby trash bin and politely waved at her and Marissa. "See, he's nice," Helen whispered as she raised her hand in return. "Oh, he's coming this way," she mumbled while pinching Marissa on the back of her arm.

Marissa discreetly yanked her arm away from Helen as he got closer. Donovan took off the matching cap to his nicely fitted polo shirt as he walked within a few feet of where they were seated.

"Hi, how are you ladies doing?" He gently shook both of their hands. "My name is Donovan."

His smile could brighten a dark room. He had a face that would make a woman take a second look. Donovan was visually appealing, ever so suave, with alluring glances that were subtly seductive. Marissa's eyes moved from his professionally tapered hairline down to the barely detected veins in his arms. She could tell that he was a dedicated weight trainer—his form made that obviously apparent. His fingers were absent of rings and although Marissa wanted to appear uninterested, she inwardly hoped that he found her as attractive as she did him.

"We're doing fine, *Donovan*. I'm Helen and this is my friend, Marissa." She placed a hand on Marissa's shoulder.

Marissa gently cleared her throat as she looked away from Helen to Donovan. "It's nice to meet you." She bashfully waved.

"The pleasure is all mine." The sound of his smooth voice enticed Marissa even more.

Within minutes they exchanged pleasantries about themselves.

Moments later, Talia started back in their direction. Her footsteps stalled as she met eyes with Donovan again. A wave of confusion muddled with nervousness came over her. She couldn't believe that he was talking to her friends. In an attempt to conceal her emotions, Talia immediately cleared the dazed look from her face as she reached Marissa and Helen.

"Oh Talia, meet Donovan," Helen introduced him.

"*Talia*?" Donovan said in a mystified voice. "*Talia Peterson, is that you?*"

She glared at him, wondering what he was up to.

"Oh, do you two know each other?" Helen inquired.

"Uh yes," Talia reluctantly improvised. "He's an old friend." Her eyes skirted away from his.

"Yes, it is so nice seeing you again. You've hardly changed." Donovan gently touched her arm as he had only moments ago. "How is your family?"

Talia uneasily shifted her weight from one foot to the other. "Everyone is just fine."

"This works out even better," Helen interrupted.

Everyone looked at her, unsure as to what she meant.

"Well, Donovan just mentioned that he's in town on a work assignment and wanted to see a couple of the sights around the city. I figured that since you know him, he's safe to go out with Marissa."

Marissa and Talia both donned similar expressions for two very different reasons.

"*Helen*," Marissa gasped. "Who told you that he needs an escort while he's in town?" Although he aroused her interest, she didn't want to appear desperate. With an apologetic expression, Marissa looked at Donovan and said, "I'm sorry, you'll have to excuse my friend." She then glanced at Helen with an irritated glare. "She's the eternal matchmaker."

"That's all right," Donovan replied as he grinned. "Well, are you single? I would love to take you out."

Marissa slowly parted her lips, mesmerized by his aroused interest.

"Don't answer right away," Donovan insisted. "Here, take my card and call me later if you decide to take me up on my offer. Besides, Talia can vouch for me." He then looked to his past conquest and questioned, "Right, Talia?"

Everyone then looked in her direction. Talia tried to conceal the fact that this man was just attempting to rekindle the romance they once had together. The thought of him with a friend stirred puzzling emotions inside of her.

"Talia, are you all right?" Helen asked as she shook her friend's arm.

Talia snapped from her daze and nodded. "Uh yes, I'm fine. I was just thinking that Rhea will be here in five minutes, so we better get our racquets since she won't be able to join us at my house later."

"But we brought our racquets in with us." Helen motioned with her eyes to the racquets that rested beside the barstools.

"Oh, that's right." Talia embarrassingly nodded. "Well, you two better get changed since she has to show a house," she stammered. "I just don't want us to delay her."

"Oh, okay. Well, I better call my sweetie. I told Vincent I would call him before we started playing." Helen noticed how her friends stared at her as she hopped off the stool. "*What*? His flight won't get in until late tonight and he doesn't want to wake me knowing that we have worship service in the morning." She clutched her purse with one hand and extended the other one to Donovan. "Again, it was nice meeting you." Her new exquisitely crafted tennis bracelet, a surprise gift from Vincent, gently moved as she shook his hand. "Hopefully we'll be seeing more of you." Helen giggled as she walked towards the women's communal changing area with a phone in her hand.

"So, Marissa, just give me a call. Maybe we can grab a bite to eat or something." Donovan then turned away from her to Talia whose eyes held countless questions. "It was nice seeing you again, Talia. Take care. And you ladies enjoy your day."

Marissa draped her hands on Talia's arm as Donovan strolled away. "Talia, why didn't you tell me that you knew ... *someone like him*? He is single, right? I mean, *really* single because I don't care to get mixed up with a man who's on the rebound." She grunted. "You know the on again, off again type. Well, I would think that he is really single since he said you can vouch for him. He just seems too good to be true. So nice, so polite," Marissa incessantly rambled.

Talia nodded, although not completely forthcoming with the response she gave to her friend of three years. "Yes, he's single ... uh recently divorced."

Marissa's eyes glistened as she stared down at his business card. He became an even bigger catch when she noticed that he was the owner of the construction company noted in the news for working on a large project in the immediate area. "*Oh, I'm calling him tonight.*" There was a curious glint in her eyes. "We'll see how he feels about God. In fact, I think I'm going to invite him to church."

Talia suddenly stared at her friend, hoping that she'd see through Donovan's façade. She was sure that he was just using Marissa to get at her, and the sad part about it was that it was working. All through the tennis doubles played with her friends, Talia obsessed about Donovan. It seemed as if she had become weaker for him than she was before arriving at the club. Her wondering mind contributed to a losing streak three times in a row. Rhea was spent trying to cover Talia's missed swings, but the distracted woman barely noticed. After an intense hour of playing, the women quickly showered so they could join Talia at her home for lunch. Rhea apologized again for not being able to spend the afternoon with them, but they each committed to a standing date for the following week.

As Talia left the country club, she glanced back and noticed Donovan standing at the entrance, beckoning her with his eyes. She quickly looked away and slid behind the wheel of her Mercedes. Although she was married to Franklin, Talia hated the fact that Donovan was going to date one of her friends. He was her private past, a forbidden memory that she often tried to forget. Now with him offering to take Marissa out, he had become a tangible reality woven into her inner circle.

As she nervously adjusted the wedding ring on her finger, Talia remembered that she wasn't able to resist the temptation of the man who tested her fidelity years ago. After seeing him today, she hoped—*prayed*—that she would be able to now.

# CHAPTER 4

KARA'S SHOULDERS SLUMPED as the polished, black Cadillac Escalade pulled in front of her old, faded brick building. She slowly grabbed her ragged duffle bag from the floor, the box of left-over food from the seat, and the hanging garment tote which housed the beautiful evening gown she had elegantly worn the night before. The memorable evening with Wendell and the celebratory breakfast with Melissa had temporarily caused her problems to become a distant memory. However, as Kara longingly watched the vehicle disappear down the street, she was unwillingly transported back to reality. Her shoulders lowered even further in despair.

"Cinderella back from her ball?" Phillip shouted from the crowd of teenaged boys on a basketball court across the street from where Kara was dropped off.

Kara sucked her teeth as she steadied the duffle bag on her shoulder.

"Hey, I'll be right back," Phillip said, breaking up the basketball game with his group of friends.

"Man, at least leave the ball," a boy shouted while others joined in with similar sentiments as Phillip darted across the street.

"I'm coming right back, y'all, dang." Phillip waved them off as he jogged with the ball tucked underneath his arm to catch up with Kara. "Hey what's up, Kara?"

Kara nonchalantly shook her head as she started towards the entrance of the brick building.

"So, when are you going to hook me up with that cute friend of yours?" Phillip annoyingly bounced the basketball around Kara as she walked.

"Phillip, could you please leave me alone? Melissa doesn't want you," she grumbled, leaving him on the outside steps.

Phillip grunted as he simply waved her off too. "I wonder what her problem is," he mumbled to himself as he rejoined the group of teenagers to finish their game.

Kara made her way up six flights of stairs because the elevator was broken for the third time this month. She shuffled her way past a drunk who was brave enough to pull at her tattered tan bag. *Friday night drinking must just now be catching up with him,* she thought.

With a hand resting on the discolored doorknob that led inside of her Section 8 home, Kara peered upward. She needed strength from God to face what awaited her behind that door. It was always something with her sister.

"Meme, I'm home," Kara pleasantly announced upon entering the apartment home she shared with Miriam.

"It's about time." Miriam's tone reeked of bitterness. "I need you to run to the store for some grits and washing powder." Her words stalled as she rolled closer to where Kara was standing. With a grunt she said, "I guess the good folks let you use their expensive soap. I could smell you all the way over there."

Kara kept a straight face as she pulled her freshened duffle bag closer to her body.

"Humph." Miriam adjusted her frumpy old T-shirt and oversized sweatpants as she stared her sister up and down. "The money and food stamp card are on the table," she grumbled.

The SNAP (Supplemental Nutrition Assistance Program) card, where she received food benefits from the state, was often used as a financial bargaining tool. On several occasions Miriam would exchange it for a reduced cash value with others who lived in the building. If someone wanted to buy food for half of what it would ordinarily cost them, Miriam was their broker. She sold the benefits by allowing use of her state-issued card and then pocketed the money. Although she had lost her job and the decent income that came along it with, her clever business savvy was still intact.

"Make sure you hurry back because I'm hungry and you need to start a load of clothes." Miriam's voice was cold and domineering.

Kara balled her lips as her sister rolled away in her new leather sewn wheelchair provided by the government. "But I have practice at the church in a little while."

Miriam stopped mid-stroll and glared back at her. "Well, I guess you better hurry up then. You should've thought about all of that before spending the night out. *What,* you think you're supposed to have clean clothes and I'm not?" Miriam released a groan as she parked herself in front of the thirty-two-inch, flat screen television set recently donated by a local charity. "And don't even *think* about leaving my clothes in those machines unattended," she snapped. "I can't afford to have anything stolen."

In an attempt to sweeten the sour mood her sister had grown accustomed to, Kara politely said, "Meme, I brought you some food. I'm sorry for not getting back earlier." Kara raised the rectangular box by the neatly tied strings surrounding it from the memorable evening with Wendell. "I know how you like chicken and red potatoes," she said to her in a tempting voice.

Miriam looked back for the second time and recanted her scowl. "You brought me chicken?"

Kara nodded with hope that this would allow her to escape going to the store just this one time. "Yeah, there's asparagus and a buttered roll in there too."

Miriam spitefully shook her head. "Thanks, but I'm more in the mood for some grits right now. Now go on and do what I told you to do." She shooed her away.

Kara dropped her duffle bag onto the kitchen floor and draped her dress across the backside of the chair. She cut her eyes away from Miriam and snatched the money and food stamp card from the table. *I can't wait to graduate*, she thought as she reached for the front door knob.

"Oh Kara, bring back a box of pancake mix too!" Miriam called out in between bouts of laughter while watching a scene from her favorite sitcom.

Kara contained her anger and grumbled, "Yeah," before rushing out the door. She hurried down the stairs while glancing at the gold and white Juicy Couture watch Melissa had bought for her last Christmas. Kara knew there was no way she'd be able to finish chores and make it to practice on time. Before landing on the bottom step, she discreetly stuffed the watch back inside of her coat pocket. If anyone knew she had it, it was sure to be stolen. She constantly reminded herself to never wear it while at home.

"Your sister got you back on the beat, huh?" Phillip pounced on Kara as soon as she got outside.

She carelessly shrugged. "Something like that."

"You mind if I roll with you?"

Kara stared at him and nonchalantly shrugged again. "Whatever." She decided that it was better to have a male escort than not, even if it was Phillip from around the way.

Miriam sat frozen for several moments as she gazed at a photo taken on her college graduation day. She was dressed in a deep burgundy cap and gown with a gold honor cord draped around her neck. Miriam stared at the picture where she stood in between her loving mother, Gwendolyn, and generous stepfather, Kenneth. Kenneth, Kara's Caucasian father, had stepped in and taken care of Miriam like she was his own.

Miriam's birth father became a causality of war when she was just four years old. Although she doesn't really remember him, she found comfort in the countless childhood photographs her mother took of the two of them during the ten days leading up to what would be his final deployment. Gwendolyn grieved almost five years before she entertained the idea of marrying again. When she did find herself walking down the aisle, the entire family was surprised that it was to a white man from up north.

The phone rang and shook Miriam from her nostalgic daze. She picked up the cordless within arm's length and saw *The Juilliard School* scroll across the caller ID. Miriam hesitated on answering. She finally decided to allow the machine to pick up.

"Hello, this is Lois Chow from The Juilliard School. I am calling to speak with Ms. Kara Bentley about prepping for an audition for admission into our undergraduate program. Judging by the performance last night I would be delighted to work with you. Please give me a call back."

Miriam's face crumbled as the lady pleasantly rattled off a series of numbers for her direct extension. She mentioned that she was in the office for a couple of hours this Saturday and needed Kara to call back no later than three that afternoon. Miriam glanced up at the clock which read twelve fifteen before forcefully pressing the delete button, maliciously erasing the urgent message.

The familiar frowns on Miriam's twenty-seven-year-old face often challenged her chronological age. Ever since losing the use of her lower extremities roughly two years ago, she had lost a piece of herself too. The plans she had never included confinement to a wheelchair for the rest of her life. As she looked down at her lifeless legs, she knew she'd never forget the moment when a part of her freedom was stripped away.

Miriam flinched as the phone rang again. This time it was Melissa calling for Kara. After Melissa left a message, Miriam quickly turned the answering machine off, tired from all the attention her younger sister was getting. As much as she hated to admit it, her baby sister had grown into a beautiful young woman. They shared distinctive features characteristic to only their mother's side of the family. The only thing that separated their resemblance was skin color and hair texture. She and Kara looked so much alike.

Although their physical features were similar, the way they carried themselves was completely different. Kara enjoyed bright, dazzling colors while Miriam, since her accident, had grown fond of dark earth tones. Kara made the cheap clothing she wore look stylish as she dressed them up with trinkets from discount stores, a trade she had picked up from their late mother before her passing a few years ago. Miriam, on the other hand, had lost her zest for style, succumbing to the dreary environment in which she had become accustomed.

Miriam angrily pushed the wheels of her chair from the living room into the kitchen. She stared at the white box Kara had left on the table for her. Her stomach released a thunderous roll as she inhaled the aroma from the carefully prepared meal. It was indeed her favorite, chicken and red potatoes. She took the box from the square table with metal edges and slid it into the small counter microwave. Only a slice of remorse penetrated her heart as she thought about the way she had spoken to Kara. However, it immediately disappeared at the sound of the microwave's beeping buzzer.

Miriam groaned in satisfaction as she allowed the food to melt into her mouth. She hadn't been able to enjoy a meal like this since last year at the church where Kara attended. It was the church's twenty-fourth anniversary celebration where Kara played for the youth choir. Convinced by Deacon Jackson to leave the home on that particular Sunday morning for worship service, Miriam hadn't been back since.

After polishing off the last forkful of potatoes, Miriam casually tossed the empty box into the swing top trash can. With a self-gratifying moan, she stared down at her body and gently rubbed her stomach. Miriam had put on a considerable amount of weight in the preceding year, but she could care less that the food she had just eaten coupled with half of a refrigerated pie she had devoured earlier mocked any thought she conceived to battle the bulge.

"Who's there?" Miriam called out as someone knocked at the door.

"It's Deidra."

Miriam grunted to herself as she wheeled closer to the door and unlocked it. "What are you doing here? I told you that I didn't want any company," she rudely said, looking the tall, slender woman up and down before she spun her wheelchair in the opposite direction.

"I know, I know. I came by to see if you needed any help." Deidra Collins, the neighbor from downstairs, walked inside of the apartment and closed the door behind her.

"I've already told you ... *no*." Miriam rolled her eyes away from her. "I can handle things, Deidra."

"Well, I've heard differently. Now where are your clothes?"

Miriam frowned with contempt as she turned back around to face one of the two only friends she had left in the city. "Did Kara come bothering you?"

"No, no, leave that girl alone. I saw her outside and asked what she was up to—"

"And she talked about that church again, didn't she?"

Deidra slowly shrugged. "Well, it is a good thing that she's going. You know it's not such a bad idea that you go every now and then." Deidra glanced around the apartment with her eyes landing on the old, tattered tan curtains and faded placement rugs. "It'll do you some good to get out of here once in a while."

"I know what's best for me *and* my sister," Miriam grumbled. "Those clothes are going to be sitting right here until she gets back."

Deidra casually scratched the side of her neck. "Well, I told her that I'd take care of it."

"You did what?" The disdain burning in Miriam's eyes reflected the mounting hatred her heart harbored against Kara.

"Look Miriam, I don't mind," Deidra tried to convince her. "I was about to do laundry myself."

"You wait until she gets her little narrow behind back here." Miriam furiously folded her arms.

"Well, you're going to be waiting a long time. I had Phillip run down to the store for you so Kara could go to practice at the church."

"You had no right," Miriam growled through clenched teeth. "That was her place to do that!"

"I'm sorry." Deidra smirked as she defensively raised her hands. "I didn't know you were so touchy about people handling your intimates."

Miriam defiantly shook her head. "I'm not in the mood for jokes, Dee."

"When are you ever?" Deidra raised her voice back at her as she spotted two stuffed blue laundry baskets beside the sofa in the living room. "Is this it? I'll just take them and be back in a couple hours. In the meantime, think about the life your sister is trying to make for herself."

With that being said, Deidra picked up the stacked laundry baskets and firmly closed the door behind her.

Miriam was alone again, relentlessly bitter by the incident that left her wheelchair bound. She still blamed Kara for everything.

It was one late night of rehearsals at the church for Kara who had called her sister before she got off from work. As a human resources recruitment manager, Miriam used to work late on Mondays, so Kara knew it wouldn't have been out of her way to walk with her, especially since the church was only a few blocks away from where they used to live. She would have ordinarily had Deacon Jackson to see her home, but this was the only way Kara found to get her sister inside of the church walls for somebody else to talk to her about Jesus.

After leaving the sanctuary, Kara went on and on about how much she enjoyed playing for the youth choir and that it was a window of opportunity for her to make a little bit of money teaching students. In the midst of Kara's banter about the parents who had inquired about lessons for their children, a darkly dressed man quickly approached them and started grabbing at Kara's backpack. Miriam screamed and took hold of the man's hoodie as he tried to get away. When she wouldn't let go, the hooded stranger pulled out a gun and shot her.

Miriam shrunk into her chair, remembering the plans she had for herself. She thought about the job she had to give up due to her inability to effectively perform the duties required of her. Miriam hated to file for social security disability, but she had no choice. Over the years, resentment had made a firm home in her heart and all of it was geared towards Kara.

The twenty-seven-year-old had given up on life and vicariously lived through her only sibling. Miriam wanted it to be her whom people called day and night. She longed for the attention Kara received. Miriam was smart and beautiful too, but it was buried beneath layers of anger and pain. She had become hardened by jealousy and resentment. Somehow Miriam had lost her passion to be the person she once was. When she no longer possessed use of her legs, Miriam felt that she had lost herself as well.

*It's not fair*, she thought. *I was the one who sacrificed to raise that girl. I was the one who was there when members of her father's side of the family wanted nothing to do with her. I was the one who made sure that she had food in her mouth and clothes on her back. It was me, but she gets all of the attention because she can play a stupid piano.*

Miriam picked up the phone again and scrolled back to the recent call list. This time as she held the phone, she spitefully pressed a button that permanently erased all of the numbers from the caller ID, including the number to where Kara longed to build upon her talents for a professional career—Juilliard.

# CHAPTER 5

"THIS IS NOT going to work!" Wendell frustratingly sighed into the ear of a timid looking young woman. "None of the people we've seen can even act. I *need* star power." He slumped down onto a pale blue plastic chair, suddenly realizing his outburst. "Look, I'm sorry. I shouldn't have raised my voice at you. But answer this for me," he said in a lowered voice as he slid to the edge of his seat, "were you trying to do some friends a favor?"

"I'm so sorry." July's face reddened as her blonde razor-cut hair edges swayed with the slightest movement of her body. "It's my first day as a casting associate," she admitted, "and ... I, uh ... well, I guess I blew this one." July had been working as best she could on such short notice. "My boss had an emergency out of town. Since the other casting director took her place at a meeting in Los Angeles, I was given this opportunity. I was chosen over the other assistant." Tears welled in her eyes as she sighed in a defeated tone, "There goes my reputation and my job."

Wendell groaned with compassion, but business was business. There was no way that he could take any of the talent she had presented him with. The schedule was tight, and the budget was small. Not to mention that he was still trying to make a way for himself as a noteworthy director. He sympathized with July as it was definitely a burdensome situation. The principal lead had recently backed out of the project for a supporting role in her first high profile film. Wendell knew that this small independent project didn't pay what studio films did, but he had a lot riding on it.

It was a sizeable challenge to find actors willing to give up their entire Saturdays and most weeknights for the next three months on the pay he and his friend were able to afford. Financiers had sealed their commitment to the venture. All Wendell and his colleagues had to do was deliver the finished project. His partners Michael Gregory and Wayne Reynolds were unable to sit through auditions today. Michael, the production manager of the film, was out of town and Wayne, the assistant director, was absent because his day job required him to work at least one Saturday out of the month. So, it was up to Wendell to make the final call before his independent film moved into its next phase.

Exasperated, July and Wendell both turned their heads towards the entrance after a knock on the door.

"Look, get that. Let me see if I can sort some things out." Wendell picked up his cell phone.

The casting call today was for a curvaceous African-American female who looked to be in the age range of 25-32 and a model-type. She had to be attractive with a strong athletic build and commanding presence. Before Wendell's call connected, Leslie Brunson walked across the threshold, depicting a picture perfect reflection of the advertised character Monique.

"Am I too late?" She curiously glanced back at the large wall clock above her head. "I saw an *Out to Lunch* sign on the door, but this is my appointment time. I hope I'm not interrupting."

July made eye contact with Wendell who gave a slight nod.

"No, you're fine. We're reading for the part of Monique. Has your agent prepped you?" Wendell inquired as he uncharacteristically reached out to shake her hand.

Leslie momentarily folded in her lips before responding, "Uh, no agent as of yesterday, but yes I've reviewed the part." She held Wendell's hand a beat before releasing her grip.

"Well, do you have a copy of the side?" Wendell asked, searching her vacant hands for any sign of the movie script.

"Uh ..." Leslie began rummaging through her large shoulder bag. "I know I had it in here." She then frustratingly rested her hand on her forehead. "You know, I think I left it on the subway."

July motioned for Leslie to retrieve a copy of the selected scene from the stack on the wooden table just outside of the room. Wendell stared at July as Leslie left the room and shook his head. Moments later, Leslie returned carrying the script with highlighted lines.

Wendell sat down and pressed a button on the black video recorder resting upon an extended tripod. Leslie nervously smiled as the red light alerted her that she was on. She allowed her shoulder bag to slide down to the floor and quickly straightened the posture on her five-foot-eight-inch frame.

"Would you please slate for us," July said to Leslie.

Leslie nodded and rattled off her name. July then nodded for her to begin with the lines given to her. Only holding the paper in view for mere seconds, Leslie perfectly recited the lines verbatim, just the way Wendell had hoped.

After the audition, Wendell looked at July who quietly exhaled a sigh of relief.

"I signed the sheet outside beside my appointment time. Did you need any other information?" Leslie inquired.

With a delayed response, Wendell answered, "Yes." He slowly flipped Leslie's headshot over to the backside where he quickly glanced over her impressive résumé. "A secondary phone number."

Although Leslie's pleasant smile fondly reminded him of Kara's, Wendell clarified his request, "For a possible call back."

The excitement rapidly drained from Leslie's face. "Oh, okay." She tossed her shoulder length, midnight hair to her back and scribbled down her number on a pad July had slid in her direction. "Well, thank you for your time," she nervously said.

"Thank you too," July spoke up after pressing the stop button on the video recorder.

Leslie lingered before slowly retrieving her bag from the floor.

"Is there anything else?" Wendell questioned as he slapped a black baseball cap across his freshly cut hair.

"Uh no, nothing else ... thanks again." Leslie tugged on the sassy lyric skirt hugging her size eight thighs.

He gave a brief nod and nonchalantly instructed, "Please close the door on your way out."

Wendell turned to July as Leslie briefly rested her hand against the wide black belt tucked around her petite waistline. He picked up a stack of headshots and waited until she was out of the room.

"*So?*" July nodded, lifting her brows for an answer. "What do you think?"

As he folded his arms Wendell's blank expression transformed into one of satisfaction. "I think we can work with that." He pointed towards the door Leslie had just closed when she left the room. "Is there anyone else on the list?"

July shrugged as if she were empty of prospects. "She was the last one."

"She'll do." Wendell confidently pointed at Leslie's headshot. "Give her a call later on and tell her she's got the part. We begin shooting in one week. See if she can make the schedule. And make sure she has the full script to start memorizing lines."

July jotted down a few notes before both she and Wendell gathered their things to leave. They parted ways after exiting the building.

Wendell headed for his car in a nearby parking garage before catching a glimpse of the woman he had auditioned only moments ago. He looked on as she stood near the edge of a sidewalk and angrily shook her head.

"Is everything all right?" Wendell asked as he carefully approached her.

Leslie swung around, surprised to see the attractive, dark-skinned director heading her way. "Oh ... hey ... yeah, everything is fine."

"Okay," Wendell said as he resumed walking toward the parking garage with a bag stuffed with the video camera and retracted tripod in his hand.

"Uh, well no," Leslie called out after him.

Wendell gazed back at her.

"This is kind of embarrassing, but I just missed that stupid bus to take me across town to a job I may lose because I'm late again," she rambled. "I'd never make it in time if I walked."

Wendell glanced at his watch and then asked, "Why don't you just take the train?"

"Well to tell you the truth, I think my metro card is the same place where I left that script," she pathetically admitted. "The bus driver left because I don't have any cash on me." She heaved a sigh.

Wendell's eyes drifted from her pouty lips down to the form-fitting skirt wrapped around her body. He pulled in a deep breath and slowly exhaled.

"But this won't interfere with my ability to get to set," Leslie assured him as she stuffed her hands inside of her waist length jacket. "I'll do whatever I have to do *if* I'm called back." Her eyes held a hopeful gaze.

Wendell tugged on his cap as he eyed her again. Leslie's gaze practically begged for the part. Aside from her good looks, Wendell truly felt that she could act. "I guess I can tell you now, the wardrobe and lines were on point, you got the part. You *are* Monique."

Leslie's lips curled into a broad smile of absolute delight. "Are you serious?"

Wendell modestly nodded. "Yeah."

"Yes!" Leslie exclaimed, momentarily drawing attention from those around them. She quickly composed herself, temporarily removed from her recent dilemma. "Thank you so much. I won't disappoint you." She cupped her hands over her mouth while excitedly bouncing in place.

Wendell appreciated her gratitude. "If you do as well as you did on the audition, I'm sure that you won't."

Leslie blushed as she swiped a few strands of her hair behind her ear.

"Look, I don't usually do this, but I can give you a ride. I'm in the parking garage a block over. Being that I know a little bit about you and have your information," he halfheartedly chuckled, "I think I'm safe."

Leslie smiled with a slight giggle.

"So, would you like for me to give you a lift?"

"Yes, if you don't mind."

"If I minded, I wouldn't have asked." Wendell tightened the baseball cap on his head. "You do work here in Brooklyn, right?"

She gently nodded.

"All right, come on, I'm just over here." He waved for her to follow his lead.

Leslie glanced down at her wardrobe again as she followed Wendell to his car. She hoped that the part wasn't all she had captured today.

# CHAPTER 6

"ELIJAH'S MOTHER IS here, Kara," Deacon Jackson called from a pew.

Kara turned from the piano and waved as Jacqueline Stewart, one of the more active members of Faithful Christian, stood at the side door of the main sanctuary. "He's only got one more scale to finish."

Mrs. Stewart nodded at Kara and walked towards the front row of pews.

Seven-year-old Elijah waved happily at his waiting mother. He then turned and stroked the piano's keys, having only missed one note in the process. *"Ah man*, I almost had it." He snapped his fingers in disappointment.

Kara rested her arm around his shoulders. "That's okay. You did very well. Next time I bet you'll nail it." She raised her hand into a ball while Elijah followed suit and they gently pounded their fists together. "See you in church tomorrow, little man."

Elijah smiled at Kara before jumping down from the piano bench and rushing to his mother's side.

"Thanks so much, Kara. I'll have some money for you tomorrow before service." Jacqueline handed her son his backpack and jacket. "You take care and have a good night."

"Thanks, Mrs. Stewart." Kara waved goodbye to them both.

"Are you ready for me to take you home?" Deacon Jackson asked as he cut the lights off in the rear of the choir stand. "I have a date with my wife, and she doesn't like to be kept waiting." A wave of warm emotions swept over his youthful face. He wore sixty very well.

Kara grabbed her brown coat from the floor and skipped a few steps down that lead from the choir stand. Deacon Jackson answered his ringing cell phone as he waited for Kara near an exit.

"Yes dear, I'll be there in about thirty minutes after I drop Kara off at home. Are you dressed yet?" Deacon Jackson turned off the remaining lights in the sanctuary and followed Kara out into the foyer. He activated the alarm system for the church and held the door open for them to exit. "Great. I promise I won't be long." He ended the conversation with his wife as he and Kara walked outside.

Deacon Thomas Jackson was a dedicated follower of Christ. He has faithfully served the church, commonly known for its outreach work in the community, for the past five years. His duties around the church consisted of countless tasks performed out of the kindness of his heart. Deacon Jackson loved being a Christian and he enjoyed helping those in need.

"Thanks again, Deacon Jackson," Kara expressed her gratitude. "I'm sorry practice ran a little long tonight."

He gave Kara a fatherly hug as they walked along the busy street. "Don't mention it, dear. You do so much to help our young children that it's the least I could do for you. The youth choir has really come to life since you joined us three years ago. Even though there are so many talented people in the city, I really don't know where we'd be without you." Deacon Jackson's charismatic laughter tickled Kara's ears. "You have managed to pull out of those kids in a matter of months what the youth director had been trying to do for years. You're truly a prodigy in more than just music."

Kara humbly smiled as Deacon Jackson complimented her. "Thank you. And I really appreciate you taking the time out to let me use the piano for extra practice this past week."

Deacon Jackson wore a question on his face. "Oh yeah, how did the performance go? I was so wrapped up in the staff meeting we had upstairs that I forgot to ask you about it."

Kara stuffed her hands in her pockets and answered with a repetitive nod, "It went *really* well. I was even listed in the playbill. Can you believe it?"

Deacon Jackson's eyes lit up. "Oh my goodness, that's great Kara! I told you that you're going to go far. I'm sorry that I missed it. My wife and I would've been there, but our grandbaby had a little debut of her own." He proudly leaned in her direction. "Can you believe that she's only five years old and already doing fashion shows?"

Kara giggled as they rounded a corner. "I can believe it. I was doing shows around that age." Admittedly she added, "Not modeling shows, but I could find my way around a keyboard. My mother was so happy when she saw me playing with the electric keyboard she had bought for Miriam one Christmas. Not even a month later, I was taking lessons."

Well aware of how dearly Kara missed her mother, Deacon Jackson cautiously asked, "Now, exactly how old were you then?" before they climbed into his vehicle.

Kara zipped her coat up closer to her neck and replied, "Five and a half when I started taking lessons. Being that I caught on so quickly, I soon became the talk of our small town."

Deacon Jackson chuckled. "Well, that's just great because it's sure a big help to the church. I'm glad that you're using your gift for the Lord."

Kara grinned. "Yeah, me too."

Deacon Jackson started his engine and drove Kara home. He didn't mind staying a little while after ministry meetings to help Kara make some money of her own. He was quite familiar with the previous spending habits of Kara's older sister Miriam and so was the pastor. Since the budding pianist gave so much to the growth of the youth ministry, especially being considered a youth herself by age, the Administrative Board didn't mind giving back where they could.

Since Kara joined the church three years ago, many of the parishioners had become well aware of her needs. Many of them went out of their way to help her since both of her parents were deceased. It troubled Deacon Jackson that Miriam refused to come to church with Kara. He had personally witnessed to her twice, but it seemed as if he just wasn't getting through to her. However, he refused to give up on a lost soul since God hadn't given up on him when his heart was just as hard.

As Deacon Jackson sat in his vehicle outside of Kara's home while he waited for her to gather her things, it pained him to see that the neighborhood he used to live in hadn't changed much. It was a great miracle that he was blessed to get out of that same block of projects where Kara now lived. Remembering the drug dealings he used to take part in, Deacon Jackson released a helpless sigh and waited with a heavy heart until Kara was safely inside before pulling away from the sidewalk.

Miriam and Kara used to live in a lovely two-bedroom condominium when they first relocated to New York City. After the death of their parents, Miriam learned that she had a trust fund that was to be allocated to her thirty days after graduating college. Initially, she was puzzled because her mother hadn't said anything to her when she first came home that fateful summer the deadly fire happened. Miriam began to resent the fact that her mother had quietly looked on while she struggled to find gainful employment. She had apparently forgotten how much her parents provided during her tenure at Tulane University.

Upon finding out that both she and Kara each had two hundred and fifty thousand dollars held in trust, Miriam cut loose like she had just hit the jackpot. Her money was payable immediately since it was four days past the waiting period when she found out about the inheritance.

Kara's trust was held until she reached the age of eighteen when she could then allocate her funds for a college education. Although Miriam had to wait until she graduated from college before she could access the funds, there wasn't an extended waiting period for Kara. Noticing something different in Kara from Miriam, their parents didn't place a stipulation on how Kara was to use the money. Both Gwendolyn and Kenneth were absolutely confident that it would be spent to advance her musical career.

At the time of their parents' death, Miriam volunteered to take care of her younger sister. It was just as her stepfather had predicted, she was there for Kara. With her natural father's demise and then losing her mother, Miriam felt that Kara was all she had left.

By applying for jobs in New York, Miriam was convinced that she would find employment more quickly in her field than in the Deep South. With two years of internship experience just a short three weeks later her theory proved true. After securing a position that paid a decent salary, Miriam used a sizeable portion of her trust money on a down payment and closing costs to purchase the condominium she later ended up losing to foreclosure. The lavish shopping sprees and frequent dinners out barreled to a screeching halt when she was shot.

In a single moment, everything in her life had suddenly changed.

"So, you finally made it home," Miriam squawked as she stared at Kara with hate-filled eyes. "Next time don't call Deidra to do your work for you." She pointed as if to dare Kara to argue with her.

Kara sucked her teeth as she was not in the mood for an argument again tonight. It had been a long, enjoyable day and the last thing she wanted was for Miriam to ruin her high.

"Aren't you going to say anything? I know you hear me talking to you." Her words hit the airwaves like bleach on colored clothing. The splash of Miriam's verbal corrosion drained the room of all colorful emotion. Immediately, the upbeat tempo of Kara's day had taken on the diminuendo of a dreadful cadence. This was not how she wanted her evening to end.

"Yes ma'am, I heard you," Kara respectfully answered.

Those words *yes ma'am* had deflated Miriam's chest that heaved with hot air. She shook her head as if she had suddenly become at a loss for words. Instead of prodding her further, Miriam rolled her eyes away from Kara and wheeled herself to her bedroom. She slammed the door behind her.

Kara pulled in a deep breath and then heavily sighed. She locked the front door behind her and slowly took off her coat. She wondered why God allowed Miriam to treat her this way, but then she quickly recanted her thought. It was a blessing to have a blood relative care for her even though it came with an occasional argument or angry glare. Kara justified that at least Miriam wasn't physically abusive. She may hurl harsh words her way, but Miriam never attempted to lay a hand on her. Kara was learning how to deal with the enemy who shared the same home as her. *There has to be a good reason why I'm going through all of this*, she thought.

Wise beyond her years, Kara knew that her trust was in God and in Him was where it had to stay. She had learned through countless Bible studies that the enemy comes to steal, kill, and destroy. It was a struggle to maintain her composure, but Miriam was her sister. Kara had to remember that although her sister was unreasonably nasty and filled with bitterness, Miriam had sacrificed to raise her. Often, Kara considered going back to her small hometown in rural Mississippi, but she had hope—hope that kept her in the books and practicing the piano. She had found a way of escape from Miriam and her cruel, degrading words by immersing herself in school and music. She had to for the sake of sanity.

Kara removed her pink scarf and placed it beside her coat on the sofa. She gently ran her hand across the soft tassels that hung from the scarf. This was the same scarf worn when Kara realized that she had feelings for

Wendell, feelings that ran much deeper than a casual acquaintance-ship. It was an article of clothing in her favorite color that Melissa had given on her birthday earlier in the year. Being that she had such a good friend in Melissa, Kara could talk to her about anything and she often thanked God for their friendship.

*It sure would be nice to spend the night over there again*, Kara thought. However, she knew her presence wasn't welcomed by every-one in the Peterson household. Although Franklin had made it clear that he absolutely adored Kara, by this morning's reaction, Talia had made it just as abundantly clear that she felt the exact opposite. Kara wasn't sure what she had done to cause Talia to not speak to her when she waved hello, but she wanted to make right whatever she had done wrong.

Kara turned around and walked into the kitchen. The small table no longer held the box of food she had left sitting there that afternoon. As she walked farther into the kitchen Kara noticed that the box of grits and pancake mix her sister was so adamant on receiving earlier in the day was on the counter—unopened.

Kara shook her head as she washed her hands over the sink. She tugged on the refrigerator door handle and stared inside. Scanning from the top to the bottom shelf, Kara only found an onion, two sticks of butter, three eggs, and a jar of moldy salsa. The quart of apple juice and concealed package of turkey luncheon meat she had purchased were gone. Kara then looked in the freezer and found that the three frozen dinners she had bought with money she had saved from teaching piano lessons were gone too.

Instantly, her eyes blurred with tears as she allowed the freezer door to close shut. *Miriam did this on purpose*, she thought. Tempted to go off on her sister and slap her for what she had done, Kara stood motionless and struggled to compose herself. This was her senior year and all she had to do was make it until graduation. If she could make it to graduation, she'd never have to deal with the likes of her sister again.

Instead of causing another scene like the one last month when neighbors had called the police due to the excessive shouting between them, Kara quietly cleared her throat. The confrontation hadn't become physical, but it was definitely on the brink of a wild fight.

Kara picked up the phone in the living room, trying to keep her voice as normal as possible. Instead of cooking pancakes or grits for dinner for the third time this week, she called Melissa. Kara knew that Melissa would pay to have something delivered. As the call went to voicemail, Kara decided not to leave a message. She took a chance on calling the home phone.

"Hello?" Talia answered.

Kara froze.

"*Hello*?" Talia repeated. "Is anyone there?"

Kara quickly hung up the phone, glad that the phone was in Miriam's name. She knew Talia wouldn't know that it was her who had called if a name showed up on the Caller ID because she and her sister had different last names. Kara walked back over to the sofa and although it was getting late, she pulled the key from her coat pocket and slipped out the front door. She went down one flight of stairs to see if Deidra was at home.

"Girl, shouldn't you be getting ready for bed?" Deidra asked as she allowed room for Kara to enter her apartment. "I thought you have to play in the morning."

With her head lowered, Kara said through a shaky, embarrassed voice, "I do ... but I'm hungry."

Deidra's eyes poured with all of the compassion she could muster. Touching Kara gently on the shoulder, she asked, "Didn't Miriam go shopping this week? She gets her stamps the same time of the month I do."

Kara shrugged, knowing that Miriam probably did go shopping with the woman who lived on the first floor. She always went shopping with her when funds were loaded onto her EBT card. Refusing to go shopping with Deidra was a way Miriam could keep her out of her business. Since she had grown so fond of Kara, Miriam loathed the fact that Deidra gave Kara things she'd rather her sister not have.

"Well, come on in, baby. I hope you like broccoli stir-fry with a side of my famous red cabbage," Deidra said with a smile as she knew it was Kara's favorite. "I'll even throw in a few extra pieces of the teriyaki glazed wings just for you." Deidra tried to make light of the situation.

"Thank you, Deidra." Kara's flushed cheeks rose in anticipation of the meal.

"You don't have to thank me. That's what friends are for." Deidra closed the door behind her. "Now, go on and have a seat."

The hospitable neighbor showed the famished teen to her burgundy-colored sofa. Kara slid down in shame with her chin tucked toward her chest. This was the second time in the past month she'd come to Deidra with this problem, although there had been many other nights she went hungry. The last time her stomach desperately cried for food was just the week before. Kara had argued with Miriam over several cans of soup and a box of buttered crackers that had gone missing. Instead of telling Deidra, Kara simply kept it to herself and went to bed on a stomach filled with nothing but a cup full of tap water. Although Miriam cooked on occasions, Kara kept a stash of food for those instances when her sister didn't.

"I really didn't want to bother you again—" Kara's sentence was snapped in two by her loud, roaring stomach.

Deidra rested a palm on Kara's arm as she asked, "Sweetie, when was the last time you ate?"

With a defeated sigh, Kara replied, "I had a little something at the church. Deacon Jackson usually brings turkey, cheese and crackers snacks whenever I have piano lessons to teach. He keeps a stash of snacks because he has a five-year-old granddaughter that visits him and that's around the age of the students I teach. Nothing big, but he says it's better than feeding them candy. One of my students didn't show today, so he offered it to me."

Deidra looked on sympathetically.

Kara straightened her posture. "Oh, Deacon Jackson would have gotten me something to eat," she admitted, "but I knew I had food at home. But when I got in and saw that my dinners were gone ..." Kara's voice sadly trailed off. "I really wouldn't bother you, but the little bit of money I have saved from teaching lessons is in an account I'd have to go to the ATM to get."

Deidra pressed her lips tightly together before saying, "So, Miriam ate your food. That is a shame. You spend your hard-earned money for a few snacks and dinners that she can get for free. What is she doing with those stamps?" Deidra rhetorically asked. "Letting them add up?" Again, there was another question that didn't require an answer. "Well don't worry. You can always come to me. Just know that I'm here for you."

"Thank you so much, Deidra."

"And you're in for a treat tonight because I also have your favorite banana cream cheesecake," Deidra said with growing enthusiasm.

Kara practically salivated. "I thought you said you weren't going to make that until my birthday?"

"Well to tell you the truth, I couldn't wait that long." Deidra smirked as she caressed the nape of her neck. "It just so happens that's my favorite as well."

They laughed in unison.

"Besides, you deserve a little treat and I wanted to do something special for you."

Kara looked at her. "But why?" she asked, considering herself unworthy.

"For starters, you nailed that performance last night."

"You were there?" Kara questioned, surprised that anyone she knew aside from Wendell had attended this milestone event in her life.

"Now you know I wouldn't have missed that for the world." Deidra planted a hand on her hip. "It took some convincing, but I finally got someone to fill in a couple of hours for me at work. I left right after your performance because I had to finish my shift, but I just had to see you play."

"I wish you were my sister instead," Kara said as she wrapped her arms around Deidra.

Deidra returned the hug with a gracious and compassionate expression although it pained her to hear Kara say those words. She wanted the sisters to be there for one another, regardless of what had happened to damage their relationship in the past.

Deidra, at the age of thirty-two, had lived her entire life in the projects. It was expensive for her to live without public assistance in the city, which was why she had been saving her money for the past three years to move to the Midwest. It was where her younger brother had relocated after graduating high school and the open invitation for her to join him had stood for the past six years. It was an offer she would soon take him up on.

After a few moments of chatting about her performance while Deidra warmed a plate of food, Kara sat in front of an attractively arranged place setting. There on the kitchen table next to a folded piece of napkin were small bulb glasses that held miniature floral pieces. Only seconds after sitting down, Kara was presented with a deliciously appetizing and colorful dish. Deidra took pride in her cooking even though her meals were considered common by most folks. It was her dream that she'd finish culinary school and open her own little quaint soul food café where her brother lived. Something small, but something she could call her own.

"Did you want a pop?" Deidra asked as she shoveled ice cubes from her freezer into a tall glass.

"Yes please, cola if you have it," Kara answered before offering, "And I can wash those dishes for you."

Deidra sympathetically looked into Kara's sheepish eyes. "No, I'll wash my own dishes. You just enjoy your meal, girl. And when you're done just put the empty plate in the sink along with the others."

Kara humbly nodded. Deidra crossed her arms with a dish towel hanging from one of her hands and nodded knowingly as the mature young woman said a prayer over the food.

"That's a good thing that you're doing, Kara. How is it that you are so heavy into the church and Miriam wants nothing to do with it?"

Kara shrugged as she stuffed her mouth with a fork full of seasoned rice and vegetables.

"Hey slow down, girl. I don't want to be calling the ambulance on account of you choking on my food," Deidra joked.

Kara grinned, covering her mouth with the napkin that was beside her plate. "Sorry," she eased out after swallowing.

Deidra flagged the dish towel in her direction. "Girl, I'm just playing with you. I just got through eating like that an hour ago myself." She chuckled as she picked up a coffee mug. "That's probably why my date left in such a hurry." Deidra chuckled again as she dropped the towel on the counter and sat down across from Kara.

"You had a date?" Kara asked in between bites of her food.

Deidra twisted her mouth to one side. "What, I'm not supposed to date? I may not be a size six like you or have legs like yours, but I can hold my own." She playfully snapped her head away with a chuckle. "Don't think that I'm too old to have it going on." Deidra then stood and modeled the sassy outfit she donned on her size twelve frame.

Kara shook her head as she giggled, trying to keep food from falling out of her mouth. "Now, you know that's not what I meant."

"I know it's not." Deidra smiled as she sat back down. "But seriously, if you ever need anything, let me know." She then sipped sparingly from the mug while cradling the cup in the palms of her hands. "I see what you're trying to do for yourself, and I think it's a good thing. With my going to school, I'm going to live my dream one day too. So, if there's anything that I can do for you," Deidra continued as she reached across the table and patted Kara on the hand. "I mean *anything*, just let me know."

Kara nodded, challenged by her emotions. She wanted so badly for her sister to take an interest in her life like friends do. It would mean so much to her, but it seemed like such a faraway notion. When Miriam's accident first happened, Kara found it hard to even talk to her sister. It got even worse when they lost the condominium. For a moment there, Kara had actually begun to feel that her sister's shooting was indeed her fault. After the move, Miriam complained everyday about how different the Section 8 apartment was from the place they had become accustomed to living in for nearly two and a half years. She complained about bills and never allowed Kara to forget that it all would not have happened if it weren't because of her.

"Deidra, can I share something with you?"

"Sure." Deidra nodded as she walked to the kitchen sink.

"And you won't tell Miriam?"

Deidra shot her a stare that said *you know me better than that.*

"Okay," Kara said, and then confided, "There's this guy that I like."

"*Oh, somebody has a boyfriend,*" Deidra sung in a teasing tone as she filled the sink with dishwater.

Kara blushed and partially covered her face. "See, I know I shouldn't have said anything."

"No, no, I'm just messing with you. For real, what's up?"

Redness flushed Kara's cheeks again just at the thought of Wendell. She wanted to be his woman so badly and hoped that he felt the same way about her. They had been friends for months, talking on the phone mostly when she went over to Melissa's. Kara knew that after last night Wendell was going to want more. The way he remembered her birthday and asking about meeting her sister, it was only a matter of time before he asked her out on a real date. Everything up until this point had something to do with either school or performances.

"Well, I wanted to know if I could give him your phone number."

Deidra's nose crinkled in confusion. "*My number?*"

"Yeah ..." Kara hesitantly responded. "You know, so that he can call and talk to me. He's had the home number for a few weeks now, but I don't want him to have to deal with Miriam anymore. She talks really stiff to my friends and I'm just tired of covering for her attitude. Melissa offered to get me a cell phone, but I don't think Mrs. Peterson cares too much for me. She's never said anything directly, but the way she looks at me sometimes makes me a little uncomfortable. She acts as if I'm going to dirty up her place or something."

"Is she white?"

Kara shook her head. "No, she's black. I don't get it. Do you think it's because I'm half white?"

"Baby, I can't answer that for you. I've had my share of discrimination from both sides. Maybe it's the money she has, who knows."

Kara shrugged. "Well, Melissa sort of said to me that I can't come over as much because of her mother. She's nothing like her though," Kara explained, "but I don't want to cause any problems at home for her. That's why I wouldn't accept the cell. Besides, if her mother found out she would probably cut it off anyway or make-up some story that I stole it."

"*What*? Do you think she has it in for you like that?" Deidra questioned as she turned the faucet off to the sink.

"No, oh, I don't know." Kara sighed. "All I know is that I don't want anything that would cause a rift between me and my friendship with Mel. I mean, I have friends, but Melissa is the only *close* friend that I have here."

Deidra nodded as if she understood. "Don't worry, you can give him my number. I'm usually at school or working some overtime in the evenings, but my voicemail can take a message." She then sat down again across from Kara. "You can use my phone to talk to him."

Kara bounced in place. "Oh, thank you, thank you, thank you!"

Deidra grinned when she saw Kara's enthusiasm. "You're welcome, but you have to promise me one thing, Kara, and I'm serious." Deidra raised a brow.

Kara looked up from her plate, holding a chicken wing in her hand. "Sure, what is it?"

"Promise me that you won't start fooling around with him. I want you to finish school *without* any baggage." She lowered her chin and made more direct eye contact with Kara. "Do you understand what I'm saying?"

Kara shied away from Deidra's glance and said, "I know. I'm not going to do anything with him."

Deidra lowered her voice when she asked, "Are you still a virgin?"

"*Deidra?*" Kara gasped.

Deidra remained unmoved. "Answer me."

Kara's eyes widened as she exclaimed in a high-pitched tone, "*Yes!*"

"Calm down," Deidra said as she rested her back against the cushioned chair. "I kind of figured that, but I just wanted to make sure. I don't want you getting a reputation."

Kara stared at Deidra, wondering where all of this was coming from. "I'm serious about my faith and I wouldn't do that." She paused, and then added, "I guess I should tell you that he's not a high school boy either."

Deidra's eyes asked for more.

"He's twenty-two," Kara continued.

"Twenty-two huh?" Deidra shook her head. "Kara look, guys are slick sometimes. They see a young pretty thing hoping to get what they can get. You understand me?" Her eyes narrowed to a squint. "All I can say is to be careful. You're an impressionable, sweet girl. I know how attractive it looks to be with an older man but watch yourself."

Kara understood what Deidra was saying, having already had a similar talk with her aunt Frieda over a year ago. Kara was determined to not let Wendell or anybody get in the way of her future. Her virginity was going to be held for her husband and that was a non-negotiable fact. Besides, she'd have to fall pretty hard in love to even consider such a thing. And she was far from in love with Wendell. She was barely in like ... so she tried convincing herself.

# CHAPTER 7

"MOM, WAS THAT for me?" Melissa asked as she poked her head inside of her parents' master bedroom. She had missed a call on her cell phone and then heard the home phone ring once just moments later.

"No, I think it was a wrong number," Talia answered with her bedroom phone receiver still in her hand. "The person hung up." She casually shrugged.

"Oh," Melissa replied, staring down at the cordless she held in her hand. The Caller ID read *No Data*, but she figured that it was Kara, although there hadn't been an answer when she tried to phone her back after the missed call on her cell. "Well, I'm going to watch a movie in my room."

"Why don't you invite one of your friends over?" Talia suggested as she blankly stared at the television mounted on her bedroom wall.

"You mean Kara?" Melissa boldly asked as she stood in the doorway.

"*No.*" Talia gave her daughter a condemning glare. "I was referring to Natalie or Rita. Didn't you all have fun in the modeling class last summer?"

"It was all right to hang out with them, but Kara's my real friend," Melissa said as she walked away.

Talia watched as Melissa closed the door behind her. She then tapped the cordless phone on the palm of her hand, debating whether she should call Donovan. If he was trying to make her jealous by going out with Marissa, Talia would never admit that it was actually working.

"Oh Mom," Melissa said as she reopened the door, simultaneously knocking on it.

"Yes, what is it?" Talia snapped from her daze, giving her daughter her undivided attention.

"I need to get new headshots done. Do you think we can set up an appointment with the photographer who did our last family portrait?"

"Melissa, you just had headshots done six months ago," Talia reminded her.

"But my hair was different then," Melissa whined. "It's longer now and the color is a shade darker. Besides, I look more mature now."

Talia shook her head at her daughter. "You haven't changed that much."

"Mom please," Melissa begged. "This is for my career and my agent says that it's important that I reflect my actual appearance, not what I looked like six months ago."

"I thought you were going to at least consider modeling. You heard what that scout said about your bone structure. A face like yours—"

"Doesn't come along every day," Melissa finished her sentence. "Yes, I remember, but I don't want to model. Acting is not just a hobby for me. This is something that I actually want to do as a career. My teacher at school says that I have presence and believability. Now Mom, you even said that if I could prove to you that I'm serious, you'd support me," Melissa challenged her. "Well, I've gotten the lead in the school play. I have an agent and have been sent out on auditions. My grades are good and I'm never in trouble."

Talia rolled her eyes up toward the ceiling and then back to her daughter. "Okay, just remember that you have to have something to fall back on. I would love to see you model, and I don't really mind the acting, but the family business will provide you with some security." Talia raised her eyebrows. "Think about what your father has said."

Melissa groaned as she raised a hand to her mother before leaving the room again.

Talia wanted so much for Melissa what she herself didn't have in her youth. It was a blessing to be able to provide her child with many of the things she didn't have growing up. Her smile soon faded as she pondered what Donovan had said to her earlier in the day. His suggestion that she was still with Franklin because of his money irritated her. Sure, she was financially secure in the marriage, but money wasn't the only thing her husband had to offer. Franklin was good to her and had provided well, but over the years she had to admit to herself that there were many areas that had gone lacking.

As Talia thought about the times Franklin's impotence stalled their intimacy, her memories of Donovan were steadily reignited. Although things were much better between her and Franklin now, there was something ungodly drawing her away from the man she had married almost twenty years ago. Back when she was first unfaithful, Talia justified it as being the seven-year itch, but now such reasoning was absolutely absurd. As a grown woman with a professed faith in Jesus Christ, she knew better. Talia knew what the Bible said about infidelity, and it had been pounded in her head through the countless marriage counseling sessions they had completed years ago. Why was she now so interested in a man who almost tore her family apart?

Talia reasoned that it was Franklin's determination to build a strong business from the ground up that took him away for many hours at a time, creating a void in her heart. His absence began with consecutive days that grew into long, lonely weeks and then subsequent, unbearable months. Shortly after their second miscarriage both Talia and Franklin's hopes of having any more children waned. Franklin threw himself further into his work and Talia went through a bout of serious depression. When the two tried to be intimate, Franklin simply couldn't perform. His mind was so preoccupied with work and the painful miscarriages that eventually the pair grew even further apart. It was then that Donovan captured Talia's attention. They had seen one another at one of their high-school class reunions that Franklin was too busy to attend. That's when the affair began.

"Honey, I gave Douglas the evening off," Franklin said, interrupting Talia's thoughts as he walked into the room. "Did you want to order takeout? I haven't had Italian in a while."

"Uh," Talia closed her eyes as if in deep thought, but she was trying to clear her mind of the past.

"Are you all right?" he asked out of concern.

"Yes, I'm fine," Talia answered, but was deeply challenged by her cheating heart. "Uh, Italian sounds good. Just let me get my shoes on."

As Talia slid to the edge of the bed and planted her feet on the floor, Franklin lightly touched her shoulder. "You don't have to get dressed. I'll run and get it. You just relax, go over whatever notes you have for the etiquette class in the morning, and I'll be right back. Just let me know what you'd like, and I'll call it in before I leave."

Talia squeezed Franklin's hand that rested upon her shoulder. He was good to her, probably more of a blessing than she had deserved. "I want you to know that I appreciate you," she said, gazing into his eyes. It pained her that her heart was beginning to stray again. Although she hadn't acted on the illicit temptation, Talia was riddled with guilt from the way she compared the two men.

Franklin leaned over and kissed her on the cheek. "I know that you do, honey. I appreciate you too." He was a generous, loving man. Talia was grateful to God for keeping their marriage together, especially after she had confessed her infidelity. The road to recovery was a rocky one, but it was a path of healing that mended the brokenness in their relationship.

After all she and her husband had been through together, Talia knew she had to put a stop to the shameful craving that was building inside of her.

"Are you sure that you don't want me to ride with you? I don't mind getting dressed." With her subtle glances, Talia apologized for the way she felt.

"No, you rest. You've had a long day with your friends. Besides, I need to pick up a few razors. I forgot to put them on the shopping list when Douglas went out this morning." Franklin glanced at a crumpled piece of notebook paper that he pulled from his front pocket. "That and shaving cream." He chuckled. "But don't worry, I won't be long. There's a store right down the street from the restaurant."

"Okay, well I'll just take a warm bath and get my things together for tomorrow morning." Talia nodded with a soft smile. "Did you ask Melissa if she wanted anything?"

"I did and she's already eaten. She had leftovers from lunch earlier. We had seafood while going over things with the business."

"Was she more receptive this time?" Talia skeptically asked.

"Not really," he groaned, "but maybe she'll come around."

"Yes, maybe she will..."

Just then out of nowhere Franklin kissed Talia again, this time passionately on the lips. She was surprised because he only kissed her that way when he was feeling romantic, and those times had become scarce again over the past few months. The look in his eyes confirmed her thought as he lightly caressed her cheek with delicate strokes of his thumb.

"Do you mind if we turn in early tonight?"

Franklin's suggestion caught Talia off guard. "Oh ... okay." She smiled at her husband, his virility casting a shadow on her adulterous thoughts. His offer was a pleasant surprise that she greatly anticipated.

"I won't be long," he promised with a wink.

As Franklin left the room after phoning in their orders, Talia hoped the night would bring them closer. With great expectation, she eagerly awaited her husband's return.

# CHAPTER 8

"THANKS FOR THE ride home," Leslie said as Wendell parked in front of her apartment building. "I really appreciate this. I'm just sorry that you had to witness that fiasco earlier." She rolled her eyes and bashfully covered her face.

"Things happen." Wendell complacently shrugged.

Wendell hadn't planned on escorting Leslie home after only meeting her today after the audition, but when he dropped her off at the diner where she worked the manager wouldn't even let her in the door. The man ranted about her being late again and didn't care if it was due to traffic.

"Learn to leave early then," the manager protested in a thick Jersey accent.

Leslie then yanked her uniform out of the bag and furiously threw it at him. After working late hours and even coming in on her days off, she was fed up. The tips were lousy, and the hours were horrible, but she tolerated it anyway for a steady paycheck. As she stormed away from the entrance and saw Wendell still parked near the sidewalk it brought on mixed emotions of both relief and embarrassment. She was glad that he offered her a ride home but having him see her fired was humiliating.

After glancing up at the windows to her apartment, Leslie looked back to Wendell and asked, "Did you want to come up for a minute?" When she seductively batted her eyes in his direction it became obviously clear to him that she wanted more than an acting role from him.

"Uh, no thanks, Ms. Brunson. I really have a lot to do."

"Oh please, call me Leslie." She gently touched his hand that rested on the gear shift.

Wendell glanced down where her hand rested on his and slowly moved his hand away. "I better get going. I'll see you when we start shooting. July should be calling you soon with the details." He paused and then carefully asked, "Is finding another job going to interfere with shooting? Let me know now. I've already had one person drop out on me."

"*No*," she said, firmly shaking her head. "You can count on me. I'll be there."

Wendell nodded, still placing prospects in mind for a possible backup. "That's good to hear. Well look, let me get out of here. You have a good night."

Leslie nodded as she opened the car door. Even in wardrobe that complimented her well-defined physique, Wendell didn't bite. He kept a safe distance between them, behaving like the perfect gentleman the entire time she was around him.

"Thanks again for the part." Leslie lingered, flipping her hair from her shoulders to her back. "I really appreciate it."

Wendell raised his brows and answered in a monotonous tone, "You're welcome."

Leslie slowly grabbed her shoulder bag from the floor and stepped out into the night air. Wendell watched as she walked towards the entrance of the building. Leslie looked back and waved. Wendell gave a slight nod and gestured good-bye with a motion of one of his fingers. He patiently waited until she was inside before driving away.

Wendell pressed a button on his phone to speed dial Wayne's number. He wanted to give the assistant director of the film a run-down of the day's events, as well as his production manager, Michael. All three colleagues were soon merged on a three-way call as they discussed the upcoming shooting schedule and the new lead.

"Leslie Brunson?" Wayne curiously questioned. "I think I may have seen her name somewhere before. Yeah, you know what? She's that fine girl working at the diner across the street from where I work. She was in a commercial or something a few months back. I'd never forget a face *or* body like hers." He suggestively laughed.

There was something intriguing about Leslie, but Wendell reserved his comments.

"Is her schedule going to interfere with the shooting?" Michael inquired.

"Nah, everything is straight. She got fired today."

"*Fired*?" Wayne and Michael exclaimed simultaneously.

Wendell explained what happened when he gave Leslie a ride to work.

"*You gave her a ride*?" They spoke in unison again.

"Yeah, she was stranded so I helped her out."

Wayne and Michael mockingly chuckled.

"What?" Wendell questioned.

"Look man, I don't know what you were thinking about giving this girl a ride to work, but chill with all of that. At least until the film is wrapped," Michael advised. "We want to be professional about this whole process."

"Yeah. And why not wait until we ... well, *I* have a chance to check the sister out?" Wayne laughed.

Wendell was quick to dismiss their caution. "I've already told you guys, it's not like that. I know how to be professional. You both know that my credentials speak for themselves."

"Yeah, yeah, yeah, we'll see man," Michael droned. "Well, I have plans later so I need to get off this phone. We'll meet sometime next week to finalize everything for shooting. Keep me posted if anything changes."

"Okay man. Talk with you guys later," Wendell said before the three of them ended their call.

Wendell smiled to himself as he thought about their conversation. Michael has been in a committed relationship for over a year now, but Wayne was a self-professed bachelor, although several of his female counterparts would say otherwise. Wendell had been single for nearly a year and a half, ever since his last girlfriend had been tragically killed in an automobile accident. They hadn't dated long before the fatal collision, but it was one that had left a lasting impression on him to the effect that whomever he dated next would be more than just a casual fling.

Although he was young, Wendell's maturity spoke volumes. He didn't care for the way Wayne changed girlfriends almost as often as he changed underwear, but it served as a constant reminder of what he didn't want to become. He wanted to be devoted from day one and find a woman he could love as Christ loved the Church.

"Hey, how are you doing, Dianne?" Wendell said to his aunt after he answered his phone. "I gather that the show was a hit. Your theater is going to be buzzing in the city."

Dianne chuckled as she replied, "It's not like you would know."

"What are you talking about?" he questioned with a smile in his voice.

"Don't play innocent with me. I saw you leaving with Kara," Dianne admitted. "What's going on between the two of you? She looks to be your type, but isn't she still in high school?"

Wendell exhaled. "*Yes, she's in high school*," he dragged the words out. "Almost a graduate might I add. And let's not mention the fact that she had you and your Juilliard friend checking her out." Wendell spoke with confidence. "Am I right or am I right? The girl has got skills."

Dianne chuckled as if she had been caught. "Yes, I have to confess that she's talented. But is she serious about a future career in music?"

"What do you mean?" Wendell questioned as he traveled from Brooklyn to get to his place in the Village. "She heard how Kara plays. Why would you ask something like that?"

Dianne lightly grunted. "Well, I just got off the phone with Lois a few minutes ago. She said that she called Kara earlier today and left a message for her to call back, but she didn't. She even waited an hour later than the time she had left on the message for Kara and still no callback. Not to mention that Lois checked her voicemail at the office after getting home and there wasn't even a hang up."

Wendell grimaced as he thought back to any hint indicating that this wasn't something Kara wanted. "Are you sure you gave her the right number? That doesn't sound like Kara."

Dianne rattled off the telephone number Wendell had given her a few days ago. She was correct with each digit.

"I don't understand." A wave of confusion swept across Wendell's face. "Let me talk to her. Maybe she had an emergency or something. I haven't spoken to her today, but I'll get this straightened out." In a last-ditch attempt to salvage Kara's reputation, he asked, "Do you think Lois will give her another chance?"

"I don't know, Wendell, her time is valuable and she's only doing this as a favor for me. Remember, this is her last semester at Juilliard before she moves to look after her ailing father."

"Yes, I remember."

"Her husband will still be here, but he's even busier at the School than she is. Besides, he doesn't want to create any conflict of interest if Kara does make it in. You know what I mean."

"I know exactly what you mean."

"Anyway, Kara is a wonderful pianist, especially to be so young. She's tackled some difficult pieces that challenge many of the under-grads. But she just has to be serious. I don't want Lois wasting her time if Kara has no intention of following through."

Wendell released a frustrated sigh as he anxiously tapped his fingers on the steering wheel. He shook his head, wondering what on Earth could've happened that kept Kara from following up on such a great opportunity. It baffled him to no end, but he was determined to get to the bottom of things.

"I'd love to help her out further, but she has to show some initiative." Dianne paused before speaking to her husband in the background. Then she called her children to the table for dinner. "Wendell, I have to talk to you later, the kids haven't eaten yet. Let me know what you want me to do. I plan on talking to Lois later before I go to bed."

"Okay thanks, Dianne. I know this was a huge favor. I'll see what's going on and give you a ring in about an hour or so."

"No, you can't bring your toys to the dinner table," Dianne said to one of her three children. "It doesn't matter that your birthday is tomorrow. Rules are rules." She then turned her attention back to the phone conversation. "Talk to you soon," Dianne rushed her words to Wendell before hanging up the phone.

Wendell immediately called Kara's home number. He couldn't believe that she would purposely jeopardize such an opportunity. It had already been a challenge to get Lois to agree to meet with her, but now her credibility was on the line. He thought even further, acknowledging that his credibility was hanging by a thread too.

"Hello," Kara quietly answered after she caught the ringing phone only moments after slipping back inside of the apartment. She peered down the short hallway where a light glowed beneath the bathroom door of her and Miriam's small two-bedroom apartment. "Hey, Wendell," she spoke almost in a whisper.

"Hey you, what's going on? Is everything all right?" he asked as he drove past the last streetlight just before his address.

Kara eased past the bathroom, tiptoeing into her bedroom. "Yeah, everything is fine." She slowly shut the door and landed on the bed next to the night lamp she had purposely left on. Kara wanted Miriam to think she had been in her bedroom all along. Miriam rarely bothered Kara in the evenings as it was normally her TV time in bed. As long as the place was clean and her belly was full, nothing brought Miriam out of that room aside from her bowels.

"Okay, well didn't you get the message about Juilliard calling today?"

"*What*?" she gasped in excitement. "She actually called?"

Wendell parked and turned his car off. "You didn't get the message?" He blankly peered out of the window and repetitively tapped on the steering wheel again.

"No, I just got in. I was at the church most of the afternoon," she explained.

"Kara, I told you to expect a call. Why didn't you check your messages after you got in?"

Kara parted her lips at a loss for words.

"My aunt's friend waited for you at the office. I think she really wants to work with you ... to help you with your application submission, but you have to be serious. Do you really want this?" Wendell's voice carried a hint of skepticism. "I don't want to take up other people's time if this isn't what you really want."

"You know I want this. I—" Kara's sentence was snapped in two by a sharp pound at the door. "Look, I have to talk to you later." She rushed her words. "Can I call you tomorrow?"

"Kara, I'm trying to help you with your career and you want to call me tomorrow?" Wendell questioned.

This time the pounding was followed by, "Are you on that phone?"

Kara muffled the phone with her hand. She quickly removed her palm in between Miriam's pounds and hurried her words. "Wendell, I gotta go. Talk to you later. Bye." She hung up.

"Kara ... *Kara*?" Wendell hopelessly called out into dead air.

Irritated, Wendell grunted before snatching his keys from the ignition. He shoved the phone in his coat pocket and reached over to the passenger side to retrieve the paperwork stuffed beside the seat. As he leaned back to an upright position, Wendell came across a foreign piece of paper in the cup tray. He unfolded it and found scribbled in blue ink a phone number followed by *Leslie—call me.*

# CHAPTER 9

KARA RESTED HER head on the tear-stained pillowcase as she knelt on the floor. It was one o'clock in the morning and she hadn't been able to rest since Miriam practically fought her over the phone two hours ago. Instead of participating in a tug of war, Kara pushed the phone to Miriam and slammed the door to her bedroom.

Kara missed her other family members back in Mississippi terribly. It had been almost a year and a half since she had last seen her dear Aunt Frieda and cousins who still lived in the community she once called home. The only thing that kept her from going back to live in the South was her passion to get into Juilliard. If it weren't for her dream, she would've left the city and Miriam a long time ago.

The sobs grew more painful as Kara thought about the phone call she had missed from Lois Chow—a call Miriam swore she knew nothing about during their recent argument—not to mention the mounting disappointment in Wendell's voice. This was a man she had quietly fallen in love with, a fact she could no longer deny. The emotion she felt was adoringly pure. He had only been the second person she'd looked at in such an affectionate way. The first was a childhood friend she hadn't seen in almost two summers since she had last gone home to visit her family.

Timothy Jenson was the pride and joy and only heir of longtime Mayor Mark Jenson and his wife Alice. Kara had gone to school with Timothy up until her family's home burned to the ground and before she moved to New York. One year prior to moving, Kara had attended a year of private school where she had gotten to know Timothy quite well during their classes. It wasn't until she saw him at the local movie theater one evening during her last visit home did a spark of interest flutter in her stomach.

Kara peered at the boy with emerald green eyes and honey-hue skin in admiration. Timothy reminded her so much of her father, Kenneth. His sandy brown hair and charismatic smile brought back so many fond memories.

At the age of fifteen that summer, Kara was responsible enough to be left alone without the supervision of Frieda. She went into town with the company of her two other female cousins who flocked to Aunt Frieda's every time she set foot in their hometown. They were both one year older than Kara and freshly armed with state driver licenses. This was what Kara missed the most, hanging out with family, enjoying the serene setting, and not having to worry about muggers or constant bumper to bumper traffic.

Although Timothy piqued her interest, nothing ever came of the juvenile feelings she once had for him. They were both shy teenagers, although Timothy spent most of his time in front of cameras at political events. At one event he even tried sneaking Kara in so that he'd have someone to talk to other than his father's constituents and their children. But when Mayor Jenson found out he made sure to have his wife put an end to their friendship. After that day, Kara had only secretly spoken to Timothy once before leaving town almost a year and a half ago. She hadn't been back since.

The prayer Kara sincerely uttered to the Lord tonight was an incredibly unselfish one. Her heart's plea was centered on her sister Miriam. Kara had already learned that she ought not to hold grudges against others. She built her foundation on the passage of Scripture that stated to pray for those who despitefully use you. This passage in the books of Matthew and Luke was one Kara had discovered through a conversation she had previously had with Deacon Jackson. Whenever she found herself waiting on a student for piano lessons or when he took her home, Deacon Jackson asked about her home life.

It had become a comfortable refuge for Kara to share her problems with this man whom God had obviously blessed her to know. She remained forever grateful to Deacon Jackson who had convinced her sister to attend worship service that one time to personally hear a soul-stirring sermon. Despite how cold Miriam had grown toward the Word of God, Kara knew that Deacon Jackson wasn't one to be deterred by that. And although Miriam hadn't been back to the church despite Deacon Jackson's urging, Kara hoped that one day God's Word would penetrate her sister's iron-clad heart.

The days were growing more intolerable inside of the small, gloomy apartment. It was as if jagged icicles hardened on Miriam's lips each time she spoke. The guilt Miriam tried to impress upon Kara weakened her defenses daily. Kara felt an impending breaking point and needed a reprieve. She just didn't know how much more she could bear.

After she finished her prayer, Kara reached inside of a letter pouch mail carrier hidden beneath her mattress and pulled out a recent letter Aunt Frieda had mailed to her. Kara remembered that Frieda had told her to call whenever she wanted or needed to. The long-distance number troubled her as she knew Miriam would scold her about the charges. Instead, Kara stuffed the number in the side pocket of her purse after deciding to ask Deacon Jackson if she could use the church phone in the morning. Christmas break was coming up soon and Kara had decided that she would take a trip down south to her hometown. There was no way she could stay in the apartment with Miriam all day *and* night for nearly two weeks.

With the money saved in an account she told Miriam nothing about, Kara had enough to get home on a coach class one way ticket. She was sure Aunt Frieda would pay her way back to New York.

In just over three weeks, the break she prayed for would be a reality.

# CHAPTER 10

*VICTORY IS MINE, victory is mine, victory today is mine ...*

The choir was indeed making a joyful noise unto the Lord. Kara sat poised at the piano, effortlessly working her fingers across the black and white keys. The upbeat tempo of the song caused her to sway with the music. This was not her usual Sunday to play, but after the head organist reported an emergency in the family Kara gladly substituted in his absence.

*I told Satan to get thee behind, victory today is mine ...*

The congregation filled the airwaves with glorious praises to God. In jubilantly uplifted spirits this morning many of them stood and proudly clapped their hands together. Despite the depressing night before, the words of the song moved joyfully within Kara. Her heart poured out to God as she struck each key on the board. It was as if she was in the sanctuary all alone with her Maker.

When the song drew to a close, the pastor took to the pulpit and delivered a touching message based on the Scripture from the twenty-third Psalm. Pastor Wyatt began by passionately reading the passage that consisted of six verses in its entirety.

*"The LORD is my shepherd; I shall not want. He makes me to lie down in green pastures; He leads me beside the still waters. He restores my soul; He leads me in the paths of righteousness for His name's sake. Yea, though I walk through the valley of the shadow of death, I will fear no evil; for You are with me; Your rod and Your staff, they comfort me. You prepare a table before me in the presence of my enemies; You anoint my head with oil; my cup runs over. Surely goodness and mercy shall follow me all the days of my life; and I will dwell in the house of the LORD Forever."*

After this initial reading, Pastor Wyatt uttered a prayer of humility. And then the congregation sat down in their respective places on the pew.

"As I begin this morning, I want us to focus on what the Word of God is saying to us. This is a familiar passage that I'm sure many of you may have even memorized." He paused, smiling as he adjusted his gold-trimmed eyeglasses. "But remember that it is just as important that in all our getting that we get understanding."

Many of the congregants nodded as the pastor made mention of his insightful Bible study session from the previous week.

"Let's first ask ourselves a couple of questions. When we lose heart at the first sign of adversity, are we remembering what God has spoken in His Word? When an unfavorable report comes our way, are we remembering what the Lord has promised?" Pastor Wyatt looked out over the crowd before peering back down at the Bible that rested on the pulpit. "You see when David talked about the valley of the shadow of death, he also made mentioned that God was with him. He recognized the fact that God's Word is true—He will never leave us nor forsake us even as we go through troubles. Understand that this was a man whose life was being sought, but *also* a man who trusted in the Lord. Do we trust God at His Word?"

Pastor Wyatt's question lingered in the sanctuary.

"Many are hearers of the Word, but not all are doers," he fervently preached. "And those of us who are doers must trust God even when the things we see tell us different. Even when the people we may have known all of our lives turn their backs on us. The devil doesn't care about us ... the enemy will use whatever and *whomever* to get us out of the will of God."

Pastor Wyatt then read verse five of the twenty-third Psalm again. Kara held her Bible and buried her eyes upon the fifth verse as it seized her attention this time around with grave importance: *You prepare a table before me in the presence of my enemies; You anoint my head with oil; My cup runs over.*

Pastor Wyatt explained that God thoroughly equips His children for any type of battle. "It doesn't matter what your obstacle or hindrance may be. *God has the answer.*"

In a sidebar, the pastor included relevant verses from the book of Ephesians where the Apostle Paul encouraged the saints to put on the whole armor of God to be able to stand against the wiles of the devil. Kara had read about this in her Bible studies before, but this time God tuned her ears in to hear what she needed at that precise moment in her life.

Ephesians 6:12 was bold printed into Kara's mind: *For we do not wrestle against flesh and blood, but against principalities, against powers, against the rulers of the darkness of this age, against spiritual hosts of wickedness in the heavenly places.*

Wrestling against spiritual hosts of wickedness was exactly what Kara felt she was in battle with. The relationship with her sibling had been amicable most of her life, but then evil forces—spiritual hosts of wickedness—clouded the love Miriam said she had for her sister. When their parents perished in that house fire years ago, Miriam held Kara close as if for dear life and promised to be there for her just as she believed their parents would have wanted.

New York was to be a fresh start for them both. Initially Kara was hesitant about moving so far away from the closest people in her life, but she was encouraged by her mother's sister Frieda. She reminded her of the innate talent God had blessed her with along with incredibly supportive parents for the time that she had them. Parents who often sacrificed to hone the skills God had given. Even at the tender age of twelve, Kara soon recognized that although her parents had died in that tragic fire didn't mean that her dream had to perish too.

Pastor Wyatt's message from God stirred in Kara's heart. She began to understand more that enemies could be those people closest to you as well as those who wanted to keep you at bay. It was incredibly hurtful for Kara to even think about the harsh rejection as her eyes discreetly drifted to Talia. With a quiet sigh, Kara gently shook her head at the woman who sat on the far left side of the sanctuary in between Franklin and Melissa. Although Kara could sense the baffling disapproval a mile away from her best friend's mother, Talia was still the least of her worries. Kara's biggest enemy, presenting itself in the natural, was her own blood relative.

"Before Jesus left this world, He promised that He would send us a Comforter," Pastor Wyatt continued. "Now we know that God is not a man that He should lie. He is not a covenant breaker. The Lord followed through on His Word and sent us *Whom* He had promised," he emphasized. "The Holy Spirit *is* the Comforter, He is the Guide. All we have to do is receive the promise."

Kara, at that moment, wasn't sure what the preacher meant by receiving the promise. She had already accepted Jesus Christ as Lord and Savior. She had been studying the Holy Bible just as much as she studied her school books. She wondered what he was trying to convey as he impressed the need to receive the promise. Her heart's thoughts were heard by the Almighty as the answer was soon delivered.

"Christians encounter adversity and dark moments in life. But when those times come we must remember that the Lord is with us. When we take a look at that word *receive* it simply means to take or acquire something that is given. Basically, it is to be a recipient of something, in this case *Someone*. When God blessed us with His Holy Spirit, He gave us more of Himself. So, when trials come we have the Lord's help if we are open to receive it." Pastor Wyatt looked out at the congregation where some faces appeared comforted while others seemed equally as confused. "Let me put it this way, when you get food at a restaurant and the waiter sets the plate on the table, have you received it yet?" He looked out at the crowd again where some shook their heads while others emphatically nodded. "It's been made available, it's yours for the taking, but you haven't *received* it yet until you have eaten it. Knowing that His goodness is available is totally different from partaking in it.

There are many people who know about the goodness of the Lord through other people's accounts but haven't really *experienced* it for themselves. This is because some bring their problems to the Lord, yet take it right back from Him, figuring that they can handle it more quickly or better than God. Or maybe they allow doubt and worry to set in, but God's Holy Word tells us that we should be anxious for nothing," Pastor Wyatt enlightened. "It also teaches us that when we go to Him we must believe that He is able to do what He says He can do. That's called faith, saints!" he exclaimed. "We must have faith because it is impossible—" He then abruptly paused before shouting, "Oh thank you, Jesus! Teach us Lord!" Pastor Wyatt briefly looked upward before he peered back over the crowd and stated purposefully, "It's *impossible* to please God without it." He then swiped his forehead with a white handkerchief before passionately adding, "We have to understand and remember that along with faith comes *faithfulness*."

At that moment, Talia uneasily crossed her legs while quietly clearing her throat. Her faithfulness was fleeting, especially last night when she fell asleep before Franklin returned from the store. She had taken a warm bath and dressed seductively for the evening, but her ability to stay awake was not there. She awoke angry at Franklin because he hadn't woken her. She didn't bother to disturb his sleep since it was three o'clock in the morning. It was a humiliating revelation when Talia realized that she had momentarily gotten her husband confused with Donovan. During the times she met with Donovan when Franklin was out of town, he would always awaken her with surprises she enjoyed. The memories and recent dreams she had about this man were troubling, even more so than seeing him seated just two rows over with Marissa Stevens at his side.

Franklin placed a hand on Talia's bouncing knee. He leaned over and whispered in her ear, "Is everything all right?"

Talia couldn't bring herself to look into her husband's eyes. She simply nodded and peered back down at her Bible. Franklin squeezed her hand followed by a subtle pat before he released his grip on her. After scribbling down a few random words, Talia steadied her ink pen into a crevice of her Bible. The longer Pastor Wyatt preached, the more she fidgeted. Within minutes, Talia closed her Bible and placed it on the seat next to Melissa.

"I'll be back," Talia quietly said to her husband before heading for the sanctuary doors.

Franklin watched as his wife hurried into the foyer, disappearing behind stained glass windows. His eyes met with Melissa's who appeared just as concerned. Donovan looked at Franklin, noticing that he did not follow his wife. It was then that he realized things weren't as perfect at home as Talia had led him to believe.

Kara's attention shifted away from the message being delivered to the swinging sanctuary doors, but only momentarily. Receiving what God wanted her to hear was far more important than a distraction from the pew. The answers to her heartfelt petitions were being realized and Kara wanted to ponder each sentiment the pastor delivered.

"When we look further into Ephesians 6, we discover that God has specific armor for us in this kind of battle. We must be equipped because the enemy has all sorts of fiery darts he wants to hurl our way. With this armor on, no weapon formed against us will prosper. It may be formed, but it won't prosper."

Kara gently closed her eyes and pondered God's words: *no weapon formed against us shall prosper.* Undoubtedly, she knew this to be true, but was challenged in the midst of her storm. It seemed as if each time

Kara broke free from Miriam's mental hold there was something else she said to weaken her defenses all over again. They were the fiery darts Pastor Wyatt was in fact preaching about. The fiery darts that were meant to force her to give up on her dreams and abandon the hopes for her future.

"As we look back to the focal passage of Psalm 23, consider the oil that's mentioned," Pastor Wyatt continued. "The Scripture states that after the table is prepared, the head is anointed with oil. The oil is protection, a covering so to speak. David's valley was the shadow of death, but yours may be something else. Your rough time may be periods of despair, moments that lack understanding, bouts of pain, and times of loneliness and neglect," Pastor Wyatt expounded. "But in the midst of this, Christians are to fear no evil because the Lord is always present. He hears your fervent prayers and knows your pain." He patted his side as he slowly moved from behind the pulpit. "Don't allow your enemies to steal your peace. They're not the ones who gave it to you."

His sermon prompted many to wave their hands in the air and reverence God.

"Now, when God prepares anything, we know that it is good for us. The table leads me to believe that there is food there. Just as natural food builds up our physical body, this *spiritual* food nourishes our spiritual life. When we look at the table God places before us, it takes the focus off the enemies and places it on the things of God.

In Matthew 14, when Peter walked on water to go to our Lord, distraction came upon him and he began to sink. What happened? Peter took his eyes off Jesus and placed it on something else. We're to focus on God and what *He* has for us to do. Allowing doubt and distraction to enter our minds can hinder us," the pastor pointed out.

He further encouraged the congregation to look to the Lord where help comes from, but Kara felt as if he was having a one-on-one conversation with her. She slowly realized that this table being spoken of was there to strengthen and nourish her in the spiritual realm similarly to what physical food does for a body in the natural realm.

"This table accompanies us along the way. So, as our spiritual strength is built, we must continue to eat from the table. When we start to feel weary, we need to eat. When we become worn and tired, eat!" the pastor belted out with startling enthusiasm. "When we feel beat up or just plain beat down, *eat* because God placed that table there for such a time. What's more amazing is that God supplies us with enough to give to somebody else." The pastor looked out over the crowd, and in a more calmed voice he added, "Allow your cup to overflow into someone else's life."

Many in the congregation were once again on their feet. Kara peered around wondering if any of them were going through anything remotely similar to her. As she cried herself to sleep the night before, she didn't search for a Scripture to read. She just didn't have the strength. But she did remember the comfort she felt when her aunt Frieda was placed on her heart. She wondered if this was something that had been placed on *her* table.

After worship service, Kara called out to Deacon Jackson just as he walked through the foyer on his way to Sunday school class. He turned around to see where the insistent voice was coming from.

"Ah Kara, how are you?" Deacon Jackson smiled as Kara eagerly approached him.

In a lowered tone, she answered, "Good."

"Glad to hear it," he said, wrapping his arms around her shoulders. "The choir really sung their hearts out this morning."

"Yes, they sure did," Kara agreed.

"And you played very well. I look forward to hearing you play at the Lincoln Center one of these days."

Kara's smile broadened. It was nice to have people around her that truly believed in the talent God had given her. The compliments were plenteous, but when they came from the genuinely few like Deacon Jackson, Deidra, and her best friend Melissa, Kara cherished the sentiments even more. Just as she prepared herself to ask if she could use the phone, Jacqueline Stewart, Elijah's mother, walked up.

"Good morning, Deacon Jackson." Jacqueline shook his hand before turning to Kara. "Doing okay?"

Kara pleasantly nodded. "Yes ma'am."

"Good, good. I wanted to catch you before I went up to class." Jacqueline reached into her purse and pulled out a white envelope and handed it to Kara. "This is for the piano lessons I owed you, plus a little something extra. I wasn't able to catch you before service, but I'm glad that I caught you before classes began."

"Thank you." Kara graciously clutched the envelope in her hands. "Where's Elijah?"

Before Jacqueline could answer, Deacon Jackson said, "It was nice seeing you ladies, but I really have to get to class. I'm teaching this morning and am on schedule for devotional in the second service. You two have a good afternoon." He gently touched their arms as he spoke.

Kara's lips parted and her shoulders slumped when Deacon Jackson swiftly started down the adjoining hallway.

Jacqueline asked her, "Is everything okay?"

"Yes ma'am."

"Are you sure?" Jacqueline placed a hand on Kara's shoulder.

Kara pulled in a deep breath and then said, "It's just that I was going to ask Deacon Jackson to use the office phone."

Jacqueline nonchalantly waved her hand. "Oh, you can use my phone. What is it? Did you need a ride home?"

"Well, I do need a ride home, but that's not why I wanted to use the phone. I need to call my aunt in Mississippi. It's long distance."

Jacqueline gazed at Kara's naivety and lovingly said, "My cell phone has free long distance, and my minutes are included in the plan. Here you go, sweetheart." She handed Kara the simply made basic black phone from a side compartment of her purse. "Just meet me back here after classes and I'll take you home."

"But your phone," Kara called out as Jacqueline started in the same direction Deacon Jackson had only moments ago.

Jacqueline looked back at her. "I'll get it after class. You go on and call your aunt and tell her I said hello."

Kara remembered that Jacqueline had met her aunt Frieda when she had come to visit for three weeks just after Miriam's accident. In between helping with Miriam's recovery, Frieda took time out to visit the church twice while she was in town. She had made a favorable impression.

"Hi Aunt Frieda, how are you?" Kara asked as she strolled near the glass doors in the foyer.

"Kara, is that you?"

"Yes ma'am, it's me." Just the sound of her aunt's voice brought on fond memories.

There was an immediate bump up in the tone of Frieda's voice. "Well, good morning to you. I'm just getting myself together for church. Aren't you attending service this morning?"

Kara giggled from the slight twang in Frieda's voice. "We just got out of the first service. I'm on my way to Sunday school."

"Oh, that's right, I forget sometimes that you have that early morning service and are an hour ahead. Well, I'm just finishing up breakfast. About to get my clothes on and head out the door for Sunday morning class myself."

A nostalgic glaze floated over Kara's face. She missed the hearty breakfasts, especially on a Sunday morning, her aunt prepared whenever she visited home. Kara yearned for the homemade country biscuits and gravy, the thick creamy grits, and oven cooked sausage patties. Not to mention Frieda's signature strawberry preserves. Oh how she missed home.

"Well Aunt Frieda, I wanted to know if I could come home for Christmas. I have enough money saved up for a one-way ticket, but I'd probably need a way to get back."

Frieda's voice held a smile. "Oh baby, you know you can come home. Don't worry about how you're going to get back. I'll make sure that you get back. I have a little money saved and I'll just purchase the round-trip ticket myself."

"But I have money. I can pay for the way there—"

"Listen, I told my sister that I would look out for you, Kara. A few dollars ain't gonna hurt me one way or the other. Besides, I was going to call you this afternoon if you hadn't called me. For some reason, you were on my mind heavily this morning."

Kara did everything to keep her eyes from welling. Uncontrollably, her vision blurred with tears out of gratitude anyway. She knew God had heard her prayers.

"I'll call you back this afternoon after service, and we can talk more then. Your cousins will be excited to hear that you're coming home."

"Aunt Frieda, please don't tell them," Kara pleaded. "I want it to be a surprise."

Frieda chuckled in compliance. "All right, dear. Well, let me go and get myself together for church. I'll talk to you this afternoon."

Kara held the phone close to her heart, inwardly praising God for answering her prayers so quickly. She slid the phone into the one good shoulder bag she owned and rushed off to her Sunday morning class.

# CHAPTER 11

THE STREETS WERE busy with incoming and outgoing traffic. Many patrons were piling in and out of the church doors to leave Sunday school while others shuffled in to make it on time to hear Pastor Wyatt's riveting message during the second service. The scheduled service and class times was a perfect set up for those who slept in on Sunday mornings or for many who loved to get started with God's Word for their lives in the early morning hours. Either way, Faithful Christian served as a gratifying spiritual hub to many busy New Yorkers who loved that down home country feel from the current pastor.

Pastor Wyatt, a South Carolina native, had been the senior pastor for just under ten years. He and his expectant wife, Sylvia, have been residing in the area for almost fifteen years, attending Faithful Christian the entire time. Due to the previous pastor's unexpected demise, although he was pretty well along in years, the congregants elected Dr. James Wyatt to be the church's next installed senior pastor. He had served many years in the capacity of Youth Pastor before moving to the area and his glowing reputation preceded him. It became evident by the way he immersed himself in the thick of building the presence of Faithful Christian not only in the neighborhood, but in surrounding communities as well. Since his inception, the congregation has grown by a couple thousand. This was mainly attributed to Dr. Wyatt's no-nonsense approach to preaching from the Holy Bible. He refused to take credit for the Lord's work, encouraging others to reverence God the same in their own lives.

"What a word Pastor delivered on this morning," Helen said as she pulled her car keys from her coat pocket. "I know Vincent would have just enjoyed that sermon." She stood alongside her friends in the church's attractive courtyard where coiled vine branches wrapped beautifully around iron-rod poles.

"Yes, it was a moving message," Marissa agreed. "I found myself jotting verses down left and right. You should've ordered the CD for Vincent."

"I did." Helen giggled. "I'm sure he'll enjoy it when he gets back. He took two older messages with him that Pastor had preached last year. When he travels, Vincent listens to them on the plane. After a quick download to his iPod, he is set for any kind of flight. Babies can be crying, people snoring, laughing, talking, or whatever, Vincent is in his own world." Helen chuckled again. "Whew, he makes it so easy being married to him." Helen grinned, absolutely smitten with even the thought of her dear Vincent.

"*He makes it so easy being married to him*?" Marissa mocked, and then winked at Talia before looking back at Helen. "Girl, what to do you mean by that?"

"I mean that it's so much easier being married to a saved man. I'm talking about a man who's saved *for real*. We have our little spats, but after twenty years what do you expect? But I know that he's not going anywhere," Helen confidently said as she smoothed a few strands of hair that had escaped her neatly arranged bun. "I don't have to worry that he's going to look for the next young thing and leave me in the lurch."

"How can you be so confident, Helen?" Talia teased, but only lightly as there was some admiration in her voice. "Men are unpredictable at times."

Helen delivered a knowing glance at her friend. "Uh, it's been twenty years and we're still together. We've been honest with one another from day one. We tell one another the truth even when what we have to say may hurt. I tell you what though, it has saved us a whole lot of unnecessary grief and money from going to marriage counselors." She erupted into laughter.

Talia grunted underneath her breath.

Helen composed herself to gravely add, "But seriously I'm telling you, communication is the key."

Talia pondered Helen's words. If communication was the key, then there was a whole lot that she and Franklin needed to discuss.

"So, I see that you and Donovan are getting along well," Helen said to Marissa as she waited for Donovan to drive the car around from the parking garage a block away. "We're going to have to do a couples night out when Vincent gets back in town."

"Yes, we may have to do that." Marissa peeked out of the narrow view she had of the street to ensure that she'd know when Donovan arrived. "It's hard to believe that I just met him yesterday. It seems as if we've known each other forever."

"How so?" Talia curiously asked. Her eye narrowed as she anxiously awaited Marissa's response.

"Well because we spent so much time talking." Marissa practically glowed as she spoke. "Over dinner, whispering in the movie theater, and even—"

"Oh, I'm sorry, honey, I just had to finalize a few things in the Trustees' office," Franklin said, unintentionally cutting off Marissa's banter. "Melissa made a stop at the restroom, but she'll be out shortly." He kissed Talia on the cheek and then acknowledged her smiling friends, "Good morning, ladies. It's nice seeing you both again. I hope you two weren't as worn out as Talia was from that tennis game on yesterday." He gave both Marissa and Helen brief, yet warm hugs. "Last night she was out like a light."

The two women chuckled along with Franklin, but the reminder of last night only brought sour memories to Talia. She forced an amicable smile that faded within seconds of its arrival. It had taken nearly two hours for her to get back to sleep after waking up in the middle of the night. Talia's mind raced relentlessly until finally teetering off in exhaustion. Thoughts of Donovan had held her captive while she was in bed next to Franklin. She was then challenged and now convicted even further after hearing Pastor Wyatt preach about faithfulness.

Talia nervously brushed the nape of her neck while subtly glancing back and forth between Marissa, Helen, and the doors of the church, successfully avoiding eye contact with her husband.

"Well Franklin, the exercise was great, and I have to say that I was in my bed early too," Helen said with an engaging smile. "I think Marissa was the only one who had enough energy to go out." She chuckled while winking at her dear friend.

"Oh Helen stop." Marissa blushed as Helen playfully tapped her on the forearm. "I was at home before eleven. And besides, Franklin doesn't want to hear about that."

Franklin chuckled in response.

"Well, how did the rest of your date go, Marissa?" Talia curtly asked with folded arms.

Helen peered at Talia, noticing a hint of annoyance in her tone.

"To tell you the truth, it's not over yet." Marissa winked as Donovan drove up and parked her car beside the sidewalk leading to the courtyard where they stood. "Since the kids spent the weekend over at their father's, Donovan and I are going to lunch before they get back home this evening." She giggled like an elementary school-age girl.

All three women looked on as Donovan emerged from the driver's seat and waited beside the passenger door. Franklin studied his wife, whose attention was fixed on the unfamiliar gentleman who waited on Marissa.

"What is he your butler now?" Talia astutely grumbled under her breath where Marissa couldn't hear, but her words were clearly audible to Helen who stood right next to her.

"You all have a good afternoon. If my day is anything like last evening, I know I will." Marissa waved with her fingertips as she hurried towards her vehicle.

"Can you believe that she already has him driving her car?" Talia judgmentally shook her head. "She doesn't even know him."

"Well, you remember how we were when we first started dating," Franklin gently reminded her, noticing the faraway look in her eyes. "So, I guess I better go get our car too before you start comparing them to us." He lightheartedly chuckled and then said goodbye to Helen.

After Franklin disappeared into a sea of people, Helen stared at Talia, wondering why she had a sudden interest in Marissa's love life. She had known Talia far longer than the both of them had known Marissa and this was an attitude that she rarely saw. Helen slowly folded her arms, looking back and forth between the taillights to Marissa's car and Talia's glare, questioning whether there was something to her suspicion. The suspicion that maybe there was more to Talia's concern for how close Marissa had gotten to Donovan in such a short period of time.

Helen held her peace, hoping that she was reading too much into things, but something was telling her that there was more than meets the eye.

# Chapter 12

LESLIE STOOD IN front of the subway tracks as the train whisked past her and barreled towards a screeching stop just ahead. She squinted as her shoulder length hair flailed from the impact of the brisk wind. Dressed in a pair of blue jeans, gray accented sneakers, and a mint green, cotton knitted sweater underneath a double-layered hooded coat, Leslie stood with a newspaper firmly tucked beneath her arm. The subway doors opened, and she squeezed inside of the car as patrons shuffled past her on their way out.

After she dropped down onto an empty bench, Leslie unfolded the paper and perused the wanted section. Her computer had crashed for the second time this week and her internet service had been disconnected that morning. She didn't care what job she had to take because she was living paycheck to paycheck. Her previous commercial royalties had dwindled, and she was down to her last fifty bucks in the bank.

Despite her depressing circumstances, Leslie believed that her role in Wendell's new movie was her golden ticket out of her spiraling decline. It was just the role she needed for others to take serious notice of her acting skills. As she pondered the possibility of dating the director, Leslie was sure that with the help of Wendell her struggling career would be catapulted to stardom. Wendell was attractive, had a little money in the bank, and as far as she knew, he was single. He was just her type, a man with a dream and the determination to fulfill it.

Leslie ruffled the newspaper as she turned to the next page. She had to get another job in order to escape her dreadful reality of being broke. The rent was due in a little over a week and her last check from the previous diner job she had lost was only enough to cover two-thirds of what she owed. If she could find work today, there was a possibility that her roommate would loan her some cash knowing that she was good for it.

"Is anyone sitting here?" A woman who looked to be in her early fifties asked Leslie before she sat down beside her.

Leslie smirked because no one ever asked her that question on the subway. "No," she answered, and then quickly stared back down at her newspaper.

"*Ah*, the want ads," the woman said, shamelessly leaning over Leslie's shoulder. "What kind of work are you looking for?"

In a fit of frustration, Leslie looked at the woman with a raised eyebrow, and then grumbled, "Anything ... I really don't have much of a choice right now."

The woman leaned back in her seat and pulled her pantyhose wrapped legs away from the center aisle and nodded knowingly. "Have you ever cleaned rooms before?" She casually patted her soft sole shoes against the grimy train floor.

Leslie's face contorted into a question mark. "Yes, many times. Why? Do you know of anybody who needs a housekeeper?" She stared into the woman's curious eyes.

"As a matter of fact, I do." The woman cordially extended her hand. "My name is Selah and I'm one of the housekeeping managers at the hotel on the next stop. We had someone quit on us yesterday and I was going to place an ad this morning, but ..."

Leslie looked hopeful, instantly taking on a pleasant disposition.

"But if you can follow my directions and be on time to work, I'll give you a job today." Selah's voice lapsed into employer-mode as she spoke. "It's a mad house around there and I need someone now."

"Are you serious?"

Selah nodded. "I'm *very* serious. If you want the job, it's yours. We're expecting two group conventions next month and I need to get reliable workers on staff."

Leslie held back the full range of her excitement and graciously shook Selah's hand. "You just don't know how much I appreciate this."

"Hey, you need a job and I need a worker," Selah said, her voice overtly optimistic. "We just need to take care of a few preliminary items and you should be good to go." She then looked up as the train slowed. "Well, I'm getting off at the next stop." Selah secured her coat belt around her waist. "Why don't you come in with me and we can fill out the paperwork."

"Okay ..." Leslie's response was slow. She hoped that the new job didn't interfere with her upcoming shooting schedule. In a careful tone, she asked, "What are the hours?"

"I'm mainly looking for early mornings to afternoons. We pretty much have our evening staff covered." Selah then appeared concerned as she stood from the bench and held onto a handrail strap. "Will that be a problem?"

Noting how cohesively the new schedule would mesh with her already existent one, Leslie peered up at her and answered with confidence, "Not at all. That would be perfect."

When the train reached its next stop, they both got off and Leslie confidently tossed her crumpled newspaper into a trash bin.

# CHAPTER 13

KARA PULLED HER wavy hair loose from the ponytail holder it had been restrained in for most of the day. She walked alongside Melissa as they exited the school building.

"Were you going by the church today?" Melissa asked as Douglas drove their family vehicle around to meet her by the sidewalk near the front entrance.

"No, I have some studying to do," Kara answered, bearing a faraway gaze. "Besides, I need to get the rest of my materials together for Juilliard before I leave town."

Melissa curled her lips to one side and folded her arms across her chest. "Leave town?" She raised a brow as her face took on an inquisitive stare. "Where are you going and who are you going with?"

"It's nothing like that and you know it." Kara nudged her on the shoulder. "I'm going home for Christmas break."

"I thought we were going to hang out during Christmas break." Melissa's concentration broke from Kara momentarily as she waved to a passing classmate. She looked back to her and asked, "What happened to our girl get-together?"

"Mel, things are kind of rough at home and I need a break from my sister. Besides, you remember what your mother said." Kara then held her hands up defensively as if to convince Melissa to also surrender to Talia's demands. "I just don't want to cause any trouble."

"You aren't causing any trouble." Melissa propped her hands on her hips as Douglas rounded the vehicle to open her door. And then as if she had just had an epiphany, she asked her driver, "Douglas, would you mind giving Kara a ride home today?"

"Not at all," Douglas replied as he opened the back door.

"Mel, I can ride the bus," Kara insisted, clutching her friend's arm.

Melissa simply shook her head as she tossed her bag on the floor in the back of the vehicle. "Thanks Douglas." Her eyes drifted to Kara's, which bore a tenacious glare, before shifting back to Douglas. "I'm sorry. Would you give us a minute?"

He complied and retreated to the driver's side of the vehicle.

Once Douglas was out of view, Melissa closed the door as she shook her head from side to side. "Kara, we're best friends. When are you going to stop acting as if I'm a stranger taking pity on you? You are not some charity case to me."

They both fell silent. Only the noise and bustle from the other students and loitering cars filled the sound waves around them. Kara brushed her hands across her head as she looked away. It pained her, even at her age, to be dependent upon anyone for anything. Although Melissa was indeed her friend and not a random stranger offering a handout as if she sat on a street corner with a box nestled in front of her filled with coins, Kara felt she had taken too much from her already.

Kara anticipated the day, just a few short months from now, when she would be able to stand on her own two feet and give back to those who had graciously given to her.

"You are my girl and no matter what, I've got your back. And don't forget, you've been there for me too."

"I hear you, but your mother is just—"

"Don't worry about her. She isn't going to find out that I gave you a ride home. Douglas is cool. He sees what kind of person you are." Melissa successfully drew a smile out of Kara. "Now come on before we get a ticket for loitering," she joked, motioning for her friend to get in the car.

Afternoon traffic was a little more hectic than usual as Douglas navigated across town. With an elbow propped on the door, Kara gazed out of the window. People were everywhere going about their business. Some carried briefcases while others lugged instruments. There was a diverse mixture of just about everybody purposefully moving about. Men in business suits, women in jeans and sneakers, students in leotards, were all bustling around with barely any recognition of the others' existence. The inhabitants of the city intrigued Kara, but she missed home. She longed for the loving comfort of her family.

"*Hello*, are you listening to me?" Melissa pulled Kara back into her world. "What are you over there thinking about?" she prodded further.

Kara looked at her, and then a knowing smile crept upon her face as she said, "Home."

Melissa pouted. "So, I guess I can't change your mind, huh?"

Before the words came from her mouth, the look in Kara's eyes had already answered Melissa's question. However, Melissa persistently added, "You know she's not going to even be in town the entire break and Dad doesn't mind if you come over. He's a *real* Christian, you know."

Kara helplessly giggled. "Now, you know you shouldn't be talking about your mother like that."

Melissa sucked her teeth and said with a smirk, "Well, it's the truth. I love her, but I'm so glad that I'm not like her." In one last ditch attempt, she asked, "So, are you going to stay or what? You know we'll have fun."

Kara's words idled. She glanced away from her friend and considered the invitation. When Kara looked back at her, Melissa raised her eyebrows as she motioned for an answer. Kara pressed her lips together tightly as if in deep thought before saying, "I wish I would've known this sooner." She shook her head and then with downcast eyes added, "But

I've already called my aunt." She looked back at her friend. "I can't, Mel. She's already bought the ticket."

Melissa nodded and then perked up as if an idea just struck her by surprise. "Hey," she said, lowering her voice to a whisper as Douglas peered in the rearview mirror. "Why don't I go with you?"

"You want to go to Mississippi?" Kara said in a startling tone. "*To the country?*" Then her head fell backwards as she erupted in laughter.

"What's so funny?"

Kara composed herself as Douglas navigated through the busy streets. "Mel, Dadenville is not Club Med and at Aunt Frieda's the only breakfast on a tray you'll have is when you're taking it out of the oven yourself."

Melissa placed her manicured fingers on top of her already crossed legs and said in a confident tone, "Well, a little hard work never killed anyone. Besides, it beats staying at home," she droned. "You know what Dad will have me doing."

Kara nodded as they responded in unison, "Going over the family business."

Both girls shook their heads critically.

"Well, I should have the flight information this afternoon. Aunt Frieda said she was going to book the flight first thing this morning since there was a bad thunderstorm on yesterday when I spoke to her."

Melissa appeared puzzled. "What does a thunderstorm have to do with booking a flight?"

"Back home in the country, we don't talk on the phone, or do much of anything, when it's lightning outside," Kara enlightened her.

"Wow, now that really is country." Melissa impulsively laughed.

"Whatever." Kara smirked. "And I can promise you that it'll be coach class."

Melissa shrugged. "So, I can do coach. You act like I've never flown coach class."

Kara skeptically raised a brow, slightly tilting her head to the side.

"Okay, okay I haven't," Melissa admitted with a smile. "But so what? There's a first time for everything, right?"

"Yeah, but you know you aren't coming with me. Your mother would go crazy. No, I take that back, your mother would go crazy on you." Kara laughed.

Somewhat embarrassed by the truth, Melissa pondered Kara's words. She often likened Christmas time in their household to a circus: parties and guests, decorators and caterers, constant deliveries in and out that left little room for meditation on the true meaning. Since befriending Kara, many things had come into perspective for Melissa. In the past there was often a thrill for her to receive packages from family across the country, but in the beautiful, attached notes there was rarely any mention of Christ.

"I know. You're right." Melissa solemnly nodded. "But it would've been nice."

"Yeah, it would've been."

Kara opened the car door and stepped out in front of her building. She leaned back inside and said, "Call me over at Deidra's." And with a slight roll of her eyes, she added, "I'm not sure what kind of mood Miriam is in. Besides, I plan on doing my homework over there anyway."

"Okay, talk to you later, girl."

Just then Phillip walked up behind Kara and gaped inside of the vehicle. "What's up, Melissa?"

Melissa stared at the boy gripping a basketball underneath his arm. "What's up?"

*What's up?* Kara made a face.

"Has Kara told you that I've been asking about you?"

Melissa curiously looked at him, answering, "No."

"Melissa, we really must be going," Douglas interrupted. "Your mother has a dinner party tonight."

"Okay, in just a minute," she answered him.

Phillip looked towards the front seat, and then back to Melissa. "Man, you got it like that? That's what's up. I'm going to have that one day. You watch and see. And you're gonna be mine." His eyebrows danced with assurance as he tossed the ball from one hand to the other.

"Oh really?" Melissa was intrigued by his confidence. She had heard from Kara, as well as through media coverage, that Phillip was the star basketball player at one of the local high schools. He was confident, attractive, and saying all of the right things to her.

"*Yes really*," Phillip boldly declared.

Melissa's gaze momentarily lingered on Phillip. His stature was just her type: tall, dark, and handsome. And it didn't hurt that he was rumored to have the NBA in his near future.

"Come on, she has to go, Phillip." Kara placed a hand on Phillip's arm as she noticed the glossed look on Melissa's face.

"Wait a minute." Melissa shifted her eyes to Kara. She scooted closer to the window and whispered to where Douglas was out of earshot, "Want to hang out this weekend? My mother is going out of town this weekend to pick up my grandmother from Florida and fly back with her next week so she can spend Thanksgiving with us."

"Oh shoot, I can't." Kara sighed. "I have a student to teach on Saturday, plus I have to put the finishing touches on my application," she explained. "Didn't you have to work on your app as well? You know they tell us to not wait until the last minute because Juilliard does not accept late submissions under any circumstance."

"Oh girl, I know." Melissa nonchalantly waved her off. "I'm almost done with it. I just want it to be perfect. Every time I look at it I find something that could've been said better. You of all people know how that is." She then causally chuckled. "Well, since you can't hang out...." Melissa then looked away from Kara to Phillip as she added, "Maybe we can go somewhere."

Kara read the unsettling innuendo in Melissa's voice.

"That's what's up." Phillip grinned as he took a step closer and propped his elbow on the roof of the vehicle. "So, what'd you have in mind?"

Melissa coyly batted her eyelashes and blushed.

"Hey, why don't you come to my game on Friday?" Phillip asked her before looking to Kara. "Surely, you can take off one night to see the next big baller take to the court."

Kara shrugged. "Well, maybe I can take one night off." She then looked at Melissa. "We can hang out then if you like."

"Sure, it sounds good to me," Melissa agreed. "And I look forward to seeing your moves, Phillip. That is *if* you're as good as you say that you are." A mischievous smile crept across her face.

Kara suspiciously stared at her friend. She was acting out of character.

"Melissa, we really must be going," Douglas urged, looking back from the front seat.

"She has to go, Phillip." Kara quickly snatched Phillip back by the arm before squinting at her girlfriend. "Bye Melissa ... and call me," she added before firmly shutting the door.

Melissa lowered the window and waved at Phillip with wiggling fingers.

Phillip licked his lips as the luxury SUV rolled away. "Your girl is diggin' on me. She's going to be mine. You watch and see." He dribbled the ball between his legs then successfully balanced the twirling ball on one finger.

"Whatever." Kara grimaced at him. "So, I guess you're the next big thing in basketball." She waved him off and started in the opposite direction.

"You've read the papers, you tell me," he answered, following behind her. "Wait, you can be a child prodigy, but I can't play pro ball?" he scoffed. "I think somebody's hatin' on me."

Kara slowed her steps and faced Phillip's accusations. "No, I'm not *hatin'* on you. I just don't want you to string her along like you've been doing every other little girl around here like she's nothing." She tossed a hand on her hip and pointed a finger at him with the other. "It's not happening under my watch."

Phillip shook his head and pushed her hand down. "You really shouldn't listen to rumors. Aren't you learning anything at that church you go to?"

"So, are you saying that it's not true?"

"*No, it ain't true.*" Phillip angrily grounded the ball and placed a foot on top of it. "Everybody's trying to get up out of the projects, Kara. And some of these girls are just looking for a meal ticket. I'm not stupid, you know. I'm not messing with any of them." He emphasized his point by the dramatic gestures of his hands. "People may call me a jock, but I'm nobody's fool. I've seen what my mom had to go through and believe me, she's the *only* woman I'm taking up out of here with me. Mark my words on that one."

Kara paused, soaking in Phillip's words. Without realizing it she had judged him by what others had said. "I'm sorry, Phillip. I guess after Shantel came up pregnant, screaming about it was your child, I just believed her."

"See, that's the problem." He critically pointed in her direction again. "You know me, Kara. You could've at least asked." Phillip grunted as he shook his head from side to side.

"Yeah, you're right."

Phillip grunted again.

"Look, I said that I was sorry. Do you forgive me?"

Her sheepish gaze softened his attitude. "Yeah, I guess so. But you know how you can make it up to me?"

Kara rested a hand on her hip and cocked her head to the side. "And how's that?"

Phillip laughed uncontrollably at her stance.

"What's so funny?" she asked.

He waved his hands back and forth in front of him, trying to compose himself. "It's just that you don't look like a projects chick, but you sure know how to act like one when you get ready."

Kara tried popping him upside the head to no avail. He dodged her advances as if he was on the court. She soon abandoned her attempts to successfully land a hit.

They both broke out into laughter.

"I'm just too quick," Phillip mocked. "And you know I'm just kidding with you about that projects crack. You're straight. Anybody can see that you have it going on. I see why you got older guys wanting to get with you."

Surprised by his remark, Kara parted her lips. "Older guys?"

"Don't play dumb, you know who I'm talking about."

"How did you know?" She quickly flipped through the archives of her mind, wondering if she had arbitrarily said something to him she shouldn't have.

"I have my ways," Phillip said, and then picked up his ball. "Word travels fast." He bounced the ball a couple of times before tossing it from hand to hand again. "Don't worry though, your secret is safe with me."

Kara stood motionless and dumbfounded. She apprehensively looked away from Phillip and started up the walkway towards the building. As she neared the door, Phillip drew her attention back to him.

"For real, Meme won't hear it from me. I know how things are."

Kara smoothed the stray strands of her hair back and carefully asked, "So, how did you know? He's never been around here."

"You don't remember inviting my mom to your show?" His eyes asked the question again.

"Performance," she corrected him.

"Whatever."

Kara then wore a telling smile. "You know, now that you mention it, I do. I remember her saying that she may have to work. And I didn't bother inviting you." She shrugged, and then caught the backpack that slipped from her shoulder in the process and readjusted it. "I just assumed that you wouldn't be interested or maybe had a game."

"See, that's what you get for assuming," Phillip cautioned her, and then smiled as he said, "But you did good, young gun."

Kara grinned at his lighthearted compliment. "Thanks for coming, Phillip. You never cease to amaze me."

"Just when you thought you had me figured out," he joked. "And I saw how happy you looked backstage. That's tight. Mom and I decided not to disturb you."

Kara modestly pressed her lips together as she readjusted the book bag that slipped from her shoulder again.

Deidra, Phillip and his mother, along with Wendell had all cared enough to show up to one of the most important events in her life, but her own blood sister thought it was too much trouble to leave the apartment because it was simply too cold for her. Kara smiled at her friend who often gave her a hard time, but supported her vision as much as she did his. Ever since they met when she and Miriam had moved into the projects, he looked out for her even when she didn't know that he was.

"Do you think your mom will say anything to my sister?" Kara carefully asked. "Miriam really doesn't want me dating even though I'm old enough to have a boyfriend," she grumbled. "I just don't want to hear her mouth or have her embarrass the heck out of me. I have enough to deal with and don't care to fight her on that too."

Phillip opened the door to their building, allowing Kara to enter. "Nah, she knows what's up. Besides, my mother said it's none of her business. She believes you know how to handle yourself. You don't have anything to worry about there. But you make sure to keep your eyes open. Don't be a fool, Kara."

"Yeah, thanks," she answered, and then walked inside.

"And remember, you have to put in a good word with Melissa," Phillip called out behind Kara with a shameless grin plastered across his face.

"Do I even need to?" Kara mumbled as she loaded the elevator.

"What'd you say?" He walked closer to where she stood.

"Never mind." She casually dismissed her offhanded remark.

"You know she wants me. You saw how she was looking at me," Phillip confidently spoke. "So, you may as well give me her number."

"I can't just give her number to you." Kara scowled.

"Well, I probably would have gotten it myself if somebody wasn't blocking," he responded. "So just call and ask her. I'm checking back with you tonight. Or you can just give her mine."

"You sound like the one who's got it bad." Kara raised a brow as she pressed a button for the elevator.

"Seriously, I'm not playing. I'm checking back with you tonight." He held the door to the elevator.

Kara pushed his hand away and pressed the close door button on the control panel. "*Bye Phillip,*" she sang, playfully waving as the elevator doors closed in front of her.

# CHAPTER 14

"HEY MOM, WHO was that on the phone?" Melissa asked as she grabbed an apple from the granite-top island in the kitchen. "My cell battery is dead, and I was expecting a call from my agent about an upcoming audition." She took a large bite from the piece of fruit and chewed vigorously.

Talia held the phone close to her chest with her back turned. "How many times have I told you to keep our home number private?" She turned to face her daughter. "This line is supposed to be for friends and family only. I get enough calls from your father's *important clients* as it is," Talia snapped.

Melissa drew back a few steps with her hands raised in the air. "*Sorry*, I'll tell him not to use it again. Forgive me for trying to be serious about my career." Melissa shook her head as she turned and started for her room.

"Melissa, come back here." Talia sat the cordless phone down on the counter and extended her arms. "I'm sorry, dear. It's just that I was expecting a call from a friend."

Melissa dabbed the corners of her mouth with a napkin as she hesitantly approached her mother.

"Come here, I shouldn't have snapped at you. It's just that with the upcoming trip out of town and getting things organized for you and Franklin before I leave, the last thing I want to do is talk business with anyone else."

Melissa squinted as Talia squeezed her arms around her. This behavior was odd, especially for her ordinarily distant mother who rarely gave out hugs or any physical sign of affection.

"Well, I'm sorry, Mom," Melissa apologized again as she released their embrace. "I'll just give him Dad's office phone as a secondary number." She warily walked to the other side of the room and tugged on the refrigerator door handle.

"You know, we don't do enough together." Talia casually folded her arms. "How about when I get back from picking up Mama we have a girls' day, all three of us?" Talia suggested, determined to occupy her idle time by getting closer to her daughter.

The convicting sermon Pastor Wyatt had delivered on the day before challenged Talia to no end. In fact, just before Melissa had walked into the kitchen, she was prepared to phone Marissa to share everything about her past with Donovan. Talia figured that if she got it all out in the open now, it would be easier than waiting until after Donovan used and discarded her friend as if she was a toy.

"Mom, are you feeling all right?" Melissa asked, biting into her apple again while tossing a loaf of bread and a package of sliced cheese onto the counter. "We never do anything together. *And now with Grandma?*" She smirked.

Talia nodded knowingly. "Well, it's time for a change." She rhythmically tapped her fingers on the countertop. "It hit me that when this school year is over, you'll be off to college."

Melissa stared at her. "Mom, you're just now realizing this?" She then giggled. "And I'll be right at Juilliard."

"I thought we discussed your becoming a business major. You know that—"

"Mom, please," Melissa emphatically said as she tossed the remnants from the apple into a nearby trashcan. "It's my life. I'm not a little kid anymore. If I fall flat on my face with the acting thing, then that'll just be my mistake." Annoyed, Melissa ruffled the plastic that was gathered at the end of the bread bag. "If it doesn't work out, then maybe I'll think about the business. But until then, can we just let this go?"

Talia raised a hand as if surrendering with a white flag. It was more of Franklin's idea than hers, but she was trying to learn how to be on one accord with her husband. This was something their marriage counselor, Pastor Wyatt, had suggested in one of their many sessions together. It was one of the numerous recommendations Talia found on the worksheets she had dug out on last night. When she saw Donovan open the car door for Marissa yesterday, those old feelings had resurfaced with a vengeance. Rather than succumb to the losing battle of her flesh, Talia searched for their counseling notes where home activities were listed that carried her through the reconciliation period years ago. And mending any noticeable brokenness was a key objective she decided to tackle first. This was one main reason why she wanted to make her relationship with Melissa better, second only to her intimacy with Franklin.

Melissa sighed through her irritation and faced her mother. "Mom, I'm sorry. I shouldn't have said it like that. It's just that I really want to give this a serious shot. If I don't do it now, I'll never really know where my career could go."

Talia softened to Melissa's plea. She had a point. It was her life and if she made a mistake, it would be her mistake to make. At the age of seventeen, Melissa's mind was pretty much decided. She took after her father in many respects: determined, focused, and ready to execute her plans. Talia just didn't want Melissa to rely on her and Franklin to fund her future. She knew that they would not always be there to protect her from the harsh blows the world may deliver, but the more Talia listened to Melissa the more confident she became in her daughter's ability to care for herself.

"Okay, I understand." Talia nodded. "Maybe I can talk to your father about it before I leave this weekend."

Melissa was taken aback. "Mom, are you in there?" she teased, slowly waving a hand back and forth in front of Talia's face. "What have you done with my mother?"

Talia chuckled, surprised by her own outburst. This was what she earnestly wanted in her relationship with Melissa. They rarely laughed, maybe because Talia was so focused on creating an image for others to admire that she neglected to nurture the bond with her own child. If it wasn't a brunch, a weekly tennis match, teaching the etiquette class at church, or going on the bi-annual mission trips, Talia would be out of town enjoying the fruits of Franklin's labor. She never thought it would come to this, but she was actually beginning to feel unsatisfied and not just at home with her husband. Something was missing and she was determined to fill that lingering void.

"Am I really that bad?" Talia asked, now pondering the image she had portrayed in front of her daughter.

Melissa raised an eyebrow as she placed two slices of bread on a saucer. "Well, it's just that you've never really supported me in my career choice. I mean, of course I'm grateful that you got my pictures done and allowed me to go to a public performing arts high school, but I know in the back of your mind you were probably never going to stop with the modeling thing and dad with the business." Melissa smiled as she scooped a sliver of butter from the round container and spread it across one side of the slices of bread. "I was kind of glad when you decided to just side with Daddy about the business."

Talia's nose crinkled in confusion. "And why's that?"

Melissa shrugged. "Well, at least I wasn't being pulled in two different directions."

Talia tapped her fingernails on the counter again. "Hmm, that surprises me. I figured you'd think we were double-teaming you." A telling smile crept across her face.

"I did at first, but not anymore," Melissa said as she placed a wedge of cheese in between the slices of bread. "I figured that it's better to deal with one of your choices than two," she quipped, turning a knob on the stove top.

"You're smart. But don't count on your father letting go so easily." Talia wagged a finger at her daughter.

"But you said you'd talk to him," Melissa whined.

"Talking to him and actually getting him to change his mind are two different things." Talia walked to where Melissa stood beside the stove and placed a hand on her shoulder. "And don't fill up on a greasy grilled cheese sandwich." Talia turned the stove off and handed Melissa a bag of fat free veggie chips from the snack basket a few feet away. "The dinner party for your father is tonight."

Melissa glared at the bag of chips and then up to her mother's eyes. She recalled Douglas mentioning the gathering earlier when he picked her up from school. "Dinner party for what?"

"Uh, have you forgotten his birthday?"

"But you've never had a dinner party for his birthday."

Talia pondered her daughter's comment. It was true that over the years they had been married Talia had never thrown her husband a birthday party, dinner party, celebratory party, or any kind of party for that matter. But it wasn't because she hadn't wanted to. It was simply out of respect to Franklin's request. He was a humble man who never wanted people to fuss over him.

"So why now?"

"Well, your father has worked hard for our family and instead of having dinner out as usual I decided to invite a few of our friends over to celebrate the occasion. It's a surprise, so don't say anything to him," Talia instructed. "Since his birthday isn't until Friday, I know he won't suspect a thing. I just hope some of his friends can make it on such short notice. I've only gotten confirmation from five people so far. I'm waiting on a few others to call me back."

"How long have you been planning this, Mom?"

"Well ... just last night," she admitted. "I wanted to do something before I left town. But I did buy his gift weeks ago. With tomorrow being his half workday where he starts a little later in the day, I figured tonight would be perfect." Talia appeared to second guess herself as she skeptically asked, "What do you think?"

Melissa's eyes widened as she shrugged. "I don't know. I guess it sounds okay. Daddy will be happy with whatever."

"You're right about that." Talia nodded. "It doesn't take much to please your father." She then retrieved her purse from a barstool and fished her keys from the side compartment. "Well, I have to run out for some last minute items. Your father isn't due home for a couple more hours. If he comes home early, just remember to keep it a secret that this party is for him. He won't suspect anything since I occasionally hold dinner parties anyway."

"Okay." Melissa nodded as she opened the bag of chips in her hand. "But I haven't gotten him a gift yet. I wasn't planning on going shopping until tomorrow."

"Don't worry, I picked up a little something from both of us last week."

Melissa enjoyed giving her own gift, something that she wanted him to have from her own acting earnings. It was the least she could do with all that he had purchased for her throughout the years.

"So, what did *we* get him this year?"

"*We* got him that new set of golf clubs he's been thinking about buying."

"Oh great, golf clubs. What an exciting gift," she droned.

Talia ignored Melissa's sarcasm. "Well, I had them engraved with his initials. So, I'm sure he'll love that. It'll go perfectly with the new golfing attire I bought him."

"Yeah, I guess so." Melissa shrugged. "But Dad's not going to play golf in this weather, Mom."

"Miss Smarty-pants, I'm also surprising your father with a weekend trip to Verona where there's an indoor dome for golfing," she replied. "Just a little relaxing retreat while I'm gone. Now, what do you think about that?"

"That's great, Mom," Melissa approved. "Now that's something I think he will really like."

"Yes, especially since his busy season is just around the corner." Talia sighed.

"I know." Melissa slightly lowered her chin while lifting an eyebrow. "Once he's in work-mode, he's really locked in."

"Don't remind me," Talia mumbled.

"Well, I guess I'll go do my homework. What time is the party?"

"At seven-thirty. If anyone calls, let them know they can reach me on my cell. It's all charged now."

"Okay, I will."

Talia grabbed a piece of paper from underneath the cordless phone she had placed on the counter earlier where she had a list of items scribbled down. "When Douglas returns, tell him to hide the cake in the oven. If he puts it in the refrigerator, Franklin will see it." Talia patted down her pockets and gave the kitchen area a once over. "Okay, I think that's everything." She looked back to Melissa and said, "I won't be long." She held up a hand and exited the front door.

Ignoring her mother's instruction to not fill up on a greasy grilled cheese sandwich, Melissa turned the range back on. She placed the black saucer that held her bread with cheese on the stove next to it. She anxiously rubbed her hands together because this snack was one of her favorite foods. Just as she placed the sandwich into the heated pan, the phone her mother had abandoned only moments ago began to ring. She picked the phone up and cradled it between her ear and shoulder as she pulled a spatula from the side drawer.

"Hello?" she answered.

"Hi ... *Melissa*?" the woman on the other end inquired.

"Yes."

"Hey, this is Marissa. Is your mother there?"

"Uh no, she just left," Melissa slowly answered as she adjusted the heat underneath the pan. "Are you calling about the party?"

"Yes, I am. Your mother is a genius to be able to plan a party in a day." Marissa chuckled.

"I know," Melissa said, slightly distracted as she carefully edged the spatula underneath the sandwich. "I just found out about it a few minutes ago. Did you want me to see if I can catch her? She just left."

"Oh no, that's all right. Just let her know that I'll be there tonight. I'm about to leave work now. Once I get home and get the kids squared away with dinner, I'll be there."

"You can call her on her cell," Melissa said, interested more in her sandwich than writing down the message that Marissa had called.

"No, I just wanted to call before I left the office. Her text message invite stated plus one and to call back on the home phone. Just tell her that I'll be there, and that I do plan to bring a friend."

"Okay, I'll tell her." Melissa smiled as she successfully flipped the sandwich to the other side without disturbing the perfect shape of the food. Marissa gave her the name of the guest she was going to bring, and Melissa made a mental note of the count.

"Thanks. See you later on, Melissa," Marissa said.

"Okay, bye."

Melissa hung up and quickly grabbed a pen and piece of paper before she forgot the message. She jotted down Marissa's and her guest's name and then trotted back to the stove. After securing the snack onto the waiting saucer, Melissa poured herself a glass of ginger ale. As she took an appetizing bite from the sandwich her eyelashes fluttered while she moaned in satisfaction.

Melissa finished her meal in a matter of minutes and wiped the filmy residue from her hands with a piece of paper towel. Before leaving the kitchen she positioned the message from Marissa in the center of the counter where her mother would see it. It read, *Marissa plus guest, Donovan.*

# CHAPTER 15

"HEY KARA, THERE'S someone named Wendell calling," Deidra whispered as she covered the phone with the palm of her hand. "Is this him?" Her eyes asked the question twice.

Kara's face lit up like a Christmas tree as she sprung from the floor where she was doing her homework. "Yes, that's him," she whispered back.

Deidra pushed the mute button on the phone as she pointed a finger at Kara. "Remember what I told you," she said in a serious tone before handing the phone over.

Kara nodded with intent. "I know."

Deidra then picked up her shoulder bag after Kara took the phone. "Well, I'm off to night school, but you're welcome to stay here until I get back." Deidra looked towards her kitchen. "There are leftovers in the fridge, so feel free to help yourself."

"Okay, thanks." Kara watched as Deidra exited the apartment before placing the phone to her ear.

She pressed the mute button again to release the silence. "Wendell?"

"Yes, it's me." He sounded spent. "Was that your sister?" he carefully asked with a slight hesitation in his voice.

Kara sat down on the nearby sofa and slowly rested her free hand on the armrest. "Uh no, that was a family friend." She quietly cleared her throat. "I see that you got my message."

"Yes, the new number." His voice was distant, teetering on the edge of anger. "Thanks for leaving me a voicemail."

There was an uncomfortable moment of silence.

Kara hoped that his respect for her hadn't waned. She tilted her head back and raised her eyes upward, inwardly praying for God to give her the words to speak, the words that would fall upon a receptive heart.

"So, did you give it to Mrs. Chow?" she cautiously asked. "I want her to know how sorry I was for not getting back to her on Saturday."

The entire situation just soured her stomach. The mere thought of a well-respected faculty member reconsidering the offer to work with her caused Kara's insides to churn.

"I gave it to my aunt who gave it to her. You know, this really made me look bad." He paused, separating his resentment from the conversation. "What's going on? I thought we were getting, you know, closer. And I thought you were serious about a music career."

"Wendell, I *am* serious. I haven't been more serious about anything except when I accepted Christ into my life," she tried to convince him. "I wouldn't play around with something as important as this. Being a student at a music and performing arts high school should tell you that." Her voice became slightly defensive. "You know that I wouldn't work so hard on getting the submission materials in if this was just a game for me."

"Then why did you hang up on me the other night?" he questioned in a tone again salted with anger.

Kara paused, embarrassed by his question. "I-I had to go. My sister wanted the phone, and I just didn't want you to hear us argue." Her voice then grew delicately thin. "I'm sorry, Wendell. I didn't even know Mrs.

Chow had called until you told me. Now that you have my new number, I'll make sure that it never happens again."

Kara's humility reminded Wendell of why he had quietly pursued her. Although he couldn't gaze into her eyes at that moment, he knew that they revealed her apologies just as he had heard in her voice.

"I'm sorry," she repeated, this time with a crackle in her voice.

Wendell released a calming sigh. There was something about this young woman that captivated him. He had only entertained the idea of dating twice since his previous girlfriend passed—both of them older—over the past year, but neither prospect seized his attention the way Kara had.

As he paced the floor, rigorously rubbing the top of his head back and forth, Wendell fought to keep his feelings in check, wanting to wait until after Kara's eighteenth birthday to reveal them to her.

Kara slumped on the cushioned microfiber loveseat, gently biting on her thumb nail. She glanced around the room, wanting to tell this man all of her secrets—but she couldn't. Her mind roamed about whether or not he would truly understand. *What if he thinks less of me because of where I live? What if he's pretending and I've fallen for an unsaved man like friends that I know? What if he tries to pressure me out of my virginity? What if....*

"Look, I'm sorry too," Wendell apologized, interrupting her thoughts. "Maybe I shouldn't have come down on you so hard. I just wanted to be sure that I wasn't pushing you into something you didn't want to do. My aunt loved your performance and Lois is willing to review your submission materials. Do you think you could meet her after school sometime this week?"

Kara could hardly contain her excitement as she blurted out, "Yes!" Quickly withdrawing her enthusiasm, she repeated in a sedated tone, "I mean, yes."

They both laughed, melting away the iciness of their conversation.

"Did you need a ride?" Wendell smiled through his words. "I can pick you up from school, say this Thursday afternoon. Is that okay?"

Kara nodded with excitement, but calmly answered, "Yeah, that'll be fine."

"So, do you think we could grab a bite to eat afterwards?" Wendell wanted to refrain from asking her out on any sort of date again, but his mind was fighting a losing battle with his heart. Not only was Kara absolutely gorgeous in his eyes, her glowing innocence mesmerized him. And even with those two striking attributes, it was her heart for God that absolutely arrested him. "I start the production phase with the film this week and my schedule is going to be kind of tight for the next couple of months."

Kara considered his request and warmly replied, "Yes, I would really like that."

Shortly after ending her call with Wendell, Kara stood in Deidra's kitchen and held the phone against her chest. After she glanced at the homework she still had left, she hurriedly dialed Frieda's number since Deidra had assured her that it was okay to call long distance from her home phone.

After the phone had rung for the fifth time, Kara peered up at the clock, wondering why her aunt hadn't answered yet. Just before she hung up, Frieda finally picked up. In a southern drawl, Frieda explained that her hands were sticky with homemade biscuit batter and had delayed her in getting to the phone.

"Now auntie, why did you have to go and start talking about biscuits?" Just the thought of Frieda's signature buttermilk biscuits triggered Kara's mouth to water. "I'm already homesick as it is."

"Well child, when you get home, you'll have biscuits coming out of your ears." Frieda chuckled. "You remind me so much of Gwen. She loved my biscuits. She would always say that they tasted just like how Mama used to make them."

"Mama sure did like to eat biscuits," Kara remembered. "She used to bring a fresh pan home every Saturday night to have for Sunday morning breakfast. Ever since we moved back to Dadenville from Boston, Mama would get you to make them for us."

"Yes, she did." Frieda grinned, partially showing the gold caps trimmed on her front teeth.

"All except for the last time." Kara rubbed the sides of her jeans as she walked back to the sofa in the living room. At moments, it was challenging for her to even think about the final moments she saw her parents alive.

"You all right, baby?"

"Yes ma'am, I'm okay. I just really miss them sometimes."

"I know what you mean."

Kara smiled through her reminiscent thoughts. "We had those pecan Danishes that night instead." The images of her parents that night years ago were still as clear as if it were yesterday. She'd never forget the flowing emerald dress Gwendolyn wore or the green and white pinstripe shirt with khaki shorts that Kenneth sported. The nostalgic images of that sunny summer day were forever imprinted into her memory.

"You keep on remembering your parents, baby. God gave us memories for a reason. Enough to keep us going forward, but not too much to keep us in the past. Keep that in mind, Kara. God has given just enough to get us through."

Kara pondered Frieda's insightful words. She understood her aunt's old wisdom that was always salted with revelations she had received from the Lord. Although the days following her parents' death were difficult, Kara came to understand that God had saved her for a reason. When a fireman presented her with a Bible where only the delicate edges had been singed, Kara clung to God even more. It was the Bible she had read to her father on that fateful night, the one that bore her silver engraved name on the front cover. The Bible she kept safely in her bedroom.

"So, how's Miriam? Is she going to be okay there alone?"

At first Kara was at a loss for words. It wasn't in her to trouble Frieda, who'd had her fair share of hospitalizations. Kara didn't want to add any unnecessary stress to Frieda's life by discussing her and Miriam's sibling discord.

"Meme will be okay," Kara answered, successfully masking her agitation. "There are people here who will look out for her. I just have to get out of here." Kara's last few words came without hesitation in a hopeless, almost desperate manner. "Aunt Frieda, I really need a break."

"Oh?" Frieda's voice spilled with concern.

"I'll talk to you about it when I get home. I'm on the neighbor's phone and still have some homework to get done," Kara explained.

Frieda released a troubled sigh. "Okay ... and I need to talk to you too. I'm glad you're coming home. We'll have plenty of time to catch up."

"Is there something wrong?"

"Nothing's *wrong*," Frieda said in a somewhat unconvincing tone. "I just want to sit down and talk to you about some things. You're getting ready for college, and I know how hard the past few years have been on you without your parents and all."

Thoughts of having to grow up without Kenneth and Gwendolyn pilfered Kara's smile. "Yeah, it has been hard without them, but thank you for being there for me."

"Oh baby, you don't have to thank me for that. You and Miriam both have always been like my own children." Frieda smiled through her words. "Gwen was blessed to have had you," she sympathized.

"And I was blessed to have had her as a mother."

Frieda nodded as she held the phone to her ear. She paced the cemented floor of her screened-in porch while gazing out at the acres of land surrounding her secluded home. It was a haven for her, away from the bustling, busy streets of where her son lived in Atlanta. Frieda stared as she saw her husband's pickup truck from a distance meander down the dirt road. He had been gone an hour longer than she had anticipated, but as he got closer she was glad to see Simon's head subtly bounce up and down with a slight jiggle from side to side in that old truck of his. He absolutely adored Kara, and Frieda couldn't wait to tell him that she was going to be there for her Christmas break.

"Well, I guess I'll see you in a few weeks. Your uncle is coming down the road, so I better get his food on the table." Frieda lightheartedly chuckled. "Did you want to hold on to say hello?"

"Oh no, that's okay. Just tell Uncle Simon I said hi. And thanks again, Aunt Frieda."

Kara held the phone in her hand for a few seconds after Frieda had hung up. She wondered what was on her aunt's mind. Frieda never expressed a need to talk in person about anything, at least not with such gravity in her voice, but today she had.

In just a few short weeks, Kara would see her aunt face to face and discuss what was on her heart.

# CHAPTER 16

MELISSA SAT AT the desk in her bedroom and perused the internet. She glanced over at the pink piece of paper next to her computer where she had doodled Phillip's name. He was a change from the guys her mother wanted her to date: a little rough around the edges, from the projects, but still down-to-earth.

Just beyond that pink sticky note was the newspaper in which Phillip had been featured. He was already a star in his own right. Melissa rested back in her chair as a smile crept across her lightly made-up face. Engrossed in a sea of delightful thoughts, she accidentally knocked over a tube of mascara as she repetitively tapped the tip of a pencil nestled between her fingers on the desktop.

"Are you dressed yet?" Talia called out from behind Melissa's closed bedroom door as she insistently knocked.

Melissa looked to the door as she answered, "Yes, I'll be down in a minute."

"Don't be long," she told her, and then with a hint of optimism added, "Quentin called while you were in the shower."

Melissa rushed from her seat to the other side of the room and flung the door open. "What did he want?"

Talia stared at her daughter's panic-stricken face. "He wanted to talk to you."

"Why didn't he call my cell?"

"Maybe because you changed your number a while back."

"Well, why didn't you tell me he called?" Melissa folded her arms as deep defining creases embedded her face. "I hope that you didn't invite him tonight."

"Like I said, you were in the shower. And I'm telling you now," she defensively answered. "And why would I invite him? It's Franklin's party, not yours."

"I'm sorry." Melissa dropped her folded arms and walked towards her dresser.

"Are you sure that you two are through for good this time?"

"Mom, I haven't talked to him in over a month. Of course we're through. Ever since ..." she abruptly paused with a wave of her hand and turned her back. "Oh, never mind."

"What is it?" Talia walked inside of the room and closed the door behind her.

"It's nothing. He's just not my type." She shrugged, facing her mother again. "We barely have anything in common."

"Now you know that's not true," Talia objected.

"No, it's true," Melissa insisted.

Quentin and Melissa met during the first day of a summer enrichment program they both had attended a year and a half ago. The two were practically inseparable over the past year before Quentin graduated from his private school and went off to college.

"He was your type a few months ago," Talia reminded her. "What happened?"

"Mom, let's just leave it alone."

"All right, all right. I just thought that a respectable young man like Quentin would really complement you ... being that he's a Harvard student and all."

Melissa fidgeted with the earrings from her jewelry box. "Maybe I'm not sophisticated enough," she scoffed.

"But he's only a year older than you." Talia struggled to gain eye contact with her daughter. "Where is all of this coming from?"

Melissa gave her mother a telling look. "Uh hello, sometimes people change after going away to college. Besides, like I said he's just not my type anymore."

"Not your type anymore? Well, what exactly is your type?" Talia probed.

"Mom, can we not talk about this?" Melissa rolled her eyes as she swiped her hair to one side and clasped on one of her earrings.

"Okay ..." Talia conceded. "Just remember that I'm here if you want to talk."

Melissa closed the jewelry box and smirked. "Okay, I'll remember that."

Talia answered her with a playful roll of the eyes.

Melissa watched as her mother's long legs started towards the door. Just as Talia took her second step, she almost fell when her feet cradled the stranded tube of mascara on the floor. Talia reached back and grabbed hold of the computer desk to break her fall.

"Oh Mom, are you okay?" Melissa rushed to her side. She looked down and watched the rolling tube hit a nearby baseboard. "I'm so sorry. I dropped that earlier and forgot to pick it up. Are you okay?"

"I'm fine." Talia regained her balance as she pulled her hand away from the desk. Melissa's pink sticky note had inadvertently attached itself to her hand. Melissa saw the note and snatched it away.

"What's that?" Talia asked as she readjusted her shoe.

"It's nothing." Melissa crumbled the pink slip of paper with Phillip's name on it and tossed it in the waste basket beside her desk. "Are you sure you're okay?" She picked up the tube of mascara and tossed it back onto the desk.

"Yes really, I'm fine." Talia tested her weight on her ankle for confirmation. She then straightened the locket dangling from her necklace and opened the door. "Just try to be downstairs soon."

After Talia closed the door, the sound of her clicking heels soon tapered away.

Melissa walked back to her desk and stared at the crumpled note in the trash. If only she could invite Phillip over the way she could Quentin. She vacantly stared at the newspaper article again and thought to herself, *maybe one day I will*. With a smile on her face, she slid the newspaper inside of her desk drawer.

After reapplying a thin coat of shimmering lip gloss that complimented her complexion perfectly, Melissa gave her belted sequin-lined dress a once over in the body length mirror. Satisfied with her appearance, she slipped on her matching heels and headed downstairs to the parlor floor.

"Where's Dad?" Melissa questioned as she neared the dining area where elegant art pieces were strategically placed about the room.

"He's still upstairs getting dressed and doesn't suspect a thing that the party is for him." Talia raised the beige tablecloth draped across the marvelously carved console table centered on a side wall of the room. "Our gifts are right here already wrapped," she proudly announced.

Melissa returned her smile just as the doorbell rang.

"Oh, that must be our first guest now." Talia smoothed the front of her red ribbon shoulder style cocktail dress against her body. She slowly exhaled, hoping that this evening would bring her even closer to her husband. Talia was determined to resume what she and Franklin had planned from last Saturday night. After purchasing a new negligee in his favorite color, she was sure that things would improve in her marriage. She turned around to a nearby mirror and needlessly repositioned the large spiral curls of her hair that was styled at the beauty salon earlier that morning.

"Douglas, will you get that?" Talia called out to him as she meticulously straightened the tablecloth she had recently disturbed.

Douglas abandoned the cream-colored ceramic dessert plates on the kitchen island where there were several foil-lined containers and walked towards the entry door. After opening the door, he announced two of Franklin's longtime friends, Janice and Curtis Banks. The couple entered with Janice holding a square, blue envelope in her hand.

Talia smiled as she opened her arms to welcome them into her home. "It is so good to see you both." Her eyes drifted to the envelope dangling from Janice's fingers. "Oh, I thought I told you that you didn't have to bring anything. Your presence is enough. Besides, on such short notice I didn't expect anyone to bring anything aside from an appetite." She waved a hand in their direction and chuckled along with her laughing guests.

"Well, come on in. Right this way." Talia showed them to the dining area, and then excused herself to the kitchen.

When Talia checked with Douglas the time needed to finish skewering the thinly sliced chicken hors d'oeuvres, she noticed a slip of paper near the base of the double door stainless-steel refrigerator. After reading the note her eyes seemed to balloon to twice their size. She didn't even hear Douglas when he explained that the chicken hors d'oeuvres had already been skewered. He just needed to know when she wanted them served.

Absolutely distracted from everything around her, Talia's faraway gaze on the note held her undivided attention. She simply could not believe that Donovan was going to be in her home. The home she shared with her husband and daughter. Talia placed a hand over her abdomen, and then nervously exhaled. Douglas, who stood at the counter dutifully shining the dessert plates, looked away from his chore and to her in concern.

"Is everything all right?" he cautiously asked.

Talia's eyelashes fluttered as her concentration broke. And as if to be sure that she had read it correctly, she glanced down at the note again before acknowledging Douglas. "Uh yes, I'm fine." She gently waved the piece of paper in her hand, staring at it yet again as if in disbelief. "Did you take this message?"

"Let me see." Douglas reached for the piece of paper in Talia's hand and studied its contents. "Oh no, I found this note on the counter when I brought the food in about an hour ago. It must've fallen off the counter when I began prepping everything." He then met Talia's gaze. "Is there something wrong? We have plenty of food. There's enough to accommodate at least five unaccounted-for guests. When the restaurant found out that the meal was for Mr. Peterson's birthday, they increased the portion sizes." Douglas approvingly chuckled. "It's made my job a whole lot easier."

Talia couldn't even muster up a fake smile. "Oh, that's great ... and th-thank you for ensuring that we have enough food," she nervously stammered, and then cleared her throat. "Excuse me, Douglas. I'm going to see if I can delay Franklin from coming down before all of the guests arrive." She quietly sighed. "Please make sure everyone gathers in the drawing room and have plenty of drinks and hors d'oeuvres."

"Yes ma'am." Douglas nodded as Talia left the room.

Before she passed through the dining room on her way upstairs, the doorbell rang again. Talia paused at the bottom of the staircase, anxiously waiting to see who had arrived. Melissa opened the front door to find another one of Franklin's friends on the other side. Talia slowly exhaled as she smiled in their direction. She greeted the man with a warm hug and told Melissa to show him to the living room where the other guests were gathered.

"And please tell everyone that Franklin will be down in fifteen minutes. I want them all to shout surprise when he enters."

"Are you sure everyone will be here by then?" Melissa skeptically asked.

Talia apprehensively glanced at the wall clock. "Well, they should be. It's seven-twenty now and the party is set to begin at seven-thirty. So, that'll give anyone else another five minutes to get here." Talia leaned to one side as she looked out of the front room windows. "There are two cabs outside now." She then looked back to her daughter. "Fifteen minutes. If anyone shows up afterwards it'll be fine. I don't know if I can keep your father in our room much longer than that."

Melissa's eyes gazed past her mother's to the top of the staircase. "Well, I'd be surprised if you can keep him another fifteen seconds from coming down those stairs," she whispered, discreetly pointing.

Talia peered back and saw Franklin starting down the stairs. She quietly gasped and rushed up to meet him as Melissa started in the opposite direction. "Honey, uh, you're wearing that tie?" Talia questioned, momentarily glancing behind her.

Franklin clutched the silk tie with his right hand and frowned. "Why? Don't you like it?"

Talia intertwined her arm with his and led him back up the stairs. "Of course I like, I bought it. I just thought the one with splashes of red would go better." Talia subtly stroked the side of his face as she said, "Especially since it would match perfectly with this dress I'm wearing."

Franklin grinned as his eyes scaled the curves of his wife's body. "By the way, you look absolutely gorgeous." He gently kissed her on the lips.

Talia almost lost herself, but then she heard murmurings from the guests entering through the front door. "Well, we better get that tie changed." She quickly took Franklin by the hand and pulled him inside of their bedroom on the second floor.

"Does it look that bad?" Franklin smirked.

Talia chuckled as she closed the door behind them. "No, of course not. I told you that I like that tie, I just think the other one would look better. Besides, Melissa picked it out for you months ago and if you don't wear it soon, she may think that you don't like it," she cleverly improvised.

Franklin carelessly shrugged as he untied the knot from the necktie. Talia looked on as he strolled into their walk-in closet. She sat on the edge of their king-sized bed and crossed her legs. Her eyes drifted to the photograph Franklin had placed on a corner of the nightstand near his side of the bed. It was an older picture of her and Franklin in their early years together. The snapshot served as a constant reminder to Talia of the poverty they once knew. She glared at the simple rags she wore, and her disgust grew even more as she stared at the front steps of the raggedy place they once called home. The luxurious abode she now resided in coupled with her fashionable wardrobe all made her modest beginnings with Franklin a distant memory.

Talia's past and present were like night and day, as they were so incredibly different. She had wanted to remove the picture on many occasions, but Franklin wouldn't hear of it. He said that it served as motivation for him to continue working harder so that they wouldn't have to see poverty-stricken days like that again. Moreover, he often reasoned that it was a continual inspiration in which to praise God for how He'd provided over the years.

"How do I look now?" Franklin asked as he emerged from the closet. He looked down and smoothed the tie between two of his fingers.

Talia nodded approvingly. "Perfect." She then glanced at the clock and noticed that only five minutes had passed. She still needed to keep him in the room for at least another ten minutes.

"Do you think Melissa will notice?" Franklin asked as he walked to where Talia was seated.

"I think she will," she answered, gently caressing the tie.

Franklin tilted his wife's chin with a slight nudge of his finger. "Is everything all right?"

Talia peered up into his waiting eyes and patted the empty space next to her on the bed. Franklin slowly sat down beside her. At first no words were spoken, only subtle glances were exchanged. Franklin then placed his hand on Talia's knee and delivered a gentle squeeze. She placed her hand on top of his and returned the gesture.

"So, what's bothering you, sweetheart?"

Talia gently sighed, unsure if this was the right time to tell Franklin about Donovan. It just seemed daring, foolish even that he would even be allowed to step foot across the threshold of their home. In a flurry of guilt Talia's eyes slid away from Franklin's, hoping that he'd understand that she had no idea that Marissa was going to bring the man she had cheated with as a guest. But even more, Talia feared that Franklin would be upset since she hadn't said anything about Donovan even after seeing him at church yesterday.

"Do you want to talk about it?" Franklin attentively caressed his wife's knee.

Talia forced a convincing smile as she adamantly shook her head. "It's nothing." Talk about it? How could she talk about a man that had all but seduced her last Saturday afternoon? This was a man who had once left her breathless to flirt with the shameful memories they shared.

Troubled by her past, Talia abruptly broke from Franklin's hypnotic gaze and glanced at the clock. "We better get to our guests." She patted his hand that was still perched upon her knee. As he squeezed her knee before removing his fingers, Talia had to admit that her husband's display of affection wooed her.

"This must be some dinner meeting you're having this evening." Franklin gently ran the backside of his forefinger up and down her arm. "This is a new dress." Holding a lock of her curled hair, he inhaled the sweet fragrance. "And your usual day at the hairdresser is Friday."

Talia parted her lips slightly, amazed that he noticed such detail about her life. They hardly spoke about her daily activities aside from charity work, but he was obviously aware of more than she had given him credit for.

"I know that I've been working a little more than usual over the past few months, but I promise things won't get like they did last time."

Talia looked away, uncomfortable again from the shameful reminders of her affair. Despite Franklin's preoccupation with work that led to his temporary impotence and her straying heart, she was still the one who had broken the sacred covenant they had vowed to one another.

Franklin nudged her chin back in his direction and stared into her eyes. "But I'm glad you told me what was going on. You could have kept it to yourself and I would've never known, so that tells me how much you really wanted things to work."

Talia nervously twiddled her thumbs.

"It was the main reason why I had to forgive you." He gently grasped her fingers. "But trust me, soon things will be back to normal." He winked as he said, "*Better than normal.*"

Desperately trying to decipher his hidden code, Talia searched his eyes for clues. Franklin rarely showed his affections, which one reason why his intimate suggestion on Saturday evening and the way he just smelled her hair and touched her knee caught her by complete surprise. And now to watch his mustache twitch from side to side in failed attempts to conceal an emergent smile, she wondered what he meant by *better than normal*.

"I have something important to tell you."

With widened eyes, Talia curiously questioned, "What is it?"

"Well," Franklin began in a jovial tone, almost as if he was throwing a surprise party for her right there at that very moment, "I'm thinking about selling the business."

Talia's eyebrows took a nosedive as her lips unconsciously parted. She glanced away, shaking her head in miniature rotations back and forth as if to completely digest what Franklin had just said to her. After releasing a telling grunt, she faced him again and in a demoralizing tone replied, "*You're thinking of doing what?*"

Franklin returned an expression that would've been followed by some colorful language a few years ago if he hadn't been saved by Jesus Christ. "Well, with Melissa not really showing an interest in taking over—"

"Wait, don't you think we should talk this over before you make a final decision?" Talia's patronizing tone further emphasized her dramatic mood change. "Are we okay with money? What would you do for income?" She firmly folded her arms across her chest.

"I thought this was what you wanted."

"No, I never said that I wanted you to quit working," Talia huffed. "I don't want to go back to the way we were living before, Franklin," she stubbornly protested.

"Listen, nothing is final yet, but money won't be an issue," he assured her. "The deal that I'm looking at includes more than fifty million dollars. Our home is paid for and we have plenty of reserves in the bank, not to mention our overseas accounts." Franklin gently clutched Talia's shoulders. "We are financially set. I just didn't want my long work hours to interfere with our marriage again."

Just then there was a knock on their bedroom door. Melissa slowly opened the door before her presence was acknowledged. "Excuse me, but I think all of the guests are here, Mom."

"Oh my goodness," Talia gasped as she noticed that twenty minutes had passed since she had left Melissa downstairs. "We'll be right down."

"Okay, and Dad you look sharp. I really like your cravat." Melissa smirked as she left the room.

Momentarily removed from their heated discussion, Franklin proudly touched his necktie. "You were right, she noticed." He casually chuckled. "She's trying hard to get that spring break trip to Paris." Franklin smiled, but Talia's face was still bent.

"We can finish this conversation later." Talia furiously edged past him towards the door.

Franklin stood with a hand parked at his waist while the other one partially covering his mouth and nose. Talia stood at the threshold and glared back at him. "Are you coming?"

Franklin shook his head as he began untying the knot from his necktie. "No, you go on. It's your dinner party anyway."

Talia pulled in a deep breath and cleared the angry expression from her face. "Look, I'm sorry. I shouldn't have blown up like that." She walked over to where her husband stood with the tie now clutched in the palm of his hand. "It's just that you've worked so hard and we've sacrificed so much to get to where we are." She sighed. "I just don't want you to give away a business that's been so successful for us."

Franklin shook his head again as he pensively folded in his lips. "Talia, did you not hear what I just said? I'm being offered millions of dollars," he said through clenched teeth. "I can still work as a consultant. Besides, don't you know that God is our Provider anyway? Something could happen tomorrow and wipe out all that we have—"

"Don't say that," Talia shushed him.

Franklin paced in the opposite direction.

"Is that what you want? To start over?"

"Listen, of course I don't want that to happen, but we've got to keep things in perspective. Think about what happened to Job in the Bible. With all that he lost, God restored." Franklin grunted. "I'm not about to put my trust in any amount of money."

"It's not just any amount. We are talking about *millions*, Franklin, like you just said. And besides that, you clear about seven or eight million every year," she grumbled. "Sometimes even more. How are you going to give that up for a one-time payment?"

Franklin just stared at Talia. His face was void of emotion as he sat back down on the bed. Talia looked on as Franklin threaded the tie through his fingers back and forth.

"Well, say something," she urged him.

Franklin looked up to her and calmly said for clarity, "The offer amount is for over fifty million dollars *plus* a generous consulting salary that's guaranteed for at least the next five years." In disappointment, he sighed. "I thought you wanted me around more. Is it me or the money, Talia?" he boldly confronted her.

Those words challenged Talia. She blinked back the effects of his insulting words, trying to keep her make-up flawless. It hurt that two totally different men in her life had mentioned her hunger for money in less than seventy-two hours.

"I hope there's no one else," Franklin said with a callous stare.

"*What?*" she gasped. "Why would you say a thing like that?"

Suddenly, there was another knock at the door. Talia dabbed the corners of her eyes with the tips of her fingers and walked towards the door. Before she responded to the second set of knocks, Talia looked back to him with her hand resting on the knob. "I didn't want to tell you, but there's a party going on downstairs in your honor."

As a wave of confusion floated across his face, Franklin stood from the edge of the bed. "What do you mean *in my honor*?"

"I arranged a surprise birthday party for you."

Franklin dragged his hand down across his mouth.

"But I'll just tell them that you're not feeling up to it." Talia opened the door where Melissa stood on the other side.

"What's taking so long?" Melissa whispered.

"Your father isn't feeling up for company tonight." Talia glanced at Franklin and then looked back to Melissa. "Besides, he knows that the party is for him."

"Ugh, you know *and* you're not coming?" Melissa stared at her father. "I just spent the last fifteen minutes explaining to people as they arrived what to say when you enter the room and you're really not coming," she dramatically ranted.

Franklin raised a hand to quiet his rambling daughter. "I'm coming, I'm coming."

"Well, come on then. And don't forget to act surprise," Melissa said as she pulled her father by the hand.

Talia watched as they walked ahead of her. She peered back once more across the lavishly decorated master suite before turning the dimmer lights out. Seconds later, she followed her husband and daughter downstairs.

"Happy forty-eighth! This year is going to be great!" the crowd bel-
lowed in perfect unison.

Franklin chuckled as he looked on at his friends laughing and clapping. "Oh my goodness, thank you everyone!" His deep voice carried
across the room. Franklin stared down at Melissa, who measured just
a few inches shorter than him, and hugged her around the shoulders.
"You did well. That was a great introduction, sweetheart," he whispered,
tenderly kissing her on the forehead without even a glance at Talia.
"Anybody hungry? Who wants to pray?" He looked up to his friends
again from where a gamut of responses emanated. Everyone confessed to
being hungry and some admitted they had no idea that he was forty-eight
years old while others urged him to pray over the food. "Okay, okay,"
Franklin said, chuckling amidst the rumbling voices. "I'll pray."

As Franklin lowered his head, Talia held her chest as a radiating pain
pierced her heart. She had worked tirelessly over the past twenty-four
hours to make this evening one that he'd remember for years to come,
and he did not even acknowledge that she was in the room. Silently
recovering from the deeply penetrating words her husband had candidly
spoken only moments before, Talia exhaled a rehabilitating breath. She
needed to play the part of a happy wife, even though she felt anything
but that.

When Franklin finished praying, Talia raised her head only to meet
eyes with Donovan. He cautiously smiled in her direction while his arms
rested comfortably around Marissa's waist. Talia looked away only to
answer a question that Douglas had posed about serving dinner.

"Have everyone gather in the formal dining room," she quietly instructed him with a hand resting across the front of her neck. "Be sure
to start the music ... playlist number eleven." She swallowed the uncomfortable lump in her throat.

Douglas nodded and then began ushering people from the drawing room into the formal dining room. Franklin glanced back at his
wife as she quickly escaped to the nearest powder room. His attention

shifted away from her only when a colleague hugged him and offered their personal congratulatory remarks. Other friends soon followed with comments of their own as they all retired to the dining room.

Talia snatched several pieces of tissue from a box holder as she sniffled helplessly. She had lost the fighting battle that waged between her tears and the will to remain unemotional. It appeared as if every attempt she made to get closer to her husband, the farther apart they became. Talia couldn't understand why it was so difficult for Franklin to understand that she wanted only the best for their family, the best of everything. It was beyond her why he translated her desire to live in the lap of luxury as more of a love for money than him. As she stared into the mirror, Talia reluctantly admitted that maybe there was some truth to what he had said.

"Yes, who is it?" Talia answered to the knock at the bathroom door.

"It's me, Mom. Are you all right?" Melissa questioned.

Talia looked away from the door and peered in the mirror as she responded, "Yes ... I'm fine." She then pumped soap from the dispenser. Talia turned the faucet on and began rubbing her hands together under the warm stream of water.

"Are you sure?" Melissa prodded.

"Yes, I'm sure," Talia sighed as she bypassed the hanging embroidered towels and dried her hands with subtle pats from a soft cloth she kept in the second drawer. "I just need to rinse something out of my eyes." Talia retrieved a small vial of eye drops from the oval mirror medicine cabinet to avoid a flood of inquiries surrounding her reddening eyes. "I'll be out in a minute."

"Okay," Melissa answered.

Talia listened as her daughter's footsteps tapered away. She then made good on her words and tried to flush the reddening color away with several cleansing eye drops. After gently patting the corners of her eyes with a piece of tissue followed by a few quick fans of her hand in front of her face, Talia slowly exhaled. She stared into the mirror again, noticing that the pinkish color on the whites of her eyes was fading away.

With a somewhat renewed confidence, Talia smoothed her hands across the sides of her waist. There was a room full of people she had invited and as much as she'd rather hide out for the remainder of the evening, she knew that was not an option. Despite the way Franklin unloaded on her, Talia was resolved to enjoy the party she had worked tirelessly to plan. Besides, if Donovan recognized the slightest hint of tension between her and Franklin, he was sure to rub it in her face.

"Yes," Talia answered to another knock at the door, "I'm coming now, Melissa." She folded the tissue she held in her hand into a waded ball and tossed it into the floral designed porcelain waste basket. Just as she swung the door open and raised her eyes from the floor, Talia flinched at the sight of Donovan.

"Well hello, Tee." His eyes roamed her body just as Franklin's had only moments prior. "I thought this was supposed to be a party. Why are you hiding out in the bathroom of all places?"

Talia peered behind him, noticing that the living room was clear as everyone had retired to the dining area. She then glared at Donovan while pointing a finger in his face. "What do you think you're trying to prove?" Still shaken from her argument with Franklin, Talia snapped at Donovan. "You show up here with Marissa after coming on to me just minutes before meeting her. And then you had the gall to come to our church?" she whispered in an angry voice.

Donovan smugly grinned. "Are you jealous?" He then delicately held a lock of her long, curled hair in his hand.

She slapped his hand away from her. Talia's nostrils flared as her lips gathered to make up a scrunched quarter-sized circle. With an angry squint, she grabbed him by the paisley print tie around his neck and jerked him closer. "This is my home. How dare you disrespect me and my husband like this? And to toy with my friend Marissa is just low."

Donovan grabbed Talia's wrist and yanked it away from him. "If she was such a friend, then why haven't you told her about us?"

"*There is no us*," Talia growled as she attempted to walk past him.

Donovan pulled her back by the arm. "Are you sure about that? What about those tears in your eyes?" Donovan flattered himself to think Talia's weeping was because of him. "I can tell that you've been crying."

Talia grimaced as she abruptly slapped Donovan across the cheek with her free hand. She quickly snatched her other arm away. "Just leave me alone," she snarled. "I don't want to *ever* see you here again." Without even a glance back at him, Talia marched away from him and into the dining room.

Donovan massaged the side of his face as she walked away. In all of the recent years of knowing Talia, she had never been able to truly resist him. He momentarily stood at the threshold of the bathroom door and shook his head before following in the same direction.

After Donovan rejoined the party, he and Talia both kept their distance from one another as he watched the fierce body language between her and Franklin. When Marissa gently caressed the cheek unbeknownst to her that had been struck in the hallway, Donovan guiltily returned her smile. Thirty minutes later, he suggested that they leave so he could get some rest for work the next morning.

"So, did you enjoy dinner with my friends?" Marissa asked Donovan on the drive back to her house.

Donovan barely glanced in her direction as he answered, "Uh ... it was nice."

Marissa was hopeful that they would enjoy more dinner meetings with friends. She was beginning to envision him as a permanent fixture in her life. It had been a long time since she had connected so well with someone. Men had come and gone in her life that simply left her hopelessly disappointed. There were men that sometimes behaved as immature boys while others were senselessly indecisive about whether or not they wanted to be in a serious relationship. Marissa had no time to waste on either as she desired someone who wanted to be with her as much as she did him.

As she gazed at Donovan under shades of the filtered city night lights, Marissa was convinced that he was different from the rest and that the best was yet to come.

# CHAPTER 17

THE ELEGANTLY DECORATED room was absolutely breathtaking. Leslie's eyes drifted from the handcrafted armoire to the soft pattern of the bonded leather chaise lounge. She could only dream of spending a night in one of the suites exclusively reserved for elite and wealthy guests. Despite her present circumstance, Leslie envisioned that one day she wouldn't be cleaning a room like this, but she would indeed be a guest herself.

The white and grey housekeeping uniform wrinkled at the waist as she stooped to retrieve a wadded piece of paper from the floor. Leslie quickly tossed the paper in the trash but was slow to stand again. Since being hired she had worked tirelessly for the past few days, desperate to pay back the money she borrowed. Her soft sole shoes were deeply creased on the top due to her wearing them everywhere for the past few days. She was determined to make things happen for herself and return all that she owed.

Leslie dutifully moved the feather duster over the furniture as she reminded herself to pick up her roommate's dry cleaning and favorite snacks from the grocery store. It was the least she could do since her friend had covered rent for the next month. Money was tight even before she was fired from her diner job, but Leslie was convinced that her financial slump wouldn't last long. She figured things were sure to turn around for her. In just a few weeks, she would have enough to catch up on her financial obligations and maybe even save a little for a rainy day.

With two more rooms to clean, Leslie tossed the feather duster aside and fiercely tugged at the stubborn extra-large pillow stuffed inside of a white standard-size case. As she yanked for the fourth time, the sudden release of the pillow sent her stumbling a few feet backwards to the floor. Leslie's shoulders lowered as she tiredly blew the misplaced strands of hair from her slightly dampened face.

"Is everything all right?" Selah entered the room with a clipboard in her hand and a smile on her face. Her bright eyes and rosy cheeks seemed to always carry a pleasant disposition. "You look like you could use some help." She raised an eyebrow in a questionable, yet amusing way.

Frazzled, Leslie shyly smiled at the woman who successfully oriented her on the ins and outs of the housekeeping job in just a matter of days. Selah nodded knowingly, remembering what it was like during her first week at the hotel. She always kept a cool head even in the midst of training others that would ordinarily send another manager into a tizzy. Although employees would periodically quit during busy months, Selah handled the pressure to keep a full staff with ease. Many often complimented her, saying that she was practically created to operate in such a position.

"Looks like you're having a little trouble here." Selah raised the white clipboard she carried from one side of her full hips and secured it underneath one of her arms. She then offered Leslie a hand.

"Uh, just a little." Leslie grinned as Selah helped to pull her from the floor. "Those pillowcases are practically painted on." She softly chuckled and straightened her clothes once she was on her feet.

Selah looked away from Leslie and carefully examined the pillow tags against the pillowcases. She then scribbled a few notes down on a piece of paper attached to the clipboard.

Leslie hesitantly looked on with folded arms. "Did I do something wrong?" she nervously asked.

With an ink pen positioned between her fingers, Selah waved her hand and responded, "Oh no, it's not your fault. These cases were just supposed to be temporaries." She split her attention between Leslie and the notes she had jotted down. "We had a little accident with a couple of our washers early last week and tons of pillowcases were ruined. The order for replacements has come in, but since this room has been vacant for the past couple of days the cases haven't been changed. Not to mention that the cleaning wasn't up to par." Selah then crossed her wrists in front of her body as she gave Leslie her undivided attention. "It was a big mess and I had to let someone go. But I digress ...," she sighed, "just put all of these cases in a special stack for emergencies only."

"Okay," Leslie replied. "Anything else?" Her voice was still a little uneasy.

"Just finish up in here and I'll go get you the right cases from the laundry room. I think this floor was the only one affected, so make sure to double-check the other vacant rooms." Selah turned to walk away, but quickly looked back and added, "I hate to throw this at you, but one of my supervisors was off this week, so I'm a little slow in getting some things finished that should have already been done. I will also need you to make sure there are extra toiletry items in the Paradise Suites. The last customer complained on a survey that they had to call down for extras."

"I'll take care of it." Leslie nodded. "I'll be sure to check those rooms."

The Paradise Suites were a step down from the Executive Suites. They had more of a honeymoon feel than the current chamber they stood inside of, but still ritzy nonetheless.

"Thank you." Selah walked away, flipping through the pages of her clipboard.

Leslie turned around and quickly vacuumed the carpet. She wasted no
time as she started for the bathroom. She double-checked the counter for
the complimentary items Selah had just spoken of and verified that each
toiletry vial was full. She made sure to place extras beneath the sink in a
beautiful linen-lined basket.

After buffing the sink to a reflective shine, Leslie scornfully scrubbed
the toilet. She hated this part of the job but was convinced that she
wouldn't have to endure for too long.

When Selah returned with the pillowcases, Leslie was putting the
finishing touches on the mirrors.

"This looks very good." Selah's voice carried a tune of satisfaction. Her
thick, red ponytail swung from side to side as she gazed around the room.
"You work fast. I like that in an employee." She smiled as she looked back
at Leslie.

Leslie peered at her boss in the crystal-clear mirror reflection and said,
"Thank you."

Selah proudly raised her hand, clutching a clear bag. "I'll just put this
on your cart."

Leslie nodded and pulled the rubber gloves off her hands. She then
slipped the cases on with ease and pushed her cart up the hallway, checking each room on her stretch along the way. Just as she entered her last
cleaning assignment for the day, the cell phone in the front pocket of her
apron vibrated.

"Hello?" Leslie quickly slipped inside of a vacant room, noting the
unfamiliar number on her Caller ID.

"Leslie Brunson?" the high-pitched voice asked.

With uncertainty in her tone, Leslie replied, "Yes, who is this?"

"This is July ... from the new film you auditioned for last week."

Leslie's voice softened. "Oh yes, July. How can I help you?"

July explained the details of the film's shooting schedule, informing
her of the meeting time for the next day. Leslie scribbled down the
location and time.

"What is your email address? I can just forward the call sheet to you."

Embarrassed that her internet service was off, Leslie asked, "Um, can you fax it?"

July quietly cleared her throat. "What's the number?" she asked with a sigh.

Leslie pulled a complimentary hotel notepad from her pocket and read the fax number off to her. "Are you going to send it now?" she questioned.

"I just did."

"Oh, okay." Leslie glanced at her watch. "If it doesn't come through, I have another number you can send it to."

"If it doesn't transmit, a notation on my computer will let me know. Either way, I can still give you a hard copy tomorrow. So, we'll see you then."

"Oh, before you go, do I need to—"

"Ms. Brunson," July interrupted, "all of your other questions will be answered before shooting. So—"

"Um, is there a chance that I could speak with the director?" Leslie impatiently inquired.

"Yes, tomorrow. He'll be there along with the AD and producer," July informed her before abruptly saying, "Good-bye."

Leslie stared at the dead phone and grimaced. "*She acts more like his bodyguard than casting agent,*" she muttered to herself as she shoved the cell phone back into her pocket. It didn't matter that she hadn't heard from Wendell since she left her number in his car, she would see him face to face tomorrow.

With a hopeful gaze, Leslie rushed downstairs to retrieve July's fax.

# CHAPTER 18

KARA SHOOK HER head as she walked out of the bathroom. She had hoped that the rumors circulating around the projects for the past few days weren't true, but the suspicions about Miriam had been confirmed. The truth rattled Kara as she approached the kitchen. She avoided eye contact with her sister and reached for a bottle of vitamins from a side drawer beside the stove. Miriam peered at her through angry eyes as Kara chased the pill with a small cup of water.

"You need to wash that cup out and put it back in the cupboard where you got it from," Miriam scolded.

Kara sighed to herself before she replied, "Can I finish using it first?" She cut her eyes away from Miriam as she took another gulp. Kara then poured the remaining liquid down the sink and scrubbed the cup with liquid soap long enough to silence Miriam's tyrannical rant. She wiped the excess water away and quickly returned the plastic cup to the second shelf over the kitchen counter.

"And where do you think you're going?" Miriam interrogated with folded arms as she stared Kara up and down. "You know that trash needs to be taken out." She cocked her head to the side, further emphasizing her nasty mood.

"If you had checked the garbage can before coming at me like that you would have noticed that it had been taken out fifteen minutes ago," Kara snapped, and then rolled her eyes away.

Miriam grimaced as Kara pulled a coat from the front closet. "You think you're something don't you?" she bitterly growled.

Kara shook her head as she turned around with the coat draped across her arm. "And just what are you talking about?"

Miriam adjusted the old floral print housecoat wrapped around her body and rolled her wheelchair closer to where Kara stood. "You know what I mean."

"I don't know what you're talking about." Kara grimaced as she slid inside of her coat. "Look, I have to go. I'll be back later on."

Miriam grunted as she fiddled with her everyday ponytail. "Later on, huh? Well, I know one thing, you better not bring any babies up in here. If you think I'm taking care of you *and* a baby, you have got another thing coming," she snidely remarked.

Kara scowled at the gall of her sister. "You know what, I don't have time for this. I come home every day and mind my own business around here. I stay out of trouble and on the honor roll, but it seems as if you can't be happy about anything I'm trying to do, Meme." Kara snatched her key from the kitchen table and shoved it inside of her fleece pocket. "I am getting tired of this!" Her eyes shifted away from Miriam who had a permanent glare painted on her face, but Kara turned back just seconds later to say in a slightly lowered voice, "And if I wanted to have sex, don't you think it would've happened by now? I mean really, Meme, can you at least give me some credit about that?" Kara steadied her book bag onto her shoulder. "If you cared anything about yourself, you'd stop doing what you're doing instead of assuming I'm the same way. You're so concerned about the trash in the kitchen, but what you should've been trying to get rid of is that garbage in the bathroom. You claim that wheelchair keeps you from working, but it sure doesn't keep you from doing other things." Kara grunted and slammed the door shut behind her.

Miriam sat unmoved, challenged by her sister's outburst. She had been so careful in concealing her deeds while Kara was at school. And with her disability, she figured no one would think twice about her sleeping around. The fact that her medical condition left her legs paralyzed, Miriam still maintained full function of her reproductive organs.

With a delayed reaction of panic, Miriam wheeled herself to the bathroom just a few feet away and stared into the waste basket beside the toilet. There she saw the gold condom wrapper torn on the side that was left by the man who had spent a few hours with her in the middle of the night.

As she thought back to how Kara had shamed her, Miriam's eyes angrily narrowed. *She must really think she's better than me now. Humph, I can do what I want to do with my body, I'm grown.* The mere thought of how well her sister had it together infuriated Miriam even more. She hated the physical condition she was forced to live with and the guy she was left to live without.

The boyfriend Miriam had left soon after her accident along with all of the money she once made. *It's all her fault why I have to do this anyway,* Miriam blamed. *I could have been living in a three-story mansion with Gary if none of this had happened instead of struggling to pay overdue credit card bills,* she supposed. *If I can't have what I want out of life, then neither can she ... I'll make sure of that.*

Kara held a hand up to Melissa as she walked into the sandwich shop known for its fresh-squeezed lemonade and tomato and cheese blended soup.

"Girl, what's up with the sour face?" Melissa asked Kara as she sat down at a table across from her. "Did Wendell say something to upset you?"

Kara waved her hand to the contrary and then sipped from her insulated paper cup. "No, it's not Wendell. We actually just had a nice lunch together." She momentarily smiled, but it soon faded. "It's Miriam."

"What about her?" Melissa asked as she pulled her coat off at the sleeves and hung it across the back of the wooden chair.

"I don't want to talk about it right now." The distant look on her face coupled with the annoyance in her voice made for a convincing argument. "It's not important anyway."

"Okay." Melissa knew her friend well enough to drop the issue. She then dragged the rectangular menu towards her from the middle of the table. "Do you know what's good here besides the soup? I feel like trying something different for a change."

"Well, Wendell and I had the turkey and cheese with lettuce and tomato on a croissant." At the sound of his name Kara's withdrawn glare turned to a faraway gaze. "It was so nice being close to one another." She rested her chin upon her clasped fingers.

"Are we still talking about the sandwich?" Melissa grinned as she closed the menu.

Kara snatched the paper menu from Melissa's hands and hit her on the head with it. "You know that I'm talking about Wendell." She helplessly giggled and tossed the menu aside. "He's the one, Melissa. I just know it."

"The one, huh? Well, uh, did *the one* say that it was all right for me to sit in during shooting?"

Kara nodded as she took another sip of her cocoa. "I told you that he wouldn't mind. It's cool, trust me."

"But did you *ask* him?" Melissa widened her eyes.

"*Yes*, I asked him. And he said that it was all right."

"Well, you know, I just didn't want him looking at me all crazy when we walked in." Melissa grinned. "Anyway, how long have you been here?"

Kara flipped a few pages of her math book and shrugged. "Mm, I don't know, maybe forty, forty-five minutes. After my meeting with Mrs. Chow, I went home for a minute before meeting Wendell here."

"Oh yeah, I thought he was supposed to pick you up from school and take you by her office."

"He was, but something about his film came up, so I went alone," Kara explained. "She was so cool and down-to-earth, Mel."

"That's great. It sure would've been nice if she worked in the drama department," Melissa said, wanting her application to stand-out among the countless others in her intended major too. "So, where's Wendell now? You said he met you here?"

"Oh, he left about fifteen minutes ago." She pointed through the window that had red, white, and blue squiggly writing on the glass. "He said that we can just meet him at the soundstage a few blocks over." Kara glanced at the clock on the wall. "Oh, they should be starting soon. We better get going. You're just going to have to eat over there. You don't mind, do you?"

"Girl no, that's fine. The opportunity to see a film produced first-hand from the start just doesn't come along every day." She pulled a bill from her pocket and handed it to Kara. "Will you order that sandwich for me while I call Douglas? If I don't check back with him soon, he'll tell Mom and she'll have the police scouring the city for me." Melissa giggled. "I don't know what she's going to do when I graduate." She shook her head and pulled out her cell phone. "I'll be glad when I turn eighteen and the restrictions on my driver's license expire." Then an inquisitive look floated across her face. "I bet the country don't have all of these hoops to jump through as the city does, right?"

"Not like here." Kara half smiled as she stood and walked toward the counter.

Melissa's relationship with her mother reminded Kara of how protective her own mother had been. The country may have fewer restrictions than the city, but none of the benefits offered could ever compare to what she really valued. Kara wondered if her mother would have outgrown her protectiveness over the years. From what Frieda told her, Gwendolyn was guarded because of Kara's ethnic background. Although Kara didn't remember, Frieda had explained to her that Gwendolyn had always remembered the biracial insults and dirty looks from white patrons when their family would go out to dinner. It didn't matter that the 1950s and 60s were long gone, their family was reminded of the lingering racism often enough.

"Would you like a drink to go with your sandwich?" The cashier looked up to Kara after keying in Melissa's order.

Kara looked back at Melissa who was just pulling her cell from her ear. "Did you want a drink?" she asked her.

"No, I have a bottle of water with me," Melissa answered as she slid back inside of her coat.

Kara shook her head at the cashier as she handed over the hundred-dollar bill.

"Do you have anything smaller?" the woman asked as she held the money in her hand.

"Uh," Kara started as she looked back to Melissa.

The manager quickly tapped his employee on the shoulder and whispered, "Its fine, we'll make another a drop in the safe. I have enough smaller bills in the other register to make change."

"Okay," the cashier responded, adhering to her supervisor's approval to keep a large bill in the register just before the evening rush. She looked back to Kara and handed over the change and a receipt. "Your food will be up in a few minutes."

"Thanks," Kara said as she moved aside for the next person in line to place their order.

Melissa had already begun packing up Kara's book bag. Kara slowly approached as her friend slid her math book and corresponding notebooks inside of her orange backpack. She observed how Melissa took care in handling her belongings. This was different from how Miriam would push her things aside and then complain about how she couldn't pick them up from the floor due to her crippled legs. Kara thanked God for her bond with Melissa who came into her life at a time when she really needed a friend. Not just a friend, but someone as close as she'd hope her own sister would be.

"So, did you get a hold of Douglas?" Kara questioned.

Melissa nodded as she handed Kara's backpack to her. "Yes, thank God. You know my parents. They insist on having me driven around like I'm some movie star or something. I don't need that. I'm not famous..." Melissa then paused with a quirky grin on her face. "Well, not yet anyway."

"That's right, *not yet*. But you will be." Kara genuinely smiled as she tagged her friend on the shoulder. "You better speak that thing into existence." She pointed and through the movement of her fingers, a coin accidentally fell from the palm of her right hand. "Oh, I almost forgot. Here's your change." Kara reached down to pick up the dime that slipped from her hand. She then handed the ninety-two dollars and twenty-one cents to her friend.

Melissa cleared strands of hair from her face as she emphatically shook her head. "No, you keep it."

"What?" Kara's nose crinkled. "Why?"

"I can give you more if you need it," Melissa offered.

Kara gently sighed. "Melissa, you don't have to keep on giving me money or gifts. I'm okay, really." She pushed the money back to her. "Trust me, you've given me more than enough."

"But I know how things are with your sister. I just want to look out for my best friend." Melissa discreetly folded the money back into Kara's hand. "Besides, you give to me too ... just in different ways. I would've never passed that math test without your help."

Kara smiled at the generosity of her friend. "Well, after I turn eighteen, I'll be able to get the money my parents left, so—"

"*So*, until that time, just know that I've got your back. Besides, that's what friends are for, right?" Melissa winked as she walked toward the counter where the cashier held up a white paper bag. She retrieved her sandwich, and they left the busy diner.

After walking a few blocks to the where Wendell was shooting his movie, Kara and Melissa entered through a door that led down a short hallway. They reached a second set of doors that was unlocked by a security officer where Wendell met them near the entrance.

"Are you sure we won't be in the way?" Kara asked Wendell as Melissa glanced around the sound stage.

"No, you're fine. Tonight is going to be a short night anyway. Just take a seat in one of the chairs over there and observe." He gently touched her on the shoulder.

"Thanks Wendell, I really appreciate this. Maybe you can cast me in one of your movies." Melissa rotated a smile between him and Kara.

Wendell grinned before giving Kara the eye. "We'll see. If you can stop the giggles, I just might take you up on that. But time is money and on my project," he said, becoming serious as he raised an eyebrow, "I don't have any to waste."

Melissa narrowed her eyes as Wendell walked away to meet with his cast. "You know, if you didn't have this thing for him I would give him a piece of my mind," she fussed, turning to Kara who giggled uncontrollably, "and that's not funny."

"Uh, yes it is." Kara continued to laugh. "Besides, you had no business playing that British role anyway."

Melissa sat beside Kara in one of the chairs backed against the sidewall. "And I thought we were best friends."

Kara nudged her girlfriend on the arm with her elbow and smirked. "Now you know that Wendell was just kidding around."

Melissa shrugged. "Yeah, I guess so."

Kara then jokingly added, "At least I think he was."

They both muffled their laughs, careful not to disturb the actors as they prepped for their recorded scene.

Seeing Wendell in action brought on a new respect for him. Kara crossed her legs as he addressed the cast and crew. It was at that moment when she truly saw a future with him. The strong stance he took in front of others was what she desired in her own life. She wanted him to be their head of household. He embodied all of the characteristics she desired, the ones that really mattered to her: intelligent, honest, *and* saved. She had since discarded her unfounded *what-if* suspicions. In her mind, he was as authentic as they came. Wendell was the real deal and if ... *when* he decided to express how she thought he truly felt, she was there to reciprocate.

"Are there any questions?" Wendell asked the cast and crew after his introductory spiel.

Noting that he had answered all lingering questions, shooting began.

Wendell, Michael, and Wayne were all pleasantly surprised at how natural the dialogue flowed between the cast members. They prayed that the cast would sound just as good throughout the rest of filming.

In between scene takes, Leslie leaned toward the man who played opposite her lead character and asked, "Who are they?"

The man's eyes followed hers to where Kara and Melissa sat. "Beats me." He shrugged as he looked back to her and then flipped through the pages of the script.

Leslie's eyes skirted away from Kara and Melissa as the director motioned for a redo of the last take.

"Marcus, I need that with a little less anger, but still just as serious," Wendell instructed the male lead. "You're upset, but don't let that overshadow the importance of what you're saying."

As Wendell addressed Marcus, Leslie hung off of his every word. The tone of his voice effortlessly serenaded her ears. When Wendell made eye contact with her she anticipated his directions, but he simply told her to repeat what she had just done. Her confidence bolstered as Wendell saw no need to adjust her performance.

The crew then prepared for another take. Leslie turned around to stand on her mark and inadvertently met eyes with Wayne. As he smiled in her direction, she returned a wary glance. She quickly looked away and gazed at the floor. She dared to look up again, but in the opposite direction. There her eyes landed on the man who captivated her from the moment they met. She aimed to please him. And when he said, "Action," Leslie did not disappoint.

After a performance that satisfied even the critical Michael, who was a director in his own right, the crew wrapped up for the night.

"That was a good scene," Wayne said to Leslie as the other cast and crew members dismantled, each leaving the building through the side door exit. "You're a natural," he added, straightening the coat on her back.

"Oh thanks," Leslie said, her shoulders rotating away from him as he touched her.

"Judging from tonight, there's a pretty good indication that the rest of the shoots are going to be smooth sailing." Wayne nodded as his eyes roamed her body.

"Yeah, I sure hope so," she answered while her eyes hungrily searched the room for Wendell, oblivious to Wayne's predacious glares. "I'm glad there's chemistry between the cast members." She forced a smile as she looked back at him.

"Yeah, me too." Wayne took a step closer to her. "Well, you let me know if you need anything." He gently tapped her on the arm with a lingering gaze before walking away.

Leslie modestly looked away as Wayne started for the side door. She waited until he was out of view before walking in the same direction.

Her footsteps stalled as she heard faint voices emanating from around a corner. The familiar tone garnered her undivided attention. Leslie smoothed her hair over and secured her purse across her shoulders. With an air of confidence about her, Leslie sashayed toward Wendell where he stood talking to Kara and Melissa.

"Hey Wendell," she said, breaking into his conversation. She leaned in closely with a seductive smile. "Good scene, huh?"

He stared at her, almost annoyed. "Yeah ... good job."

Leslie then looked at Kara and Melissa. "You two must be the stand-ins."

Wendell crossed his arms as Kara and Melissa suspiciously stared at her.

"Uh no," Melissa answered with raised eyebrows. "Stand-in work is good, but that's not why I'm here."

"And I'm not an actress," Kara added.

"Oh ... relatives?" Leslie shamelessly continued.

"No, we're not related." Kara frowned as her bewildered eyes drifted from Leslie to Wendell.

"At least not yet," Melissa interjected, and then poked Kara in the side. Kara flinched but held her composure.

"Is there something I can do for you, Leslie?" Wendell drew her attention back to him.

"Uh, I ..." Leslie hesitated, somewhat distracted by Melissa's outburst. She curiously glanced at Kara before making eye contact with Wendell. "I just wanted you to know that I really appreciate the ride home the other night. I'm sorry you couldn't stay, but maybe next time." She gently touched him on the shoulder. "But in the meantime, I'm going to work on memorizing the rest of these lines." She held the script up for effect. "I promise ... I won't disappoint you." Leslie delivered a lingering stare to him as she walked away.

"*You went to her place?*" Kara looked to Wendell for an honest answer. Although they weren't in a long-standing relationship or any kind of commitment for that matter, she harbored feelings for Wendell that she simply could not discard. "Are you two dating?" Her eyebrows rose as she sought clarity about Leslie.

"No, we're not." Wendell dismissed her questions with a shake of his head. "Please, just ignore her. I gave her a ride home after her audition with me. It was nothing." He sighed and then impassively said, "Did you two want to get something to eat before going home?"

Kara's eyelashes fluttered from the painful twinge that burned across her chest. "No, I don't think so," she rashly said before turning to her friend. "Melissa, let's go."

Melissa understandably nodded as she grabbed her coat from the folding chair and then they started for the door.

Wendell quickly grabbed Kara by the hand. "Wait..." He stared into her eyes and soon recognized her pain. "May I talk to you for a minute?"

Melissa took a second glance at Kara and too noticed the unspoken pain on her face. "Hey, let's just go."

After a few silent moments Kara raised a hand. "It's all right, Mel. Let me talk to him. I'll only be a minute," she assured her.

"All right, but I'll be waiting over there by the door." Melissa hesitantly surrendered. "I'll go ahead and call Douglas to meet us at the sandwich shop." She then warily looked at Wendell before walking away.

"I can give you guys a lift home, you know," Wendell said, making a peace-offering.

Kara picked up her bag and steadied it across her shoulders. "No, we're fine. Thanks." She successfully avoided eye contact with Wendell until he gently moved a lock of her wavy hair from her eyes. Kara carefully pushed his hand away as she looked in another direction.

"Just so you know," Wendell said, drawing her eyes back on him, "I'm not interested in Leslie ... *at all*. The only thing we have in common is this movie," he tried convincing her.

"Okay," Kara said with a nod, "You don't owe me any explanation. I mean, it's not like we're in a relationship or anything." She shrugged. "Anyway, I hope your movie is a big hit."

"I hope so too," Wendell responded, not entirely persuaded that she believed what he had said about Leslie.

"Well, I better get going. I don't want to keep Melissa waiting." Kara's eyes drifted to the floor as she started in the opposite direction.

"Wait," Wendell abruptly said as he pulled her back again. "I want you to know that I really enjoyed lunch today. I'm sorry again about not being able to pick you up from school. Making sure everything runs smoothly with this film is so time-consuming," he explained.

"Oh yeah, I understand," she nonchalantly answered with her hands tucked around the straps of her bag, wondering if the man she cared for truly had a love connection with someone else.

"I'm glad the meeting went well with Lois."

"I am too." Kara tried to mask the crack in her voice. "Mrs. Chow was very nice. You know, going over my application to make sure everything looked okay and everything. I was a little disappointed to hear that she thought my showmanship on the prescreening audition video was a bit stiff, but she advised me on how to improve that." Kara successfully blinked back the tears that threatened to fall from her eyes. "She gave me some great pointers for the live audition if I'm scheduled."

Wendell slowly took her hand. "Now, you know you're going to get scheduled."

"Yeah ... maybe ... uh, look I have to go." Kara could no longer hide the tears that now fell from her eyes that were first formed in her heart. Just the thought of him with someone else crushed the image she had of the two of them together. "I'll—"

Before Kara could finish her sentence, Wendell passionately kissed her on the lips. He tried to contain his emotions, but they simply overtook him. Kara resisted at first, but then fell limp to his advances. Moments later, the two stood almost breathless.

"*Whoa*," Kara said as she guardedly glanced around the room. Everyone in the crew had already left the building. The only other person still there besides them was Melissa who was around the corner out of view.

"I didn't mean to catch you off guard, but I wanted you to know how I felt." He gently wiped the tears from her face. "How I really feel."

Kara's chest inflated with a deep breath before she slowly exhaled. "*Wow* ... that was, uh ... that was something." She softly chuckled, delicately touching the curvature of her lips with slightly shaky fingers. "But what about that woman?"

Wendell grabbed her around the waist and carefully kissed her lips again. "Now does that answer your question?" He cleared the remaining wetness from her cheeks with soft strokes of his thumbs.

Kara bashfully lowered her chin as she demurely smiled. He stirred emotions inside of her that she could no longer hide from him. It flattered her that Wendell's interest wasn't merely a physical attraction. He sincerely cared about her feelings and her future. Something Kara not only desired, but the encouragement she needed at this time in her life.

"I wanted to ask you if we could be ..." Wendell casually shrugged, slowing dragging his thumb and forefinger around the corners of his mouth, "you know ... us."

Kara stared at him with such innocence, softly answering, "Yes."

The two shared soft laughter along with a warm embrace. Kara rested her head on his chest as she carefully surrendered her heart in his care. She had only cared about one other young man remotely similar in this way, but even that couldn't compare to the mature emotions she now carried for Wendell.

"Look, we better get out of here before Melissa comes looking for you." Wendell grinned as he lightly caressed her cheek again.

Kara giggled with a stomach flurrying with butterflies. "Yeah, we better."

# CHAPTER 19

MELISSA WALKED THROUGH the front door and met eyes with her father who stood at the bottom of the staircase. They smiled at one another as Franklin held onto a thermos filled with his favorite chai tea. His sullen mood brightened as Melissa slid her arms around his waist and they hugged.

"Before I forget, here are the keys to the SUV. Douglas was in a hurry to get somewhere, so I told him that I'd bring them inside."

"That's right, he had plans for this evening," Franklin recalled. "Actually, for the weekend."

Melissa raised an eyebrow. "Oh, I didn't know. I wouldn't have had him stop for ice cream after the game."

"Game?" Franklin inquired as he peered down at his daughter. "Last night it was research on a film production and tonight it's a game?"

"Yes. Last night *I was* on the set of an independent film. And Daddy, you knew Kara's friend was playing in that big game tonight. The Friday night game I mentioned earlier this week," Melissa tried to remind him.

"No, I don't remember you telling me that." Franklin sparingly sipped from his thermos. "Is this the same friend that's been in the news?"

"Yes, it's the same friend." Melissa coyly grinned. "But I sure hope that I didn't spoil things for Douglas."

"*Uh-huh* ..." Franklin gave his daughter the wary eye. "Well, I'm sure if it was a problem he would've let you know. Douglas is quite forthcoming when he needs to be." He then chuckled. "Besides, if he dropped you off, he probably did what he had to do while you were at the game. I'm sure driving around in the SUV didn't hurt his reputation." Franklin grinned as he dropped the keys inside of his front pocket. "So, how's Kara?"

With her lips slightly parted, Melissa peered at her father. "Why would you assume that I was out with only Kara? I have other friends too."

"For starters, Natalie called while you were out—"

"Oh, I forgot to turn my ringer back on," Melissa sighed as she gaped at her cell.

"And Rita is out of town with her parents," Franklin continued. "I'm not aware of any boyfriend since you broke up with Quentin ... unless there's more to this friend you've been talking about," Franklin hinted. "We agreed that all boyfriends go through me first." He tapped on his chest.

"No Dad, there's no boyfriend." Melissa then giggled with a hand on her hip. "Why are you so protective?"

"You're my daughter ... it's my job to be *so protective*." He winked.

Melissa smirked as her father hugged her again. "So, were you about to go to bed?"

Franklin peered down at his blue, monogramed chambray robe and quipped, "Did my clothes give me away?"

Melissa jokingly jabbed her father in the side and he flinched. The two burst into laughter again. The joyful sound drew Talia out of the master suite. She closed her housecoat as she looked down from the stair balcony.

Over the past few days Franklin hadn't shown her nearly as much attention as he had their daughter. It seemed to be a chore for him just to say hello. Ever since the argument they had just before the birthday dinner she had planned in his honor, Talia hadn't had a decent conversation with her husband. Their marriage had become strained once again, but she held out hope that they would reconcile before she left for the airport the next morning.

"Oh hey, Mom!" Melissa waved as Talia clutched the banister's curvature with one hand while she raised the other. "Are you all packed?"

Talia nodded as she forced a smile for her daughter's sake. "Yes," she sighed, "I'm all packed. My flight leaves at six in the morning."

Melissa glanced at the petite frame of her crystal sundial wristwatch before looking between her parents. "Oh wow, well you better get some sleep. It's already after eleven-thirty."

Talia's eyes briefly drifted to Franklin who then took a sip from his thermos, breaking the gaze she had with him. She looked back to Melissa and gently smiled. "Well, I better get my hug now since I know you're not going to be up at four-thirty when I leave."

"Uh yeah, you better because even if I get up, I'll probably think I'm hallucinating or something when you come into my room." Melissa laughed as she left her father's side and started up the stairs.

Talia hugged Melissa while gazing at Franklin over her shoulder. His eyes reluctantly met hers as she smiled. Franklin returned the simple gesture and calmly sipped from his thermos again.

"Have a safe trip and—"

Talia held up a hand with closed eyes as she said, "And bring you something back."

Melissa chuckled as she pulled her mother's hand down. "I was going to say be sure to call us as soon as your plane lands."

Talia stared at her daughter with a surprised look. "*What*, you didn't want anything? You always want something when I go to pick up Mama."

"Uh-uh, I didn't say that I didn't want anything," she corrected her, motioning with the sway of a single finger, "I'm just not asking for it."

Talia warily glanced at Franklin before looking back to Melissa.

"What I'm saying is that you and Daddy have given me a lot …" A sullen expression cascaded across her face as she continued, "More than what I needed. And in a few months I'll practically be on my own."

"Now Melissa, I'm not too comfortable about you living on campus alone."

"Mom, that's a requirement. Besides, I won't be alone … Kara's applying to Juilliard too."

"And where is she going to get the money to attend?" Talia suspiciously questioned.

"Ahem," Franklin angrily grunted. "When did we make a final decision on Juilliard?"

"*Oh, here we go* …" Melissa rolled her eyes while Talia ignored Franklin's question.

"Is anybody going to say anything?" he questioned, staring between the two of them.

Melissa peered at Talia out of the corners of her eyes before looking at her father. "Daddy, Mom and I talked earlier this week and she agreed that I should pursue my dreams."

"*Mom and I talked*?" He placed his thermos down on a nearby coaster, and then pointed between the two of them. "So, I had no say in this?" That query he directed to Talia. "I guess compromise was out of the question. That school does not offer a minor in business or accounting."

"Franklin, she doesn't want to study business or accounting … or have anything to do with investment banking. Besides, things are much different now than they were when you made most of your money," Talia reasoned on her daughter's behalf. "She's old enough now to know what she wants to do with her life."

"You know—" Franklin huffed, but abruptly paused. "Melissa, excuse us. Your mother and I need to talk."

"But Daddy, I want to go to Juilliard," she pleaded.

"Melissa, what did I say?" Franklin kept his eyes on Talia as he spoke to his daughter. "Leave us alone."

Melissa stared at Talia who concurred with downcast eyes, "Do what your father says."

Furious, Melissa strutted up the stairs and slammed her bedroom door.

"Oh not in my house." Franklin started after his daughter. "She's got to know that disrespectful behavior is not tolerated here."

"Let it go, Franklin." Talia pulled him back by the arm. "You're not angry with her, it's me."

Franklin pulled in a deep breath and sighed before facing his wife again.

"What is it that you have to say to me? Obviously, you have more on your mind than just Melissa and that school. You've barely said five sentences to me today." Talia's eyes pierced his. "What is it? *What* have I done now?" She held her arms out and then dramatically dropped them at her sides.

Franklin picked up his thermos from the sofa table. "Nothing Talia, *as usual*, you've done nothing," he sarcastically said before turning away from her and walking in the direction of his home office.

"Aren't you going to say anything else?" Talia tightened the belt to her housecoat around her waist and followed him into his office.

Franklin reserved his response until after the door was closed. "Sit down, Talia."

She looked at him with questions pouring from her eyes. Franklin sat behind his cherry oak desk and toggled the mouse to his computer. As the light from the screen shone on his face, Talia pursed her lips and crossed her legs, impatiently tapping her fingers on the chair arm.

"I want you to see something." Franklin turned the monitor around to where Talia could see the display.

"What is it?"

"A record of what you've spent over the past year."

Her brows furrowed as she glared at him. "*A record*?"

"*Yes*, a record." Franklin emphatically nodded. "Since you seem to think that I'd be better off running this business for a few more years, working long hours while you go out and spend just about half of what I make."

Talia pushed the monitor back in Franklin's direction. "How dare you keep tabs on me!" Talia quickly realized her outburst and lowered her voice. "I was here when you had nothing," she sparred through clenched teeth, "so don't you try this *record-keeping* mess with me."

"I expected this out of you. Every time I try to talk to you about money, well, about *saving money* you just go off." Franklin rested against the back of his chair. "I tell you, I've worked hard for years and yes you were there, but where are you now?" His glare asked the question twice.

Talia slammed the bottom of her fist onto the desk as she stood. "What do you mean *where am I now*?"

"I'm talking about where your heart is, Talia. It seems as if we were happier before we had all of this." Franklin gestured with his hands. "The house, the cars, the jewelry, the money ..."

"No, *you* may have been happier," she said, forcefully pointing a finger at him. With a hand on her hip, Talia shook her head and walked to the other side of the room. "I tell you what, I'm glad that we have all of this." She mimicked Franklin's earlier gesture of when he mentioned what their wealth had accumulated. "What's wrong with being able to go on a weekend trip at a moment's notice?" she impudently questioned. "To be a member of the city's most elite country club?" Her eyes glistened as she carried on. "It feels *good* to wear designer clothes and have money in the bank. This is what we've always dreamed of."

"No, this is what *you've* always dreamed of." Franklin pointed back at her. "I was fine with living a comfortable life within my means. To not have to work seventy-five, eighty hours a week or go without seeing my little girl at night. Sure, things are different now," Franklin argued with regret in his eyes. "Melissa is about to leave home and I'll never be able to get that time back. So, why is it wrong of me to want to spend these last few months with my daughter? To not have to tell her that I can't make her school play or I'm too busy to watch a couple movies?"

"Well, if you weren't so busy trying to shove the business down her throat, maybe you could spend some quality time together." Talia raised her eyebrows, almost daring him to challenge her.

With a heavy grunt, Franklin stared at the computer monitor again. "Do you even care about how much I've sacrificed?"

Talia looked at him in annoyance. She had heard the *sacrificial* spiel before, and she didn't care to hear it again. Her heart was hardening to Franklin again, the man who certainly sacrificed more than she'd ever know. He had worked through sickness he'd never spoken about and only recalled important milestones in his child's life through cherished photographs. Talia assumed that she had heard all of Franklin's sacrificial spiel, but she didn't know half of it.

"Go on Franklin," she chided, "tell me how much you've given up as if I wasn't here suffering through two miscarriages. I've had it rough too you know."

Franklin's eyes narrowed as he asked, "What did you say?"

"I said I've had it rough too you know," she harshly repeated. "Who do you think raised Melissa? Who do you think was there to bathe her, help her with homework, and go to school meetings?" Talia counted off the things she listed one by one on her fingers. "I've done more than you give me credit for, that's for sure."

Franklin still had a dumbfounded glaze on his face as he prodded, "No, I want you to repeat what you just said."

"Is this some sort of joke?" she scoffed. "Are you trying to make me angrier than I already am?" Talia rolled her eyes. "I just repeated myself and you're asking me to do it again? Didn't you hear me the first time?"

Franklin looked at her with a menacing glare. "Did you hear yourself the first time?"

"What are you talking about?"

"You just said you suffered *two* miscarriages." Franklin stood from behind his desk, unintentionally pushing his chair against the wall in the process. "But we had *three*. Did the last child not mean anything to you? Each of my children, whether they survived or not, has a place in my heart." He grimaced at her. "I at least thought we had *that* in common."

"I-I just made a slip of the tongue, that's all." Talia nervously clutched the gold pendant dangling from the chain around her neck. "You always make a mountain out of a mole hill. You know what I meant."

"Do I?" Indignation gripped his voice.

"Yes, you do," she snidely replied.

Franklin walked toward her and halted his footsteps just inches in front of her. They stood facing one another, each weathering the warmth of the other's breath. Talia looked away, hoping to mask her deceitfulness. The deceitful past she shared with Donovan and the child they had aborted.

"Is there something that you want to tell me?" Franklin lingered in front of his wife, struggling to regain eye contact with her.

"What would I have to tell you?" Talia nervously took a step back while simultaneously pushing him away.

Franklin ceased his pursuit and studied her movements. He gathered that she didn't want his hands anywhere on her body. "You don't really love me, Talia. Not like how a wife should her husband." Looking disappointed, Franklin shook his head and placed a hand over his heart. "I can feel it in here."

"Franklin, that's not true." Talia reached out for him, but inwardly knew that what he said was fairly true. His stark honesty challenged her, but just as before Talia wanted to work at her marriage. She desired to revive what brought them together in the beginning. "Look, I'm sorry. Maybe I shouldn't have raised my voice, but you made me angry. How could you go behind my back and detail every little purchase I've made? We've been together for twenty years."

Franklin reconsidered her feelings. With nineteen years of marriage and almost a year of dating, he and Talia were just months shy of sharing a twenty-year milestone together. Franklin often hoped that things would return to how they were when they first met. The long days and countless hours he labored were to fund their future, to secure Melissa's education, and once she left home, afford the opportunity for him and Talia to travel—*together* for a change. He loved his wife dearly and it pained him that her feelings may not be reciprocated.

"I do love you," Talia gently whispered in Franklin's ear.

He gazed into her now submissive eyes, still troubled by her lust for money.

"Maybe we just need to spend some time together ... alone." Talia's voice sounded different as she removed the hair clip that restrained her long hair. "I don't want to go away on this trip angry. Four days is a long time," she added with an apologetic smile, "to be angry."

In an instant, Franklin's desire for her grew as his resistant anger began to melt away. His eyes followed the locks of her hair that flowed past her shoulders. Talia slid her hand into his as she moved closer. Franklin became somewhat hypnotized as he inhaled the tantalizing aroma of her soft hair.

"Why don't we turn in and talk about this later?" Talia enticed him. Her remorseful actions successfully diverted her husband's attention.

With one hand planted at Talia's waist, Franklin reached across his desk with the other and pressed a button on the monitor. He abandoned his distrustful thoughts and the lighted screen soon disappeared. He peered into her eyes, but she nervously looked away.

"What's wrong?" he asked.

"Well," she said, slowly moving around him towards the door. "I just thought that we should go to our bedroom before things go too far."

Franklin nodded while noting the hesitation in her movements. He turned the lights out to his office and followed his wife to their room. Inwardly, he prayed that whatever she was harboring in her heart would soon come out. In order for him to have peace about their longstanding marriage, this was something he needed to know.

Oblivious to Franklin and Talia's private conversation, Melissa emerged from her room and stood at the winding stairwell. After she heard the door to her parents' room close, she took a few steps down to their floor. She wondered if they were going to stay up half the night arguing about the educational path for her future. After she stood for several seconds and watched the lights under the door to their suite go out, the question to her thoughts was soon answered.

Melissa capped the bottle of water she sipped from and meandered back inside of her room. After tossing aside a brochure to Juilliard, she picked up her cell and called Kara, the only other person she knew who truly understood what it meant to attend that school.

"Hey, what's up girl? Are you busy?"

In a dejected tone, Kara replied, "Nope."

"What's going on?"

"Miriam as usual," Kara sighed. "Thank God the woman from downstairs convinced her to watch a movie in her apartment."

Melissa listened as Kara carried on about her sister. She had only seen Miriam twice since meeting Kara although she had heard her voice numerous times over the phone. To Melissa, she didn't sound as bad as Kara made her out to be. Nonetheless, she gathered that the terrible reputation that preceded Miriam had to carry some weight coming from her best friend.

"Enough about Miriam," Melissa said, shifting Kara's attention. "What's up with Wendell? Are you over there waiting on him to call?"

"*No*," Kara responded, blushing from the mere suggestion. "I'm not waiting on Wendell to call."

"Girl, you know you're going to have to tell me about that serious lip-lock he had on you."

Kara giggled as she twirled a finger through her hair. "Well I started to tell you on the way home, but your little phone call from Phillip seemed to be more important."

"Now Kara, you know the boy has it bad for me. I had to at least give him enough attention to let him know that I'm interested. The boy is fine!"

"Girl, you are too much. I've never seen you carry on about a boy like this before."

"Yeah, well, I've never seen you carry on about anybody like you have about Wendell. Did he say anything else about that Leslie chick?"

"Nothing other than what I've already told you. Just that he's not interested in her," Kara replied, trying to change the subject from being about Leslie. "He wants me to be his girl."

"Well, that'll mean that he can't date anybody else," Melissa said with an offhanded grunt.

In a somewhat offensive tone, Kara questioned, "Why'd you have to go there?"

"Girl, I'm just saying. You saw how that Leslie chick was all up on him."

"I'm not worried about her." Kara deflected Melissa's comment. "If Wendell wanted her, he wouldn't have been all up on me."

"Uh-huh," Melissa said, echoing her earlier sentiments.

"Anyway, what is up with you and Phillip? Ever since I told you what he said, you suddenly became his sideline cheerleader. At the game, you just about knocked me over when he slam-dunked the winning shot."

"Me and everybody else," Melissa said in defense. "It was a home game, girl. Where's your team spirit?"

"Yeah, whatever." Kara casually dismissed her.

Melissa smiled as she rolled her eyes over to the cheap bottle of perfume Phillip had given to her. Although the fragrance was pungent, she appreciated the thought, especially after seeing how nervous he seemed when giving it to her after the game. It was exciting as she watched Phillip hype the crowd up with his amazing athletic skills. Although she hadn't admitted to Kara, Melissa knew that anybody could tell how interested she really was in him by the way she flocked to Phillip after the game. She saw potential in him, and even if he didn't make it as a professional athlete Phillip would still be successful, Melissa was sure of it. But it troubled her that Talia may find out.

*If Mom only saw people the way I do*, Melissa thought.

"So, are you saying that I shouldn't talk to him?"

"Girl, no I'm not saying that. Phillip is cool. I'm just surprised that's all."

"Why?" Melissa inquired.

"Well, you know how your mom doesn't want me coming over. What would she say if Phillip wanted to visit you or something?"

Melissa quietly cleared her throat and pondered that. It was a challenge just to get her mother to see that Kara was a trustworthy friend—regardless of where she lived or how much money her family *didn't* have—but if she dared to invite Phillip over as a potential boyfriend, Talia would probably throw a fit.

"You're right, Phillip does have it bad for you. I can honestly say that he's been asking me about you for a long time—"

"He has?"

"Yes, he has. But he won't hold his tongue with your mother the way that I have," Kara warned. "He's respectful, polite and all of that, but he would light into a person in a minute."

"I hear you." Melissa chuckled, figuring that about Phillip. "Oh, hang on a minute." She quickly pulled the phone away from her ear. Her lips curled into a blushing smile as she looked at the screen display. "Girl, Phillip is calling me."

"Oh, so he has your number now."

"Oh please, Wendell has yours."

"And we've been talking for months."

"You're too slow for me," Melissa teased. "Look, I'll call you back in the morning. Mom is leaving early and Daddy says you can stay over if you want to. You can pick out some things from my closet that you want to take on your trip *down south*."

"Okay, I'll talk—"

"Oh gotta go, girl. The phone just beeped again. Bye!"

Before Kara attempted to say anything else, Melissa was off the line. She stared at the dead phone and shook her head. Kara rested back on her bed and thought about how Melissa carried on about Phillip. After the game, she had introduced herself to Phillip's mother before she left for her night shift job and even waited until he returned from showering in the locker room. Melissa had watched as a swarm of girls crowded around Phillip after the game, making goo-goo eyes at him, but she was bold enough to break through the huddle and lead him away by the hand.

Kara was happy that Melissa had found someone who genuinely wanted to date her, unlike her previous snooty boyfriend, Quentin. Phillip wasn't rich by any means, but similarly he wasn't a run-of-the-mill guy living in the projects either. He had dreams along with the determination to make them come true. Phillip spent as many hours on the court as Kara spent practicing the piano or studying the history of classical composers.

She had previously shielded Melissa from Phillip, misjudging him by what she had heard from others. Kara realized that she was wrong by assuming that he had slept with the girl who claimed he was the father of her child. She had underestimated him, but now felt that he would make a good match for her best friend.

Kara held out hope for the best as she got on her knees and prayed for those closest in her life. Even a sincere prayer was offered up for Miriam. The relationship between them was strained, but she was still her sister. Kara remembered how Miriam took her in after their parents passed, regardless of how nasty she had become over the years. Maybe she couldn't break through the cast-iron hatred Miriam had barricaded herself in, but God could.

God can do anything, that's one thing Kara was sure of.

# CHAPTER 20

"NOW BOARDING FLIGHT 2344, nonstop to LaGuardia," the gate agent announced for the second time in a row.

Talia slowly looked up from her sleek, onyx eReader and gazed at the dwindling line of patrons. The direct flight from Fort Lauderdale was unusually light for a Thursday afternoon in December. She had enjoyed the week-long visit with her mother during Thanksgiving week so much that she decided to fly back to Florida not just as the normal escort, but to stay with her mother for a few weeks into December. This time of the year often caused Talia to drift into a depressive state, ever since her father had passed two years ago.

On many occasions Talia had tried to convince her aging mother to move with her to New York, but she adamantly refused. In Ms. Shirley Vaughn's words, *New York has a lot to offer, but Florida weather isn't one of them.*

Talia smiled at the wittiness of her mother. The woman who was bent on staying in the old house she had shared with her husband for over three decades. It was simple, quaint, but as her mother would also say, *most importantly it's paid off.*

"Ma'am, are you on this flight?" the gate agent asked Talia as he moved from behind the counter.

"Uh yes, is there something wrong?" Her eyes drifted from the agent to the empty gate.

"No, nothing's wrong." He tugged at the jacket of his crisp uniform as his glance followed Talia's gaze before drifting back to her. "I was just wondering if you were one of the three passengers that we're waiting on. Once we get everyone onboard, we may be able to push back early."

"Oh." Talia quickly uncrossed her legs. She hurriedly picked up her designer shades and gathered her other items into a large shoulder bag. After a glance back to ensure nothing was left behind, Talia followed the agent closely down the jetway and stepped onto the plane.

First class was practically empty as she took her typical seat by a window on the last row.

"Would you like something to drink before we take off?" a flight attendant asked while simultaneously extending a pillow in her direction.

Talia dumped her bag on the vacant seat next to her and shook her head. "No, nothing to drink and I have my own pillow, thank you." She offered a gentle smile in return. "But would it be all right if I used the restroom?"

The attendant glanced back at the darkened sign just above the lavatory at the front of the aircraft and then looked back to Talia. "Yes, it's vacant and we're still waiting on two more passengers."

Talia slid out of the row and walked towards the front lavatory. With her body slightly wedged between the open door, she half-smiled at the flight attendant who stood in the galley. She interrupted the woman who was in the middle of securing the carts that held alcohol minis, canned sodas, and carbonated water.

"I hate to do this to you," Talia started with a hand on the doorframe of the lavatory, "but I think I will have a drink after all."

"Oh, no problem," the attendant replied as she stood from her stooped position. "What'll you have?"

"Coffee, decaf, one sugar."

"Sure, I'll have it for you when you come out."

Talia nodded at the woman with a pleasant disposition and closed the door behind her. She soon found herself smiling at the thought of her mother again. The time they shared over the past few weeks reminded her of what things were like when her father was still alive. Tons of photographs were shared as well as two unplanned trips to the mausoleum at Talia's urging. Ms. Vaughn admitted that she rarely visited the vault that held her late husband's remains. *This place is for the dead, and I'm alive*, were her sentiments. Although she had loved her spouse dearly, Ms. Vaughn was strong enough to know that she had to let him go for her own sanity. It was difficult and challenging when he first passed, but as time went on she realized that she still had more life to live and she couldn't do it by constantly revisiting the past.

Talia held onto her mother's insight for dear life, especially when she opened the lavatory door and saw Donovan. She cautiously watched as he tossed a bag into an overhead bin. Her eyes then drifted to the floor. The past had once again revisited her.

"Ma'am, here's your coffee." The flight attendant handed the warm cup to her with two square-shaped napkins wrapped around it. "Our last passengers have arrived, so we'll be pushing back shortly after the young woman returns. She had to run back out to get something she left on a bench in the lobby. So, I'll have to take the drink after the safety demo."

Talia nodded aimlessly as she took the drink and started to walk towards her seat.

Donovan clutched a small pillow and blanket underneath his arm as he shut the overhead bin with his free hand. When he looked toward the head of the aisle, there stood Talia wearing a puzzling glare on her face.

"Tee?" His voice rang with surprise. "What are you doing on this flight?"

"I was uh ...." She stalled as her eyes drifted down to the cup in her hand and then to the flight attendant standing in the galley. Talia gently smoothed her hair back that was secured in an elegant French braid as she looked away from the woman and back to Donovan. "I was visiting my mother."

"I see." Donovan looked away from her as he tossed the blanket and pillow onto the empty seats of his row. "How is she?"

"Good." Her eyes roamed from the empty seats to the three other passengers in first class.

Donovan nodded as his eyes shifted away from her again. "That's good." He sat down in an aisle seat and fastened his seatbelt. "Next time, tell her I said hello." After picking up a magazine from the empty seat next to him, he casually flipped through the pages.

Talia glanced behind her at the open main aircraft door. She raised an eyebrow, and then with a hint of jealousy in her voice asked, "Traveling with someone?"

Donovan chuckled under his breath as he looked up from the sports magazine. "Why? Are you?"

Talia's eyes narrowed to a squint as she marched past him. She sat down behind him on the opposite side and stared out of the window. Curiosity drew her eyes back on Donovan as she waited to see if the mysterious stranger who had just walked onto the plane was his travelling companion. Talia watched as the petite Hispanic woman who looked to be in her mid-twenties passed through first class and into the main cabin.

Donovan looked back at Talia and met her gaze as the woman passed by. He smiled at her, noticing the subtle hint of relief on her face. Talia's eyes shifted away and she slid on her sunglasses. She quietly cleared her throat and sipped sparingly from her cup of coffee. Donovan shook his head and turned around in his seat.

The flight attendant delivered a final head count of the passengers onboard to the gate agent and then the main aircraft door was closed. After collecting all cups and paper products, the attendants showed the safety demonstration as the plane pushed back and rolled onto the runway.

Donovan summoned one of the flight attendants as she walked through the cabin. She stopped at his row and he motioned for her to come closer.

"What is it?" she asked, keeping a respectable distance between them.

"Once we take off, I'd like to move to the seat behind me since it is empty. Is that all right?"

She stood from her leaning position and nodded. "Oh yes, that'll be fine. Once the FASTEN SEATBELT SIGN is turned off, you can change seats at that time." She smiled and then the pilot made an announcement for the flight attendants to take their seats in preparation for takeoff. "I have to get to my jump seat, but feel free to move at that time," she repeated before walking away.

Donovan glanced back at Talia again who blankly stared out of the window. He turned around and rested his head against the seatback as the plane elevated at a steep incline. When the plane leveled off and the FASTEN SEATBELT SIGN darkened, Donovan was fast asleep. It had been a busy week for him as he checked on the house he had built in his hometown after he and his wife split, but also a late night from visiting a family member who suddenly fell ill while he was in town. Talia noticed his freefalling head nod helplessly and her defenses melted. She shook her head at the fact that he wasn't using the pillow on the seat right next to him.

Talia repetitively tapped her thumb on the eReader she held in her hands. She reluctantly admitted her relief that Marissa was not travelling with Donovan. Ever since she had struck him on the face and watched her friend kiss him on the same cheek only moments later, Talia was enraptured once again. As much as she tried to deny her feelings, even after the passionate, spontaneous evening with Franklin before she left for Ft. Lauderdale to escort her mother back to New York, Talia still dreamt about her past paramour. The hold he had on her seemed unnatural as she had promised to share her life with someone else.

Talia nudged Donovan on the shoulder as she whispered, "I guess this seat isn't taken."

He flinched from his sleep and looked at her with a long, bewildering stare. "Huh?"

Talia motioned her head toward the empty seat beside him. "Do you mind if I sit down?"

"No," Donovan said as he sat upright in his seat. "Not at all." He stood and allowed Talia to slide to the window seat beside him. "As a matter of fact, I was going to come and talk to you."

Talia nodded as she knew he shared her mutual feelings. "I'm sorry about the way I treated you at my house last month," she whispered.

"No, I was way out of line." Donovan shook his head. "You were right, that's your home with your family. Besides, you had already told me at the club where I stood. I don't know, I just didn't think you were serious ... not until that night." He gently smiled at her. "You know we go way back. And I guess I never really accepted that things were over between us."

Talia closed her eyes and released a menacing groan. "I shouldn't have reacted that way." She opened her eyes and stared at him. "It's just that when I saw you with Marissa again, it just stirred up some old emotions that I thought were dead."

His lips parted, stunned by her confession.

"What are you doing with Marissa?" Talia delicately placed her hands on top of his. "You know she's not who you want."

When Donovan looked into her eyes, he could see that she was serious. As serious as he was when he told her that he and his wife were no longer together. Although he had grown to like Marissa, it was true that she was not who he really wanted.

"I don't want her to get hurt behind you." Talia amended her response and tenderly said, "Behind us."

"Neither do I." Apologies were written all over his face. "I was actually going to tell her tonight after I got back. The contract for the building project is about to end and I just can't let her think that I'm going to stay in town for her."

Over the past few weeks he had grown to know Marissa as a lovely female companion. The late-night movies and frequent dinner dates had all but sealed the notion for her that they were dating exclusively. However, when Marissa introduced him to her children a few short hours before he left town for Ft. Lauderdale, Donovan knew that she saw more in him than a casual date. He knew then that he had to find a way to let her down easily, regardless of his ties to Talia.

"Yes, you need to tell her, but does it have to be tonight?" She squeezed his hand as a suggestive smile crept across her lips. "My family isn't expecting me until tomorrow."

Donovan looked into her eyes just as he had so many times before. But this time he saw his old flame, the woman he went to high school with, the woman who had carried his child, the woman who was willing to jeopardize all she had again—just to be with him.

"Well," he began, wetting his lips, "I think tomorrow will definitely be better." He then returned the squeeze to her hand and agreed, "Yes ... I'll just tell her tomorrow."

# CHAPTER 21

KARA DREW THE curtains to her window on the dawn of a beautiful morning. Although it was only six o'clock, the streets were filled with patrons bustling and moving about with purpose. She felt good knowing that she could now proudly declare that she was a Juilliard applicant.

After spending hours at the library in front of a computer screen a couple weeks ago, Kara finally submitted her application materials to the college. In the midst, an overwhelming sense of nostalgia swept over her. It was her faith being realized from a childhood dream.

Today was a particularly special one for Kara. Not only was she leaving to go home for a couple weeks to Dadenville, but it was her mother's birthday. Christmas break did not begin until Monday, but on this Thursday morning Frieda agreed that two days out of school wasn't going to hurt the student who was consistently on the honor roll, all except for one semester after her parents passed. Frieda sympathized with Kara's longing to be around family, especially during this time of the year.

After her morning prayer that flowed from a grateful heart, Kara flipped the page on her daily devotional calendar. Her fingers lingered on the page for today's Scriptural passage, Proverbs 15:1: *A soft answer turns away wrath, but a harsh word stirs up anger.*

Kara pondered today's passage as she thanked God for His Word. The devotional went on to describe moments when speaking a kind word may be challenging, especially if there's someone shouting at you or attempting to do you harm. Kara read further, and soon the word reaction caught her attention. *Your reaction does not have to mimic their ungodly action. You have the freedom to choose how you will respond to a negative situation. Shouting at one another tends to stir up anger. So, be like Jesus and speak a gentle word.*

She closed her eyes and inhaled a deep breath. With pleasant thoughts dancing through her mind, Kara peacefully exhaled. Moments later, she double-checked the suitcase by her bedroom door to ensure that she had her audition repertoire packed. Although there weren't any music applicants scheduled as of yet, she wanted to ensure that her classical selections, from the scales to her preferred work from the repertoire list, were skillfully polished. Kara was sure that she would get scheduled, as sure as she was that Melissa would do great on her audition that had already been scheduled to take place in a few short weeks. They both would have to wait until after the New Year though to find out the next step on their individual journeys.

Kara pondered Melissa's third date with Phillip last weekend as she stuffed her devotional calendar in the front pocket of the suitcase. They had gone to the movies, but when Kara asked her about the details of the date Melissa barely shared anything with her. It struck Kara as strange because Melissa always shared the specifics of her dates with her—whether good or bad. Lately, it seemed as if their conversations were only about the agents who scouted Phillip.

With a meditative expression drawn on her face, Kara looked down at the cell phone Wendell had bought her and rolled her luggage to the front door. Despite her attempts to convince him that she barely had any time to talk on the phone, he insisted. It shamed her to hear him say, "I know that you can afford to buy your own things, but let me do this for you." Kara pensively sighed as she stood at the front door of the apartment, lowering the handle on her suitcase.

The apartment was still fairly dark, but faint movements could be heard coming from Miriam's bedroom. When Kara went back into her room to secure her Bible from the nightstand, she overheard murmurings. She looked toward the bottom of Miriam's door and noticed that the lights were out. Kara walked past the door once more and slid the Bible into her carry-on bag that also sat by the front door.

This time when she walked back to her room there was a soft glow beneath Miriam's door, but the voices had stopped. Kara shook her head and repeated to herself, *a soft answer turns away wrath*. It had been particularly difficult for her to even sleep under the same roof with Miriam over the past few weeks. Ever since Kara revealed to Miriam that she knew about her promiscuous lifestyle, it was as if a license was given for all of her boyfriends to have full reign of the apartment. As she looked back at the closed door Kara simply shook her head again, eager to get on the plane and out of Miriam's sight.

"*Oh Lord, I miss my mother ....*" Kara gazed at the outfit hanging from a nail on the back of her bedroom door she had set aside to wear and ran her fingers across the beautiful fabric. Since it was her mother's birthday, she had chosen to wear one of Gwendolyn's blouses in her memory.

Noticing the dwindling time to be at the airport, Kara called a taxi to pick her up in thirty minutes. She then grabbed her outfit and toiletry bag and rushed into the bathroom. After a quick shower she hurriedly flat-ironed her long hair that flowed attractively to her shoulders. Then with a paddle brush, Kara carefully smoothed her new bang that covered a portion of her forehead. It was a sleek do that she had held onto since Deidra's friend had clipped and shaped her ends a couple weeks ago. It didn't hurt either that Wendell absolutely adored the straight hairstyle on her. Anything he liked on her, Kara looked to enhance. Since making it official, she could hardly contain her excitement about their budding relationship. Kara looked forward to sharing the news of her new love with Frieda, hoping that her aunt and boyfriend would meet at her upcoming graduation at the end of the school year.

"Kara, hurry up out of that bathroom!" Miriam shouted as she pounded on the door.

Kara flinched from the persistent pounding.

"Chris needs to use it," she said in a voice already laced with layers of anger so early in the morning.

Kara rolled her eyes upward and then back to her reflection in the mirror. After applying a thin layer of clear lip gloss, she tossed the applicator inside of her toiletry bag and zipped it closed. Since it was a challenge for her to say anything nice, Kara simply ignored Miriam as she attached her earrings and adjusted the cute top her mother once owned.

"*Hello*, didn't you hear me the first time?" Miriam struck the door again.

"I'm so glad that I'm out of here until the New Year," Kara mumbled before she opened the door.

Miriam glared at her sister. "Were you going to stay in there all morning?"

Kara stared down at her older sister parked just outside of the doorway. "No, I'm leaving for the airport now." She grabbed her toiletry bag from a nearby shelf and head rag from the bathroom sink. "Excuse me." She edged past Miriam who barely allowed a foot of distance between the door and her wheelchair.

"Must you where that hideous top?"

Kara halted at the top of the hallway and peered down at one of the few items retrieved from the fire years ago. There were several items salvaged from a metal encased chest tucked away in a spare bedroom of their parents' home, but this article of clothing she treasured above them all.

"*Hideous?*" Kara faced Miriam as she extended the hem of the blouse. "This was one of mom's shirts."

Miriam swallowed hard and abruptly shifted her face towards one of the barren walls. "Well, take it off."

Kara stood unmoved, challenged by her sister's sour attitude. "*Why*? You said I could have it when I grew into it."

"Well, I changed my mind." Miriam looked back at her sister who had filled out since she had made that promise five years ago. "I said take it off!"

"*No!*" Kara shouted back and then reached for her shoulder bag on the floor.

In a fit of rage, Miriam grabbed the hem of the blouse and growled, "Don't play with me, girl! You better remember who's taking care of you."

"How can I forget? You remind me every chance you get." Kara slapped her hands away. "Now, let go of my clothes!"

"I don't have to take care of you, you know," Miriam threatened her.

Kara grunted as she managed to free herself from Miriam's grasp. She then turned away from her sister and started up the hallway. Miriam grabbed her from behind and accidentally ripped the shirt down the side seam.

There was a sudden stark break of silence.

Kara stared at the backside of the shirt she had cherished since their mother died. She looked up from the rags she now held in her hands and questioned, "*Why?*"

Miriam shrunk into her chair. "You ... you should have taken it off when I asked you to," she rationalized. The tense rippling of her jaws intensified as she fought off the remorse that attempted to penetrate her heart.

As the open material flopped against Kara's body, the straps of her shoulder bag slid down her arm. She stared at Miriam and sniffled, "I guess you got what you wanted."

The looming tears soon streaked down her face as she slowly pulled the blouse over her head. Kara tugged at the white tank top she wore underneath and marched to her bedroom. She scowled at Miriam and dropped the torn material onto her lap along the way.

Suddenly, Chris emerged from Miriam's bedroom shirtless, wearing only a pair of blue jeans. "What's going on?" he asked, scratching the back of his head.

Miriam glanced at him before shifting her attention back to Kara. "You better lose that attitude in my house."

"Whatever." Kara sucked her teeth as she stood at the threshold of her bedroom door. Her eyes then shifted to Chris who smugly looked on. "And you just need to leave."

Chris surrendered, raising his hands as he went back into Miriam's bedroom.

"He doesn't have to go anywhere," Miriam defended him. "Why don't *you* just hurry up and leave?"

"Trust me, I'm trying to get out of here as fast as I can." Kara turned away from Miriam and stormed inside her room. She pulled on the second-hand dresser drawer that was off track, struggling to get it to open.

"What did I just tell you about your attitude?" Miriam argued as she rolled inside of Kara's room. "You owe me an apology."

Kara dropped her hands to her waist in defeat and faced her resentful sister. "I'm sorry, okay," she offered in a sarcastic quiver. "I'm sorry about the blouse you obviously hate and just ruined. I'm sorry about us living in this beat-up old apartment. I'm sorry about you getting shot ... I'm sorry about everything!"

Miriam drew back, astonished by Kara's outburst.

"But it's not my fault! Stop blaming me for you getting shot, stop blaming me for your disability, and stop blaming me for *your* decision to raise me!" Kara smeared the tears away that poured from her eyes with the back of her hand. "Aunt Frieda would have been more than willing to take me in."

Miriam simply stared in response, gripping the arms of her wheel-chair.

Kara deserted her attempts to open the stubborn dresser drawer and instead grabbed the knob to her closet door. The frail shutter-style door collapsed to the floor. After kicking the door, Kara snatched a sweater from a wire hanger that was equally as nice as the blouse Miriam had ruined. It was a present Wendell had recently bought for her.

"Where'd you get that from?" Miriam pried, rolling farther into Kara's bedroom.

"Wouldn't you like to know?" Kara rolled her eyes as she stood in front of the dresser mirror. She quickly slipped into the top and turned to the side, smoothing the bottom of the sweater over the slacks that hugged her hips. The outfit fit beautifully across her mature body.

Miriam shook her head in judgment. "If Mama could see how you turned out."

Kara scoffed at Miriam's last attempt to completely break her down. "*No*, if she could see how *you* turned out." She turned away from Miriam and noticed through the window a taxi pulling up near the sidewalk. Kara snatched her keys from the dresser and hurriedly grabbed her coat from the armchair in a corner of her room. Without even a glance back at her sister, Kara secured her luggage and walked out the door.

All the way to the airport and through the security check-point, she fought to not let anger consume her. As she sat with her boarding pass in hand, Kara's mind tirelessly reviewed the day's devotional message: *A soft wrath turns away anger...* She shook her head and lowered her eyes to the floor as passengers unloaded the plane she was about to board. *How am I supposed to give a soft answer to someone who is so evil?*

After she pulled her Bible from the shoulder bag that was on the seat next to her, Kara flipped aimlessly through the pages. Her fingers paused at the recently highlighted passage: *You prepare a table before me in the presence of my enemies.* She raised her head as if in reflection and exhaled a deep breath. The wrinkling on her forehead slowly rippled away. The

fact that God, the ever-present I AM, is with her even in the midst
of adversity was a comforting reminder.

"Oh, excuse me," a stranger said as she accidentally bumped Kara's
feet in passing.

Kara nodded with a kind gesture of the hand as she moved her
feet underneath her seat. She opened the flaps to the shoulder bag
again and slid her Bible back inside. As she looked toward a nearby
restroom, her eyes inadvertently landed on her best friend's mother.
Kara's lips parted at the sight of Talia walking alongside an unfamiliar man. Her eyes drifted from the smiles they shared between one
another to the slow separation of their clasped fingers.

"Oh, I think I left my shades on the plane," Talia said with the tips
of her fingers perched just above her eyebrow.

Kara slid down in her chair as Talia stood just a few feet away from
where she was seated. She pulled her freshly pressed hair forward and
pretended to search for something in her bag. Seconds later, Kara
discreetly looked up and watched as the man rested his hand on the
small of Talia's back.

"I'll ask the agent if she can get them," he offered.

"Thanks, Donovan," Talia replied, gently touching his forearm as
he started back toward the jetway.

*Donovan?* Kara stared at the mysterious stranger and wondered
if she had ever seen him before. *Maybe he's a relative*, she thought.
Kara watched as Talia nervously rubbed her hands up and down the
sides of her arms. When Talia looked in the vicinity of where she was
seated, Kara buried her face in her bag again. Having not noticed
Kara, Talia fidgeted with her dangling earrings as she looked back in
the direction of where Donovan had gone. She brushed the nape of
her neck and smiled at his return.

"Here they are," Donovan announced as he proudly extended the
shades in her direction. "The flight attendant was just about to leave

them with the gate agent. I guess there are still some honest people in the world after all," he quipped.

"I guess so." Talia hesitantly smiled as she took her shades from his hand.

"So, did you want me to call the hotel?"

Talia reluctantly nodded. She lowered her eyes and slipped the designer shades inside of a leather-sewn case.

Donovan's brows puckered as he noticed the guilty look on her face. "Tee, are you okay?" He moved closer to her.

"Yes," she quietly answered, trying to mask her apprehension. "I just need to unwind."

Donovan nodded knowingly. "Once we get to the Waldorf, your troubles will be a distant memory."

Kara watched as the man delicately kissed her best friend's mother on the cheek. Talia subtly pushed him away with a slight shake of her head. Kara craned her neck to hear the remainder of their conversation, but their words became inaudible as they walked away.

The first thought Kara conceived was to tell Melissa. *How do I tell her that her mother is cheating on her father*? She reached for her cell phone and held it in her hands. Thoughts cycled through her mind of what she should say to Melissa. She tapped her thumb repetitively on her thigh, wondering if she should mention any of what she saw to her best friend. Just as she was about to call Melissa her phone rang.

"Hey, did you make it to the airport okay?"

"Yes, I made it here just fine." Kara gently smiled at the sound of Wendell's voice. "What are you doing up already? I thought you were going to sleep in after the late night you had?"

Wendell chuckled. "Well, I had to hear your voice this morning before you left. I miss you already, girl."

"You know, I miss you too," Kara whispered, blushing behind her admission.

"Besides, we were supposed to pray together this morning," Wendell reminded her. "Did you forget?"

Kara practically glowed as she answered, "Aw, look at you. You are so considerate. And just so you know, I didn't forget. I just figured since you had a late night that you'd want to sleep in. I didn't want to disturb you."

"No call from you is a disturbance," he said in a serious tone. "Remember that."

"Yes sir," she joked.

"Besides, we're taking a break on the film until after the first of the year. I hate to see you go just when my time has freed up a little."

"I know ..." Kara moaned, "but I have to go see my family. With the way things are between me and my sister, it's best that I get away for a little while."

Wendell had been Kara's sounding board for the past few weeks. She finally opened up to him about Miriam's overbearing ways which was what initially prompted him to buy her a cell phone. Their relationship had matured exponentially over this time and Kara knew that she would have to soon tell him everything about her, including where she really lived. She found solace in the hope that her residence was of no importance to him, but it was still troubling since she had led him to believe that she lived at the Peterson mansion. His busy shooting schedule with the film and her long days studying kept them from visiting one another. This was only a temporary barrier that Kara knew would eventually collapse.

"Hey beautiful, I have to go, but you call me when your flight lands."

Kara smiled at his pet name for her. "Okay, I will."

"Talk to you later."

Kara ended the call and sat motionless, staring at the flashing time on the screen of her phone. She looked up and noticed that her flight was boarding, and then to the long corridor where Talia had disappeared. Although Kara hadn't had a serious girl talk with Melissa since things heated up between her and Phillip, after witnessing what she had today, she was convinced that this was one conversation they had to make time to have.

# CHAPTER 22

"LESLIE, OVER HERE!" Wayne called out as he waved his arm in the air.

Leslie took her hand off the door handle to a pizzeria and glanced around. Her eyes mechanically scanned the busy sidewalk and soon found Wayne's familiar face in the crowd. She shuddered inwardly, but plastered on a phony smile as he came within steps of where she stood.

"Hey, what's going on?" Wayne was slightly out of breath after he reached her.

Leslie's eyes took a sharp left to the pizza place before looking back to him. "Just grabbing a bite on my lunch break."

"Oh, you work nearby?" Wayne appeared more interested in what she was wearing than her answer to where she worked.

"Uh yeah ..." She moved aside to allow a patron to exit the restaurant. "Just a block down at the hotel."

"Well, I'm on my lunch break too. Do you mind if I join you?"

"Uh ... no." Leslie casually shrugged. "But I only have about twenty minutes to eat."

"No problem, it usually only takes me ten," he revealed with a smirk.

Leslie rolled her eyes out of view as Wayne held the door open for her.

The restaurant was busy, but the employees kept the ever-growing line moving. After Leslie placed her order Wayne held up his hand and motioned that they were together. Leslie stared at him as he paid for their food.

"You know you didn't have to do that." She held up a ten dollar bill. "I could've paid for myself."

"You're welcome," Wayne sarcastically said as he looked away from her. He stuffed the receipt from the cashier into his wallet, and then moved out of line. Leslie followed him to a table.

"Look, I'm sorry about that. It's just that with the filming still going on, I don't want there to be any misunderstanding." She sat down across from him. "You know what I mean?"

Wayne propped his elbows on the small square table and clasped his fingers together as he matter-of-factly asked, "And what misunderstanding would that be?"

Leslie looked him square in the eyes, but Wayne's stance didn't waiver. She twiddled her thumbs, careful as to her choice of words. "Well, you know ..."

Wayne smiled at her coyness, knowing that wasn't her usual character. Since working with her on the set, he had become well aware of Leslie's boldness and the natural confidence behind her words. The change in her demeanor was amusing to him.

"Did I do something that I shouldn't have?" He toyed with her. "All I did was pay for a slice of veggie pizza."

Although Wayne was certain that Leslie wasn't interested in him, that still didn't deter his desire to be with her. No more than it did for the woman who had just entered the restaurant.

Leslie looked behind her to see what Wayne's eyes was fixed on. Without even a glance back at Leslie, Wayne stood up. "I think our food is ready." He then approached the woman who returned his same hungry stare.

*Unbelievable*, she thought.

Leslie watched as Wayne stood with their food in hand while talking to the woman whom he obviously knew. Wayne stared in Leslie's direction and gestured as if he was trying to explain something to the mysterious stranger. Leslie turned back around in her seat and crossed her legs as they walked up to her.

"Leslie, this is Simone, a friend of mine." Wayne introduced the woman. "And Simone, this is Leslie, an actress in that film I'm working on."

Leslie hesitantly nodded. Simone acknowledged her with a smile before she whispered into Wayne's ear. Wayne placed the food on the table and watched as the woman walked away. Simone grabbed a bag from the cashier and winked at Wayne on her way out of the restaurant.

"Girlfriend?" Leslie inquired as she slid her pizza in front of her.

Wayne sat down and grinned. "No."

Leslie peered at him skeptically, and then down at her plate.

"What does it matter anyway?" Wayne questioned with a smirk on his face. "You're obviously not interested ... not in me anyway."

Leslie looked up from her plate with an inquisitive glare. "What's that supposed to mean?"

Wayne chuckled as he pushed a straw into his cup of lemonade. "Leslie, the entire set can see that you have a thing for Wendell." He complacently shrugged. "I just thought I'd give it a shot."

She blankly stared at him.

"Hey, you can't fault a brother for trying." He then smiled at her. "You are one beautiful woman, but you don't stand a chance against his girlfriend."

"Girlfriend? I didn't know that he had a girlfriend." She unconsciously admitted her feelings through her reaction.

"See, I knew you had a thing for him," Wayne said as a wave of jealousy came over him. "Well, you may as well give me a chance since you don't have one with him."

"Who is she? Someone on set?" she probed, ignoring Wayne's flirtatious behavior.

"Oh, you've seen her on set alright," Wayne hinted. "She's the one who's sat in the back on and off when we first started filming, barely saying anything. She hasn't been there over the past couple of weeks, but they're still together." He ardently worked to get Leslie to see that she didn't have a fighting chance with Wendell just as she had done with him.

"Oh, I didn't know she was his girlfriend. Well ... I wasn't sure." Leslie looked away.

"If you asked me, she's got nothing on you," Wayne said, hating that Leslie preferred his business partner over him. "But hey, it's Wendell's loss, right?" He gave her a lingering stare, and then picked up a slice of his pepperoni pizza.

Leslie fell silent and picked at her food.

The resentment Wayne harbored against Wendell was unjustified. He envied the fact that Wendell knew a slew of prominent backers and seasoned contacts in the movie industry. To know that Wendell held the attention of a woman he wanted as a personal conquest only fueled his jealousy. He hoped that one day he wouldn't need Wendell or Michael to help him get a movie off the ground. And Wayne was determined to make that day come sooner than later.

Ever since Wendell had shared with Wayne the names of a couple of the silent partners for his current film project, Wayne had secretly begun submitting correspondence to them for his own independent picture. Wendell had shared with Wayne, as well as Michael, a fresh idea for a new film. Unbeknownst to Wendell, Wayne maliciously passed the idea off as his own to those silent partners Wendell had told him about in confidence. It was only a matter of time before he heard back from some of them about the project he desperately wanted to start before Wendell made his new venture public.

"I guess some guys just like young women." Wayne grinned under his breath.

"I suppose ... she's probably twenty or so." She then suddenly realized what he had just said. "Wait a minute. Are you calling me old?" Leslie questioned, staring at him as if he had just assaulted her. "Hey, I'm only twenty-eight years old. Most people think that I'm as young as she is."

"Well, you'd have to drop a few more years." He smirked. "Kara's only a teenager."

"*A teenager?*"

"Yes, a teenager."

"*She's just a child,*" Leslie huffed.

"Tell me about it, but the law says differently. At seventeen you can do just about anything." He picked up his drink and slurped from the straw. "But you on the other hand are definitely all woman."

Leslie rolled her eyes at him and dismissively said, "Yeah, just like the woman who was here not even five minutes ago?"

"But that was my sister." His lie was unbelievable.

"Whatever," Leslie said, annoyed with him. "And how do you know that she's seventeen?"

"Well, she's graduating this year. I just kind of figured. Seventeen, eighteen what does it matter, she's still a teenager."

Leslie sat back in her seat and folded her arms.

"But I must say that the girl has her stuff together."

"What are you talking about?"

"Well, from what Wendell tells me, she's applying to Juilliard." Wayne then smugly added, "I've heard her play and the girl's got skills."

Leslie dropped a crumpled piece of napkin onto the table as she scooted her chair backward. "Look, I have to get back to work." She stood and grabbed her small purse. "Thanks for lunch."

Wayne nodded as he swallowed the food in his mouth. "No problem." He then scrambled to his feet. "Maybe we can do it again."

Leslie didn't reply. She simply turned and walked in the opposite direction towards the exit. With a determined glare on her face she thought, *no teenager is going to stand in my way*.

# CHAPTER 23

FRANKLIN SIGHED IN relief as he peered out of the living room window at the parked vehicle, then allowed the drapes to fall across the window. After making a quick call to Douglas, he placed the cordless phone on an end table and walked out the front door. His smile brightened as the cab driver sat Talia's bags on the sidewalk.

"Thank you, I'll take it from here," Franklin said as he pulled some cash from his pocket and slid it into the driver's palm.

Talia secured her purse across her shoulders as she met her husband at the gated entrance. "Hi."

"Well, hello to you too." He looked her over with an endearing smile, and then warmly hugged her. "I almost called your mother to make sure you didn't miss your flight." His eyes momentarily shifted to the taxicab that drove out into traffic.

"Well, you don't have to call my mother," she griped, and then snidely added, "I have a phone."

"Yes, I know, but it was turned off."

"Oh ... my battery must be dead." Talia quietly cleared her throat as she walked past him toward the front steps. "I'll use the house phone to call Douglas to let him know that I'm here."

"I already phoned," Franklin quickly spoke. "After I saw the cab pull up, I called him. He'll be back after picking Melissa up from school."

Talia slowly nodded as she walked through the front door. She started up the stairs and momentarily peered back where Franklin walked closely behind carrying her luggage. He smiled, but she looked away, unable to bear looking at him. After the forbidden, yet passionate night she had spent with Donovan, guilt penetrated her soul.

When they reached their master suite, she shed her coat and asked Franklin to place her suitcase on the bed. He followed her instructions and then took her in his arms again.

"Hmm, you smell good," Franklin moaned as he massaged his wife's shoulders and kissed the nape of her neck. "I'm glad to have you home." Her hair felt like silk between his fingers.

"Please don't ..." Talia uneasily rolled her shoulders backward as she squirmed away from him. "I'm a little tired. I just want to get unpacked and settled."

"Oh ... okay." Franklin lightly rubbed his hands together as he took a step backward. "So, uh, how was the trip with your mother?"

"The trip was nice." Talia avoided eye contact with Franklin as she leaned over and unzipped her suitcase. He on the other hand studied her movements. "She's looking forward to visiting again this spring."

"That's good." Franklin sat down on the bed next to Talia's suitcase and watched as she paced back and forth between the bed and dresser. On the third trip, she pulled off her high-heels and tossed them into the walk-in closet. Her movements were mechanical as she indeed appeared to be worn-out. Talia's eyes were puffy, and it wasn't normal for her to go out in public without any make-up. To Franklin she was still beautiful, more attractive than when she wore lipstick and foundation, but today her pure look was somewhat contaminated.

"She said to tell you hello and not to be a stranger."

Franklin slowly nodded, noting the melancholy in his wife's voice. The coldness of her actions reminded him that this was still a difficult time of the year for her.

"It was good to spend some more time with Mother."

"Did you visit your father's grave?" He treaded gingerly on the subject.

"You know I always do." Talia sighed as she placed her jewelry box inside of the armoire. "But Mama didn't go with me to the mausoleum this time."

"Why not?"

"Well, you know her. Maybe she didn't want to see me in tears." Talia complacently shrugged as she reached into her suitcase again.

Franklin pulled his wife towards him and hugged her as he stood. "I'm sorry, sweetheart. I knew that you missed your father, but I didn't know that it still bothered you so much."

"I'm fine." Talia gently moved away from him again, despite the fragrance of her favorite cologne on his skin. "It's just that the memories become so fresh when I'm down there visiting. The house holds constant reminders that just make me miss him all over again as if he'd just died." Talia resumed pulling items from her suitcase as Franklin looked on. "I don't care what anyone says, *time* does not heal all wounds," she said in a slightly irritated tone.

Franklin nodded as he sat back onto the bed. "You're right about that. Time doesn't heal all wounds, baby, God does."

"*Could you not call me that?*" Talia snapped. "I'm not a baby, I'm a grown woman. Just call me by my name." She grunted as she cut her eyes away from him.

Franklin suspiciously gazed at his wife. He quickly recognized that his gentle words were not going to soften her sour mood. Talia had been home no more than fifteen minutes but was already behaving as if she wanted to leave again. Being the kindhearted man that he was, Franklin had cut his workday short to spend some time with her. Reservations had been made at her favorite restaurant and he had even placed a sparkling new Tiffany's bracelet in her top drawer. Over the past few weeks, he had missed Talia terribly and desperately wanted to make up for the time they had been apart.

"What's going on with you?" he questioned, discarding the compassion from his voice. "You've never acted this way before about my calling you *baby*."

"Nothing is going on with me. I just don't like you calling me that," she argued.

"Well, it never bothered you before." He frowned, suspicious of the unwarranted anger in her voice.

"That's right, *Franklin*, there are a lot of things that never bothered me before that do now," she scoffed and looked at him with disgust.

"What are you talking about?" His brows puckered.

"For starters, what's this?" She grabbed his side and squeezed.

He instinctively pushed her hand away.

"Just look at you. You have fat everywhere!"

Franklin swallowed his humiliation. He was taken aback by her rage.

"I mean, you don't even workout anymore. You used to be in better shape than me, but lately you act as if you're allergic to a treadmill!"

"*Because I've put on a few pounds you're angry*?" His voice had lowered to a raspy grunt.

"Franklin, it's more than just your weight, I'm tired of you trying to control my every move."

"Talia, you just got home after being gone three weeks! What are you talking about *control your every move*? How can I control you when you're hardly here?" Franklin shook his head and paced to the other side of the room. "No, there's more to this." He stared her in the eyes, reluctant to face his suspicions about her. "What is going on with you?"

"*What's going on with me*?"

Franklin glared at her and said through clenched teeth, "*Yes*, please tell me."

"I just told you." She angrily stared back at him. "Why are you questioning me?"

"Because I'm your husband and you're supposed to talk to me!" Franklin pounded on his chest.

Suddenly, there was a beep from the alarm control panel in their room.

Both Franklin and Talia stared at one another, realizing that Melissa had arrived home. Franklin cleared his face of all distressing emotions and started for the bathroom. Talia sighed as she propped a hand on her hip. He abruptly stopped at the door and faced his wife.

In a much calmer voice, he said, "I thought our relationship, *our marriage*, was for better or worse. Most people fight over much deeper issues like infidelity," he paused with a sigh, "but we've even managed to get past that."

Talia's eyes shifted away and landed on the familiar photo Franklin kept on the nightstand. She folded her arms and gently shook her head. He was not the same man as when they first met and nor was she the same woman. Talia desired different things in life than her husband. They had both grown over the years, but regrettably it was apart.

"But if my weight is really a problem for you, I'll lose it." Franklin dragged his hand down across his mouth. He exhaled a deep breath and then admitted, "Because I love you." He stared at her and compassionately repeated, "*I love you, Talia.*"

With slightly parted lips, Talia's arms drifted to her sides as he closed the door behind him. She collapsed onto the bed and dropped her head into the palms of her hands. She was torn on the inside and sniffled uncontrollably as tears fell from her eyes.

Through her blurred vision, she looked back at the closed bathroom door and sorrowfully whispered, "*But I don't love you....*"

# CHAPTER 24

KARA CLOSED THE black metal mailbox scribed with white stenciled letters. She glanced back to the dirt road she had just walked down and raised her hand to a relative who drove speedily past Frieda's house. Kara smiled as she had just ended a busy day herself with cousins, now retiring to her aunt's home on the brink of dusk. The tall, oak trees had cast their shadow over the close-knit community and the beautifully adorned street lamps were just illuminating. Kara stood amid the serene setting and exhaled. Aside from being near Wendell, she didn't miss New York at all. It was good to be home.

As a nostalgic glow floated across her face, Kara patted the letters against her thigh and carried them inside of the house. The appetizing aroma of fried fish soon infiltrated her nostrils. She closed her eyes and remembered what it was like to come home to her mother's cooking. Aside from the way Gwendolyn used to design her own clothing, Frieda seemed identical to her in every other way.

"Another long day with your cousins?" Frieda looked at Kara as she walked into the apple orchard themed kitchen. "You've been home for a week now and we've barely had a chance to really talk other than that first night." She smiled, revealing a gold trimmed tooth as she carefully lowered cornmeal battered fillets into a pan of piping hot grease. "I thought we were going to catch up."

Kara nodded with a tender smile on her face. She had been home for exactly one week and nearly two full days. And ever since she arrived in her hometown it had been like a nonstop carousel of sleepovers, skating dates, and sightseeing of the festive Christmas lights draped around town.

"I'm sorry, Aunt Frieda. You know how things are with Kendra and Monica when I come home." Kara placed the mail onto the kitchen counter. "But tonight they have dates and I don't want to play the third wheel."

"Those girls have dates on Christmas Eve?" Frieda said in a high-pitched tone. "Things sure have changed since I was a teenager." She shook her head as she turned around to face the stove again. "Christmas Eve, *as well as Christmas*, was a time for family."

"So, you and Mama weren't allowed to have boyfriends?" Kara giggled as she took a seat.

" *Well*, I wouldn't exactly say that," she replied with a slight chuckle. "We had friends, but they had to court us at home where Daddy could keep an eye on things." Frieda smiled with a wistful twinkle in her eyes.

"You mean you dated more than one guy at a time?" Kara joked as she tugged at her sleeves and climbed out of her coat. "Wow, y'all weren't playing around."

With a metal spatula in her hand Frieda pointed at Kara while she propped the other hand on her hip. "Now you know that's not what I meant. Gwen had her friend and I had mine. *One* each." She chuckled, holding up a single finger for effect before she faced the stove again. "Anyway, the only man I've ever dated was your uncle Simon."

Kara smiled as she understood her uncle Simon was the only man in Frieda's life. The pictures from childhood and school dances served as proof. Simon had been a permanent fixture in their family for decades.

"I sure hope things work out for me and Wendell like they have for you and Uncle Simon."

"Let me tell you, we've had our ups and downs," Frieda admitted, splitting her attention between her niece and the stove. "We've gotten through them, but it hadn't been as easy as it may look. I guess what I'm saying is to be careful what you ask for." She tipped her head at Kara, driving her point home. "So, things are pretty serious between you and, uh, Wendell?"

"Yes ma'am," Kara shyly answered, intentionally neglecting to reveal Wendell's age. "I understand what you're saying. Trust me, Wendell is a really good person. Someone I can talk to about just anything."

"I'm glad, Kara. You've always been a good judge of character. As long as he's a true Christian, he'll treat you the way that you're supposed to be treated."

"Oh, yes ma'am! He's a true Christian," Kara defended her boyfriend. "We talk about God and how Jesus is the foundation of our lives." The excitement grew in her voice. "Not to mention how supportive he is of my musical career. I think he's as excited about my applying to Juilliard as I am." She bubbled with enthusiasm.

Frieda grinned as she wiped her hands on a red and white checkered dishtowel that hung from the stove handle. "I'm so proud of you, Kara. Just think, this time next year you'll be a freshman in college." She then adjusted the layers of paper towels inside of a large foil pan in preparation to receive the final batch of cornmeal battered fish fresh from the sturdy black skillet. "Gwen would just be beside herself with happiness if she could see you now."

Kara nodded, optimistic about her future and how much she was still encouraged by both her mother and father's words. And she was even more grateful to have family like Frieda and Simon, carrying the torch her parents once had. If she hadn't had the support of relatives like them, while dealing with the likes of Miriam, Kara would have given up a long time ago.

"So, do you need any help with dinner?" Kara walked to the kitchen sink and rolled up her sleeves.

"Oh no, I have everything under control." Frieda waved the dish towel in her direction.

Kara scrubbed her hands with soap underneath the running water. "What about for tomorrow's dinner?" she questioned, looking over to the clear canister of flour and white bowl of boiled sweet potatoes. "I can't cook like you, but I can surely bake."

"Trust me, I remember." Frieda peered at her with a knowing smile. "To be so young, you sure bake like nobody's business."

They both erupted into laughter.

"But no, don't you worry about it. All I have to do is finish the filling for the sweet potato pies and cook a pot of rice," Frieda said as she checked the collard greens simmering on the back burner.

"Okay, just remember that I offered," Kara surrendered, playfully backing away with raised arms.

"Oh, there'll be plenty for you to help with. After dinner tonight, you can help with the pile of dishes that'll be stacked in the sink," Frieda countered.

Kara laughed as she pointed a finger at Frieda. "I knew there was a reason why you didn't care about my helping to cook. Well, I don't mind washing dishes. It's almost second nature for me to clean anything that looks dirty. Sometimes, I feel like Cinderella without even a ball to go to living with Miriam."

Frieda couldn't even force herself to smile at Kara's wisecrack. It pained her to know that her niece was going through such sibling rivalry with her sister. She and Gwen had their moments growing up, but never encountered such hatred as what Kara had described upon arriving back home last week.

"Have you spoken to Miriam at all this week?"

Kara scowled as she shook her head. "*No* ... besides I have nothing to say to her."

Frieda slowly looked away to the window over the sink, wearing a faraway gaze.

"I think I'm going to move out when I get my trust money." Kara sat at the counter and twiddled her thumbs. "You know, if I had it now, I wouldn't even go back to that apartment ... other than to get my things and leave again."

Frieda met Kara's pensive stare that further emphasized her point.

"Well baby, it won't be long now," Frieda commented as she walked back towards the counter. "Your birthday is just around the corner."

"I know, and I can't wait to get out of there," Kara stressed with a frown still etched on her face. "But enough about her, I want to enjoy my break." She lightheartedly chuckled, pulling her hair up into a clip retrieved from her coat pocket. "Anyway, will Samuel be able to make it home for New Year's? A few days ago he still wasn't sure."

"Oh, Sam will make it home," Frieda spoke optimistically of her only child. "He may not be here for New Year's Day, but I'm sure he'll find a way to see you before you leave town."

"I sure hate that he couldn't come home for Christmas. There's never a dull moment with him. He keeps me laughing around the clock even when I don't feel like it," Kara reminisced. "Man, that job of his doesn't let up."

"Well, the hospital is a twenty-four seven operation," Frieda quipped, proud of her son. "But he enjoys it, nonetheless. Being an anesthesiologist is a dream come true for him."

"Yeah, I know. Hopefully, he can make it to my graduation this spring."

"We all plan to be there. You know I wouldn't miss it for anything, Lord willing."

Kara smiled knowingly as she peered down at her cell. She had phoned Melissa two days ago and when she returned her call, they had only talked for mere minutes before Phillip interrupted the conversation by beeping in on the other line. It was hard for Kara to bring up the subject about

Talia, but when she finally gathered the nerve to say something it was trumped by Melissa ending their call to take Phillip's.

"*Oh no*," Frieda gasped as she stared into the fridge. "How could I forget the butter?"

"Can't you borrow from somebody?"

"A stick or two, maybe, but not a whole two boxes." Frieda pushed the fridge's door closed in frustration and looked up at the wall clock. "I can still make it to the store before it closes in an hour." Frieda unraveled the strings of her apron and hurriedly tossed it aside. "Did you want to ride with me?"

Kara twisted her lips to one side, contemplating the commercial frenzy of Christmas Eve. The mere thought of the commotion reminded her too much of the busyness she had temporarily escaped.

"Traffic ... last minute shoppers? Uh, I think I'll pass." Kara shook her head and glanced down at her cell again. "Besides, I can get some practice in on the piano."

Frieda nodded as she pulled her coat from the hallway closet. "Okay then. You'll have the place all to yourself for a little while." She glanced at the clock again. "Simon isn't due home for another forty-five minutes to an hour or so. He got a call and went out just before you came in."

"Again?" Kara questioned. "It seems like every time I come home, he's always so busy."

"I know, baby. But being that it's Christmas tomorrow, he'll be here all day." And then with a smile she added, "I'll see to it personally." After she put her coat on, Frieda hugged Kara from the back around the shoulders.

"What was that for?" Kara turned around on the counter stool and peered at her aunt.

"No reason, other than I'm glad you're home," Frieda said as she fastened the buttons on her coat. "And that I love you."

After a slight pause, Kara replied, "I love you too." Oddly enough, she hadn't realized how much she really needed to hear those words.

"Well, if you're hungry now feel free to get a piece, *or two*, of fish. There's green lettuce as well as potato salad in the fridge."

"But I thought the potato salad was for tomorrow." Kara walked over to the fridge and tugged on the door handle.

"Child, you know I always make an extra bowl for the house," Frieda reminded her.

"Oh yeah, I should have known." Kara giggled as she pulled the smaller of the two bowls of potato salad from the refrigerator and placed it on the counter. "There's only one thing missing."

"What's that?"

"Those pecan Danishes from the downtown bakery."

"*Oh, I know.* Too bad the place closed down last year." Frieda adjusted her purse onto her shoulder. "When old lady Helen took sick, her nephew just couldn't run the place from out of town. And then when she died, everything about the business sort of died right along with her."

"Those Danishes were the best with vanilla ice cream," Kara moaned, practically salivating. "I sure miss it."

"Well, after you try my crust covered sweet potato pie with ice cream, those Danishes will be a distant memory."

Both Kara and Frieda laughed.

"I better get out of here before that store closes on me." Frieda grabbed the keys from her purse and walked towards the door.

"Okay Auntie, see you when you get back." Eagerly anticipating the home-cooked meal, Kara piled a healthy helping of potato salad onto a bed of green lettuce. Beside it she placed a golden piece of fried whiting fish.

Frieda placed a hand on the doorframe as she stalled at the kitchen entryway.

Kara stared at her and questioned, "What is it?"

Frieda shook from her daze and responded with an unpersuasive smile, "Oh sweetie, it's nothing for you to be concerned about."

"Are you sure?" Kara suspiciously questioned, temporarily abandoning the focus on her meal.

"Yes, I'm sure," she replied, this time with renewed confidence. "I'm just glad that you're home."

"I am too, Auntie."

Frieda raised a hand to Kara and quickly disappeared to the living room and then behind the front door.

There was something different about her aunt, something that made Kara grateful again that she had decided to visit Mississippi this Christmas. Time was dwindling for her to return to New York City, but as she gazed at the plate of food in front of her, Kara was determined to savor every moment she had left.

It was the break she had prayed for, and she was going to enjoy it.

# CHAPTER 25

"I CAN'T BELIEVE he did that to me," Marissa cried into Helen's ear. "He's met my kids and even gone to church with me." Her tears rolled uncontrollably down her flushed cheeks. "And to think he would do this right before Christmas," she balled.

Helen rubbed the shoulders of her dear friend, consoling her the best way she knew how. After a romantic dinner with her husband, Vincent, leaving his side to see about Marissa was one of the last things she wanted to do. Especially since this was one of those rare moments when they had the house to themselves for a few quiet hours. Over the past week, family members had arrived in town for the Christmas occasion.

"I'm so sorry, Helen. I know Vincent just got home again, but I couldn't reach Talia and I didn't have anyone else to call," she sniffled. "Thank God the kids are with their father until tomorrow. I couldn't bear to let them see me like this." Marissa dabbed her nose with a crumpled piece of tissue. "How could I be so naïve thinking he would be the one?"

Helen pulled a fresh piece of tissue from the nearby holder and handed it to her friend. "You were not naïve, Marissa. I guess I should have just left well enough alone. I practically pushed you two together. I am so sorry," Helen apologized, and then wrapped her arms around Marissa's shoulders.

Marissa waved her hand to the contrary. "No, no it's not your fault." She then discarded the overused piece of tissue in a small waste basket beside a wooden end table. "I'm a big girl. I just moved too fast," she sighed and shook her head, "like I always do. If I had only taken things a little slower or—"

"Why are you blaming yourself?" Helen questioned. "What happened exactly? You said that he broke it off, but why? Did Donovan say anything about this sudden change of heart?" she relentlessly grilled.

After a deep breath, Marissa nodded. "Yes, he said there was someone else." She folded her arms and slowly walked towards the fireplace. "He admitted that he was sorry, but he cared too much for this woman to let her go and too much about me to string me along."

"The nerve of that guy," Helen said through tight lips. "Who does he think he is? He's acting as if he was doing you a favor."

"I know right." Marissa's confidence slowly returned. "I don't know who this woman is, but she has got some hold over him. I just don't understand when he's had time to see her. We've been out on dates just about every other day," she explained, gesturing with her hands. "When he wasn't over here, I was with him ... or on the phone. Everything seemed fine when he left for his hometown, but after he came back last week to pick up a few important items and release his crew until after the New Year, I don't know, things just changed."

"Changed how?" Helen questioned.

"For starters, we didn't even talk, let alone see each other right after he got back. I spoke to him before he boarded the plane, but not even a word from him until a couple days later."

"Are you serious?"

"Yes, so you can imagine what a wreck I was." Marissa sighed. "I didn't know if he had missed the flight, if there was an accident, or if he was in the hospital somewhere."

"So, what did he say when you did talk to him?"

"At first, there was nothing said about another woman, I'll tell you that," Marissa grumbled as she gave Helen a knowing look. "He took me out to lunch the next day and said that he was tied up and that's why he hadn't called me. He wasn't very talkative, but things seemed somewhat okay, you know. I just didn't press the issue." She shrugged her shoulders as if to get compliance from Helen that she was right for not interrogating him. "I figured he had a lot on his mind about work, so I didn't think too much of it. But when I received a text that he needed to talk to me about something important, I left my desk at work and called him right away."

"And this was today?" Helen stared at her through slightly squinted eyes.

"Yes, about an hour before I got off from work. Since things were really slow there, we talked." Her words momentarily diminished. "But if I knew that he was going to say what he said, I would've waited until I got home. It was so hard to keep a straight face in front of my coworkers. *Could you imagine?*"

Helen shook her head as she shifted her eyes in another direction. "No ... I couldn't."

Marissa placed a hand on her hip and the other on the beautifully decorated fireplace mantel. "What does she have that I don't?" A million questions poured from her eyes. "I mean, is there something wrong with me? I'm not fat, I'm not lazy, and I don't think I'm clingy." She then flippantly bragged with a mischievous grin, "And I have my own money ... thanks to my ex-husband."

Helen shook her head and playfully rolled her eyes at the light-hearted break in her friend's tireless rant.

"But seriously, do you think it's because I have children and he doesn't?"

"Now Marissa, you know what I've told you about that." Helen pointed a finger at her. "If a man can't accept your children, then he can't really accept you. Besides, if that was the reason, why would he have dated you for this long?"

"Honestly Helen, I don't know. I'm just confused ... and hurt. I want to be married again so badly." Marissa curled the hand that rested on the fireplace mantel into a fist and slammed it onto the hard surface. "I'm only thirty-eight years old and he's almost fifty! Am I not good enough? I mean who does he think he is?"

Helen stood up and complied, "That's the spirit!" She walked over to where Marissa stood and egged her on, "If he can't see what a gem you are then who needs him?"

Marissa's eyes quickly displayed the recanted thoughts burrowing through her mind. "I do ..." she sniffled.

Helen consoled Marissa as she burst into tears again. It was a good front she had put on, but Helen knew that her friend's façade wouldn't last long. She could tell that Marissa truly cared about this man. Compared to the others she had dated, Marissa often raved that Donovan wasn't a project that she had to mold into a compatible partner. He came as a complete package that treated her like a princess. He bought her flowers on occasions, opened doors and pulled out chairs, and always seemed to have time for her. She couldn't identify one clue that would lead her to believe that Donovan was a player.

After Helen and Marissa retired to the kitchen table, the two spent nearly an hour over cups of hot chamomile tea still discussing the likes of Donovan Carson, despite his sudden departure for another woman. Helen allowed Marissa to empty her emotional vault of the painful remnants Donovan had left behind, although she figured it would be replenished by the time she walked outside to her car. In an attempt to keep that from happening, Helen offered a heartfelt prayer to God on her behalf. It was a genuine request for comfort and peace that caused Marissa's painful tears to transform into redeeming waters.

"Sweetie, please try to get some sleep tonight," Helen said after drawing the prayer to a close. "He doesn't deserve anymore of your tears," she added, holding Marissa's hands. "Christmas is tomorrow and let's just be thankful to God that Donovan decided to walk away before your children got too attached."

"I guess you're right." Marissa met her gaze as she swiped a single finger beneath her eyes. "They've met him, but they're nowhere near being attached. For that I am grateful."

"Good ... well, I better get back to Vincent. His parents are probably back at the house by now and wondering where I am." Helen stood and carried her empty mug to the sink.

"Thanks for coming over. I really appreciate it." Marissa exhaled a deep breath.

"Hey, that's what friends are for. Now come on and walk me to the door."

Marissa gently smiled as she led her friend through the kitchen to the front door.

"Remember to keep your head up and try not to lose any sleep," Helen instructed in a motherly tone.

"Sure, I'll try," Marissa dryly answered as they walked outside. "Who knew that a trip home to Ft. Lauderdale would make him change his mind about us?"

Marissa's rhetorical question lingered a while before Helen asked, "Ft. Lauderdale?"

"Yes, that's where he's from," Marissa clarified. "Too bad I never got a chance to visit. I know Florida has some beautiful weather, aside from those pesky hurricanes of course."

Helen peered at Marissa strangely but kept the recent revelation to herself. She knew that Talia had been home to Ft. Lauderdale recently

and the fact that Donovan had been there too didn't seem like a coinci-
dence.

"Is everything all right?" Marissa questioned, noticing how Helen
lingered at her car, peering off into the night.

"Uh ... yes. Everything is fine," Helen stammered.

She simply told Marissa that she'd call her tomorrow and then quickly
retreated inside of her vehicle. The two women waved to one another as
Helen started the engine.

Just before entering the street Helen dialed Talia's number, but there
wasn't an answer. She cleared the line and thought to herself, *I'm sure I
know who made Donovan change his mind.*

Burdened with suspicion, Helen shook her head and drove home.

# CHAPTER 26

"I PROMISE I won't be in the way, and I'll clean up after myself and everything," Kara tried to persuade Deidra. She held the phone wedged between her shoulder and ear while dutifully wiping down the kitchen countertop. She wanted the kitchen to be spotless when her aunt and uncle returned home since Frieda had gotten up early to prepare one of her famous country breakfasts. "I just can't go back to that apartment. I just can't," Kara protested.

The closer the time neared for her to return to New York, the more urgent it became for her to find another place to live. Kara could no longer fathom the idea of going back to live with Miriam. It became ever so clear when she called her sister at Frieda's urging. The gesture of reconciliation was destroyed when an unfamiliar male's voice answered the phone. This was the final straw for Kara.

"Baby, it's all right, really," Deidra replied. "You don't have to convince me. You are more than welcome to stay for as long as you need to. With this being your last year in school and all, you don't need to deal with all of that stress. You tell your aunt that I'll look out for you like you're my own sister."

"Oh, thank you, Deidra!" Kara exclaimed with relief. "As soon as I get back tomorrow, I'll move some of my things in while Miriam is out shopping."

"Girl, you sure know your sister's schedule like the back of your hand."

"Yeah well, it's practically the same every week. Besides, on the first of the month she never misses a chance to go grocery shopping," Kara scornfully said. "It's beyond me how she eats so much in such a short period of time. It seems like there's never any food in the house."

"Well, she has put on a considerable amount of weight over the past year. And eating like that sure isn't going to help her lose any of it," Deidra offhandedly said. "But anyway, let me go before I'm late for work. I'll have an extra key for you when you get back in town." She then stacked two small plastic containers and a bottle of water inside of her shoulder bag. After grabbing her coat and glancing across her living room once more to ensure she had everything, she said, "Be safe and I'll see you when you get back."

"Thanks, Deidra. See you then."

Kara smiled as she placed her phone on the counter. This New Year was going to be a new start, a fresh start. *Out with the old and in with the new*, she thought. The prospect of attending Juilliard in the fall with Wendell at her side kept her in good spirits, despite her previously depressive state. God was making a way for her. The table prepared before her was definitely a saving grace.

A nostalgic glow crept across Kara's face as she placed a black iron skillet inside of a cabinet beneath the countertop. Breakfast this morning and dinner last night was one she would remember for a long time. Samuel had managed to come home for a couple of days, making Kara's last few nights in town lively ones. She hated to see him go this morning. As Kara thought back to the familiar Gospel hymn, she played on the piano last night, she was still astonished at the sound of her aunt's voice.

Frieda had sung alongside her in perfect pitch and clarity. She was no stranger to singing soul-stirring solos, and Kara knew this, it was *how* she sang the song this time that amazed her. It was as if she was alone, singing directly to the Father. Kara stared at Frieda while Simon and Samuel harmonized in the background, and then she saw her aunt cloaked in peace. It was then that she truly grasped what Frieda had said to her the night after she returned from the store on the evening of Christmas Eve: *In due time baby, God will make all things new.* Considering her own situation, Kara knew those were words to live by.

Startled by the ringing phone, Kara shook from her daze. When she saw that it was her cousin, Monica, calling Kara answered and told her that she'd talk with her and Kendra later in the afternoon. After they made plans to get together later in the evening, Kara resumed her housekeeping duties.

Once she straightened up the guestroom she was staying in, Kara picked up her phone again. Aside from her brief chat with Melissa last night they had barely spoken over the past few days. It had become a frustrating pattern. The secret about Talia was tearing at Kara on the inside and she didn't want to stand by and watch Franklin be made a fool of, especially since he had been so nice to her over the past couple of years. She reasoned that something had to be said.

After casting aside her anxieties, Kara dialed Melissa's number.

"Hey girl, what's going?" Melissa answered on the second ring. "I am so sorry about not calling right back like I said I would, but Phillip—"

"But Phillip called … yeah, I know," Kara finished her sentence.

Melissa laughed, but Kara kept her impassive composure. "So, what's going on?"

Kara swallowed, still searching for the right words to break her silence.

"Are you still there?" Melissa asked.

"I'm here."

"You sound different. Is everything okay?"

Kara sighed as she peeked out of the guestroom window, overlooking the vacant driveway. She didn't expect her aunt and uncle back for another hour or so, which she hoped would give her some uninterrupted time to talk with her best friend.

"Okay Kara, you're concerning me. You rarely have a loss for words. What's going on?" Melissa pressed.

In an attempt to divert attention away from the real reason for her call, Kara questioned, "What's going on with you and Phillip?"

Melissa cackled as if Kara had just cracked a hilarious joke. "What do you mean what's going on with us? You know that we're going together. He's my boyfriend."

"Since when?"

"Oh Kara, stop it. You know that we've been going out and talking for the past month."

"How would I know that if we barely talk anymore?"

"Now you know how it is with boyfriends," Melissa quipped. "I didn't say anything when Wendell gave you that phone and you just kicked me to the curb."

"That's not true, Mel," Kara defended herself. "Between practicing and school, we don't talk that much."

"Well, Phillip helps me with studying." Melissa's voice turned serious. "Besides that, I try to make it to his games. You know, just like you going to Wendell's film shoots."

Kara disregarded Melissa's last statement, and then asked, "Have you told your mother about him?"

"Uh, *no*," Melissa sarcastically answered. "She doesn't need to know right now. I'm about get up out of this house and be on my own ... I'll tell her then. I don't need her trying to break us up."

"Are you ashamed of Phillip?"

"What kind of crazy question is that?" Melissa scoffed. "You mean because he's from the projects? Kara, have I ever been ashamed of you? Come on, where is this coming from?"

Kara inhaled a deep breath as she prepared to tell Melissa about the deep, dark secret that had relentlessly troubled her over the past couple of weeks.

"Uh, *hello*? Are you going to say something?"

"Mel, I have something to tell you."

"Well ... what is it?"

Kara sighed. "It's about your mother."

"*My mother*? What about my mother?"

"I ... I think she's cheating on your dad," Kara blurted out.

Kara explained about seeing Talia at the airport when she was leaving for Mississippi. She described how she attempted several times to tell her, but she was either on the phone with Phillip or out with him.

"You spend so much time with him that I've barely had a chance to talk to you."

"Are you for real?" Melissa nervously scoffed. "I don't believe you would go this far to keep me away from Phillip."

"*What*?" Kara gasped. "Keep you away from Phillip?" Folds of skin gathered on her forehead.

"I thought he was your friend. Now it makes sense why you tried to keep us apart that time I had Douglas drop you off at home," Melissa carried on. "But I never thought you ... *you* of all people would stir up such vicious lies about my mother because I now spend more time talking to him than you," she huffed. "You know, Phillip told me about the time you thought he got that girl pregnant."

"That's what Shantel said," Kara quickly defended herself again against Melissa's accusations. "And-and I apologized to Phillip for that."

"Oh yeah, he told me that you said you were sorry, but now you think you saw my mother at the airport with another man. Are you going to later say you're sorry for that too?" Melissa sucked her teeth. "What's next, Kara?"

"*I did see her*," Kara insisted. "Why would I make something like that up?"

"I don't know why, but what I do know is that you're no friend of mine," Melissa argued. "My father is a trustee in the church and my mother has been married to him for almost twenty years! *Are you crazy?*" The sound of her voice maliciously darkened. "I've given to you and given to you, and now you come at me with this ... *this mess!*"

"*Melissa—*"

"No, don't you say another word to me! If you know what I know, you better be worried about that Leslie woman trying to get with Wendell and leave my parents' marriage alone." Melissa grunted. "You know, maybe my mother was right about you ... maybe you just want the life that I have."

"Mel, how could you say that to me?" Kara tried to reason with her. "We're best friends."

"No, we *used to be* best friends. I'll give your best friend bracelet to Phillip for you—"

"But ... but that's yours..."

"Not anymore. You can just find somebody else to give it to because I've got nothing else to say to you!" Melissa hung up the phone and threw it on her bed.

Melissa marched to the other side of the room and snatched the doors to her armoire open. After rummaging through the contents of her black velvet encased jewelry box, she clutched her half of the BEST FRIENDS ornament that dangled from a silver bracelet. Melissa unfolded her hand and stared at the engraved word FRIENDS on the half of the silver heart she had had for over two years. As it rested in the center of her open palm all sorts of mixed emotions invaded her heart, but the one that overpowered the others was pain.

"Knock, knock, sweetheart," Franklin said as he stood outside of Melissa's open door. "Is everything all right?"

Melissa discreetly cleared the pooled tears from underneath her eyes, and then turned to her father. "Uh yeah, sure ... why?"

"Well," Franklin started as he wiped his dampened forehead and cheeks with a short beige towel, "when I got upstairs, I could hear you yelling all the way from the second floor." He had just finished a stringent work-out in their home gym.

"You eavesdropped on my conversation?" Melissa carefully asked.

"No, I didn't eavesdrop in my own house." Franklin glared at her as he draped the towel across his left shoulder. "You were just loud."

"I'm sorry, Daddy," Melissa quietly sighed.

Franklin's glare melted away. "Besides, I couldn't make out what you were saying, but it's pretty obvious that you were upset with that person. Who in the world were you talking to?"

"An *old* friend." Melissa indifferently shrugged as she sat on the edge of her bed. "Someone who doesn't matter anymore. I can't stand when people lie to me." She simply couldn't fathom the idea of her mother cheating on her father. "But that's the past now." After exhaling a cleansing breath, Melissa stared at Franklin's sweat suit. "So, I see you've started your New Year's resolution early," she said in a feeble attempt to erase the upsetting thoughts from her mind.

Franklin nonchalantly nodded. "Something like that ... but hey, don't go changing the subject on me. Who was the old friend? It wasn't Quentin, was it?" Franklin raised an eyebrow. "I've noticed how much time you've been spending talking to that Phillip guy."

"Oh Daddy, don't worry, my grades are still up." She somewhat blew him off with a casual wave of her hand. "He's not a bad influence, you know. He's smart, athletic, and your favorite—well-mannered."

Franklin cast a smirk in his daughter's direction. "Well-mannered, huh? Well, we'll see about that. Just remember, no dates until I meet him for myself."

"Daddy, for the *umpteenth time* I know...." Melissa then looked away, wondering how she was going to pull off seeing Phillip now that she's torn Kara from her life. She was always able to justify her frequent interest in the local high school basketball games because one of Kara's friends was playing. But as of five minutes ago, things had drastically changed between them.

"I know you know, but do you hear me?"

"*Yes, I hear you,*" she groaned, folding her arms across her chest.

Franklin stepped inside Melissa's room, still with a considerable amount of distance between them. "Look, I know you're older and will soon be making decisions for yourself. I just want to protect you."

She looked up at him. "Daddy, I've heard this speech before."

Franklin took another step closer. "I know you hear me, but are you listening? I'm a man, but I was once a teenaged boy too." He lowered his chin, still maintaining eye contact with her. "I know what most teenaged boys see in teenaged girls."

Melissa gasped. "*Daddy.*"

"No, hear me out," he insisted. "Phillip may be a nice guy, but is he saved? What do you know about him other than being a great basketball player? Where does he go to church? Does he even go to church?"

Melissa parted her lips at a loss for words. She soon realized that her father was right; she had never discussed Jesus with Phillip. They had great conversations and a ton of things in common, but it hadn't crossed her mind to investigate his spiritual life. She knew that was something she'd have to address.

"Baby-girl, if you really want to date him, he has to see me first. I mean it."

"Even if he lives in the projects?" Melissa stared at her father with suspicion in her eyes. "If you approve, then what about Mom?"

Franklin stood with his hands parked at his waist, contending with his emotions. He knew Melissa was well aware of how he didn't contest Talia's decision to bar Kara from their home. He had simply decided to let his wife have her way even though he felt that her reasons were wrong. As Franklin pondered his daughter's query even further, he supposed this was why Talia so often lashed out at him—he had allowed her to.

When he questioned or challenged her decisions, she often defied his authority.

"*Dad*, did you hear me?" Melissa drew him back into the conversation.

Franklin peered at his daughter as he answered, "Loud and clear."

"So, do you really want to meet him?"

"Of course I do."

"Really?" Melissa's eyes brightened. "You mean it?"

"Yes, I mean it. How about this weekend?" Franklin improvised. "Sunday after church he can have dinner with us ... I'll talk to your mother about it."

"Oh thanks, Daddy!" Melissa hugged him, but then grimaced as she backed away. "Whew, you must've had a hard workout." She playfully waved her hand in front of her face.

"It did have me practically out of breath," Franklin confessed as he flapped his arms like chicken wings.

"Daddy!" Melissa screeched. She pushed her father away while fanning a notebook in his direction. "Whew!"

"What, you don't like it?" he joked.

"No!" she playfully shouted.

Talia appeared on the floor by the staircase banister just as Melissa closed Franklin out of her bedroom.

"A little sweat never killed anybody," he called out behind her closed door. Franklin swiped his forehead and chuckled. As he turned away from the closed door, he met eyes with his wife. Surprised by her sudden appearance, Franklin paused momentarily. "Hey." The happiness quickly drained from his voice.

Talia reluctantly smiled. "Hi." Her eyes drifted from his, down to the moistened T-shirt he wore. She faintly admired Franklin for his effort to get into better shape, but inwardly felt he would never look as good as Donovan. No matter how hard he tried.

"Well, I better get showered if we're still going out to dinner." Franklin winked.

Talia nodded, but her face was void of emotion. She simply walked past him as she responded, "Okay, I'll be in the computer room. Let me know when you're ready."

Before Franklin could say anything else to her, she was behind the closed glass doors opposite to the terrace where Melissa's room was nestled in between the two. He watched as his wife steadied herself in front of the granite top computer desk and placed her cell phone in the hutch beside the pen and pencil holder. Her freshly curled hair bounced with the slightest move she made, and her make-up—remarkably flawless. Talia was beautiful, but at times Franklin wondered why he tried so hard to please a woman whose love for him seemed to sway whichever way the wind blew, regardless of how attractive she was.

Downtrodden, Franklin slowly looked away as he started for the master suite. He knew there was more to their marital problems than his weight but didn't want to accuse his wife of infidelity without proof. The last time he suspected her of cheating, Talia admitted her adulterous affair. This time Franklin supposed she may not be as forthcoming, ever since he caught her sifting through his financial earnings paperwork the night after she arrived from Ft. Lauderdale. He didn't believe for a moment that she was simply looking for the password to their new joint bank account. He recalled that she had previously admitted to memorizing that code.

Suspicious, Franklin figured that even if Talia had forgotten it, she was well aware that it was Melissa's birthdate. Determined to handle their situation delicately, Franklin cautiously prepared for a romantic evening with his wife.

*Maybe I'm just being paranoid*, he thought. Despite how hard he tried to shake off the notion that his wife was seeing another man, Franklin was making departure preparations of his own. If she was planning to make an exit from their marriage, this time he was not going to be blindsided.

# CHAPTER 27

KARA'S EYES DRIFTED from the attractively arranged bouquet of flowers resting atop the glass shelf in the corner of her aunt's living room to the familiar family portrait hanging on the front wall. As the sun barely penetrated the sheer secondary lining of the embroidered curtains draped over the living room window, the delicious aroma of homemade buttermilk biscuits baked well over thirty minutes ago still lingered in the air.

The peaceful sound of the quiet early morning practically serenaded Kara's ears, aside from Simon's occasional grunting just outside. Kara gazed out of the window behind her and watched as Simon dutifully checked the tire pressure and oil gauge, preparing his truck for the forty-minute drive to the airport. After securing Kara's luggage onto the back seat of the double cab, he wiped his hands on a dark blue handkerchief that hung from the back pocket of his blue jeans. Moments later, he started up the steps to the front porch and then poked his head inside of the house.

"Is Frieda still in the kitchen?" Simon asked Kara.

"No, she went to the restroom."

"Well, I need to fill the truck with gas. Just let her know that I'll be back in about fifteen minutes."

"Okay, I will," Kara answered, splitting her attention between him and the wall clock.

"Did you want anything from the store?" Simon asked while simultaneously glancing down at his cell phone.

Kara shook her head. "No, I'm fine. Thanks."

Simon nodded, placed the phone to his ear, and then closed the door behind him.

Kara sat on the sofa with an elbow resting on the chair arm. Her eyes wandered over to the wall calendar that reminded her once again that it was New Year's Day. This year was going to be a new beginning in more ways than one. Amongst all the good things happening in her life, the fact that she no longer had a best friend overshadowed them all.

"Hey, where's Simon going?" Frieda asked as she entered the room, noticing through the curtains his truck backing out of the front yard.

"Oh, he said to tell you that he was going to get gas." In a melancholy voice, she added, "He'll be back in about fifteen minutes."

Frieda looked at her niece with concern. "Why the long face?"

Kara gently smiled and softly said, "I'm just gonna miss you guys that's all. This visit went by really fast."

"Yes, it did." Frieda nodded knowingly as she took a seat on the sofa next to Kara. "But it was good. You got to see your cousins and I got some extra help in the kitchen," she quipped.

With a grin, Kara replied, "I know, and I enjoyed every minute of it." She then leaned her head on Frieda's shoulder.

"Oh baby," Frieda sighed as she caressed Kara's head. "Maybe things will get better between you and your sister, and you'll enjoy being in the kitchen with her as much as you do with me."

Kara raised her head and responded with a slight grunt, "No, that'll never happen."

"Never say never, Kara." Frieda waved a single finger in her direction. "God has a way of putting people back together. And you know how that is, right?"

Kara wore an expression that sought clarity.

"It's called forgiveness."

With uncertainty in her voice, Kara responded, "Yeah, I know..."

"No matter how bad things may get or seem, you have to forgive Miriam for her actions. One day she'll come around," she spoke optimistically.

"But Auntie, you don't know what it's like living with her," Kara debated her point. "She treats me like a child. I'm practically a grown woman."

"That you are." Frieda smiled as she patted Kara on the knee. "I just hate that it has come to you moving out."

"Well, it'll be better for me to live with Deidra than her. I just can't take it anymore."

"I understand. Deidra's a good person ... I'm sure she'll look out for you." Frieda stood and walked over to the window where she needlessly straightened the overlapping curtain layers. "Before your parents died, I promised your mother that I would look out for you guys."

"Oh, Aunt Frieda, you know you've looked out for me like I was your own daughter. I couldn't have asked for a better aunt."

"Thank you, baby." Frieda glanced back at her. "I'm glad I haven't failed you."

"Failed me? Of course not. Whenever I needed anything, you were there for me. You've always looked out and steered me right." She abruptly paused, and then continued with a smirk, "Even when I didn't want you to." Kara giggled as Frieda smiled. "You may not have always told me things that I wanted to hear, but it was what I needed."

Frieda covered her mouth and fought to stifle the mist clouding her eyes.

"Is everything alright?" Kara walked over to where her aunt stood and placed a palm on her shoulder.

Frieda nodded with an endearing smile as she covered Kara's hand with her own. "I'm fine." She wiped the drops of tears from the corner of her eyes. "It's just that over the years I've come to see all that Gwen has missed." She sniffled in between a couple of disturbing coughs. "You have always been like a daughter to me." She then offhandedly chuckled after clearing her throat. "Isn't it funny? I just asked you why the long face and here I am blubbering like a baby."

"At least you're not jumping for joy to see me go," Kara joked. "It's good to be wanted. We'll see each other soon."

Just then, Simon blew the horn of his truck.

Frieda looked up and stared through the curtains. "Well, you better get going. Men don't keep long waiting in a car." She laughed aloud, but inwardly wondered why Simon was on his phone so early in the morning. "Call me as soon as you get in, sweetie."

"Are you sure that you can't ride with us to the airport?"

Frieda emphatically shook her head. "As much as I would like to, I can't. After my visit with the doctor yesterday morning, I think it's best that I stay out of the cold air. I don't want to make this chest congestion any worse."

"Yeah, you're right," Kara agreed. "So, I'll just give you a call when I get there. I have one connecting flight, but the layover isn't long at all."

"That's good." Frieda hugged and patted her on the back as she said, "You be careful now."

"I will."

At that moment Simon sounded off with his horn again. Frieda and Kara looked at one another with similar amused expressions.

"I better go before he drags me out of this house." Kara laughed.

Frieda smiled as she opened the door and waved at Simon. "She's coming!"

Kara gave her aunt one last hug and hurried to the truck where her uncle waited. The two backed out of the driveway and Frieda waved once more as the vehicle disappeared down the road.

All the way to the airport, Kara thought about Melissa and how angry she sounded on the phone. Never in a million years did she imagine that her best friend would accuse her of lying, let alone jealousy. She had known Phillip for years, even before they had become friends. So, it was beyond her why Melissa would figure that she wanted to keep them apart because she was no longer getting her attention. It was a crazy and downright childish notion in Kara's book. And to mention the fact that Leslie flirted shamelessly with Wendell was an even lower blow. Especially since Melissa knew how she felt about Wendell.

As she boarded the plane, Kara figured that maybe the way she told her friend about Talia was all wrong. She went over and over in her head about how she could have better broken the news to Melissa. No matter what solution she came up with now, it would not change what's already been said and Kara regretted that. Her friendship would never be the same.

Being back in New York City presented so many challenges, but Kara was determined to get through them all. She had a new place to stay and that alone alleviated some of her mounting stress. Although things were strained between her and Melissa, she still had Wendell to lean on. After her plane landed, they talked for a little while, but still she hadn't built up the nerve to confess where she really lived. Kara convinced herself that she just needed to keep this secret from him until they got closer. Wendell obviously cared for her, but Kara wanted to ensure that her address didn't change his feelings about her.

"Hey, young gun," Phillip saluted Kara as the cabbie unloaded her luggage in front of their building. "Did you need some help?"

Immediately drafted back into the argument she had with Melissa the day before, Kara coldly cut her eyes away from Phillip. With stiff shoulders and an attitude to match, she grabbed the handles of her two bags and began to drag them away. "No, I think you've helped enough as it is."

"What's wrong with you?" Phillip grimaced as she shuffled past him. "You take a little plane ride and now you're all of that?"

Kara glared back at him and shook her head. "Whatever ... just leave me alone."

"Girl, what's up with you now?" Phillip's eyebrows furrowed. "We were cool when you left town, but now you're up on this attitude?"

Kara stopped short of the front entrance and faced him. "Phillip, you know, some things are better left unsaid." Then with a snarl in her voice and a bent in her face, she added, "If I haven't learned anything, I've at least learned that."

Phillip stood dumbfounded as she jerked her neck away from him and dragged her bags inside.

When Kara reached her floor, it was as if a dark cloud hovered over her. She pulled in a deep breath and unlocked the door. The lights were off, and the apartment was void of life. As predicted, Miriam was out grocery shopping with the neighbor downstairs. The small notepad she always used to write out her grocery list and red pencil on the kitchen table testified to that fact.

"Good," Kara mumbled to herself. "She's not here."

She hurriedly picked up the phone and dialed Deidra's number. When she answered, Kara asked if she could help her move her clothes and personal items to her apartment. After Deidra agreed that she would be there in five minutes, Kara abandoned her bags at the front door and headed for the bathroom. She cleared her designated shelf in a matter of seconds by sweeping the items inside of a white, plastic bag. Kara then went into her bedroom and secured all her shoes from underneath the bed and trinkets that she had left on the dresser.

Once she had quickly filled an old duffle bag with most of her belongings, Kara realized that her letter pouch mail carrier was missing. She hadn't taken it with her on her trip and distinctly remembered leaving it in the top drawer of her dresser. After searching the four corners of her room, Kara stood in the middle of the floor with folded arms. Letters from Frieda, her cousins, amongst other mail were secured inside of that pouch.

A few moments later, she walked across the short hallway to Miriam's bedroom. Kara cautiously looked to the front of the apartment again before she walked inside of the room. Upon crossing the threshold, she stumbled over a pair of her sister's shoes. Kara regained her balance by placing one hand on the bed to break her fall. She then turned around and flipped the light switch on. The room was a mess. "And she's always on me for keeping the kitchen clean," Kara angrily mumbled to herself.

After tossing aside shoes, papers, and head scarves Kara made her way to the other side of the room, searching for her letter pouch. It was nowhere to be found. Before abandoning her efforts, she opened Miriam's dresser drawers and her forehead wrinkled at what she saw. There were cookie boxes, jarred peanuts, bags of potato chips, and packages of snack-sized candy bars stashed inside. Kara could barely believe her eyes. As far as she knew, Miriam never bought this much food at one time. Or at least she had never seen this much food in the apartment at any given time.

"Hey, what are you doing in here?"

Astonished, Kara looked up and met eyes with Deidra.

"I knocked on the door but came on in since it was open ..." Deidra's words slowed as she walked inside of Miriam's bedroom. Her eyes drifted from Kara's down to the open drawers that housed layers of food inside. "Where did all of this come from?"

Kara's mouth hung open as she shook her head in disbelief. "I ... I don't know." She shoved the top drawer closed and then flung open the closet door. "I just don't believe this."

Deidra and Kara both stared in astonishment at the cans of soup and bottles of soda tucked away in a cardboard box on the floor.

"Oh my goodness." Deidra's eyes widened. "I saw her about an hour ago with the neighbor from downstairs. This is what she must've been helping her to do," she paused, and then met eyes with Kara, "... to hide food from you."

"So, she went shopping early because she knew I was coming back this afternoon. You know, Deidra, this is why I have to get out of here," Kara complained. "This is my sister and look at how she treats me. She's actually been hiding food from me when she gets money for taking care of me." Kara placed a hand on her forehead while the other one rested at her waist as if to calm herself down. She then grunted and waved her hands, signifying that she had had enough. "You know what, it doesn't even matter anymore. Please help me get the rest of my things so I can just get out of here." Kara stormed past Deidra.

Deidra looked on as Kara dragged bags from her bedroom to the front of the apartment. She then looked back at the food Miriam had hidden around the room and shook her head. After closing the closet door and dresser drawers, Deidra turned the lights off before leaving the room.

The two women made several trips back and forth to Deidra's place, carrying as many of Kara's things as they could before Miriam arrived back home. At times Deidra would notice the flushed look on Kara's face, but she didn't say anything about it. She was aware of how her young friend was feeling. After gathering most of her things, Kara locked the door to the residence she once shared with her sister, placed the key inside of her pocket, and followed Deidra back to her apartment.

"Is there anything else that you need to get?" Deidra asked as Kara plopped down on the sofa in the living room.

"No, not right now." She shook her head. "Besides, I have nowhere else to put anything."

They both glanced around at the small apartment Deidra rented and smiled. Kara's things filled the front closet that had been cleared out for her and a corner of Deidra's bedroom. She now had her own drawer in the bathroom and a computer to use that Deidra had bought over the Christmas holiday.

"Well, it's only temporary. Soon, you'll be gracing the campus of Juilliard. Just don't forget about me when you become rich and famous," Deidra joked as she took a seat on the arm of the sofa. "When do you think you'll hear something back?"

"Sometime this month," Kara optimistically said. "I've been practicing practically nonstop and praying about it just the same. People have called me a child prodigy since forever, but I'm smart enough to know that it is only by the grace of God that I have the skills that I have. I don't want to take it for granted."

Deidra nodded in compliance. "That's right, Kara. Keep God first, no matter what, and just do your best. Nobody can ask any more of you."

"I will. Thanks."

"Well," Deidra began as she stood, "I need to run to the grocery store. Are you hungry?"

They both momentarily stared at one another, each remembering the smorgasbord in Miriam's bedroom.

"Since it's been a long day, how about we order in and watch a movie?"

"That sounds good. There's no telling when I'll be able to kick back and relax this semester. Between school, church, and Wendell, my schedule is going to be pretty tight."

"I know what you mean. Having today off is a rare treat. No school or work just doesn't come along every day. Girl, I want to enjoy this." Deidra pulled a folded piece of paper from the kitchen counter and stuffed it into the front pocket of her jeans. She then looked up at Kara with a smile. "Hey, I just had an idea."

"What is it?"

"Why don't you invite your friend over? I don't mind. Besides, I'd love to meet him."

Kara smiled dimly, shifting her eyes away. "Well, I don't know. He's about to start shooting again and when I spoke to him after arriving at the airport, he sounded pretty tired."

"Oh, okay. Well, we can make it a girl's night then." Deidra grabbed her wallet from the dining room table and reached for her leather jacket hanging from the back of a dining room chair.

"Did you want me to come with you to the store?"

"No, that's all right, I won't be long." Deidra slid into her coat and retrieved her keys from the counter. "You've been on a plane half the day and then moving your things for a good part of the other. Relax and help yourself to anything in the fridge. I'll be back shortly."

Ashamed of her thoughts about where she lived, Kara slowly nodded as Deidra left. She knew this was something she'd have to discuss with Wendell ... sometime soon.

# CHAPTER 28

"SERVICE SURE WAS good this morning," Franklin said to Talia on their way out of the sanctuary on this cold Sunday morning. "Well actually, it's always good," he grinned, correcting himself. "Anywhere the presence of the Lord is guarantees a person to be in good company."

Before Talia could respond to her husband, a fellow trustee tapped Franklin on the shoulder. "Glad I didn't miss you. We need you in the back office for a second." He then looked to Talia and Melissa, and said with a smile, "Ladies, I won't keep him long."

Franklin nodded and then turned to his wife. "You and Melissa go on home. Sometimes a second can turn into thirty to forty-five minutes. I'll catch a ride."

"Oh mom, I can drive," Melissa eagerly volunteered.

"I'm sure you can," she answered and then acknowledged Franklin by saying, "Okay, we'll see you at home."

As Franklin walked away, Talia watched as Helen greeted him with a warm hug before strolling in her direction.

"Uh Melissa, go on and pull the car around." Talia quickly retrieved her keys from her purse and handed them to her daughter along with her Bible. "I'll be waiting out front."

Melissa happily took the keys from her mother's hand and waved to Helen on her way out of the church's foyer.

"She's such a mature young lady," Helen complimented as she wiggled her fingers inside of a pair of leather gloves. "I know that you are just absolutely proud of her."

Talia looked to the double glass doors where Melissa had exited the building and then proudly nodded. "Yes, I am. Thank you."

There was an uncomfortable moment of silence between the women, a lingering silence familiar to the one during their last phone conversation a couple of days ago.

"So, did you ever get a chance to talk to Marissa? You know she's still a little down about things ending between her and Donovan."

"No, I haven't spoken to her. I called her yesterday but didn't get an answer."

"Oh, I see." Helen cleared her throat with a slight grunt. "Well, did you leave a message?"

"Uh no, I didn't," Talia answered sharply in a lowered voice. "And what's with the third degree?"

"Why are you so upset?" Helen pleasantly smiled, momentarily making eye contact with some of the patrons who passed them in the busy vestibule. "It was just a question because I'm concerned about *our* friend." Her eyes then pierced Talia's. "She is still your friend, right?"

"What do you mean?" Talia returned her glare. "Of course she's my friend."

"Over here." Helen led Talia off to the side and sighed as she smoothed the fibers of her warm cashmere coat.

"What is it, Helen? What's going on?" Talia defensively asked, folding her arms.

"Donovan," Helen abruptly answered.

"*Donovan?*" she questioned with a scowl. "What ... what about him?"

Helen looked around at the bustling crowd before inching closer to Talia. "Can you really tell me that there's nothing going on between the two of you?" she whispered.

Appalled by the insinuation, Talia propped a hand on her hip. "Of all places, Helen, you're really asking me this in the house of God? You really have some nerve."

In a calm and unwavering tone, Helen responded, "I was hoping that the house of God was one place you wouldn't lie."

"I'm not going to stand here for this." Talia began to walk away.

"She may not be able to see it, but I can," Helen called out behind her. "And one thing's for sure, Franklin will be able to too." The outburst of their conversation caught the attention of several bystanders.

Talia looked back, plastered on a counterfeit smile to deflect Helen's comment, and then quickly slipped out the door. She neared the edge of the walkway where Melissa had just pulled up and hurriedly opened the door.

"So, did you need to go anywhere before—"

"No, Melissa, just drive home," Talia sternly answered.

Melissa's eyebrows furrowed at the tone of her mother's voice. "What did I do?"

With her eyes glued to the outside, Talia stiffly answered, "Nothing, just drive home."

"Well, I needed to stop at the store for some—"

"Melissa, either you drive straight home or get from behind the wheel," Talia snapped.

Melissa's lips parted in confusion. Instead of further infuriating her mother, she simply edged into traffic and drove home. When she parked in front of their house, Melissa peered over at Talia who stepped out of the vehicle with a faraway gaze on her face.

"What's wrong?" Melissa asked as she followed her mother indoors.

"I just have some things on my mind, that's all," Talia said as she stifled the house alarm.

"Well, we're all going to still have dinner together, aren't we?"

Talia slipped off her shoes at the base of the stairs, securing one hand on the banister. "I don't know, I'm thinking about having brunch with a friend."

"But we always eat Sunday dinner together."

Talia faced her daughter. "Well, not today. I'm going out." She then started up the stairs.

"But you're supposed to meet Phillip today."

Talia stopped mid-step and turned around. "Meet Phillip? Who's Phillip?"

Melissa sighed as she rolled her eyes upward. "You mean Daddy didn't talk to you?"

Talia started back down the stairs. "Talk to me about what?"

"About Phillip having dinner with us today."

Talia parted her lips to say something, but she rescinded her callous comment about Franklin and instead said, "This is the first I'm hearing about this."

Melissa took a couple of quiet steps towards her mother. "Well, he told me that it was alright and that he would let you know."

"*Let me know*? So that's how things are done around here. He was not going to discuss it with me, but simply let me know?" Talia shook her head and groaned, "*Unbelievable*."

Melissa simply stared at her mother.

"Who's this Phillip? I thought Quentin had started calling you again?"

"Oh Mom, Quentin is old news. He's definitely in the past. I talked to Daddy about Phillip, and he said that it would be okay to date him after meeting him."

"Oh really? Where is this Phillip from? How old is he? Where does he live?" Talia interrogated.

Melissa's shoulders shrunk in intimidation. She just couldn't tell her mother that he was a friend of Kara's.

"Are you going to answer me?"

"He's only seventeen, Mom." Melissa fidgeted and picked at her fingernails. "He's a senior like me and a very nice guy."

"Where is he from and what does he plan to do after graduation?"

Just as Melissa parted her lips to answer, Talia's phone rang. Melissa looked on as her mother rummaged through her purse and pulled out her cell. It seemed strange to Melissa that from the moment her mother glanced at the screen on her phone her entire demeanor changed.

"Hey, could you hold on a minute?" Talia pulled the phone from her ear after muting the call and turned her attention back to Melissa. "Look, I have to take this. I'm sorry but meeting your friend today is out of the question. I have plans later and will be leaving here in about fifteen minutes."

"But Mom, can you wait until after he leaves," Melissa begged. "Phillip's not going to be here long. I really like this guy."

Talia gave her daughter a stern stare. "I'm sorry, but your father should have told me. How many times has he skipped out on Sunday dinner with us?"

"Dad only does that when he's busy with work," Melissa justified. "Besides, he always made it up to us."

"Okay, well I'll make it up and just meet him another time," Talia coldly responded.

Melissa stared as her mother turned away and placed the phone back to her ear. She watched as Talia hurried up the stairs, and then she went to her room. After placing her Bible on the bed, Melissa pulled her cell phone from her purse and called Phillip. Barely ten minutes later, she slipped out of her room and watched as her mother hurried down the stairs in a fresh change of clothes. Talia rushed through the entrance, carrying her coat across her arms, and soon disappeared from view.

"No, she's gone now," Melissa spoke into her phone as she went back inside of her bedroom. "But I think my dad is going to love meeting you. Just be yourself and I'll see you in about an hour."

"All right," Phillip answered. "And Mel, I enjoyed myself the other night."

Melissa could hardly contain her emergent smile. Phillip practically swept her off her feet. The entire time they were together she felt that he was the perfect guy who said all of the right things. Even though he didn't come from money like her last boyfriend, Phillip had a way about him that captivated Melissa's mind and was on the verge of capturing her heart. She simply knew that her father would love him too.

"I can't seem to stop thinking about it either." She blushed.

"Did you tell Kara what happened?"

Melissa stalled, and then cleared her throat. "No, I didn't tell her. We're not exactly on speaking terms."

"You too? She about bit my head off when she got back in town last week. I wonder what's up with her."

"She's acting really crazy right now, but she'll be alright." Melissa grunted. "But I really don't want to talk about that right now. All I want is to see you at my front door in forty-five minutes." She grinned, primping in front of her full-length mirror. "I miss you."

"I can't get you out of my mind ... I miss you too, baby."

"Well, hurry up and get over here. The sooner my dad approves of you, the better."

"What if your mother comes back?"

"Oh, don't worry about her. She probably won't be back until later on this evening," Melissa explained. "Now, just remember that my dad likes football as well as basketball."

"What man doesn't?" Phillip teased.

"Whatever," Melissa replied, grinning. "He's always raving about the Philadelphia Eagles and that basketball team in Oklahoma."

"Oklahoma City Thunder."

"Yeah, whatever."

Phillip laughed. "I got you, girl. But you just better learn those NBA teams because I'll either be playing with or against them one day soon. Remember, one and done," he said, referring to the NBA mandate that a player must be nineteen years old and out of high school for at least a year before being eligible to play in the league. "You can bet on that."

"Oh, I know," Melissa confidently said. "And trust me, I'll be your number one cheerleader."

"That's what's up." Phillip already had plans to play in the McDonald All-American Game while considering a pro career overseas until he qualified the next year to play in the NBA.

"Alright, I'll see you soon."

After Melissa hung up with Phillip, she modeled the beautiful waist tie shirt in front of her body. The deep, rich shade of purple complemented her skin tone perfectly. The top was adequately modest to satisfy her father's taste for her, but still shapely enough to make Phillip take notice. She slipped into her favorite pair of jeans and accessorized the outfit with a matching necklace and pair of earrings. The BEST FRIEND bracelet she usually wore would have completed her ensemble flawlessly, but she didn't want anything on that would constantly remind her of the friendship she once had with Kara. Melissa touched her bare wrist and sighed to herself.

"Knock, knock," Franklin said as he opened the door to Melissa's bedroom. "Where's your mother? I saw that her car wasn't out front."

Melissa looked to him and answered, "Oh, she said that she had plans today."

Creases immediately embedded Franklin's face. "Plans? What plans?"

"Well, she said that you never told her about Phillip coming over today."

"I thought I had. Maybe I didn't," Franklin admitted. "I've had so much on my mind lately." He stood in the doorway for a moment, motionless. "Uh, did she say what time she'd be back?"

Melissa turned and faced the mirror as she answered, "Nope."

"I see ... and what time is Phillip coming again?"

"He should be here in about thirty minutes. That'll be just enough time to heat the food Douglas cooked on yesterday and set the table."

Franklin nodded with a distant gaze on his face. "Well, you go on and get things on the table and I'll be down shortly. I just need to change my clothes."

"Okay." Melissa nodded with a smile. "I can't wait for you to meet him, Daddy."

"If he's like you said he is, I'm sure I'll like him just fine."

Franklin backed out of his daughter's room with troublesome thoughts racing through his mind. After he called Talia's cell and another man answered, his suspicions were confirmed.

# CHAPTER 29

"RAPE? WH-WHAT?" Wendell stared at his friend, Tim, like he had just lost his mind. "I've never raped anybody in my life!"

"Wendell, calm down. Man, I know you, I'm just telling you what's going on. We got a call yesterday about a statutory rape charge."

"*Yesterday*? And you're just telling me now?" Wendell grilled his longtime friend who was a few years older and an experienced detective in the local police department. "Who did I supposedly rape?"

Tim peered down at his notepad and then looked up into Wendell's expectant eyes. "Does Kara Bentley ring a bell?"

"Man, you've got to be kidding me." Wendell nervously rubbed the top of his head. "There's got to be some kind of mistake."

"Wendell," Tim said, staring Wendell squarely in the eyes, "man, be straight with me. Did you have sex with this girl?"

Wendell paced to the other side of his loft, blindsided by the accusations. He parked his hands at his waist and remembered the last time he saw Kara. It was when he had invited her to spend the night at his loft a few days after she had gotten back from Mississippi, but never in a million years would he have ever thought she would accuse him of raping her.

"Wendell, answer me." Tim's voice changed from casual to concerned. "Did you have sex with this girl and is she only sixteen years old?"

"*No ...*" Wendell stared back at him in anger. "We didn't have sex and second, she's almost eighteen years old. I checked the law," he answered snidely. "And *if* we had done something it could only be considered statutory rape if she was less than seventeen years old." He looked at his friend with a grim expression. "But let me tell you again, neither one is true. We did not have sex and she is *not* sixteen."

"Hey man, it came across my desk and I wanted to check this out for myself," Tim argued with raised hands. "I know you and I figured that it had to be a mistake." He then looked as if he remembered something. "Wait a minute, this isn't the girl you were telling me about a few months back, is it?"

Wendell sighed in response, wondering if there was a possibility that Kara may have acted out anger from seeing an old girlfriend's photo propped on a shelf in his place.

"I thought you said it wasn't that serious."

"At the time it wasn't." Wendell turned away to the window that overlooked the city. "Things changed."

"Hey man, I'm not here to judge you, I was just asking."

"Look, I'm sorry," Wendell apologized. "I know you're just doing your job and looking out for me as a friend, but you've got to know this isn't easy to hear. Somebody's got it in for me." He shook his head. "Kara wouldn't do this ..." he then corrected himself, "she *didn't* do this."

Tim nodded at Wendell's declaration about Kara. "I hear you, man." The passion expressed in Wendell's voice convinced Tim that this was a bogus claim. "I'll keep you posted. We get calls about these sorts of situations all the time, but we must take each one seriously. Since no one has come down to the station, it's probably just like you said ... somebody's got it in for you." Tim patted his friend on the arm. "Don't worry about it, the truth will come out. Isn't that what you always say?" he asked with a smile.

Wendell's mood lightened as he slowly nodded.

"Alright then. Besides, I'll keep an eye on things." Tim then started for the door. "I have to go, but you be careful."

"Yeah, I'm always watching my back. Thanks for looking out."

"No problem. We'll be in touch." Tim opened the door and left.

Wendell locked the door behind Tim and immediately grabbed his phone. Although he needed to review minor changes to his movie script before the cast and crew met later in the day, he called Kara instead.

"Come on, pick up the phone," Wendell mumbled to himself as he stared at the time on his microwave. It was past the time Kara usually got home from school. With each passing ring, Wendell grew increasingly impatient. And when the voicemail cut on, he simply hung up the phone.

Determined to get to the bottom of things and truly get a clear answer that it wasn't Kara who had called the police, Wendell got in his car and drove to the address saved in his GPS from when he dropped her off a few months ago after the opening of his aunt's theater.

This was a conversation he needed to have with her face to face.

# Chapter 30

THE HOME WAS just as he had remembered, a residence stapled with wealthy caliber. Wendell parked his car on the street and sat motionless. All sorts of thoughts raced through his mind as he remembered dropping Kara off at school after she had spent the night with him. He chastised himself about kissing her longer than she was willing, but never in a million years would he have ever attempted to defile her. Wendell admitted to himself that he found her absolutely breathtaking, and his passions dared to get the better part of him, but he still would not have classified their making out as rape or anything remotely close to it. Besides, he questioned why she would stay the night after their argument if she really didn't trust him.

Despite what he had told Tim about knowing that Kara wouldn't report such a thing, Wendell thought about how upset she had looked that morning when he dropped her off at school. The more he considered her anger from him having a photo of a former girlfriend on his mantel, the more his suspicions were raised about her actually calling in a rape charge.

"Uh, can I help you?"

Wendell's thoughts were disrupted by the insistent knocks on his car window. Startled, he looked to the woman who stood outside, and then quickly lowered the glass.

"Who are you?" Talia questioned, glancing from his front seat to the back seat, back to the front.

Wendell cleared his throat and answered, "Hi, I'm Wendell." His eyes nervously shifted from the can of mace pepper spray in her hand. "I'm here to see Kara."

"*Kara*?" Talia slowly lowered the small pink canister. "Why on earth would you be looking for her here?"

"Isn't this where she lives?" Wendell cautiously asked. "I dropped her off here before."

"No, she does not live here." Talia's lips curled into a sinister smirk. "She's my daughter's charity case."

"Charity case?"

Talia casually tugged at the bottom of her waist length leather jacket. "Yes ... try the other side of town, you might find her rummaging through some garbage cans or something."

Wendell looked at her in confusion and rolled his window back up. What she said didn't make any sense to him. After Talia gave him a look that he ought to leave, Wendell quickly started his car. Talia stood unmoved as Wendell's car disappeared from view.

"The nerve of her telling him that she lives here," she mumbled to herself.

Shaking her head, Talia retrieved the bags she had temporarily abandoned on the front steps and tossed them into the trunk of her car. This was the second trip she had made to gather her things and move them out of the house she once called her own. A few days prior, Franklin had made clear in no uncertain terms that he wanted her out of the house. It was bad enough that he had suspicions about her being unfaithful, but to have the audacity to throw it in his face by having another man answer her cell phone was downright inexcusable.

Over the past two days she had the pleasure of enjoying Donovan's company without having to check in with her husband. It was pure bliss knowing that he would care for her far better than Franklin had. Donovan was her high school sweetheart and although his means were meager some years ago, they certainly weren't now. He could afford a woman with taste like hers and she reveled in the fact that he spared no money when it came to what she wanted. With Franklin, she would always hear the sacrificial spiel of what it took to accumulate the wealth they had, but with Donovan it seemed as if nothing was too good or cost too much.

As Talia drove to the new high rise, fully furnished condo Donovan had rented for her, she thought about the way Melissa looked when she told her she was leaving. Melissa had no idea that it was because of an adulterous affair that her mother was going on an unplanned trip, and Talia wanted to keep it that way. She simply told her daughter that she had an emergency she needed to take care of, and Franklin didn't object to her explanation. If it were left up to him, he would never discuss the sordid subject with another living soul. Not again.

"Baby, I'm home," Talia joyfully announced upon entering her temporary residence. She dropped her bags at the door and walked through the spacious living room, stopping at an oval mirror along the way. Talia stared in the mirror, meticulously straightening her freshly pressed locks of hair.

"Hey you, I thought you would never make it in." Donovan strolled up behind Talia with a plush terrycloth bath towel securely tucked around his chiseled waist. He placed his strong arms around her petite body and softly kissed her on the neck. "I've been waiting here for over an hour."

Talia gazed at his reflection in the wall mirror and smiled. "Well, I wasn't sure that you would be back from the site this early." She giggled as he nibbled on her neck. "When I saw your architectural designs on the table over there, I knew you were here."

"It is my calling card." Donovan chuckled. "We're almost finished with the project, so you won't have to worry about my paperwork littering your coffee table."

Talia turned around and faced Donovan. "So, when do you leave?"

Donovan released their embrace and walked hand in hand with Talia back to the bedroom. "Soon."

She sat on the bed as he started to dress. "Donovan, you know I have to tie up loose ends with Franklin before I can move back to Florida. Not to mention, my daughter will be graduating in a few months."

Donovan nodded as he pulled a T-shirt over his head. "I know all of this, Tee. That's why I got you this place. You can stay here until everything is finalized and when you're ready, I'll be there waiting," he promised.

"So, what about in the meantime? How are we supposed to see each other if you're going back to Florida soon?" she questioned. "I don't want to be alone."

Donovan sighed as he slid into a comfortable pair of blue jeans. "Tee, you're not alone." He sat down beside her on the edge of the bed. "This is what I've wanted for a long time. *You* are who I've wanted for a very long time." Donovan then rubbed her knee. "Anytime you want to see me, you can. And whatever I can do to make that happen, I will," he convinced her. "But right now, I still have a business to run and clients that need me."

"But I need you..." Talia then realized that her words echoed what she had said to Franklin over the years. Those same familiar feelings of unfulfillment threatened to invade her new relationship. She looked away from him and for a moment, regretted leaving her husband. But when Donovan traced his fingers from the center between her shoulder blades down to the small of her back, Talia recanted her thoughts.

When Donovan kissed her this time, it felt like the first time. Talia remembered what had brought them together so many years ago and the child that they had together. He held so many secrets of her heart and so many memories of her past that it seemed as if she did need him. She needed him to complete her. So often she had been warned that that was a dangerous sentiment, especially being a professed Christian. She had been taught that her completion should come from a relationship with Jesus Christ, not another human being. But with the way Talia's emotions swayed recklessly, she could barely make the distinction. Or rather chose not to.

"How about I go with you to Ft. Lauderdale?" Talia offered. "Just for a few days. To see the house you've built, and you know, to make roots again. Besides, I wouldn't mind checking in on Mother."

Donovan exhaled but nodded. "Okay, sure. Maybe I can stop by your mother's house to say hello."

Talia stalled. "Do you think we're ready for that?"

"Well, you're the one who said you wanted to make roots again. I'm sure your mother is going to ask why you're moving back there."

"I didn't say that I'm moving just yet."

"I know, but the word is going to get out that we're together." Donovan raised his eyebrows. "Unless you need more time to think about this. You can wait until after your daughter graduates."

Talia contemplated her options and emphatically shook her head. "No, this is what I want."

"Are you sure?" he hesitantly questioned.

"Yes ... besides, I really don't have much of a reason to stay here any longer." She sighed and then snidely remarked, "I'm certain Franklin is going to blab everything to our pastor. And after the last time, I just can't show my face there." She shook her head again. "Uh-uh, no, I need a fresh start." Talia then gazed into Donovan's eyes and softly whispered, "With the man I've always loved."

# CHAPTER 31

"HEY DEIDRA," KARA said as she tossed her book bag underneath the dining area table. It had been a busy and somewhat stressful day between the cold stares from Melissa at school and the nasty words from Miriam after she got home. Although she only went to her sister's apartment to drop off a Christmas gift that Frieda had sent along, Kara regretted stopping by while she was at home. "Did anybody call me today?"

"No, I don't think there were any messages on the voicemail," Deidra answered, perusing through her email at the dining room table. "But you did get an important email today."

"An email?" Kara peered at her quizzically as she grabbed a banana from the countertop.

Deidra turned the laptop in Kara's direction. "Yes, you left your email up from last night. I didn't open it ... although I was tempted," she confessed with a smirk. "It's from Admissions."

Kara stopped in her tracks, and gasped, "*Admissions*?" The banana fell back onto the counter from her limp hand. "Juilliard?"

"That's what it says." Deidra nodded with a smile. "You've waited a long time for this."

Kara slowly placed a palm across her chest, drew in a deep breath and exhaled. "Yes ... a very long time." Ever since she submitted her application to the Manhattan School of Music as a backup, Juilliard had always been her first choice; a dream she's had since entering her first piano competition.

"Girl, if you don't get over here and open this email!" Deidra excitedly screamed.

Instantly, Kara blinked from her daze and rushed over to the table and sat in a chair beside Deidra. She quickly clicked on the email from Juilliard's Office of Admission. Her hands nervously shook as her eyes quickly scanned the contents of the email from top to bottom. She immediately broke out into a hallelujah praise when she saw that she had been scheduled for a live audition.

Deidra cupped her hands over her mouth and then wrapped her arms around the elated Kara. Since they've been living together, Deidra had witnessed firsthand how dedicated Kara was to the art of music. She had seen her study musical history and theories for countless hours when she wasn't at the church perfecting her repertoire. Deidra had never seen such a dedicated and focused teenager in her life. It had concerned her though when she learned that Kara had spent the night out, but Deidra was reassured that she had staved off distraction after acing a recent test in school.

"Yes!" Kara screamed, and then high-fived Deidra. "Oh my goodness, can you believe this? I am actually scheduled for a live audition at Juilliard!"

"Well, you've worked hard for this and now it is paying off." Deidra nodded in admiration. "You are going places, Kara, and I thank God that I know you."

Kara hugged Deidra as tears streamed down her flushed cheeks. Immediately she thought about Melissa again, wanting to share the good news with her. Although they had parted ways, she still cared about her friend, even though Melissa no longer referred to her as such. Kara wondered how her acting audition went that was scheduled for today. So much was happening in both of their lives that it all seemed so strange not sharing such important news with one another.

"I feel like this is happening to me." Deidra giggled, wiping tears from underneath her eyes. "So, when is it?"

"Not for another five weeks," Kara noted, momentarily glancing back at the screen, "but believe me, I need every minute of that time." Her smile was endless. "Now I have to prepare for the written exam as well as the musical skills eval." Kara sighed at just the thought of the work ahead of her. "I have to make sure that everything is perfect for that day."

"Oh girl, you got this," Deidra assured her. "*Wow* ... I am so proud of you. I think a celebratory dinner is in order," she offered, walking into the kitchen. "How about I fix your favorite meal tonight?"

"But I thought you had school tonight."

"I do, but that's hours from now." Deidra began pulling pans from a cabinet and her apron from the back of the pantry door. "I can whip you up something like that." She snapped her fingers. "Did you forget who you were talking to?" Deidra playfully propped her hands on her hips. "Girl, you just take a seat, finish your homework, or whatever you need to do and be ready to indulge your taste buds in about forty minutes."

Kara grinned, but reluctantly asked, "Are you sure? You really don't have to do this."

"I know I don't have to, I want to. Besides, with the way you keep this apartment clean, I feel like I owe you, girl." She laughed. "I don't know when the last time I saw this place so spotless."

"Just earning my keep," Kara quipped.

"Well, you've done that and then some. I really enjoy having you around."

Kara smiled to herself. It felt good to hear those words, especially with all she had been going through over the past few days. Wendell hadn't called her since their disagreement when she spent the night over at his place. The more she pondered their argument, the sillier she felt. It wasn't as if the photograph she saw in his place threatened what they had together, so Kara tried convincing herself. It was just that Wendell had captured her heart, and she didn't want to be a typical naïve girl who dismissed red flags when they presented themselves.

*Was it really a red flag*, she questioned herself. Or could it have been that for the first time in her life she saw him as being more than just a boyfriend? More than a guy she was dating and more than a close friend who took a serious interest in her, but in fact a potential husband.

"You're thinking of him, aren't you?" Deidra pulled Kara from her deep thoughts.

Kara's eyes shifted to Deidra's as a coy smile crept across her lips. "Yeah, I am."

"So, why don't you call him?"

"I don't know," Kara groaned. "He hasn't called me in days and I'm not about to run after him."

Deidra adjusted the heat underneath the pan on the stove and looked back to Kara. "Nobody says that you have to run after him. Don't you want to tell him about your audition? After all, isn't he the one who stuck his neck out there to get someone at the school to help you?"

Kara pondered Deidra's words. Her pride had blinded how nice and giving Wendell had been to her. He had been there for her and never asked anything in return.

"Girl, if I had someone like him in my corner, I wouldn't let him out." Deidra chuckled.

"But weren't you the one telling me to watch my back?" Kara folded her arms across her chest with a grin. "*Guys are slick sometimes*," she mocked. "*They see a young pretty thing hoping to get what they can get.*"

Deidra looked at Kara with slightly parted lips. After several failed attempts to conceal her smile, Deidra burst out laughing. "Did I say that?"

"Yeah, you did."

"I know, I know," Deidra humbly admitted, "but that was before I knew more about him."

"Uh huh," Kara teased.

"No seriously, over the past few months I've heard the way you've talked about him. It was always, Wendell did this or Wendell said that, but in a nice way. So, I know he's got to be some kind of guy."

Kara briefly looked away, remembering how she wouldn't let Wendell explain the photograph of the beautiful woman that sat on his mantel. That night when they were in the heat of kissing to a point of nearly no return, Kara's eyes inadvertently landed on a picture just inches away. When they had entered the common living area earlier in the evening, she assumed that it was a snapshot of his sister. But after noticing that the woman was wearing a necklace amazingly similar to the one he had given to her for Christmas, Kara began pushing Wendell away. She confronted him about the necklace that then hung from her neck, and he didn't deny that it was indeed the same piece of jewelry. Kara took the necklace off and pushed it back to him. She would've left, but it was late and she had school the next day. Angered, she didn't want to hear anything he had to say, all she wanted was for him to keep his distance away from her until the next morning.

"So, why don't you invite him over?" Deidra's question dissolved Kara's faraway gaze. "Whatever your little disagreement was, it couldn't have been that bad. Not with the way you're always asking if he called."

"I don't know," she groaned. "Besides, he's busy with his film and everything."

Deidra placed the large wooden spoon on the stove and gently asked, "Did something happen between the two of you?"

Kara avoided eye contact as she answered, "Just an argument. Everybody has them."

"Yeah, all relationships have disagreements at one time or another," Deidra sighed. "Did you want to talk about it?"

"Not really," Kara grumbled. "I just want to rest my eyes for a little bit before your delicious dinner." She forced a smile, and then walked into the living room.

"Okay," Deidra relented. "Just know that I'm here for you."

"I know," Kara answered, sitting down on the sofa. She removed her shoes and curled up into a fetal position with a pillow fluffed beneath her head. "And thanks for finding my letter pouch. I don't know what I would have done if I had lost it. All of my important papers are in there."

"Well, it didn't take much searching. I found it in the bottom drawer of your old dresser. I think you just overlooked it because you were in such a hurry to get out of that apartment."

"Maybe so, I'm just glad it was found."

"Did you still want me to hold onto your mailbox key? That package you were expecting from your aunt came today."

"Oh, my phone charger is here?" Kara raised her head from the pillow.

"Yeah, it's right over there on the end table beside the lamp. And you also got your bank statement too."

"Okay, thanks."

Deidra reached into her pant pocket and pulled out the key. "Here you go."

"Thanks, just leave it on the counter." Kara rested her head back onto the pillow. "I'll get it later."

Deidra placed the key on the countertop. She looked back to the stove when Kara closed her eyes and inwardly prayed for God to mend the brokenness in her friend's life. Deidra was grateful that she could help her along the way, but something about the way Miriam had spoken to her today when she saw her at the elevator suggested there was more going on between her and Kara than she was willing to admit.

Deidra had a feeling that this something could only be resolved by the Lord.

# CHAPTER 32

"THAT SCENE WAS on point," Wayne congratulated Leslie. "I like the way you improvised and added a little something extra to the lines." He then turned to Wendell who was engrossed in setting up the next scene. "Wasn't that something, man?"

Wendell looked up from the script and nodded. "Uh yeah, that was good, Leslie."

She grinned and elbowed her co-star's side.

"But next time you decide to change my lines, check with me first." He then folded the script in his hand and walked toward a group of actors slated for the next scene.

Wayne glanced between Wendell and the fading smile on Leslie's face. The demeaning tone in which he spoke was totally out of character for him. Wayne held up a finger to Leslie as if to tell her to wait a minute and walked after Wendell.

"Hey, what's up with you?" he questioned Wendell after pulling him aside from the group of actors. "You've been short with me, Michael, and now the cast. That was a great scene, better than I had seen all shoot and you scold the lead. What's going on?"

Wendell looked away and promptly dismissed the cast and crew to a break before focusing his attention back on Wayne. He sighed from frustration and then confided in him about the statutory rape charge.

"I thought you two were, you know, straight."

Still disturbed by even the slightest mention of his situation, Wendell sighed, "Yeah, me too." Concerned that someone might overhear their conversation, he led Wayne to the back office and closed the door behind them.

"So, you think somebody else has it in for you?" Wayne questioned, picking up a container of assorted nuts from the desk in the room. "And you haven't even spoken to Kara since your friend, Tim, laid this allegation on you?" He nonchalantly popped a handful of the mixed nuts into his mouth.

"No ... I tried to go by and see her, but she doesn't even live where I thought she did," Wendell explained.

Wayne shook his head as he swallowed the grounded nuts. "Sounds like you don't know her as well as you thought you did. But don't let this sideline your obligation to this movie. We only have a few weeks left of shooting before going into post-production. Keep your head focused and your nose clean," Wayne warned as he rose from his seat. "Come on, let's get something to eat. These nuts aren't doing a thing for my hunger." He put the container back on the desk and pushed it away from him.

Just as Wendell followed Wayne out of the office, his cell phone vibrated in his pocket. He stared at the number on the screen and told Wayne that he'd be a minute. Wayne nodded and continued on to the concession stand as Wendell double-backed into the office and closed the door behind him.

"Hey, what's going on?" His voice was cold and monotonous.

"Hey ... I haven't heard from you in a while," Kara softly spoke. "Are you busy?"

"Not at the moment." His icy stance remained unmoved. "What's going on?"

"Is that all you're going to say?"

"Kara, you're the one who called me. I figured that after the last time we spoke, you didn't want to hear from me. So, if you have something to say, then just say it."

She sucked her teeth. "I want to know why you had another woman's photo up, wearing a necklace that you tried to give to me."

"I tried explaining that to you, Kara, but you didn't want to hear anything I had to say."

"Well, I'm listening now."

Wendell gently closed his eyes before he said, "She was an old girl-friend, that's all."

"*That's all*? You have nothing else to say about it?" Kara questioned.

"Look, I'm working. I really don't want to go into everything here." He abruptly paused, and then carefully asked, "Don't you trust me?"

"You're one to ask that question," she said with an attitude. "You know what, *whatever*, you don't have to talk about it. I just called to let you know that I got scheduled for an audition ... at Juilliard."

After a slight pause, Wendell warmed at the mention of her news. "Juilliard, that's great news, Kara." He gently cleared his throat, and then reminded her, "I told you that you would."

"Yeah, you did," she stiffly said. "Well, I just wanted to say thank you. Do you mind telling Mrs. Chow that I said thanks for her help since she's not at the School any longer?"

"Sure, sure ... I'll tell my aunt to get in touch with her. She'd be happy to know that."

Again, there was another uncomfortable moment of silence.

"Your hard work has paid off," Wendell continued.

"Well, I still have to get in." Kara paused, and then countered her own statement, "But I'm confident that I will. I know my repertoire backward and forward."

"That's my girl," Wendell slipped. He didn't want to express any terms of endearment towards her until after they had resolved their differences.

"Am I still your girl?" she innocently asked in a softened tone. "You haven't called me or anything."

"Well, I did try to come over and see you."

"You did?" Kara's stomach churned as she imagined what happened when Wendell showed up at the Peterson mansion.

"Yes, when were you going to tell me that you didn't live there?" he questioned, redirecting the anger she had just unleashed on him.

Challenged, Kara stuttered, "I-I didn't know how."

"You didn't know how to tell me that you didn't live in that house ... or that you live in the projects?"

Kara's silence spoke volumes.

Wendell looked through the glass window on the door at the cast and crew as they made trips back and forth to the concession stand. His dream was coming true and all he wanted was to help make Kara's a reality as well. It hurt him that she felt she had to mislead him on any level or to think that he was that superficial.

He learned that she lived in the projects after calling the home number she had given him months ago. When Deidra answered the phone, not knowing that Kara had concealed where she lived, she confirmed through casual conversation that Kara has lived in the projects for the past two and a half years. It was difficult for Wendell to fathom because she was so classically grounded and intellectually mature, but he soon realized that she was a diamond in the rough.

"*Deidra told you?*" Kara questioned. "What else did she say?"

"Does it matter if it's the truth?" He challenged her integrity. "I want to hear from you why you didn't tell me?"

Embarrassed, Kara still wanted nothing more from Wendell than to be the woman he would indeed love, cherish, and respect ... no matter what. She didn't realize that in the process of assembling a façade, her pretend world was bound to crumble to pieces.

"I'm sorry, Wendell. I-I wasn't trying to deceive you," she stammered. "I just didn't know how to tell you that I didn't live in that house. After you assumed that was where I lived, I just—"

"I don't need for you to live in a mansion for me to love you," he earnestly said without the slightest hesitation.

"You love me?" Kara's voice gently sought reassurance.

"Yes ... I love you ... for you. And no matter what happens or who says what, that's the God's honest truth," Wendell confirmed. "So, don't go hiding things from me that you think will make me feel a certain way. Remember Kara, if you have to do that then it's not real love."

Kara pondered his words carefully. She understood where he was coming from and decided from that moment forward to be completely honest with him, as honest as she wanted him to be with her.

Wendell watched through the door window again as Wayne strutted back towards him with a curious expression on his face. "Look, I'm on set, so I'll have to give you a ring later." He hurried the conversation along. "Maybe this Sunday I can come by or pick you up so we can talk in person. Is that okay?"

In a somewhat relieved tone, Kara replied, "Yes."

"Alright. I'll call you later." Wendell ended the call and opened the door just as Wayne walked within a few feet of him.

"Hey man, is everything all right?" he asked.

"Yeah, everything is fine," Wendell answered, closing the office door behind him.

"So, uh, who was that on the phone?" Wayne curiously inquired. "Everything's cool with the silent partners, right?"

Wendell stared at him suspiciously. "Yeah, everything's fine with the partners. Why would you ask something like that?"

"Oh, I was just wondering since you never mentioned anything else about your new film idea."

Wendell stopped mid-stroll and questioned, "Wondering what?"

"Just if you had worked on the script yet or even shared with them your new idea like you did with me and Michael." The sudden call Wayne had just received from one of the silent partners unnerved him.

"I may have mentioned it." Wendell's eyes narrowed. "Why?"

"Nothing, just wondering." Wayne avoided eye contact, now regretting that he had overstepped his bounds of passing Wendell's idea for a new film off as his own. Despite Wayne understanding that Wendell couldn't copyright an idea, only the product once it was executed, he was still anxious about moving forward. When one of the silent partners called and asked for a copy of the script treatment, Wayne wanted to ensure that Wendell hadn't submitted his own version of the basic summary he had verbally pitched to him and Michael some months back. He feared that if he had, his credibility would be shot and his name in the industry would be ruined.

"There's a lot on my plate right now, so I may put it off until we near the end of post-production." Wendell folded his arms. "Remember what you said not even twenty minutes ago that I should keep my head focused. This film we're working on now is my baby."

"That's right." Wayne nervously chuckled. "But we can't stop the grind in the meantime, you know what I mean?"

"I think I'm beginning to," Wendell said as he patted Wayne on the back.

The two men briefly made eye contact as they started back towards the set. Along the way, Wendell grabbed an apple and a bottle of water from the concession table. He sat down in his director's chair and flipped through the pages of the script with one hand while devouring the apple with the other. There were some changes soon to be made in his life. Wendell promised himself that as soon as the movie was wrapped, so would some of the people be cut out of his life.

# CHAPTER 33

FRANKLIN SAT IN his home office, staring aimlessly out of the window. With a grim expression painted on his face, his eyes drifted back down to the dissolution of marriage paperwork on his desk. It had been almost a week since he heard another man's voice answer his wife's phone. The blatant disrespect shown to him almost caused him to act out of pure rage. He couldn't believe that Talia chose this way to let him know that she wanted nothing else to do with the marriage or the life they had built together. Nearly twenty years of marriage, months of planning a retirement to spend more time with his wife, and weeks of coordinating a special anniversary getaway of their first date was all crushed in a matter of seconds.

*Lord, I don't know how she could do this to me again*, Franklin lamented. Many heartfelt sentiments were offered up to God from him over the past few days. Divorce was something he never considered when he said I do to Talia so many years ago. In his mind, in his soul, marriage to Talia was until death separated them. It was an arduous task getting past her infidelity a few years ago, but now Franklin just felt like a fool. He had given so much to provide for their family and sacrificed selflessly to accommodate his wife's desires. But in the wake of discovering how conniving and self-absorbed she was, he wanted to take back everything he had given her: his time, his efforts, and his money.

"Hey Daddy," Melissa interrupted his thoughts as she entered the room. "Can Phillip come over and watch a movie or something?"

"Didn't you just see him last night at the game?" Franklin slid the divorce paperwork underneath a work folder.

"Yes, but I figured since Mom was out of town again for the next few days, that he could come over. Besides, I thought after the Sunday dinner we had that you really liked him."

Franklin gently smiled at the remembrance of meeting Phillip for the first time. "I do like him, but I thought we would spend some time alone today."

"Please, don't tell me that you want to talk about the family business again. I thought this was settled already," she insistently declared with a hand on her hip.

Franklin pushed his chair back from his desk and walked over to where his daughter stood. "Melissa," he began, placing an arm around her shoulders, "we need to talk ... and no it's not about the business. You're right, that is settled."

Franklin walked with his daughter through the house into the front room. When they sat down on the sofa, he explained to her the things Talia refused to discuss. Melissa was nearly a grown woman, and he knew she was old enough to handle the truth about his and his wife's situation. As he delicately described the unraveling of their marriage, omitting the details of Talia's affair, Melissa's eyes clouded with tears. It was hard for her to imagine her parents parting ways.

"Are you sure you guys can't work this out?" she pleaded. "I mean, people claim to grow apart all the time, but can't you go to counseling?"

Franklin pulled in a deep breath and exhaled heavily. "We've been that route." He placed a hand on his daughter's knee. "What I need to know right now is what you want to do."

"What I want to do?" she repeated.

"Yes, do you want to stay here with me, or do you want to go with your mother to Florida?"

"Are you serious?" she scoffed. "Daddy, I'm a senior in high school. Of course I want to stay here. Florida? The only people I know there are Grandma and my cousins Lisa and Dina."

"Okay. I kind of figured you'd want to stay, but I had to ask. I wanted this to be your decision."

"But Daddy, none of this is making any sense." Melissa waved her hand while simultaneously shaking her head. "How do two people who've been together twenty years, married almost as long, just up and decide to get a divorce? You belong to a church and believe in God. Why don't you pray about this?" She stared him squarely in the eyes as she cleared the tears from beneath hers. "Isn't that what you're always telling other people to do?"

Melissa's maturity challenged Franklin. She had no idea how many nights he had prayed for God to intervene. He pleaded with the Father to restore his marriage, but also to reveal what was wrong with it. In the process Franklin realized that his prayers were answered, just not the way he assumed or thought they would have been. Over the years his union with Talia was restored, but Franklin now understood that God was not going to remove her freewill in choosing to be elsewhere. The choice to be together was a decision that they both had to agree upon and after the way Talia had defended her relationship with another man, Franklin understood that theirs was over.

"Don't you love her, Daddy?"

Franklin initially responded with a simple gesture by nodding his head. And then he looked into his daughter's eyes again, knowing that she needed to hear him say it. "Yes Melissa, I love your mother."

"Then why can't you two work it out?"

Committed to leaving that question for Talia, Franklin responded, "That's something you need to ask your mother." He kissed Melissa on the forehead. "Things have changed, and I want you to know that I tried. I would never abandon you or your mother. Those wedding vows are sacred to me. Please believe me when I tell you that I wanted my marriage to work."

Melissa looked away as a faraway gaze glossed over her face. She stared up at the large wedding portrait of her parents above the fireplace. Just the thought of them divorcing seemed so surreal to her. Melissa's eyes drifted back to her father's. She rested her head on his shoulders and cried again. Thoughts raced through her mind of how things would never be the same. Summer vacations, birthday celebrations, and holidays would all be different now. She struggled in her mind to adjust to what was to become her new normal, a change that she wanted no part of.

"I tell you what, why don't we spend the day in the city?" Franklin proposed, squeezing his daughter's shoulders. "We can celebrate your audition at Juilliard. I just know that you did well. It'll take some getting used to, but I think I can adjust to my daughter becoming a star."

"Juilliard is the last thing on my mind right now, Daddy." Melissa shuddered at her father's enthusiasm. "Thanks, but I don't feel much like celebrating right now."

"Melissa, I know that this news was hard to hear, but sitting around the house moping isn't going to make either one of us feel any better about the situation."

Before Melissa could reply to her father, the front door opened. Both Melissa and Franklin looked surprised as Talia walked into the room.

"Oh ... I thought you would be out." Startled, Talia stared at Franklin. She then looked to Melissa and questioned, "Why are you crying?"

"I'll leave you two alone," Franklin offered, and then walked past Talia to his office without making eye contact with her again.

Talia watched as her husband strutted past her. She looked back to Melissa and asked, "What's going on?"

"Mom, I know," Melissa confessed with a sour tone. "Why didn't you just tell me the truth?"

"The truth about what?" Talia eyed Melissa as she slowly draped her coat across the sofa.

"About your marriage, about not being here and pretending that you were just going on another trip, about moving," Melissa rattled off.

Talia sat down and nervously rubbed her hands up and down her thighs. "I guess your father told you that we're getting a divorce."

"Of course he told me, but why didn't you before up and leaving the house?"

"Melissa, you need to watch your tone with me. I'm still your mother."

Melissa sighed and folded her arms across her chest.

"Now, I didn't tell you because I didn't feel that it was the right time," Talia explained. "You had your audition coming up this week and I didn't want to put any undue stress on you. I know how badly you wanted this, so I made it seem as if I was just going on another trip. And yes, I may have been wrong for that, but I was thinking of you. I'm sorry."

Melissa burst into tears again and ran up the stairs. Mystified by her dramatic reaction, Talia followed Melissa to her room. She watched from the doorway as her daughter stretched out across the bed and buried her face in a pillow. Talia quietly exhaled as she walked towards Melissa, closing the door behind her.

"Melissa, I'm sorry you're taking this so hard, but your father and I have been having problems for a while now." Talia sat down on the edge of the bed and peered at her daughter who turned her face in the opposite direction. "We just didn't want to visit our issues on you," she continued, gently stroking her daughter's head.

"Mom, it's not just that." Melissa turned her face back in Talia's direction with tears pouring uncontrollably from her eyes.

Talia stared at her in concern. "Then what is it?"

Melissa sat up, curling her feet underneath her. She grabbed a throw pillow and wedged it in front of her body as she smeared the tears from her face with the back of her hand. "I have something to tell you," her voice quivered. She looked up at her mother with reddened eyes and said, "I missed my—"

Talia held up a hand, silencing her daughter. "Please, don't tell me what I think you're about to tell me." She stared at Melissa and shook her head. Talia rose from the edge of the bed and clutched the gold locket hanging from the chain around her neck. She angrily paced to the other side of the room and gazed up towards the ceiling, and mumbled, "*Is this my punishment?*"

"Mom, I'm sorry ... I—"

"Don't say another word," Talia sternly countered. She faced her daughter again and asked, "It's that Phillip guy I've been hearing about, isn't it?"

Melissa's shoulders slumped in disgrace as she nodded.

"You jeopardized everything on some NBA wannabe?" she crassly asked.

"Mom, it's not like that," Melissa said in Phillip's defense.

"Then what is it like, Melissa?" she scolded with fire in her eyes. "Do you know this will change *everything* about your life?" The anger in her voice was mimicked in her expression. "Oh, how I didn't want you to make the same mistake I did," Talia ranted.

"Mom, I have options ..."

"*Options?*" Talia ridiculed. "There is only one as far as I am concerned." She pointed at Melissa. "You are *not* having this baby."

Astonished, Melissa's eyes narrowed. "*What?*"

"You heard me the first time," Talia stressed. "How could you be so irresponsible? Here you've missed your period and ended up pregnant by some run-of-the-mill hoodlum. It wouldn't have been so bad if it were Quentin." Talia cut her eyes away from Melissa and hopelessly shook her head. "At least we'd know the baby would have a decent father."

"I don't believe you're saying this."

"No, I don't believe what you've done. As much as we've trusted you to make mature decisions, especially in the past few months, you go and get pregnant. Do you think I really want you to have an abortion like I had to?"

Suddenly, there was a sharp break of silence.

Talia squeezed her eyes closed as she whispered, "*Oh, dear God...*"

"You had an abortion?" Melissa questioned as her eyes narrowed to a squint. "Just why would you have an abortion?" She grilled her mother, realizing now that Kara was telling her the truth about the affair.

Talia's demeanor transformed from offensive to defensive. She cleared her throat and replied, "It was a long time ago."

"How long ago, *Mom*?" Melissa hustled off her bed as Talia shifted her eyes to the floor. She stood in front of her mother and craned her neck, struggling to regain eye contact. "Was it before you were married ... *or after*?" She raised an eyebrow.

Talia's silence spoke volumes.

"Oh, you disgust me," Melissa huffed. "After all you've preached to me about saving myself for marriage and you go and break up your own."

"Melissa, it's complicated," Talia tried to explain. "You're too young to understand what's going on between me and your father."

"Too young to understand? But I'm not too young to have an abortion," Melissa mocked. "I didn't miss my period, *Mom*, I missed my audition." She callously glared at her mother. "Don't you know I may have lost my best friend forever because of you! Kara saw you with another man, but no, I didn't believe her."

Shock splashed across Talia's face.

"How could you be so evil?" Melissa's voice eerily lowered to a whisper before erupting into blaring anger. "You know, if I were pregnant, I wouldn't kill my child! All I was trying to tell you is that I'll have to depend on things coming through with my back-up schools in North Carolina and Pennsylvania. Those are my only options now. Not the option of getting rid of an innocent child!"

Franklin flung the door open and burst into the bedroom. "What's going on in here?" He stared between his wife and daughter.

"Tell him, Mom!" Melissa's nostrils flared.

Franklin stared at Talia with a scowl on his face and questioned, "Tell me what?"

Talia's chest heaved as she shook her head and stormed out of the room. Moments later, the front door slammed shut. Talia dashed away from the house, abandoning the reason why she went there in the first place. There was no way now that she'd ever be able to get close to any financial paperwork in Franklin's office again. Talia figured that Melissa was sure to tell her father about the abortion and doubted if he'd even allow her to come near the house again without court approval.

Hoping that she had enough in her private bank account to last her for a while, Talia trusted that Donovan would pick up the slack. She was sure that Franklin would fight her tooth and nail to keep as much of the family money to himself as possible.

Confident that things would work out in her favor, Talia threw her purse on the passenger seat and squealed out of her parking space.

# CHAPTER 34

"SO THAT'S THE story with you and your sister." Wendell nodded as his eyes shifted away from Kara's to the busy street. "You know you could have told me this sooner, but I know now and that's what matters." He momentarily squeezed her hand before placing it back on the gear shift as he drove.

The pair had spent most of the day together after Sunday worship service. For the first time, Wendell had the pleasure of hearing Kara play songs that ministered the Gospel of Jesus Christ. Although he had no doubt that her skills would be just as proficient, if not even more so, in playing Gospel as with classical music, it was still an amazing experience.

Before a delicious lunch at a bistro located down the street from the church, Kara confided the details of her and Miriam's dysfunctional relationship. Kara had somewhat distanced herself from becoming emotional when talking about her home life, especially after moving in with Deidra since she didn't have to relive the drama she used to endure day in and day out with her sister. And now that Wendell knew the truth, the whole truth, she finally felt completely free to be herself.

In completely opening up to Wendell, Kara thanked God that Melissa felt the same way in coming clean with her. To have her friend sorely apologize about their argument to rekindle their friendship made Kara feel that the broken pieces of her life were finally coming together. After sitting next to one another during service alongside Phillip, Franklin, and Wendell, their friendship was solid again.

"Do you mind stopping home so that I can change my clothes before going to your place?" Kara asked Wendell, still thinking about how sad Franklin looked in church.

"Uh sure," Wendell hesitated. "You're just going to run up and change or bring the clothes with you, right?"

Kara stared at him with suspicion in her eyes and then her lips spread into a broad smile. "Are you afraid to come to my *hood*?" she questioned, chuckling in between her words. "I could've gotten Melissa to give me a lift."

"Afraid, girl no," he scoffed. "And it wouldn't make since for me to visit your church for the first time and not take you home. Besides, why should I be afraid?" Wendell blew Kara off with a nonchalant shrug.

"Is that so?" Kara smirked as she opened his glove box. Inside she pulled out a gun that was tucked securely beneath a gray pouch that contained his insurance and registration information. "So, what's this for?" Her telling grin mocked him. "I noticed it when I was looking for a napkin while you were checking your tires after church." She swayed the gun back and forth in her hand.

"Put that back," Wendell cautioned, easing her hand away as he neared a stoplight. "That's nothing to play with."

"Wendell, the safety's on," she said, lowering the gun to her lap. "I'm not stupid you know. I may not own a gun, but I sure know how to use one."

"*You*?"

"*Yes*," Kara answered. She stared at the gun, testing its weight in her hand and recognizing the make. "This is an internal hammer Smith &

Wesson AirWeight." She then rotated the gun from right to left. "A 642 model, I think ... I haven't held one in a while."

"How do you know that?" Wendell glanced at her through narrowed eyes.

"You only have to see your sister getting shot once to learn a few things," she bluntly admitted. "She bought one because we were both scared to death after what had happened to her, but it didn't take long before she got rid of it. The thought of having one in the apartment freaked her out more than not having one."

Wendell nodded understandably. "I guess I'm learning a lot of things about you that I didn't know."

"Hey, don't knock me just because I'm a country girl at heart. That doesn't mean that I haven't learned a few things while living here in the city," Kara said with a smirk. "I'm not a timid prissy missy that most people make me out to be, you know."

"I hear you."

She winked, and then opened the glove compartment again to put the gun back inside.

"No, you can just leave that out. I'll keep it next to me while you go up and change your clothes," he said, avoiding eye contact.

Kara laughed as Wendell neared the street where she lived. "Really, this area isn't as bad as you're making it out to be. Now, other parts, yeah, you should be worried, but this isn't one of them."

"Sure." Wendell smiled as he neared the sidewalk to let Kara out. "I'll just humor myself." He winked, and then slipped the gun in the side pocket of his car door. "Try not to be too long."

"I won't. I'll be right back." Kara got out of the car and hurried towards the front entrance. She glanced back once and smiled at Wendell before disappearing inside.

Wendell looked around his immediate vicinity, marveling at what a diamond in the rough Kara really was: determined and on the grind to make her reality a distant memory. He thought about all she had overcome thus far in her life, things that he wasn't sure he would have been able to if he were in her shoes. But through it all, Wendell knew that there was Someone who had Kara's back that has been with her from day one. Despite the stumbling blocks, or rather roadblocks, put in her way she was steadily rising above them all.

*Boom-boom-boom-boom!*

Wendell jumped from the sudden pounding on his window. He quickly reached in between his seat and the car door as he looked up. With a sigh of relief, he pushed the gun back down inside of its hiding place.

"You are so busted. I thought you weren't scared." Kara laughed hysterically.

Wendell cleared the nervous glare from his face and pointed at her. "Get in the car, you."

Kara playfully raised her hands with a grin before she obeyed his command. She climbed into the vehicle and teased him practically the entire way back to his loft.

Kara watched as Wendell placed the gun underneath his shirt inside of an opening in a waist holster located on the small of back. After they got out of the car, she followed him inside his place and dropped her backpack at the front door. Wendell removed the gun and placed it inside of a drawer in his bedroom. As he walked back into the common area, Kara simply stared at him.

"What?" Wendell asked.

She nonchalantly shook her head. "Nothing. I was just noticing that it seems like a habit for you."

"Oh, you mean the gun?" Wendell looked behind him and then back to her with a gentle smile. "I guess you could say that. If you do things in a certain order day in and day out, it sort of becomes a habit. I'm just careful about how I do things, not taking owning a gun lightly or as a license to use it irresponsibly like some people. I'm vigilant, but not a vigilante," he joked.

Wendell took Kara by the hand and led her towards the sofa. Before they sat down, he slid his hand underneath her long, silky hair, and rested it on the nape of her neck. With closed eyes, he gently kissed her on the lips.

"What was that for?" Kara asked, smiling softly.

Wendell sat down and answered, "Just for being you."

Kara eased down beside him. "Thank you ..." Her eyes then drifted to the spot where she last saw the photo of the woman that prompted their heated argument.

Wendell followed her eyes and nodded knowingly. "Oh yeah, I took it down."

She met eyes with him again, knowing this was now the perfect time for them to have that long-awaited conversation.

"You see, she was an ex-girlfriend ... and I'm not going to lie, I cared about her ..."

Kara's eyes uncomfortably drifted down as Wendell held her hands. "But she died."

Kara's lips parted unintentionally. "You never told me about that."

"Yeah, I know." Wendell stole a moment for himself before continuing, "Because I felt guilty about it."

"Guilty, why?" she questioned.

"Because it was right after we had an argument." He resignedly sighed. "We were on a weekend getaway on the Jersey shore, and she wouldn't ... she wouldn't have sex with me."

"You tried to have sex with her?" Kara snatched her hands from his and shook her head in disbelief. "I thought you're saved?"

"I wasn't at the time," Wendell explained. "You see, I knew about Jesus and what He had done on the Cross, but I wasn't living the life ... I honestly had no desire to." He pulled Kara's hands back towards him and held them tightly. "But after that night, everything changed. *I* changed."

"So, are you telling me that you never got over her?"

"No, no, it's nothing like that." Wendell shook his head. "I guess I had her picture up as a reminder of what she taught me. She was real with her faith and stood her ground. It didn't matter to her that I had spent money on a nice hotel and bought her an expensive necklace. She was not going to sleep with me."

"Is that what you were trying with me?" Kara's eyes asked the question twice. "Is that why you gave me *her* necklace?"

Wendell sighed. "No, of course not. And just so you know, that wasn't the same necklace. But I did buy one that was similar because you reminded me so much of her."

Kara was silent.

He continued, "The way that you're dedicated to your dreams and committed to your faith ... that was her."

"But I'm not her."

"I know that." Wendell sighed. "I didn't mean it like that." He looked at her with an apologetic gaze. "I just wanted to clear the air. You came clean with me, and I wanted to do the same."

Kara softened at his gesture of good faith. The warm hug she gave him testified to that fact. There was an even deeper level of respect for Wendell after he revealed the details of the statutory rape allegation. Kara knew that he had grown to love her because he never accused her of making that call. And she confirmed in all honesty that she was not the one who had called the police.

"Trust me, I know that you didn't," Wendell assured her. "But I think I know who did."

# CHAPTER 35

*HE IS SO good for her*, Deidra thought as she stared at the decaying bouquet of flowers that Kara refused to throw away. The assorted color of roses was a part of an eighteenth birthday gift from Wendell a couple weeks prior. Although Kara had poured the clouded water from the keepsake vase, the tattered, fragile petals of the arrangement remained on a thin sheet of decorated tissue paper in a corner of the dining area.

Deidra remembered how surprised Kara looked when the delivery arrived. She hadn't expected anything since Wendell had been busy with last-minute changes to the production of his film. She was absolutely floored that he found time to send a special token of his love. And after witnessing it all, especially how polite he was the first time she met him, Deidra felt that they were a match made in Heaven.

As she prepared to leave her apartment for work, Deidra glanced at the beige envelope Kara had left on the kitchen counter. It was a certified notice received a few days after her birthday from the law office that held her trust account, notifying Kara that she was to receive the money left by her parents in the next correspondence. That payment arrived just as expected about a week ago. With a smile, Deidra recalled how Kara pensively gazed at the check and then quickly went to deposit it into her bank account.

Within minutes of receiving the letter, Kara selflessly offered Deidra some money for the kindness she had shown to her, but she outright refused. Deidra reminded her that friends helped one another out without looking for something in return. She then further assisted Kara to decide about what amount to put aside in savings and how much to keep in her checking account to assist with anything financial aid may not cover for school. Kara was hopeful that as an honor roll student she'd be approved for a scholarship from Juilliard since she had already secured three smaller ones from local organizations. The remaining amount of money she planned to save for her future years at the School. But in the meantime, the entire trust amount of two hundred and fifty thousand dollars would stay in her main account until she had time to sort through the details of exactly what she would need. She practically had her entire college career planned out, just as her parents would have wanted.

*I have to get out of here,* Deidra thought as she rushed to gather her things so that she wouldn't be late for work. There was just enough time to check the mail for her favorite magazine and grab lunch on the go before clocking in for her shift.

"Hey girl," Deidra said as she glanced at Miriam. "How you doing?" With a forced smile, she stood at her mailbox and quickly thumbed through a stack of envelopes.

"I'm fine, couldn't be better," Miriam answered, looking up from her own stack with a smirk on her face. "Ever since you took Kara off my hands, I am doing great." Her voice sounded as if she truly meant every word she said.

Deidra sighed as she locked her box and pulled the key out. "Well, did anything come for her today?" she questioned, moving closer to Miriam while stuffing her letters into a shoulder bag.

Miriam emphatically shook her head as she tucked the mail in her hand on the side of her wheelchair. "No, but you can tell her that I want the rest of her things out of that bedroom."

"You can't be serious." Deidra looked on in disbelief. "Where is she supposed to put all that stuff? My place is packed as it is."

"Well, I guess she should have thought about that before she decided to move," Miriam snidely responded.

Deidra glanced in another direction and grunted. As she looked back to Miriam, it was evidently clear to her that all Kara had said about her sister was true. She was indeed a maliciously bitter woman. Deidra shook her head, wondering how two people who came from the same womb could be so different from one another.

"So, you tell her the next time I have to mention it," Miriam continued, "I'm selling every last thing or throwing it away."

"She's moving in a few months, Miriam," Deidra tried to reason with her. "Why can't you wait until she starts college?"

With an inquisitive glare, Miriam questioned, "Oh, so she's gotten her acceptance letter already?"

"No, but her audition is tomorrow. And you know Kara, she's going to nail it."

"Whatever, I don't care." Miriam's heartless words came with a sinister scowl. "If she doesn't have the rest of her things out by tonight, they won't be there tomorrow. And tell her I want my keys."

"Are you serious?" Deidra grimaced. "What do you need all of that space for? I know you're not still talking about moving Chris in."

"And what if I am? He sure brings more money into the house than she does." Miriam rolled her neck. "I have bills just like everybody else."

"You even said yourself that you haven't seen or heard from him in over a week."

"Whatever." Miriam scoffed. "We just had an argument, but he'll be back. Chris is my man."

"This week," Deidra mumbled under her breath.

"What?" Miriam questioned.

"Nothing. But how are you going to move some man in? The state isn't going to just sit back and let you do that while living on government assistance."

"How would they know?" Miriam eyed Deidra. "What, are you going to tell them?"

"I don't have time for this," Deidra said as she started for the door. "I have to get to work."

"You just tell her what I said," Miriam called out behind her.

Deidra looked back in disgust.

"Or I will do what I said." Miriam then maneuvered her wheelchair in the opposite direction and rolled herself away.

# CHAPTER 36

"THAT IS CRAZY, *she* is crazy!" Melissa blared into the phone. "Is she for real?"

Kara paced the apartment floor as she held the note in her hand that Deidra had left posted on the refrigerator door. "If I know my sister, she'll have someone do just what she said." She tossed the note aside. "How am I supposed to move a heavy chest trunk with all of those books and that storage bin packed with papers that I need?"

"You know I would help you, but I'm having dinner out with my dad." Melissa glanced at her father through the glass window of the upscale restaurant as she stood on the sidewalk. "And you know, since Mom moved the last of her things out this week, he really needs me. We've actually gotten closer since their separation two months ago."

"Oh no, I know, Mel. Thanks anyway, but even with the both of us we still wouldn't be able to lift that chest." Kara grunted in desperation. "I wish Wendell was through with his film, but I know he's busy so I'm not going to even bother him. It's too late to call Deacon Jackson and there's nobody else around here that I really trust to help me out."

"Did you ask Phillip?" Melissa questioned. "I know he's been busy with practicing for all of those tournaments, but I'm sure he should be home soon."

"I just saw his mom about twenty minutes ago, and he hadn't gotten home yet." Kara sighed. "But I guess I can wait a little longer before I have to get some rest."

"Oh yeah, that's right, your audition is tomorrow," Melissa remembered. "What a day Miriam picked to show her colors again."

"Tell me about it," Kara groaned. "But it'll all be over soon. I'm not going to let her ruin this for me no matter how nasty she acts."

"That's right because one of us is going to go to Juilliard," Melissa said with a smile in her voice.

"Oh Mel ..."

"No, no, it was my fault for hanging with Phillip instead of handling my business," Melissa admitted. "But hey, I aced that audition with UNCSA."

"Yeah, I can guess why that school was your second choice." Kara smiled, noting that Phillip had decided to attend UNC-Chapel Hill instead of playing overseas until he qualified for the NBA. "I wonder whatever happened to living in the city and being around people like yourself."

"Hey, if it's a drama program, believe me I'll be around people who will have the same things in common." Melissa giggled as she held up a forefinger to her father who was motioning for her to come back to the dinner table. "Look, I have to go, but I'll call you as soon as we leave the restaurant."

"Okay girl, tell your father I said hello."

"I will. And try Phillip again. I'm sure he and his friend will help you, no matter how late it is."

"I plan to. I just hope he gets home soon." Kara glanced at the wall clock. "Talk to you later."

After hanging up with Melissa, Kara tried Phillip's home number again. When he answered, she thanked the Lord for small favors.

"And that's a wrap," Wendell announced with a priceless smile on his face. "Picture is in the can!"

The cast and crew cheered while some high-fived one another. It had been a grueling four months, but the movie was officially moving into the post-production phase to be edited and prepared for submission to film festivals.

Wendell shook hands with Michael and some of the crew members before he noticed Wayne walking towards him. The last five weeks of shooting had been somewhat challenging since learning of Wayne's backdoor approach to his silent partners. What Wayne didn't know was that two of those silent partners were Wendell's childhood friends who had since moved to California. It was difficult for Wendell to face Wayne, but he kept what he had learned to himself to keep the peace while trying to finish shooting his movie.

"Hey man, we did it!" Wayne extended his hand to Wendell.

Trying hard to contain his anger about Wayne's underhandedness, Wendell forced a smile. "Yeah, we did. I thought we weren't going to make it for a minute there."

"Oh yeah, shooting on location in Jersey," he sighed. "But we got through it."

Wendell nodded, briefly looking away to acknowledge a crew member in passing.

"So, the wrap party is still on for this weekend, right?" Wayne drew Wendell's attention back to him.

"Things are on schedule as planned," Wendell answered. "I have a few friends coming to town for the occasion."

"Oh yeah, is your girl coming?"

"Kara will definitely be there. She wouldn't miss it for the world," Wendell said confidently. "And of course, my family will be there along with other supporters."

"I'm thinking of inviting a few of my coworkers. They can't wait to see the film on the silver screen."

"Well, hopefully it'll make it there," Wendell optimistically spoke.

"Oh, with a face like Leslie's and a script like yours, we got this." Wayne chuckled.

"Did I hear my name?" Leslie smiled as she walked up and stood alongside Wayne.

"Yes, you did." Wayne smiled back at her. "We were just talking about the great job you did on this film."

"Well, I do try my best to please." She shifted her eyes from Wayne to Wendell. "I'm glad you liked my performance. I hope I'll have the opportunity to work on your future films."

Wendell grunted underneath his breath, but instead responded, "I have to give it to you. You are quite the actress."

"I hope to make a permanent living off of it soon." Leslie chuckled, placing a hand on Wendell's arm.

Wendell moved his arm away, and then questioned, "Have you ever performed a scene where a woman makes a bogus call to the police about a rape charge?"

Leslie's flirtatious smile faded. She grimaced at Wendell, and then nervously glanced at Wayne.

"You see, I have this idea for a film where the guy accused is cleared because the voice on the recording sounds nothing like who the caller pretended to be." Wendell folded his arms across his chest. "There's much more to the story than that, but I think you get where I'm coming from."

Wayne stared at Leslie, recognizing the fact that Wendell was indeed talking about her making the false statutory rape accusation about Kara.

"But what's even more interesting about this story is that there's also a part about one of the characters doing whatever it takes to get whatever they want." He stroked his chin but kept a stern face as he then stared at Wayne. "You know the kind, passing ideas off as their own, but in the process unknowingly sabotaging themselves. I'm thinking about calling the script *Backstabbers*. What do you think?"

Both Leslie and Wayne parted their lips at a loss for words. Embarrassed, they dodged Wendell's glares as he angrily walked away from them and to the other side of the room.

# CHAPTER 37

*THIS DAY IS finally here*, Kara thought as she entered The Juilliard School. When she sat down to take her written exam of basic musicianship skills, Kara felt at home. The questions were very familiar and presented very little challenge for her. But jitters began to claim the better part of her as she sat down in front of faculty members for her musical skills evaluation. Their eyes seemed like lasers penetrating her skin, scrutinizing her every move. Kara's palms became sweaty, and beads of perspiration lightly lined her forehead. She had come too far to falter now. Too many sacrifices had been made and far too much time had been dedicated just for her to fall to pieces. With closed eyes Kara quietly inhaled and gently exhaled a deep breath. After repeating in her mind, *I can do all things through Christ who strengthens me*, her confidence slowly began to return.

Earlier that morning, Kara had prayed diligently for God to erase the demeaning words Miriam had spewed from her mouth the night before. The way her sister had spoken to her, one would have thought Kara was the most evil person to have ever walked the face of the Earth. After praying with Frieda before going to bed Kara felt renewed, but this morning she had allowed her mind to recall the hateful bashing. Sitting at the piano Kara quickly realized that she had to make a decision: either allow the enemy to steal what God had placed before her or realize that she was more than a conqueror in Him Who loves her.

"Are you ready?" a faculty member asked, nudging the rim of his glasses away from the tip of his nose.

Kara nodded with her hands poised over the keyboard like she had done so many times before. And she played her pieces like a seasoned veteran for nearly an hour. Everything she had worked so hard for came to a head in that one moment in time. Kara decided to ignore the negative thoughts and receive God's truth instead of Satan's lies. At the conclusion of her audition, she was certain that an acceptance letter was in her near future.

All the way back home, Kara praised God for blessing her. He gave her a mind that recalled things proficiently and a heart to know that it came from Him. She immediately phoned Wendell, who was waiting for her call and told him how well she had done. He had always been optimistic that she would do exceptionally well.

After repeating verbatim the details of her day from the moment she entered the building to when she left, Kara agreed to meet Wendell later in the evening. He noted having several business calls to make, but that he would stop by briefly to see her. Kara laughed at Wendell again, remembering how paranoid he was coming to her neighborhood. She giggled even louder when he said that he wouldn't have his car due to a minor fender bender.

"Yeah right, you're just scared to park your car in this neighborhood."

"Nah, for real, my car is at the body shop overnight," Wendell explained. "If I was so scared, would I be taking the train to your side of town?"

"You didn't get a rental?" Kara asked.

"No, I figured it wasn't worth the hassle since the shop said my car would be ready first thing in the morning. Besides, one night without

a car in New York didn't kill me before and it isn't going to now."
Transportation in the City was the least of his worries.

"I hear ya," Kara said to Wendell as she rushed inside of Deidra's
apartment to answer the ringing phone. "Well, somebody's calling
on the other line. I'll see you a little later." She quickly hung up with
him and picked up the land phone which displayed Frieda's number.

"Hey Auntie!" Kara exclaimed, still flying on a natural high. "I
didn't expect to hear from you so soon. You'd be glad to know that
I nailed my audition." Without even a response from the other end
of the line, Kara chattered on, "You know, I forgot to tell you last
night that Deidra may have you beat with that crust covered sweet
potato pie." She chuckled as she cradled the phone between her neck
and shoulder while washing her hands at the sink. "She made one
on a whim the night before last. I'm telling you, that woman loves
to bake." Kara dried her hands on a towel hanging from the stove
handle and then pulled an aluminum foil pan from the refrigerator.
"You guys may have to have a bake off when you come up here for
my graduation. The winner will get—"

"Kara ... Kara," Simon interrupted her incessant rambling. "This
isn't Frieda."

"Oh, hey Uncle Simon, how are you? Does Aunt Frieda have you
making her calls again while she cooks?" Kara giggled. "I'm going to
have to get her a phone with a good speaker on it."

Simon stalled on the other end.

"Uncle Simon," Kara's voice trailed thin as she dared to ask, "what
is it?"

"Kara, I don't know how to tell you this, but Frieda is gone ...."

With a slight shake of her head, Kara tried to make sense of what
Simon had just said. "*No ... no ...* I just talked to her last night." She
immediately burst into tears. "*What happened?*"

"Kara, listen to me, Frieda was sick when you were here."

"She never said anything," Kara sniffled between her words.

"You know your aunt. She just didn't want to worry you. Her chest congestion was really an onset of pneumonia," Simon explained. "She got better for a while and then took a turn for the worse after an asthma attack this morning. The funeral home just took the body away."

Kara couldn't believe that her aunt was gone. It seemed surreal to her since she had just heard Frieda's voice not even twenty-four hours prior. Simon told her that there were a lot of people gathered at the house, but that she should pass the message on to Miriam and that he would call when funeral arrangements were made.

*Funeral arrangements ...* after hearing those words Kara was forced to accept what she didn't want to.

When Deidra walked into the apartment nearly two hours later, Kara was still curled up in a fetal position on the couch, clutching a pillow. Deidra dropped her bag on a chair and looked at Kara in concern. She sat on the sofa at her feet, figuring that Kara had botched the audition, but when she found instead that Frieda had died Deidra could hardly believe it.

"I just talked to her, you know." Kara sobbed with a crumpled piece of tissue in her hand. "She'll never know how well I did on my audition or see me graduate or anything..."

Deidra hugged Kara in lieu of words and it was as if Kara's stinging pain deepened.

Moments after Deidra calmed Kara, there was a knock at the door.

"That's probably Wendell," Kara said, glancing at the wall clock. "I hope you don't mind. He just wanted to stop by for a minute since everything went well with my audition today." Kara straightened her new sweater she had bought just for today's occasion and stood.

"Oh girl, no. You know how much I like Wendell. Besides, you need him right now." Deidra gently rubbed Kara's back.

"Thanks," she replied and walked toward the door.

Wendell smiled and hugged Kara as he entered the apartment. He looked over her shoulder and waved at Deidra. Kara hugged him back, inadvertently running her hand across the gun positioned in the small of his back. In her sorrow, there wasn't even a slight urge to kid him about wearing his gun to visit her.

After Wendell kissed her on the cheek, it was only then that he noticed her reddened eyes.

"What's wrong?" he asked, placing a palm across her cheek.

Kara closed the door behind him as she said, "My aunt Frieda has gone to Heaven."

"*What?*" Wendell glanced at Deidra before burying his eyes back on Kara. "Are you okay?"

"I am now."

"Hey, I'm going to leave you two alone," Deidra offered as she picked her bag up from the chair. "But Kara, you need to tell your sister like Simon said. Maybe after hearing the news, she'll have a change of heart about things."

Kara contentiously pursed her lips together as Deidra went to her bedroom. Wendell nodded as he took off his coat, repeating Deidra's sentiments. Conflicted, Kara folded her arms and considered what Deidra had said. Regardless of whether Miriam had a change of heart or not, Kara knew that her sister still had the right to know that their aunt had passed on.

"I'll come with you." Wendell held her hand as he nudged her towards the door.

"Okay," she reluctantly agreed.

Still holding on to the key that Miriam had earlier demanded, Kara unlocked the door to the apartment they once shared. In a rush to get out of the apartment the night before, Kara had forgotten to leave it as her sister had instructed. Miriam was barricaded in her room as usual, so she was nowhere to be seen when Phillip and his friend came to help move Kara's trunk and bin earlier into Deidra's living room.

"It's pretty dark in here," Wendell said, closing the door behind him.

.ok

"That's nothing new," Kara replied, flipping the lights on to the kitchen. She looked around for any sign that her sister was at home but found none. Even the lights in her bedroom were out. "Meme, are you here?" Kara called out, but there was no response. She looked back at Wendell and shook her head. "She's not here."

"Did you want to leave a note for her to call you or something?"

Kara stared at Wendell and grunted. "Call me? She's not going to call me ... and I don't want to leave something like that in a note."

"You don't have to write any specifics, just tell her that there's an emergency back home and you need to talk to her."

"Yeah, that'll probably get her to come over to Deidra's." Kara nodded and then walked into the kitchen. She rummaged through the drawers, searching for an ink pen. After finding one, she pushed aside an empty cup and saucer to get to the papers on the other side of it. The papers, water damaged with circular brown stains, looked to be old credit card statements mingled with junk mail that Miriam was using as temporary coasters.

"Boy, she really knows how to keep house," Wendell commented on the scattered paperwork and dirty dishes piled in the sink.

"Trust me, it did not look like this when I lived here," Kara assured him, while defending herself. She shook her head and pulled a sheet of blank paper towards her. She quickly scribbled a note to Miriam and took it to the refrigerator. There were two places Kara was sure her sister would look, and the fridge was location number one.

Just as she was about to attach the note on the door with a red square-shaped magnet, Kara flipped the piece of paper over. For a moment it seemed as if her vision was failing her. Kara's eyes widened while her lips unintentionally parted.

"What is it?" Wendell asked.

Kara froze in place.

"*What?*" Wendell repeated.

Kara met his gaze but was speechless.

Wendell snatched the paper from her hand and stared down at the bank statement that bore her name. Below the bold-printed words ENDING BALANCE, it read $5.26. He looked up at her just as the knob to the front door turned.

"What are you doing in here?" Miriam glared at Kara as her friend, Robin, who lived on the first floor, closed the door behind them. "And who are you?" Miriam glared at Wendell as she rolled herself farther into the apartment and parked near the kitchen entrance.

It was as if time stood still because those were the only words Kara heard before she erupted into unbridled fury. Instinctively, she grabbed Wendell's shirt and lifted his gun. After disengaging the safety lock, Kara pointed the weapon at Miriam.

Fear gripped Miriam as she stared down the barrel of the gun.

"You stole my money!"

Miriam's chest began to visibly rise and lower in rapid cycles with her hands defensively raised in the air. "Kara, I didn't. I-I-I promise you that I didn't do it ..."

"Don't you lie to me!" Kara hollered with a squinted eye as she steadied the gun. "How could you? You just want to take everything from me!"

"Kara, put the gun down," Wendell tried to reason with her. "Just give it to me." He slowly moved in her direction.

"Stay out of this!" Kara yelled at him with her eyes still glued on Miriam. "Now, you better tell me where my money is!"

"I-I don't have it ...." Miriam's dread-filled eyes watered in terror. "It was Chris," she confessed. "And I can't find him."

"Stop lying to me!" Kara screamed as her hands began to shake.

"I promise, I'm not lying!" Miriam declared. "Look!" She pointed towards the shelf in the living room a few feet away. "He even took my daddy's military medals that Mama gave me after graduation." Miriam hadn't noticed it missing over the past week since she always kept it tucked away on the top shelf in the living room. She figured Chris probably thought they were worth some money, but the only value they really had was sentimental. It wasn't until she opened Kara's bank statement that came in the mail earlier today that she realized Chris was never coming back.

When Kara turned her head and found that Miriam's father's medals were indeed missing, Wendell grabbed her wrist and snatched the gun away from her. She struggled to get it back from him, but he overpowered her until she no longer resisted.

"It's all your fault!" Kara frantically shouted as she lunged at Miriam and yanked her out of the wheelchair.

Wendell managed to pull Kara off her sister while Robin shielded Miriam with her body, and then dragged her back into the wheelchair. Wendell quickly pushed Kara towards the door.

"*Why*?" The high-strung energy quickly drained from Kara's body.

Miriam stared as Wendell wrapped his arms around Kara's limp waist and pulled her out the door.

Wendell practically carried his girlfriend back to Deidra's apartment. Kara cried hysterically while he and Deidra both tried to calm her down.

"Why did she do this?" Kara questioned while pounding on Wendell's chest. "How can I go to school now? *Oh God....*"

After subduing Kara, Wendell wore a grim frown as he glanced over at Deidra. "I don't think she needs to be in this building tonight. I'm going to take her to my place."

"You're right, she doesn't need to be anywhere near Miriam right now." Deidra then looked to Kara and began detangling her disheveled hair with gentle strokes of her fingers. "I think that's a good idea, sweetie."

Kara seemed dazed and confused, so Deidra packed an overnight bag while Wendell kept a close eye on her. As he buttoned up his overcoat and waited by the door, Wendell placed his hand over the gun that almost changed Kara's life and ended Miriam's. He exhaled heavily and mouthed the words *thank you* to God.

Moments later, he and Kara walked out of the building together with his arm wrapped around her shoulders. On the train ride to the Village, Kara didn't utter a word and Wendell echoed her attitude. Even after arriving at his loft Kara only said one sentence, indicating that she wanted to take a shower before she disappeared behind the bathroom door.

"Did you need anything?" Wendell cautiously asked.

"No ..." she softly answered.

Wendell stood at the door quietly and soon heard Kara's quiet sobs. There was nothing he could humanly do or say that would take her pain away. He knew this was strictly God's territory. After securely putting his revolver away, Wendell dropped to his knees and prayed to the Father. His girlfriend needed Him now more than ever. Kara needed God's comfort to endure this trial and His strength to move past it. Irrespective of how God chose to answer that prayer, Wendell promised the Lord that he would be with her in the process.

After an hour behind that closed door, Kara emerged from the bathroom with eyes that had graduated from red to a faint pink. Her hair was up in a clip with the necklace Wendell had bought her still resting against her fair skin. She sat down on the sofa where Wendell was and waited for him to end his phone call.

"How are you?" he softly asked, sliding his phone onto the coffee table. "Are you feeling any better?" He gently moved strands of hair from her eyes.

"Yeah, I am ... thanks." Kara cleared her throat as she placed a hand on his thigh. "I'm sorry ... I shouldn't have taken your gun ..." her voice squeaked as she broke down again.

"I know, Kara, I know." Wendell cradled her in his arms.

Kara hugged him back and then whispered in between her sniffles, "I want to be with you."

With a confused look washed across his face, Wendell leaned back and questioned, "What did you just say?"

"You heard me." Kara draped her arms around his neck and began kissing him.

Wendell pushed her away, but after several attempts he was swept up in the moment. He scooped one arm underneath her legs while supporting her back with the other and carried her to his bed. The two of them embraced, unleashing the passion they held bottled inside. Wendell pulled his short sleeve undershirt over his head and tossed it on the floor while Kara removed her hair from the clip. They kissed uncontrollably, showing one another in action what they couldn't in words. It wasn't until Kara grabbed Wendell's belt that he abruptly grabbed her wrists.

"Kara, stop." His voice was soft, but unconvincing. Kara squirmed away from his grasp and continued kissing him on the neck as she tried a second time at his belt buckle.

"Kara, no..."

She paused, challenged by his words that now pierced her. "*No?*"

Wendell grunted as he moved to the side of his king-size bed and sat on the edge. "Not like this. I don't want it to happen like this." He looked back at her and said, "You're hurt and angry. This isn't what you want to do."

Kara drew in a deep breath as she crawled out of bed and stood in front of him. "So, you don't want me now? Am I that pathetic?"

Wendell draped his hands at her waist as his eyes scaled her body. "I would take you in a minute ... *if* I wasn't saved. I got caught up in the moment, but you know we can't do this." He then gazed into her eyes. "Your virginity belongs to your husband."

Kara pushed his hands away from her and walked towards the window on the other side of the room. She folded her arms across her chest and hopelessly shook her head.

"This has been a crazy night for you, and I don't want you to do something you'd regret."

"Something I'd regret?" Kara questioned, staring back at him. "Silly me, thinking that you would be my husband."

Wendell smiled through her heartfelt words and walked over to where she stood. He gently wiped the tears from her flushed cheeks and whispered in her ear, "Don't you worry about that ... I will be."

# CHAPTER 38

"IT FEELS SO good being here with you," Talia moaned as she rolled over in bed, resting her chin on the backside of Donovan's bare shoulder. "How about having breakfast in bed?" She pecked the nape of his neck. "I figured we'd have lunch with Mother, you know, at that café on the marina downtown, and after dropping her off at home, spend the rest of the day on the boat ... *alone*." She shamelessly giggled.

The springtime met the adulterous couple still carousing in the throes of passion. After officially moving from New York to Florida, Talia felt that she was reliving her youth. Life, in her words, had become uncomplicated and carefree. She no longer had to sneak behind Franklin's back since she had Donovan to meet her every need, physically as well as financially. The uncontested divorce papers had been filed while Talia was having the time of her life with the man whom she felt knew her better than anyone else.

"Breakfast in bed would be nice," Donovan answered in a monotonous tone, "but I have plans later." He turned around and faced her.

Talia raked her hair back with her fingers and sat up. "Plans? I thought this week was our week together."

Donovan sighed as he rolled out of bed and slipped into a pair of drawstring pajama pants. "Tee, we've had our week together. We just got back yesterday from our cruise."

"And we still have a day left before you start work on your next project."

"Yes, and I wanted to play a few games of golf with some friends of mine." He grabbed his cell from the nightstand and began scrolling through his missed calls. "Besides, don't you still need to find a gift for your daughter's graduation before you and your mother leave in a couple days?"

"I bought a gift for her when we were on the cruise," Talia huffed. "And why do you always have to play golf with your friends every week?"

Donovan looked up from his phone and cocked his head to the side. "Isn't that what you used to do in New York?" he reminded her. "I seem to recall your weekly tennis games every Saturday morning." He then walked towards the closet on the other side of the room and pulled out a neatly pressed polo shirt and a pair of khaki shorts.

"Who am I going to play tennis with here?" Talia rolled her eyes as she climbed out of bed and into her bathrobe.

"Well, maybe if you made some new friends, you'd find out," he snapped back at her. "I can't spend all of my time with you."

Talia stared at him with her hands firmly on her hips. "I can't believe you just said that to me. When have I ever asked you to spend *all* your time with me? Since I've moved here, except for this past week, you've been out just about every evening. If it wasn't to watch basketball at a stupid sports bar it was to play cards with your buddies," she ridiculed him. "And how much money have you gambled away now anyway?"

"What does it matter?" Donovan challenged her. "It's *my* money to gamble." He pounded on his chest.

Talia swallowed her shame. This was not the same man who wooed her. She sucked her teeth, wondering how she allowed their affair to drive a permanent wedge between her and her family. Franklin would never waste money like Donovan, although she had done enough wasteful spending for them both while they were together.

"So, that's it, you're not going to spend the day with me?" Talia's hands flopped to her sides.

Donovan looked at her with a scornful glare as he dropped his attire for the day onto the bed. "You know what Tee, this isn't working." He shook his head.

"What do you mean this isn't working?"

"I mean this," he pointed between them, "*us* .... it ain't working."

"Isn't," she scornfully corrected him.

"Are you mocking me?" Donovan squinted. "Have you forgotten where you came from?"

"No, I haven't forgotten, but apparently I've learned a few things since leaving," she sparred.

"Oh really?" Donovan scoffed. "Well, how about you learn how to take care of yourself?"

"*Excuse me*?" Her eyes bulged with anger as she shook her head in disbelief. "Oh no, after all I've given up for you," she ranted. "*You* chased me, not the other way around."

"Yeah, I chased you, but if I had known that I was catching another version of my ex-wife, I would've left you where I found you."

Talia balled her lips in anger. She snatched a table lamp from the wall socket and hurled it at him. Donovan ducked and the lamp smashed against the back wall. He looked behind him at the shattered pieces scattered on the textured, wool carpet.

"Do you know how hard it's going to be to get glass out of this carpet?" Donovan stared back at her.

"Does it look like I care?" Talia shouted at him.

Donovan rubbed his temples and turned his back to her. He stared aimlessly out of the window, realizing the tragic mistake he had made by convincing Talia to leave her husband. It didn't matter that her beauty practically hypnotized him; they were just two totally different people when left to themselves. The adventurous intrigue of being with her at exclusive hotels had worn thin. It was no longer a thrill to be around her. The normal couple routine didn't suit his lifestyle and he regretted the day that he thought it would.

"Aren't you going to say anything else?" Talia questioned him, still on the other side of the room with her arms folded.

"Tee, look at us." Donovan slowly faced her. "What are we doing?"

Talia's arms slowly unfolded after she saw the seriousness in his eyes.

"Maybe you shouldn't have left your husband." He sighed as he plopped onto the edge of the bed. "We're fighting all of the time now. When we argue, it's like fire and gasoline. I put up with too much of that from my ex-wife. Asking me where I've been after stepping foot in the house and how long I'll be when I leave." Donovan then looked at her with remorse. "I didn't sign up for any of this."

Talia blinked back her tears as she stared in another direction of the room. When she saw her reflection in the dresser mirror, all sorts of emotions rushed out of her heart: humiliation, guilt, and anger. They all made her feel foolishly alone.

"When you leave for New York in a couple of days, I don't think you should come back." Donovan shook his head. "At least not to my house."

# CHAPTER 39

KARA LOOKED UP at Deacon Jackson and the entire Faithful Christian congregation as she accepted the scholarship award from the youth pastor. It was an honor to not only receive recognition from her church home, but to be able to add this money to what she had already been awarded from local scholarships and grants, the largest given by Juilliard. Kara's dreams were realized when an acceptance letter came from the School, despite the hardship she had endured. For a moment, she wanted to give up on going to Juilliard, but God ... The way He provided completely amazed her. Although her seed money for school was stolen and the culprit never found, the Lord's promise held true that He would never leave nor forsake.

"God always gives you what you need and just enough strength to get you through." Wendell smiled at her. "Isn't that what you said your aunt always said?"

"Yep, she always said that." Kara smiled nostalgically, remembering Frieda. "It's been three and a half months, but to me it still feels like yesterday." She smiled, despite all that had taken place in that short period of time.

"It's going to take some time, but—"

"In time, God will make all things new," she recounted a portion of Scripture that Frieda was known for reciting. Those words of wisdom held hope for Kara. Ever since Miriam moved back home to Mississippi to live with another relative three months ago, Kara prayed that her sister would truly change. She hadn't seen her since they were both at the graveyard after Frieda's funeral, but Kara still longed for things to return to the way they were between them almost six years ago. It was tough to get past what Miriam's friend had done, but Kara had a choice to either be depressed about the past or move forward. And she made the conscious decision to trust God in all areas of her life, regardless of how much others had hurt her.

"I'm so glad you got into Juilliard." Jacqueline Stewart hugged Kara. "But Elijah is sure going to miss those piano lessons."

"Oh, I'm going to miss teaching him. But I know my school load is going to be much heavier."

"We understand." Jacqueline smiled. "You just stay focused."

Kara nodded as she glanced up at Wendell. "He'll make sure of it."

After Jacqueline walked away, the pair stood in the vestibule as Kara hugged several other people in passing. The entire church rallied around her once they discovered the tragic misfortune she had endured by her aunt's death and almost losing the opportunity to attend the school of her dreams. After Kara told Deacon Jackson about the way things exploded between her and Miriam, Franklin and a few of the other wealthy congregants gathered together to ensure that she would be taken care of financially. As an added measure of security, Franklin volunteered to set up an account in a FDIC insured bank equipped with fraud alerts that would be virtually impossible for anyone to rip-off.

"Hey girl, in just a few days we'll be graduates and, on our way, to being college students!" Melissa excitedly ran towards Kara as Phillip and Franklin walked a few steps behind her. "Can you believe that we have gotten through our senior year? Man, I am so glad that's over."

"But the hard work is just about to begin," Franklin reminded his daughter, nudging her on the arm.

Melissa smiled as she playfully rolled her eyes. "Daddy, you really know how to kill a buzz."

Wendell, Kara, and Phillip all laughed at her lighthearted comment. After a few seconds, Franklin even cracked a smile himself.

"Hey, is your mom going to join us for lunch?" Kara asked Phillip. "I know she must be just as proud of you for that athletic scholarship to UNC-Chapel Hill."

"Oh yeah, no doubt." Phillip nodded. "She's going to meet us at the restaurant."

"That's right, she just started her new job," Kara remembered. "I hope she doesn't have to work third shift too long."

"Me too. After I leave for school, I'm not going to be able to walk with her to work." Phillip donned a reflective gaze. "But I think I remember her saying that after her probationary period is up, she'll be able to move to first shift. Something about them not having the time to train her on first shift. But hey, some of my boys will still be here to look out for her."

Phillip's mother had waited a long time to be employed as an addiction specialist at the local rehabilitation center. Ever since his father overdosed on drugs, Phillip was constantly reminded to never touch the stuff. His mother could have made it to church this morning, but it was still a sore spot for her that his father's last hit came from a stash Deacon Jackson had dealt him some years ago when he used to live in the neighborhood and before he was a saved man.

"So, how's my favorite granddaughter?" Shirley asked, covering Melissa's eyes.

"Oh my gosh, *Grandma*?" Melissa peeled Shirley's fingers away from her face and turned around. "When did you get here?" She hugged her as they easily swayed side to side with the embrace. "I wasn't expecting you for another few days."

"Well, we wanted to see you sooner..."

All eyes shifted to Talia who stood a few inches behind Shirley. She extended her arms and reached for Melissa's hands. "You look beautiful, sweetheart. I'm so proud of you for getting that scholarship." She then looked at Kara apologetically. "You too, Kara."

"Thank you," Kara responded with an emotionless nod, still somewhat sore from the cruel way Talia had treated her.

Melissa nervously smiled as her glance shifted from Kara to her father.

"Hello Shirley," Franklin pleasantly greeted his mother-in-law before his eyes shifted to his soon to be ex-wife. "Talia," he coldly acknowledged her. After quietly clearing his throat, Franklin turned to Melissa and said in a lowered voice, "I'll be waiting outside."

Melissa sighed as she watched her father walk towards the exit.

"Excuse me," Talia said as she shamelessly followed Franklin.

"*Oh boy*," Melissa mumbled to herself as she watched her mother run out of the building after her father.

"Franklin, Franklin!" Talia called out to him after getting a few feet onto the sidewalk.

His steps slowed until his body was motionless. "What is it?" Franklin turned around and faced her.

"I'm sorry," Talia admitted as she strode within a couple feet of him. "I-I shouldn't have left you the way that I did."

Franklin tightened his lips to bury the hostility that threatened to resurface. He shook his head, noting that they'd had this conversation some years ago when she first cheated on him. It was in him to forgive, but not to allow her to continuously drag their marital vows through the gutter. His promise to God was sacred, and it pained him that she obviously did not feel the same way.

"Do you think we can work this out?" she asked, grabbing his hands, noticing that he had lost a considerable amount of weight since the last time she saw him.

Franklin's eyes shifted from her fingers back to her eyes as he shook his head. "No, not this time." He pulled his hands away from hers and grunted to himself. "I gave you what you wanted ... Alimony to cover your monthly expenses and the freedom to leave. You didn't have to go behind my back to see if I was hiding more money than you knew about."

Talia looked surprised.

"Yes, I knew you were going through my paperwork, but know this ... I would've never deprived you of getting what's fair." Franklin shook his head again. "It was never about money with me, Talia." He released a cleansing breath. "And I've made peace with God about moving on."

"So, that's it?" Talia questioned in desperation. "I can't come back home?"

"*Home*?" Franklin grimaced. "There is no *home* with us, Talia. You broke all of that up when you left."

"But—"

"I said no ..." It became obvious to him things hadn't worked out with her lover as planned, but that was no longer his concern. "But thank you for at least being there for Melissa."

Talia watched as Franklin turned and continued up the sidewalk. She took a few steps behind him, refusing to accept no for an answer, but then stopped her in tracks. Talia froze, dressed in her Sunday best, humiliated for the second time in the past week. It was bad enough that she had to temporarily move back in with her mother until she found a place of her own, but now she didn't have either man to call her own. With a signature Burberry clutch—her latest score from Bloomingdale's—tucked underneath her arm, Talia turned around to walk back towards the church. She then surprisingly met eyes with Marissa.

There was an awkward moment of silence.

"Marissa ... uh ... how have you been?" Talia's eyes uncomfortably glanced back and forth between Marissa, Helen, and an unfamiliar gentleman.

"I'm good, Talia," Marissa stiffly answered. "Much better than I was a few months ago. But I find comfort in Pastor's sermon this morning. You do remember the Scripture passage, don't you? You reap what you sow." She raised a brow, painfully remembering all that Helen had told her about Donovan's stint with Talia. It became obviously clear to Helen that Talia was having an affair when she didn't deny it that day in the church's foyer. It was further evident when she had stopped attending church and abruptly left town for months without any explanation.

"It's been a while." Helen drew Talia's attention away from Marissa and the new man she held hands with. "I take it that Florida must not be treating you too well." She grinned, having overheard her conversation with Franklin.

Talia grimaced in response to Helen's flippant remark. Instead of sparring wits with her or Marissa, she simply walked away without even a glance back at them and rejoined her mother just outside of the church.

"Where's Melissa?" Talia asked her mother.

"She went to the restroom with Kara ... but let me talk to you for a moment."

After Shirley explained that it would be better if they just took Melissa out for dinner later that evening instead of joining her for lunch, Talia didn't object. It was obvious that Franklin had nothing to say to her and from what Shirley explained neither did the young man who accompanied her granddaughter. Talia was forced to acknowledge her demons; the ones that convinced her to leave a faithful husband and loyal family for an uncertain future with a deceptive bachelor.

That day Talia learned more about herself than she wanted to know. She had boxed herself into a lonely corner and was forced to relinquish her pride. Experiencing the feeling of abandonment that she had visited upon others forced her to reflect on her fateful choices. She finally realized that it was time for change; a time to be honest with everyone, including herself.

This day brought on moments of reflection for more than just Talia. As the sun began to set, Kara sat in the window of Wendell's loft, thinking as well. She pondered the trials that tested her faith, the relationships gained and lost along the way, and the strength and maturity that was developed inside of her as a result. The Lord had provided in ways she had least expected, blessing her with renewed assurance.

"Give me three words that describe your thoughts," Wendell interrupted her thoughts.

Kara placed a hand on his that rested on her shoulder. It may not have been the direction she would have envisioned, but she answered with absolute certainty, "Life is good."

He kissed her on the cheek and replied, "Yes, yes it is."

Her life may not have been perfect, but Kara knew that she would always have her Father who is.

# EPILOGUE

*Four years later...*

KARA SCANNED THE audience as she walked across the stage in her dark colored cap and gown. Amidst the president of the School and several distinguished faculty members and alumni, Melissa held up her camera and snapped a few quick shots of her best-friend with a raised thumb before she continued across the stage. This was a familiar scene for Melissa as she had recently graduated from UNCSA. Kara waved at her family members who took the trip from Dadenville to Manhattan for the special occasion.

"There's my world-class pianist." Wendell grabbed Kara around the waist after the ceremony was over and passionately kissed her on the lips.

Kara gazed into his eyes and softly responded, "Hey you, how's my award-nominated director husband?"

"Doing just fine. And oh, before I forget, my parents said they'll meet up with us later tonight after my dad's meeting."

"Okay, that sounds good. I'm just glad they made it."

"Are you kidding? They wouldn't have missed their daughter-in-law's graduation for anything." Wendell grinned.

It had been two years since the two had decided to tie the knot. With Melissa, Phillip, and Deidra, who helped to professionally cater the event, alongside other close relatives and friends, Wendell and Kara made a vow before God to honor and cherish one another until death separated them. It was a quaint ceremony at a countryside villa where they each took a short break from their rigorously demanding schedules to become husband and wife. Determined to live for the Lord, Kara honored God by keeping her virginity until their wedding night.

"I'm happy that this day has finally arrived." Wendell squeezed her closer.

"You mean that you're happy you survived all of my late-night studying and cancelled dinner dates."

Wendell chuckled. "Well, I got through it. I can't say that I was much better. Those two months away while I shot that film overseas wasn't the easiest thing for you to deal with either."

The corners of Kara's mouth rose. "No, but I think it made our relationship stronger." She casually played with his silk tie. "I mean that I missed you and all, but distance has a way of making you put things into perspective."

"Yes, it does." Wendell lowered his chin as he buried his eyes into hers.

"Can anybody else get a hug in?" Samuel joked as he held his arms open to Kara, glancing back and forth between her and Wendell.

Kara chuckled as Samuel pecked her on the cheek. The moment was bittersweet as they looked into one another's eyes, each recalling their deceased mothers, Frieda and Gwendolyn. It hadn't been long ago that the two had a heart-to-heart phone conversation about the details surrounding Kenneth and Gwendolyn's death roughly ten years ago. But the facts devastated them both to learn that Simon played a part in the grisly deaths.

Soon after the long-time mayor of Dadenville became ill, news swarmed around the small town about Mayor Jenson's last words as he laid on his deathbed. He admitted to hiring some people to set fire to the Bentley's new home because he wanted the property that it rested on, and one of those people was indeed Gwendolyn's longtime brother-in-law, Simon. Unbeknownst to Mayor Jenson that there were people in town willing to go against him, regardless of his ruthless reputation, he lost the bid to secure the property the Bentleys ended up buying. Out of anger, Mayor Jenson made sure that the Bentleys would not enjoy the money that was paid to them from the professional diggers that he unjustly considered to be his.

In hindsight, Simon's odd behavior and mysterious phone calls during the times Kara visited were explained. It took her a while to grasp that her uncle would do such a thing just to get rid of gambling debts owed to some small-time gangsters, but the way Samuel said his father explained it was that it was either his life or theirs. Samuel nor Kara held regrets that Simon was now in jail without any contact from their family.

"You did it, Kara." Samuel gently rubbed the sides of her arms. "You made the family proud. I know you have a husband now," he smiled at Wendell, "but you can still call me, you know, if you ever need to talk."

Kara hugged him again. "Of course, Sam, you know I will."

"All right, so you want us all to meet back at your place or the hotel?" he asked.

Kara glanced at Wendell before she looked back at Samuel. "It'll be easier if we meet everybody at the hotel. I already told Melissa, Kendra, and Monica. After we get changed, we can go out and celebrate."

"I thought I was going to get to meet your NBA superstar friend. It'd be nice to get some tickets next season." Samuel chuckled as he asked about Phillip.

"Oh yeah, Phillip took us out for lunch yesterday before you guys arrived. He had an important meeting with his agent today, but I think I can get you an invitation to their wedding next month and tickets to the season opener in a few months." Kara winked. "You know I got the connections."

"That's what I'm talking about, girl." Samuel smiled as he pointed at her. "Courtside?"

Kara tilted her head as she said, "Don't push it."

"Okay, okay." Samuel laughed as he held his hands up. "Let me go get changed. See you in about an hour?"

"Sounds good." Kara nodded.

"All right, later man." Samuel shook Wendell's hand and then walked away.

Just as Samuel disappeared into the crowd, Wendell noticed how disappointed Kara looked. "Are you okay?" he asked, drawing her eyes from the floor back to his.

"Yeah, I guess so. Everybody came except her." Kara shrugged with a sigh. "Well, I wasn't really expecting her to show up ... although I hoped that she would."

"I wouldn't have missed it for the world," a meek voice said.

Kara looked behind her to find Miriam modestly waving at her. She was beautifully adorned in a bright, yellow print dress that complimented her new figure. "*Oh my goodness, Meme* ... wow, look at you!" She could hardly contain her excitement. Kara's eyes drifted from Miriam's silky hair secured on one side with a sparkling barrette to her nicely manicured fingertips. Even her wheelchair looked to have had an upgrade.

"I know, different huh?" Miriam smiled at her sister. "I think the weight loss really pulls it all together."

After several quiet moments of staring at one another, they both broke into joyful tears. Wendell drew back a few steps as he patted the welling tears in his own eyes.

"How did you get here?" Kara leaned over and hugged her sister while inwardly thanking God for the reunion. "What happened to you? I mean, I've tried calling and writing you, but never got an answer."

"I know and I'm sorry about all of that." Miriam nodded knowingly. "But you know Samuel. When I told him that I wanted to surprise you, he offered to escort me."

"And he never said a word." Kara grinned as she looked around to see if she could find Samuel in the crowd, but he was already long gone.

"Anyway, I know that I should have responded to your wedding invitation a couple of years ago, but I guess I was still stuck in the past," she regretfully admitted. "But when I got your invitation in the mail for the graduation, it had already been five months since I had given my life to Christ."

"*You*?" Kara's eyes widened with surprise.

"Yes, I finally accepted Jesus." Miriam winked at her. "You were right little sis, He is the answer. I've never known a love like His. The way you forgave me after what I had done to you, I knew that it had to be something ... *Someone* bigger than yourself that helped you to do it." She then fanned her hand in front of her face to keep from crying. "Anyway, here's your wedding/graduation gift." Miriam handed Kara the rectangular, silver box with a red bow from her lap. "I just didn't know how to apologize for all that I had done or allowed to happen. Maybe this present will make up for a little bit of it."

Kara's nose crinkled as she glanced at Wendell, and then back at Miriam. "What is it?"

"Just open it." Miriam smiled, motioning for Kara to hurry.

Kara curiously removed the beautifully tied red bow and opened the box. After pulling away the glittery tissue paper, she immediately gasped and covered her mouth.

"Do you like it?" Miriam glowed from the expression on Kara's face.

Kara pulled out a framed picture along with a blouse her mother once owned and handed the empty box to Wendell. It was the same blouse Miriam had ripped one morning when she and Kara had fought with one another so many years ago, except now it was completely intact.

"*Like it?* I-I don't have words to describe how I feel about what you've done ..." Kara thanked Miriam as she held the shirt close to her chest. "But I thought you had thrown it away."

"I could've never thrown Mama's blouse away," Miriam confessed, and then with a disheartening grunt added, "even in my unsaved days."

Kara hugged her sister again as she stood amidst a crowd of elated graduates. Neither one would have imagined that after the night Kara held a gun on Miriam that they'd be lovingly holding one another today. It was a testament to God's redemptive nature. It does not expire with time, but instead weathers the most heinous storms and heals the deepest wounds.

And on this day, they had both been restored.

*Surely goodness and mercy shall follow me*
*all the days of my life; and I will*
*dwell in the house of the Lord forever.*

Psalm 23:6

# DISCUSSION QUESTIONS

1. Miriam blamed Kara for her disability and them having to move from a nice condominium to a Section 8 home. How would you handle someone who constantly blamed you for something that was beyond your control?

2. Talia looked down on those who had less than she did. Do you think she should have been in a position of leadership, giving others advice, at the church? Discuss.

3. Kara was afraid to tell Wendell that she lived in the projects. Do you think she should have told him where she lived when he dropped her off at the Peterson mansion or waited until they were in a relationship?

4. Talia appeared to have it all but complained about being unsatisfied. What do you think was missing from her life and how could she have filled that void spoken of in Chapter 14? Discuss.

5. Kara uncovers an affair between her best friend's mother and another man. If you were in her shoes, would you have told Melissa about it? Why or why not?

6. Leslie and Wayne both maliciously went behind Wendell's back, hoping to get what they wanted. How would you handle betrayal from someone you considered a friend?

7. Talia felt that she needed Donovan to complete her. What are your thoughts when professed Christians say they need someone (other than God) to complete them? Discuss.

8. There was a considerable amount of money stolen from Kara by one of her sister's boyfriends. How would you handle this situation if it happened to you?

9. Franklin had reached his breaking point and decided to divorce Talia. What are your views on Christians getting a divorce? Discuss.

10. Kara endured trials in her life, some from close family. Do you find it harder to forgive those who are closer to you? Discuss.

# ABOUT THE AUTHOR

RENEE MCCOY (known to readers as Renée Allen McCoy) is a loving wife and mother, an author, but most importantly a devoted Christian. To date, in addition to *In the Presence of My Enemies*, she has penned three novels that make up *The Fiery Furnace* series: *The Kiss of Judas*, *Confessions*, and *The Eleventh Hour*, and one novella: *The Christmas Beau (The True Love Novellas ~ Book 1)*. Also available is her first non-fiction book entitled *Soul Ties: Breaking Up with a Past That's Killing Your Future*.

Visit her online at www.ReneeAllenMcCoy.com for more information.

www.ingramcontent.com/pod-product-compliance
Lightning Source LLC
Chambersburg PA
CBHW030242030726
47493CB00023B/514